IGNITING THE REACHES

DAVID DRAKE

ACE BOOKS, NEW YORK

This Ace Book contains the complete text of the original hardcover edition.

IGNITING THE REACHES

An Ace Book / published by arrangement with the author

PRINTING HISTORY
Ace hardcover edition / April 1994
Ace paperback edition / March 1995

ISBN: 0-441-00179-3

ACE®
Ace Books are published by The Berkley Publishing Group,
200 Madison Avenue, New York, New York 10016.
ACE and the "A" design
are trademarks belonging to Charter Communications, Inc.

PRINTED IN THE UNITED STATES OF AMERICA

10 9 8 7 6 5 4 3 2 1

To Rana Van Name
Who first heard about this one
when we were all going off to dinner;
And who is special.

—1—

Above Salute

Piet Ricimer stood out like an open flame on the crowded, cluttered bridge of the *Sultan* as she orbited Salute. Stephen Gregg was amused by the young officer's flashy dress.

Well, Ricimer was no younger than Gregg himself—but Gregg, as a member of a factorial family, was mature in ways that no sailor would ever be. More sophisticated, at any rate. Realizing that sophistication and maturity might not be the same made Gregg frown for a moment until he focused on the discussion again.

"I suppose it *might* be Salute," mumbled Bivens, the navigator. Gregg had already marked Bivens down as a man who never saw a planetfall he liked—or was sure he could identify.

"Look, of course it's Salute!" insisted Captain Choransky, commander of the *Sultan* and the other two ships of the argosy. "It's just this tub's lousy optics that makes it hard to tell."

His vehemence made the landfall seem as doubtful as Bivens' concern had done. This was Gregg's first voyage off Venus, much less out of the solar system. He was too young at twenty-two Earth years to worry much about it, but he wondered at the back of his mind whether this lot would be able to find their way home.

Besides the officers, three crewmen sat at the workstations controlling the forward band of attitude jets. The *Sultan* had been stretched by two hull sections after her first decade of service as an intrasystem trader. That had required adding another band of jets.

The new controls and the sprawl of conduits feeding them had been placed on the bridge. They made it difficult for a landsman like Gregg to walk there under normal 1-g acceleration without tripping or bruising himself against a hip-high projection. Now, with the flagship floating in orbit, Gregg had even worse problems. The spacers slid easily along.

The most reassuring thing about the situation was the expression of utter boredom worn by every one of the crewmen on the control boards. They were experienced, and they saw no reason for concern.

"Sir," said Ricimer, "I'll take the cutter down and find us a landing site. This is Salute. I've checked the star plots myself."

"Can't be sure of a plot with these optics," Bivens muttered. "Maybe the *Dove* got a better sighting than I could."

"I'll take the six men who came with me when I sold *The Judge*," Ricimer said brightly. "I'm pretty sure I've spotted two Southern compounds, and there are scores of Molt cities for sure."

Ricimer was a short man, dark where Gregg was fair. Though willing to be critical, Gregg admitted that the spacer was good-looking, with regular features and a waist that nipped in beneath powerful shoulders. Ricimer wore a tunic of naturally red fibers from somewhere outside the solar system, and his large St. Christopher medal hung from a strand of glittering crystals that were more showy than valuable.

"Might not even be Molts here if it isn't Salute," Bivens said. "Between the twenty-third and twenty-ninth transits, I think we went off track."

Choransky turned, probably as much to get away from his navigator as for a positive purpose, and said, "All right, Ricimer, take the cutter down. But don't lose her, and *don't* con me into some needle farm that won't give me a hundred meters of smooth ground. The *Sultan*'s no featherboat, remember."

"Aye-aye, sir!" Ricimer said with another of his brilliant smiles.

"I'd like to go down with the boat," Gregg said, as much to his own surprise as anyone else's.

That drew the interest of the other men on the bridge, even the common sailors. Piet Ricimer's face went as blank as a bulkhead.

Gregg anchored himself firmly to the underside of a workstation with his left hand. "I'm Stephen Gregg," he said. "I'm traveling as supercargo for my uncle, Gregg of Weyston."

"I know that," Ricimer said, with no more expression in his voice than his face held.

"Ah—Ricimer," Captain Choransky said nervously. "Factor Gregg is quite a major investor in this voyage."

"I know that too," Ricimer said. His eyes continued to appraise Gregg. In a tone of challenge, he went on, "Can you handle a boat in an atmosphere, then, Gregg?"

Gregg sniffed. "I can't handle a boat anywhere," he said flatly. "But I'm colonel of the Eryx battalion of the militia, and I'm as good a gunman as anybody aboard *this* ship."

Ricimer's smile spread again. "Yeah," he said, "that might be useful."

He reached out his hand to shake Gregg's. When he saw the landsman was afraid to seem awkward in reaching to take it, Ricimer slid closer. He moved as smoothly as a feather in the breeze. Ricimer's grip was firm, but he didn't make the mistake of trying to crush Gregg's hand to prove that he was as strong as the bigger man.

"Maybe," Ricimer added over his shoulder as he led Gregg out through the bridge hatch, "we can give you some hands-on with the boat as well."

—2—

Above Salute

"Tancred!" Ricimer shouted as he slid hand over hand past crewmen in the bay containing the other two sets of attitude-jet controls. "C'mon along. Leon, get Bailey and Dole from the main engine compartment. We're taking the cutter down!"

"Bloody well about time!" agreed Leon. He was the *Sultan*'s bosun, a burly, scarred man. Leon picked his way with practiced skill through a jungle of equipment and connectors toward a back passage to the fusion thrusters.

"Lightbody and Jeude are already in Cargo Three with the boat," Ricimer said as he plunged headfirst down a ladderway toward the cargo holds.

Gregg tried to go "down" feetfirst as he would on a ladder under gravity. The passage, looped with conduits, was too narrow for him to turn when he realized his mistake. Tancred, following Gregg the proper way, was scarcely a boy in age. His face bore a look of bored disgust as he waited for the landsman to kick his way clear of obstacles he couldn't see.

Though the *Sultan* wasn't under thrust, scores of machines worked within the vessel's hull to keep her habitable. Echoes in the passage sighed like souls overwhelmed by misery.

Three crewmen under Leon were readying the eight-meter cutter when Gregg reached the hold. Tancred dogged the hatch closed, then joined the others with a snorted comment that Gregg chose not to hear.

Ricimer was at the arms locker, handing a cutting bar to a wiry spacer. "Here you go, Gregg," Ricimer called. The hold's empty volume blurred and thinned Ricimer's tones. "What do you want to carry?"

Gregg looked over the selection. The bridge had a separate arms locker, but the larger cabinet was here in Cargo Three, whose outer hatch provided the *Sultan*'s main access—except, presumably, when the hold was full of cargo.

The locker held a dozen breech-loading rifles, each with a bag of ammunition sized to that weapon's chamber. Two of the rifles were repeaters, but those would be even more sensitive to ammo variations than the single-shots.

True standardization had ended a millennium before, when hit-and-run attacks during the revolt of the outer colonies wrecked automated factories throughout the human universe. Billions of people died in the Collapse that followed.

Humanity had recovered to a degree. Mass production was technically possible again. The horror of complex systems that could be destroyed by a shock—and bring down civilization with them—remained. It was as much a religious attitude as a practical one.

Most of the locker was filled with powered cutting bars, forty or more of them. Venerian ceramic technology made their blades, super-hard teeth laminated in a resilient matrix, deadly even when the powerpack was exhausted and could not vibrate the cutting edge. Apart from their use as weapons, the bars were useful tools when anything from steel to tree trunks had to be cut.

There were also three flashguns in the locker. These had stubby barrels of black ceramic, thirty centimeters long and about twenty in diameter, mounted on shoulder stocks.

Under the right circumstances, a flashgun's laser bolts were far more effective than shots from a projectile weapon. The flashgun drained its power at each bolt, but the battery in the butt could be replaced with reasonable ease. Under sunny conditions, a parasol accumulator deployed over the gunner's head would recharge the weapon in two or three minutes anyway, making it still handier.

But flashguns were heavy, nearly useless in smoke or rain, and dangerous when the barrel cracked in use. The man carrying one was a target for every enemy within range, and side-scatter from the bolt was at best unpleasant to the shooter. They weren't popular weapons despite their undoubted efficiency.

Gregg took a flashgun and a bandolier holding six spare batteries from the locker.

Piet Ricimer raised an eyebrow. "I don't like to fool with flashguns unless I'm wearing a hard suit," he said.

Gregg shrugged, aware that he'd impressed the sailor for the first time. "I don't think we'll run into anything requiring hard suits," he said. "Do you?"

Ricimer shrugged in reply. "No, I don't suppose so," he said mildly.

Carrying two single-shot rifles, Ricimer nodded the crewman holding another rifle and three cutting bars toward the boat. He followed, side by side with Gregg.

"You owned your own ship?" Gregg asked, both from curiosity for the answer and to find a friendly topic. He didn't care to be on prickly terms with anybody else in the narrow confines of a starship.

Ricimer smiled at the memory. "*The Judge*, yes," he said. "Captain Cooper, the man who trained me, willed her to me when he died without kin. Just a little intrasystem trader, but she taught me as much as the captain himself did. I wouldn't have sold her, except that I really wanted to see the stars."

Ricimer braked himself on the cutter's hull with an expert flex of his knees, then caught Gregg to prevent him from caroming toward a far corner of the hold. "You'll get the hang of it in no time," he added encouragingly to the landsman.

The interior of the boat was tight for eight people. The bench down the axis of the cabin would seat only about five, so the others squatted in the aisles along the bulkheads.

Gregg had heard of as many as twenty being crammed into a vessel of similar size. He couldn't imagine how. He had to duck when a sailor took the pair of rifles from Ricimer and swung, poking their barrels toward Gregg's eyes.

Ricimer seated himself at the control console in the rear of the cabin. "Make room here for Mr. Gregg," he ordered Leon, who'd taken the end of the bench nearest him. The burly spacer gave Gregg a cold look as he obeyed.

"Hatch is tight, sir," Tancred reported from the bow as he checked the dogs.

Ricimer keyed the console's radio. "Cutter to *Sultan*'s bridge," he said. "Open Cargo Three. Over."

There was no response over the radio, but a jolt transmitted through the hull indicated that something was happening in the hold. The boat's vision screen was on the bulkhead to the left of the controls. Gregg leaned forward for a clearer view. The double hatchway pivoted open like a clam gaping. Vacuum was a nonreflecting darkness between the valves of dull white ceramic.

"Hang on, boys," Ricimer said. He touched a control. An attitude jet puffed the cutter out of the hold, on the first stage of its descent to the surface of the planet below.

—3—

Salute

"Got a hot spot, sir," Leon said, shouting over the atmospheric buffeting. He nodded toward the snake of glowing red across the decking forward. The interior of the cutter was unpleasantly warm, and the bitter tinge of things burning out of the bilges made Gregg's eyes water and his throat squeeze closed.

"Noted," Ricimer agreed. He fired the pair of small thrusters again, skewing the impulse 10° from a perpendicular through the axis of the bench.

The spacers swayed without seeming to notice the change. Tancred grabbed Gregg's bandolier. That was all that prevented the landsman from hurtling into a bulkhead.

"Thanks," Gregg muttered in embarrassment.

The young spacer sneered.

Ricimer leaned over his console. "Sorry," he said. "I needed to yaw us a bit. There's a crack in the outer hull, and if the inner facing gets hot enough, we'll have problems with that too."

Gregg nodded. He looked at the hot spot, possibly a duller red than it had been a moment before, and wondered whether atmospheric entry with a perforated hull could be survivable. He decided the answer didn't matter.

"Do you have a particular landing site in mind, Ricimer?" he asked, hoping his raw throat wouldn't make his voice break.

"Three of them," Ricimer said, glancing toward the vision screen. "But I don't trust the *Sultan*'s optics either. We'll find something here, no worry."

The cutter's vision screen gave a torn, grainy view of the landscape racing by beneath. A few cogs of the scanning raster were out of synch with the rest, displacing the center of the image to the right. Ragged green streaks marked the generally arid, rocky terrain.

Gregg squinted at the screen. He'd seen a regular pattern, a mosaic of pentagons, across the green floor of one valley. "That's something!" he said.

Ricimer nodded approvingly. "There's Molts here, at least. Captain Choransky wants a place where the Southerns have already set up the trade, though."

The Molts inhabited scores of planets within what had been human space before the Collapse. Tradition said that men had brought the chitinous humanoids from some unguessed homeworld and used them as laborers. Certainly there was no sign that the Molts had ever developed mechanical transport on their own, let alone star drive.

It was easy to think of the Molts as man-sized ants and their cities as mere hives, but they had survived the Collapse on the outworlds far better than humans had. Some planets beyond the solar system still had human populations of a sort: naked savages, "Rabbits" to the spacers, susceptible to diseases hatched among the larger populations of Earth and Venus and virtually useless for the purposes of resurgent civilization.

Molt culture was the same as it had been a thousand years ago, and perhaps for ten million years before that; and there was one thing more:

A few robot factories had survived the Collapse. They were sited at the farthest edges of human expansion, the colony worlds which had been overwhelmed by disaster so swiftly that the population didn't have time to cannibalize their systems in a desperate bid for survival. To present-day humans, these automated wonders were as mysterious as the processes which had first brought forth life.

But the Molts had genetic memory of the robot factories humans had trained them to manage before the Collapse. Whatever the Molts had been to men of the first expansion, equals or slaves, they were assuredly slaves now; and they were very valuable slaves.

Gregg checked his flashgun's parasol. Space in the boat was too tight to deploy the solar collector fully, but it appeared to slide smoothly on the extension rod.

Two spacers forward were discussing an entertainer in

Redport on Titan. From their description of her movements, she must have had snake blood.

The thrusters roared, braking hard. "So . . ." said Ricimer. "You're going to be a factor one of these days?"

Gregg looked at him. "Probably not," he said. "My brother inherited the hold. He's healthy, and he's got two sons already."

He paused, then added, "It's a small place in the Atalanta Plains, you know. Eryx. Nothing to get excited about."

The edge of Ricimer's mouth quirked. "Easy to say when you've got it," he said, so softly that Gregg had to read the words off the smaller man's lips.

The thrusters fired again. Gregg held himself as rigid as a caryatid. He smiled coldly at Tancred beside him.

Ricimer stroked a lever down, gimballing the thrusters sternward. The cigar-shaped vessel dropped from orbit with its long axis displayed to the shock of the atmosphere. Now that they'd slowed sufficiently, Ricimer slewed them into normal flight. They were about a thousand meters above the ground.

"You know, I'm from a factorial family too," Ricimer said with a challenge in his tone.

Gregg raised an eyebrow. "Are you?" he said. "Myself, I've always suspected that my family was really of some no-account in the service of Captain Gregg during the Revolt."

His smile was similar to the one he had directed at Tancred a moment before. "My Uncle Benjamin, though," Gregg continued, "that's Gregg of Weyston . . . He swears he's checked the genealogy and I'm wrong. That sort of thing matters a great deal—to Uncle Benjamin."

The two young men stared at one another while the cutter shuddered clumsily through the air. Starships' boats could operate in atmospheres, but they weren't optimized for the duty.

Piet Ricimer suddenly laughed. He reached over the console and gripped Gregg's hand. "You're all right, Gregg," he said. "And so am I, most of the time." His smile lighted the interior of the vessel. "Though you must be wondering.

"And there . . ." Ricimer went on—he hadn't looked toward the vision screen, so he must have caught the blurred glint of metal out of the corner of his eyes—"is what we're looking for."

Ricimer cut the thruster and brought the boat around in a

slow curve with one hand while the other keyed the radio. "Ricimer to *Sultan*," he said. "Home on me. We've got what looks like a Molt compound with two Southern Cross ships there already."

"And we're all going to be rich!" Leon rumbled from where he squatted beside the bow hatch. He touched the trigger of his cutting bar and brought it to brief, howling life—

Just enough to be sure the weapon was as ready as Leon himself was.

4

Salute

The *Preakness*, third and last vessel of Captain Choransky's argosy, spluttered like water boiling to lift a pot lid as she descended onto the gravel scrubland. Her engines cut in and out raggedly instead of holding a balanced thrust the way those of the *Sultan*'s boat had done for Ricimer.

Compared to the *Sultan* herself, the little *Preakness* was a model of control. Choransky's flagship slid down the gravity slope like a hog learning to skate. Gregg had been so sure the *Sultan* was going to crash that he'd looked around for some sort of cover from the gout of flaming debris.

The flagship had cooled enough for the crew to begin opening its hatches. It had finally set down six hundred meters away from the boat, too close for Gregg's comfort during the landing but a long walk for him now.

The roaring engines of the *Preakness* shut off abruptly. The ground shuddered with the weight of the vessel. Bits of rock, kicked up from the soil by the thrusters, clicked and pinged for a few moments on the hulls of the other ships.

"Let's go see what Captain Choransky has in mind," Ricimer said, adjusting the sling of the rifle on his shoulder. He sighed and added, "You know, if they'd trust the ships' artificial intelligences, they could land a lot smoother. When the *Sultan* wallowed in, I was ready to run for cover."

Gregg chuckled. "There wasn't any," he said.

"You're telling me!" Ricimer agreed.

He turned to the sailors. Two were still in the boat, while the others huddled unhappily in the vessel's shadow. Venerians weren't used to open skies. Gregg was uncomfortable himself, but his honor as a gentleman—and Piet Ricimer's apparent

12

imperturbability—prevented him from showing his fear.

"The rest of you stay here with the boat," Ricimer ordered. "Chances are, the captain'll want us to ferry him closer to the Southern compound. There's no point in doing anything until we know what the plan is."

"Aye-aye," Leon muttered for the crew. The bosun was as obviously glad as the remainder of the crew that he didn't have to cross the empty expanse.

"And keep a watch," Ricimer added. "Just because we don't see much here—"

He gestured. Except for the Venerian ships—the crews of the *Sultan* and *Dove* were unloading ground vehicles—there was nothing between the boat and the horizon except rocky hummocks of brush separated by sparse growths of a plant similar to grass.

"—doesn't mean that there isn't something around that thinks we're dinner. Besides, Molts can be dangerous, and you know the Southern Cross government in Buenos Aires doesn't want us to trade on the worlds it claims."

"Let them Southerns just try something!" Tancred said. The boy got up and stalked purposefully around to the other side of the boat, from where he could see the rest of the surroundings.

Gregg and Ricimer set out for the flagship. The dust of landing had settled, but reaction mass exhausted as plasma had ignited patches of scrub. The fires gave off bitter smoke.

"Do you think there's really anything dangerous around here?" Gregg asked curiously.

Ricimer shrugged. "I doubt it," he said. "But I don't know anything about Salute." He stared at the white sky. "If this really *is* Salute."

From above, the landscape appeared flat and featureless. The hummocks were three or four meters high, lifted from the ground on the plateaus of dirt which clung to the roots of woody scrub. Sometimes they hid even the *Sultan*'s 300-tonne bulk from the pair on foot.

The bushes were brown, leafless, and seemingly as dead as the gravel beneath. Gregg saw no sign of animal life whatever.

"How do you think the Southerns are going to react?" Ricimer asked suddenly.

Gregg snorted. "They can claim the Administration of Humanity gave them sole rights to this region if they like. The Administration didn't do a damned thing for the Gregg

family after the Collapse, when we could've used some help—
didn't do a damned thing—"

"Don't swear," Ricimer said sharply. "God hears us here
also."

Gregg grimaced. In a softer tone, he continued, "Nobody
but God and Venus helped Venus during the Collapse. The
Administration isn't going to tell us where in God's universe
we can trade now."

Ricimer nodded. He flashed his companion a brief grin to
take away the sting of his previous rebuke. Factorial families
were notoriously loose about their language; though the same
was true of most sailors as well.

"But what will the Southerns *do*, do you think?" Ricimer
asked in a mild voice.

"They'll trade with us," Gregg said flatly. He shifted his
grip on the flashgun. It was an awkward weapon to carry
for any distance. The fat barrel made it muzzle-heavy and
difficult to sling. "Just as the colonies of the North American
Federation will trade with us when we carry the Molts to them.
The people out in the Reaches, they need the trade, whatever
politics are back in the solar system."

"Anyway," Ricimer said in partial agreement, "the Southerns can't possibly have enough strength here to give us a hard
time. We've got almost two hundred men."

Choransky's crew had uncrated the three stake-bed trucks
carried in the *Sultan*'s forward hold. Two of them were running. As Ricimer and Gregg approached, the smoky rotary
engine of the third vibrated into life. Armed crewmen, many
of them wearing full or partial body armor, clambered aboard.

Captain Choransky stood up in the open cab of the leading
vehicle. "There you are, Ricimer!" he called over the head of
his driver. "We're off to load our ships. You and Mr. Gregg
can come along if you can find room."

The truck bed was full of men, and the other two would be
packed before the young officers could reach them. Without
hesitation, Ricimer gripped a cleat and hauled himself onto the
outside of Choransky's vehicle. His boot toes thrust between
the stakes which he held with one hand. He reached down
with the other hand to help Gregg into a similarly precarious
position, just as the truck accelerated away.

Gregg wondered what he would have done if Ricimer hadn't
extended a hand, certain that his companion wanted to come

despite the risk. Gregg didn't worry about his own courage—
but he preferred to act deliberately rather than at the spur of
the moment.

He looked over his shoulder. The *Sultan*'s other two trucks
were right behind them, but the *Dove*'s crew were still setting
up the vehicle they'd unloaded. The *Preakness* was just opening her single hatch.

"Shouldn't we have gotten organized first?" Gregg shouted
into Ricimer's ear over the wind noise.

Ricimer shrugged, but he was frowning.

—5—

Salute

The general rise in the lumpy terrain was imperceptible, but when the trucks jounced onto a crest, Gregg found he could look sharply *down* at the ships three kilometers behind him—

And, in the other direction, at the compound. Neither of the Southern vessels was as big as the *Preakness*, the lightest of Choransky's argosy. The installation itself consisted of a pair of orange, prefabricated buildings and a sprawling area set off by metal fencing several meters high. The fence twinkled as it incinerated scraps of vegetation which blew against it.

There was no sign of humans. Squat, mauve-colored figures watched the Venerians from inside the fence: Molts, over a hundred of them.

Captain Choransky stood up in his seat again, aiming his rifle skyward in one hand. The truck rumbled over the crest, gaining speed as it went.

"Here we go, boys!" Choransky bellowed. His shot cracked flatly across the barren distances.

A dozen other crewmen fired. Dust puffed just short of the orange buildings, indicating that at least one of the men wasn't aiming at the empty heavens.

"What are we doing?" Gregg shouted to Ricimer. "Is this an attack? What's happening?"

Ricimer cross-stepped along the stakes and leaned toward the cab. "Captain Choransky!" he said. "We're not at war with the Southern Cross, are we?"

The captain turned with a startled expression replacing his glee. "War, boy?" he said. "There's no peace beyond Pluto! Don't you know anything?"

Choransky's truck pulled up between the two buildings. Gregg squeezed hard to keep from losing his grip either on the vehicle or the heavy flashgun which inertia tried to drag out of the hand he could spare for it. The second truck almost skidded into theirs in a cloud of stinging grit. The third stopped near the Southern starships.

Gregg jumped down, glad to be on firm ground again. The smaller building was a barracks. Sliding doors and no windows marked the larger as a warehouse.

Gregg ran toward the warehouse, his flashgun ready. Ricimer was just ahead of him. They were spurred by events, even though neither of them was sure what was going on.

Ricimer twisted the latch of the small personnel door in the slider. It wasn't locked.

The warehouse lights were on. The interior was almost empty. A man in bright clothing lay facedown on the concrete floor with his hands clasped behind his neck. "I surrender!" he bleated. "I'm not armed! Don't hurt—"

Gregg gripped the Southern by the shoulder. "Come on, get up," he said. "Nobody's going to hurt you."

"I got one!" cried the spacer who pushed into the warehouse behind Gregg. He waved his cutting bar toward the prisoner.

Ricimer used his rifle muzzle to prod the blade aside as he stepped in front of the Venerian. "*Our* prisoner, I think, sailor," he said. "And take off your cap when you address officers!"

The man stumbled backward into the group following him. One of the newcomers was Platt, another member of Choransky's command group. Platt wore a helmet with the faceshield raised. In addition, he carried a revolving pistol belted on over body armor.

"Who else is here?" Gregg asked the Southern he held. He spoke in English, the language of trade—and the tongue in which the fellow had begged for mercy.

"What's going on?" Platt demanded.

Ricimer shushed him curtly. He stood protectively between Gregg and the newcomers, but his face was turned to catch the Southern's answers.

"Nobody, nobody!" the prisoner said. "I was in here—all right, I was asleep. I heard a ship landing, I thought it was, so I went out and all the bastards had run away and left me!

All of them! Taken the trucks and what was I supposed to do? Defend the compound?"

"Why didn't you defend the compound?" Gregg asked. "I mean, all of you. There's the crews of those two ships as well as the staff here."

Around them, Platt and a score of other Venerians were poking among bales of trade goods, mostly synthetic fabrics and metal containers. The warehouse was spacious enough to hold twenty times the amount of merchandise present.

"Defend?" the Southern sputtered. He was a small man, as dark as Ricimer, with a face that hadn't been prepossessing before a disease had pocked it. "With what, half a dozen rifles? And there wasn't but ten of us all told. The local Molts bring us prisoners and we buy them. We aren't soldiers."

"We should've landed right here in the valley," said Platt, who'd drifted close enough to hear the comment. "Cap'n Choransky was too afraid of taking a plasma charge up the bum while we hovered to do that, though."

"And so would you be if you had the sense God gave a goose!" boomed Choransky himself as he strode into the warehouse. "You got a prisoner, Mr. Gregg? Good work. There wasn't anybody in the house."

The captain rubbed his cheek with the knuckles of his right hand, in which he held his rifle. "Like a pigsty, that place."

"He says his fellows drove off in a panic and left him when they heard the ships landing, sir," Ricimer said.

Choransky stepped closer to the prisoner. "Where's the rest of your stock?" he asked.

"You can't just come and take—" the Southern began.

Choransky punched him, again using his right hand with the rifle. The prisoner sprawled backward on the concrete. His lip bled, and there was a livid mark at the hairline where the fore end struck him.

"We've got pretty much a full load," the Southern said in a flat voice from the floor. He was staring at the toes of his boots.

He touched the cut in his lip with his tongue, then continued, "There's a freighter due in a week or so. The ships out there, they don't have transit capability. The freighter, it stays in orbit. We ferry up air, reaction mass, and cargo and bring down the food and trade goods."

Choransky nodded. "Maybe we'll use them to ferry the water over and top off our reaction mass. Those ships, they've got pumps to load water themselves?"

"Yes," the Southern muttered to his toes.

Platt kicked the side of the prisoner's head, not hard. "Say 'sir' when you talk to the captain, dog!"

"Yes sir, Captain," the Southern said.

"All right," Choransky said as he turned to leave the warehouse. "Platt, get the Molts organized and march them to the ships. Ricimer, you think you're a whiz with thrusters, you see if you can get one of those Southern boats working. I'll tell Baltasar to put an officer and crew from the *Dove* in the other."

He strode out the door. Platt followed him, and the rest of the spacers began to drift along in their wake.

"Right," said Ricimer. He counted off the six nearest men with pecks of his index finger. "You lot, come along with me and Mr. Gregg. I'm going to show people how to make a ship hover on thrust."

He shooed them toward the doorway ahead of him with both arms. The chosen crewmen scowled or didn't, depending on temperament, but no one questioned the order.

"You don't mind, do you?" Ricimer murmured to Gregg as they stepped out under an open sky again. "They haven't worked with me before. You won't have to do anything, but I'd like a little extra authority present."

"Glad to help," Gregg said. He looked at his left hand. He'd managed to bark the knuckles badly during the wild ride to the compound. "Besides, I wasn't looking forward to those trucks again."

Ricimer chuckled. His dark, animated face settled. Without looking at his companion, he said, "What do you think about all this, anyway? The way we're dealing with the Southerns."

Gregg glanced around while he framed a reply. Venerians had unlocked the gate in the electrified fence and were herding out the Molts. Some crewmen waved their weapons, but that seemed unnecessary. The Molts were perfectly docile.

The wedge-faced humanoids were a little shorter than the human average. Most of them were slightly built, but a few had double the bulk of the norm. Gregg wondered whether that was a sexual distinction or some more esoteric specialization.

Viewed up close, many of the Molts bore dark scars on their waxy, purplish exoskeletons. A few were missing arms, and more lacked one or more of the trio of multijointed fingers that formed a normal "hand".

"I'm my uncle's agent," Gregg said at last. "And I can tell you, nothing bothers my Uncle Ben if there's profit in it. Which there certainly is here."

Ricimer nodded. "I'm second cousin to the Mosterts," he said.

One of the crewmen he'd dragooned showed enough initiative to run ahead and find the hatch mechanism of the nearer ship. It sighed open.

"Really, now," Ricimer added with a grin to his companion. "Though what I said about a factorial family, there's evidence."

Gregg laughed.

"All three ships are Alexi Mostert's," Ricimer continued. "In the past, my cousin's made the voyage himself, though he sent Choransky out in charge this time. I'm sure this is how Alexi conducted the business too."

They'd reached the Southern Cross vessel. It weighed about 50 tonnes and was metal-hulled, unlike the ships of the Venerian argosy. Metals were cheap and readily available in the asteroids of every planetary system; but ceramic hulls were preferable for vessels which had to traverse the hellish atmosphere of Venus. Besides, the surface of the second planet was metal-poor.

Survival after the Collapse had raised ceramic technology to a level higher than had been dreamed of while Venus was part of a functioning intergalactic economy. After a thousand years of refinement, Venerians sneered at the notion metals could ever equal ceramics—though the taunt "glass-boat sailor!" had started fights in many spaceports since Venus returned to space.

"Some of you find the water intakes and figure out how to deploy them," Ricimer ordered as he sat at the control console.

The interior of the vessel stank with a variety of odors, some of them simply those of a large mass of metal to noses unfamiliar with it. The control cabin could be sealed. The rest of the ship was a single open hold.

"What do *you* think of what we're doing?" Ricimer said to Gregg.

Then, before the landsman could reply, he added in a crisp voice, "All hands watch yourselves. I'm going to light the thrusters."

"I think . . ." Gregg murmured as Ricimer engaged the vessel's AI, "that it's bad for business, my friend."

Near Virginia

Choransky and Bivens muttered, their heads close above a CRT packed with data. The navigator grimaced but nodded. Choransky reached for a switch.

Ricimer turned from where he stood in the midst of the forward attitude-control boards he now supervised. "All right, gentlemen," he said. "We're about to transit again."

He winked at Gregg.

Gregg clasped a stanchion. He kept his eyes open, because he'd learned that helped—*helped*—him control vertigo. There wasn't anything in his stomach but acid, but he'd spew *that*, sure as the sun shone somewhere, if he wasn't lucky.

The *Sultan* lurched into transit space—and lurched out again calculated milliseconds later. The starship's location and velocity were modified by the amount she'd accelerated in a spacetime whose constants were radically different from those of the sidereal universe.

They dropped in and out of alien universes thirty-eight times by Gregg's count, bootstrapping the length of each jump by the acceleration achieved in the series previous before they returned to the sidereal universe to stay—until the next insertion. The entire sequence took a little more than one sidereal minute. Gregg's stomach echoed the jumps a dozen times over before finally settling again.

"There!" cried Captain Choransky, pointing to the blurred starfield that suddenly filled the *Sultan*'s positioning screen. "There, we've got Virginia!"

"We've got something," Bivens said morosely. "I'm not sure it's Virginia. These optics . . ."

Dole, at one of the attitude workstations, yawned and closed his eyes. Lightbody took out his pocket Bible and began to read, moving his lips. Jeude, at the third workstation, appeared to be comatose.

Two officers came in from aft compartments. They joined Choransky and Bivens at the front of the bridge, squabbling over the *Sultan*'s location and whether or not their consorts were among the flecks of light on the positional display. It was obviously going to be some minutes, perhaps hours, before the next transit.

Gregg maneuvered carefully through the cluttered three meters separating him from Ricimer. The landsman was getting better at moving in freefall. He'd learned that his very speed and strength were against him, and that he had to move in tiny, precisely-controlled increments.

Ricimer grinned. "These were easy jumps," he said. "Wait till the gradients rise and the thrusters have us bucking fit to spring the frames before we can get into transit space. But you'll get used to it."

"Where are we?" Gregg asked, pretending to ignore the spacer's comments.

He spoke softly, but the combination of mechanical racket, the keening of the Molts—they didn't like transit any better than Gregg's stomach did—and the increasingly loud argument around the positional display provided privacy from anyone but the trio at the attitude controls. Those men were Ricimer's, body and soul. They were as unlikely to carry tales against him as they were to try to swim home to Venus.

"The Virginia system," Ricimer said. "Both the captain and Bivens are pretty fair navigators. We're about a hundred million kilometers out from the planet; three jumps or maybe four."

"Why are you sure and they aren't?" the landsman asked.

Jeude turned his head toward the officers. He was a young man, fair-haired and angelic in appearance. "Because Mr. Ricimer knows his ass from a hole in the ground, sir," he said to Gregg. "Which that lot"—he nodded forward—"don't."

"None of that, Jeude," Ricimer said sharply. His expression softened as he added to Gregg, "I memorized starcharts for some of the likely planetfalls when I applied for a place on this voyage."

"But . . . ?" Gregg said. He peered at the flat-screen positional display, placed at an angle across the bridge. It would be blurry even close up. "You can tell from *that*?"

Ricimer shrugged. "Well, you can't expect to have a perfect sighting or a precise attitude," he said. "You have to study. And trust your judgment."

"I'd rather trust *your* judgment, sir," Jeude said. When he spoke, it was like seeing a dead man come to life.

"I think that'll do for me, too," Gregg agreed.

"Right, it's Virginia and I don't want any more bloody argument!" Captain Choransky boomed. "We'll do it in four jumps."

"I'd do it in three," Ricimer murmured. His voice was too soft for Gregg to hear the words, but the landsman read them in his grin.

—7—

Above Virginia

"If they don't make up their mind in the next thirty seconds," Ricimer said in Gregg's ear, "we'll lose our reentry window and have to orbit a fourth time."

"All right," Choransky said, as though prodded by the comment that he couldn't have heard. "That's got to be the settlement. We're going down."

He threw a large switch on his console, engaging not the main thrusters directly but rather the AI which had planned the descent two and a half hours earlier. The thrusters fired in a steady 1-g impulse quite different from the vertiginous throbs required by navigation through transit space.

Gregg's legs flexed slightly. It felt good to have weight again.

Attitude jets burped, rocking the *Sultan* as they counteracted the first effects of atmospheric buffeting. Lightbody spread his fingers over his control keys.

"Keep your hands off those, sailor!" Ricimer said sharply. "When I want you to override the AI, I'll tell you so."

Such images as had been available on the positioning display vanished behind curtains of light. The *Sultan*'s powerplant converted reaction mass, normally water, into plasma accelerated to a sizable fraction of light speed. When the thrusters were being used, as now, to brake the vessel's descent into an atmosphere, she drove down into a bath of the stripped ions she herself had ejected.

"Shouldn't we have told the *Dove* and the *Preakness* we were going down?" Gregg said. He pitched his voice low, not only to prevent the captain from hearing but because he didn't want to interfere with Piet Ricimer's concentration if the young officer was busier than he appeared to Gregg to be.

Ricimer pursed his lips. "One could say . . ." he replied. His eyes darted from one of the workstations to the next, checking to be sure his men were alert but not acting where silicon decisions were preferable. " . . . that Baltasar and Roon will see us going down, and that we need to land first anyway because the *Sultan* is such a pig. But one also could say that . . ."

"Communication doesn't hurt," Gregg said, not so much putting words in the spacer's mouth as offering his own opinion.

Ricimer nodded.

The *Sultan* began to vibrate unpleasantly. Gregg wasn't sure whether it was his imagination until Ricimer scowled and called out, "Sir, that harmonic is causing trouble with my controls. Can you give me—"

Choransky swore and thumbed a vernier on his console. The increment to the AI's calculated power was minute, but it kept the hull from resonating with sympathetic vibration.

Gregg frowned at the three workstations, trying to see anything different about them. "What was wrong with the controls?" he asked after a moment.

Ricimer grinned, then mouthed, "Nothing," with the back of his head to the captain and navigator. "She would've shaken to bits in time," he said, amplifying his statement in a scarcely louder voice. "And I don't know how *much* time."

He glanced at Choransky, then turned again and added, "He doesn't trust the AI for navigation, when he ought to; but he won't overrule it for something like that, harmonics that a chip can't *feel* so a man's got to."

Gregg watched as the display slowly cleared. The *Sultan* had scrubbed away her orbital velocity. Now she descended under gravity alone, partially balanced by atmospheric braking. The AI cut thruster output, so there was less plasma-generated interference with the optics which fed the screen.

Virginia was slightly more prepossessing than Salute had been. The landmass expanding beneath the starship was green and gray-green with vegetation.

The planet's main export was cellulose base, useful as a raw material in the solar system albeit not a high-value cargo. The few pre-Collapse sites on Virginia provided a trickle of artifacts which current civilization could not duplicate. There were no caches of microchips on Virginia or automated factories like those which made some planets so valuable.

About thirty kilometers of slant distance away, metal glittered in the center of an expanse of lighter green. That was Virginia's unnamed spaceport, from which drones lifted mats of cellulose into orbit for starships to clamp to the outside of their hulls. Gregg squinted at the settlement, trying to bring it into focus.

The display vibrated in rainbow colors. Something slammed the *Sultan*.

"Plasma bolt!" Gregg shouted in amazement.

Captain Choransky disconnected the AI with one hand and chopped thruster output with the other. For an instant, the starship hesitated as gravity fought the inertia of earlier thrust. Gregg's stomach flip-flopped.

Ricimer reached past Dole and mashed a control button on his workstation. "Gregg!" he shouted. "Get aft and tell the other two bands to give us side-impulse! Only Jet Two on each bank!"

A bell on the navigational console clanged. Red lights were flashing from Dole's workstation. Gregg didn't know what the alarms meant—maybe the *Sultan* was breaking up—and he didn't understand Ricimer's words.

He understood that he had to repeat the command to the sailors controlling the other two bands of attitude jets in the next compartment sternward, though.

Gregg sprinted through the rear hatch. The starship was nearly in freefall as Choransky tried to drop out of the sights of the Federation gunners. Ricimer wanted to slew the vessel sideways as well, but the impulse from his forward attitude jet was being resisted fiercely by the crewmen at the other two bands who didn't have a clue as to what was happening on the bridge.

The *Sultan* yawed. Gregg jumped over a squat power supply and through the hatch like a practiced gymnast, touching nothing on the way. "Those Federation heathens are shooting at us!" someone bleated behind him.

The next compartment was even more crowded than the bridge. The double bank of attitude-control workstations, each with an officer standing in the middle of three seated crewmen, was against the starboard bulkhead. Platt and Martre were on duty.

The port side was usually rolled hammocks and a table

for off-duty men to do handwork. Now it was stacked with rations for the Molts—fungus-processed carbohydrate bricks that stank almost as bad now as they did when the aliens excreted the residue. Half a dozen men clustered around the crates for want of anywhere better to be.

Overhead a tannoy blurted fragments of Choransky's voice. The *Sultan*'s intercom system worked badly, and the captain was nearly incoherent at the moment anyway.

"What's going on?" Platt demanded. Gregg's appearance caught him leaving his station to go to the bridge.

"Fire Jet Two, both bands!" Gregg shouted. "Not the others!"

"You heard him!" Martre said, pointing to one of his team. Choransky had dropped the men on the central and rear attitude controls into an unexplained crisis when he switched off the artificial intelligence. Martre was delighted to have someone—anyone—tell him what to do.

"What in *hell* is going on?" Platt repeated. The *Sultan* began to yaw as the attitude jets fought one another.

Ricimer came through the hatch behind Gregg and darted for Platt's control set. Platt tried to grab him. Gregg put his right arm around Platt's throat from behind and clamped hard enough to choke off the officer's startled squawk.

Platt's team members jumped up from their seats—to get out of the way rather than to interfere. Ricimer slid one control up. Tancred, off duty in the compartment a moment before, sprawled over a workstation in order to drop its slide and that of the third to the bottom of their tracks.

Lights flickered. Gregg felt hairs lift on his arms.

"*Missed* us, by the mercy of God," Ricimer said, and there was no blasphemy in his tone. He seated himself properly at the workstation he'd taken over. "But not by much."

Bivens stuck his head through the hatch from the bridge. "Stand by for braking!" he warned in a shrill voice.

Gregg released Platt.

The smaller man turned and croaked, "You whoreson!" He cocked a fist, then took in Gregg's size and the particular smile on the young gentleman's face.

Platt turned away. Leon, who'd popped up from one of the lower compartments, judiciously concealed what looked like a length of high-pressure tubing in his trouser leg. The bosun nodded respectfully to Gregg.

The thrusters cut in again with a tremendous roar, slowing the massive starship after her freefall through the line-of-sight range of the Federation guns. The braking effort was an abnormal several Gs, slamming men to the decks and causing some shelves to collapse. Gregg kept his feet with difficulty.

On the bridge, the men at the forward attitude controls were bellowing "Onward, Christian Soldiers" in surprisingly good harmony.

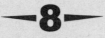

Virginia

The *Sultan*'s long cigar shape lay on its side with the landing legs properly deployed and all three cargo hatches open. The ground beneath the thrusters fizzed and snapped as heat-stressed stones cooled.

Gregg hunched in his hard suit and wondered whether he ought to drop the thick visor as well. That would mean using bottled air and seeing out through a slit, but at least it would keep the *wind* off him.

Virginia's breezes slapped harshly against skin used to the weatherless corridors of Venus. The *Sultan*'s thrusters had ignited pungent fires as she roared in to land, and miniature leaves blew from the scorched trees surrounding the starship. They were hard-shelled, and their tips were as sharp as shards of glass.

More by luck than planning, Choransky had brought the *Sultan* down at the edge of a natural clearing. The ground was so thin-soiled that only ankle-high moss grew on it. That was fortunate, because the trees beyond the clearing were thirty or forty meters high, with trunks so thin and closely spaced that they resembled a field of giant wheat.

Starships' plasma exhaust could clear landing sites in almost any vegetation, but the blazing, shattered trunks would form an impassable barrier. The debris would have locked the crew and cargo within the *Sultan* as surely as hard vacuum had during the voyage.

A Molt stumbled off the ramp and bumped a guard. "God damn your crinkly soul to Hell!" shouted the spacer as he lashed out with his boot. The chitinous alien tried to back

30

away, but one of its legs flailed spastically. It fell toward the human again.

Piet Ricimer grabbed the crewman by the collar and jerked him backward. "You!" Ricimer said. "If I hear you blaspheme that way again, you'll swab out all three holds alone! Do you think God no longer hears us because we're off Venus?"

"Sorry, sir," the sailor muttered. Gregg had expected more trouble—and was moving closer in case it occurred. Ricimer's fierce sincerity shocked the man into quiet obedience.

Navigator Bivens appeared at the edge of Cargo One. He cupped his hands before his mouth as an amplifier and shouted, "Watch out, boys. There's aircraft coming, the radar says."

"Hell *take* them!" Gregg snarled, meaning life in general. He was glad an instant later that he hadn't spoken loudly enough for his new friend Ricimer to hear.

And after all, the spacer was right. They were going to need the Lord's help here in the outer reaches of his universe at least as much as they did among the familiar verities of home.

Captain Choransky was on the radio, trying to raise the *Sultan*'s consorts and whoever was in charge of the Federation settlement. Ricimer, Gregg, and about two dozen armed crewmen shepherded the cargo of Molts onto the surface so that the holds could be washed down. So far as the men aboard the starship were concerned, Ricimer's task was the more important.

They'd loaded ninety-eight Molts aboard the *Sultan* on Salute, a slight majority of the total, with the rest split between the smaller Venerian ships. Ninety-two had survived thus far, but many of them were on their last legs, and in a confined space they stank like death itself.

A single air system served the entire starship. The *Sultan*'s human complement had been breathing the stench throughout a voyage of seventeen days.

Men checked their weapons. Only a few of those guarding the Molts had brought rifles: cutting bars were lighter and more effective, both for use and as threats. More riflemen and another flashgunner in a hard suit appeared at the lip of Cargo One a moment after Bivens called his warning.

"Don't shoot unless I tell you to," Ricimer shouted to the men spread in a loose perimeter around the Molts. "Remember we aren't here to fight. We're traders!"

"Hope *they* remember that," said Jeude as he spun his cutting bar for a test. His tone undercut the words.

Gregg thought he heard the faint *pop-pop-pop-pop* of motors. He glanced at the cloud-streaked sky. The sound didn't have a clear direction.

"Which way is the settlement?" he called to Ricimer.

Ricimer turned from the Molt he'd helped over the coaming at the bottom of the ramp. The alien was the last to leave the *Sultan*. It was either sick or very old, and the ramp's four-centimeter lip had stopped it like a slab of bedrock.

"That way," Ricimer said, pointing across the clearing toward south-southwest based on sun position. "Five klicks, a hair less. Once a ship the size of the *Sultan* commits to landing, you don't maneuver much."

Someone hammered within the starship's hull, freeing a stuck latch. One, then five more meter-square hatches swung open along the *Sultan*'s hull. The muzzle of a plasma cannon poked through the nearest opening.

Ricimer looked at the Molts, milling slowly in the midst of the crewmen. Some of the aliens were rubbing their torsos with wads of moss they'd plucked. "Move them into the woods," Ricimer ordered. "Now! Nobody'd better be in the clearing if the heavy ordnance fires."

Gregg focused in the direction of the settlement. The sound of motors was very close, though nothing was visible over the trees at the edge of the clearing. He aimed his flashgun at the expected target and shouted, "Don't fire until Master Ricimer orders!" to prevent anyone from mistaking his intent.

The *Sultan* carried ten plasma cannon, but she was pierced with over forty gunports so that the heavy weapons could be moved to where they were needed. Even in weightlessness, the weapons' mass made them difficult to shift through the strait confines of the vessel. When the crews were working here on the ground, they'd be lucky if scrapes and bruises were the only injuries before the start of the fighting.

If there was going to be fighting.

Two aircraft crossed the edge of the clearing and banked in opposite directions. They were one- or two-place autogyros, moving at 100kph or slower.

Nobody fired at them, but one of the crewmen screamed, "Federation dog-mothers!" and waved his cutting bar. Leon grabbed the man's arm and growled at him before Ricimer could react.

The first aircraft vanished beneath the treetops again. Three more autogyros appeared. One of them settled into the clearing. It bounced twice on the rocky soil but came to a halt within fifteen meters. Its four consorts began to circle the starship slowly at a hundred meters.

Choransky, Bivens, and several other officers stamped down the Cargo Three ramp. They were all armed. Martre wore the helmet and torso of a hard suit and carried another flashgun. He nodded as Gregg fell in step to one side of the command group and Ricimer joined on the other.

The autogyro's four-bladed support rotor slowed to a halt. The passenger getting out of the tandem seat to the rear was male, but Gregg noticed with distaste that the pilot was a woman. Gregg wasn't a religious zealot, but the way the North American Federation put women in positions of danger—women even served in the crews of Federation starships—would be offensive to any decent man.

The autogyro was powered by an air-cooled diesel. Gregg didn't realize how noisy it was until the passenger shouted an order and his pilot shut the clattering motor off.

"What do you mean shooting at us?" Captain Choransky shouted while he was still twenty meters from the aircraft. "Look at that!"

He pointed over his shoulder in the general direction of the *Sultan.* Through air at such long range, the plasma bolt had only scoured away a patch of yellow-brown corrosion the Venerian atmosphere had left on the starship's white hull. Even such a relatively light weapon could have been fatal if it hit the thrusters during the descent, or if the *Sultan*'s hull was crazed by long vibration.

"You have no right to be here!" the Federation envoy said shrilly. "The Administration of Humanity has awarded exploitation of this sector to America!"

The envoy was a tall, thin man with a full beard but almost no hair above the line of his ears. He wore a gray tunic over blue trousers, perhaps a uniform, with gaudy decorations on his left breast. His holstered pistol was for show rather than use, and he looked extremely apprehensive of the heavily-armed Venerians.

"Brisbane's authority is a farce!" Choransky said. He stopped directly in front of the envoy and stood with his arms akimbo, emphasizing the breadth of his chest. "The Secretary General can't *fart* unless President Pleyal tells him to."

The envoy swallowed. He met Choransky's glare, but Gregg had the feeling that was to avoid having to admit the presence of the other murderous-looking Venerians surrounding him. The Fed's courage wasn't in doubt.

"Whatever President Pleyal may be to you," the envoy said, "he is my head of state. And his orders are that his domains beyond Earth shall have no dealings except with vessels of the North American Federation."

Choransky poked the envoy's chest with one powerful finger. "Balls!" he said. "Captain Mostert turned over his whole cargo on Virginia last year. I'm *from* Captain Mostert. Don't you recognize the damned ship?"

The Federation envoy made an angry moue with his lips. "Port Commander Finchly, who dealt with your Captain Mostert," he said, "was arrested and carried back to Earth last month to stand trial. His replacement, Port Commander Zaloga, arrived with the orders for his predecessor's arrest."

Choransky seized the grip of the cutting bar dangling from his belt. He also wore a slung rifle. The envoy shut his eyes but didn't move.

"God grind your stupid bones to meal!" the captain said, his voice low-pitched but sincere. Then he went on in a grating but nearly normal tone, "Look, you tell your Commander Zaloga this. I'm bringing my other ships down, because they stink worse 'n sewers with the Molts we're carrying. And you bastards *need* Molts!"

The envoy's eyelids quivered.

"Then we'll come talk to Zaloga, and talk like sensible people. If he's looking for a little something for himself to clear this, well, I guess something can be arranged. But no more shooting!"

The envoy nodded, then opened his eyes. "I'll tell the commander," he said, "and I'm sure he'll talk with you himself. But as for your business—"

For an instant there was something more than fear and formality in the Fed's voice. "Gentlemen, you *know* President Pleyal. It's as much as a man's life is worth to cross him."

Choransky gripped the envoy by the shoulder, gently enough, and turned the man back toward his autogyro. "Pleyal's a

long way away," the Venerian captain said. "I'm here, and
believe me, I'm not taking these stinking Molts back to Venus
with me."

Ricimer stepped in front of the envoy. "Sir," he said. "Without trade your colony will die, and without outside resources
the homeworlds—even Earth in her present condition—will
die also. No orders that restrict trade can be in keeping with
the will of God for mankind to survive."

The Federation officer stared as Ricimer moved out of the
way again. "Does President Pleyal recognize a god beyond
himself?" he asked, half a taunt. He got into the aircraft.

"And no shooting!" Choransky repeated in a loud voice as
the Fed pilot restarted her motor.

—9—

Virginia

The roar of the vessels landing made bones quiver. The glare of the thrusters was so intense that Gregg felt the bare backs of his hands prickle. He'd lowered his visor to protect his sight.

They'd had to reload the Molts temporarily. With luck, the other ships could manage to avoid the *Sultan* when they landed around the edges of the clearing, but there was no way to safely mark the location of off-loaded cargo among the trees. The aliens moaned as they were forced back aboard the vessel.

From the *Sultan*'s open hatchways Gregg, Ricimer, and a score of other crewmen and officers watched their consorts land. Partly because of his filtered vision, partly due to simple unfamiliarity with the fine points of starship construction, it wasn't until the vessels were within fifty meters of the ground that Gregg understood what was wrong.

"That's not the *Preakness* with the *Dove!*" he bellowed to Ricimer. The spacer couldn't possibly hear him—and had no doubt known the truth within seconds of the time the starships came in sight, making a rare and dangerous simultaneous landing. "That's some Earth ship! She's got a metal hull!"

Whatever the vessel was, she landed neatly in the clear area. The *Dove* came down in an orange fireball fifty meters within the margin of the forest, blasting splinters in every direction.

Virginia's vegetation didn't sustain flames very well when it was green. The fire wouldn't be dangerous, but it would smolder and reek for days or longer. Ricimer, his face screened by the rosy filter which pivoted down from inside the brim of his cap, shook his head in disgust at the *Dove*'s awkwardness.

The strange vessel was about the 150 tonnes of the *Dove*. The hull was more smoothly curved than that of a Venerian ship, but there were a dozen or more blisters marring the general lines. Some of the blisters were obviously weapons installations.

Metal was easier to form into complex shapes than mold-cast ceramics. It was also easier to tack this or that extra installation onto a metal hull later, instead of getting the design right the first time.

The *Preakness* had started her landing approach. Radio was useless when a starship's thrusters were swamping the RF spectrum with ions. Gregg didn't expect to learn anything until all the vessels were down.

A personnel hatch on the newcomer's belly curve opened. The rock beneath still glowed white from the landing, distorting the vessel's appearance with heat waves.

A man—a very big man—wearing a silver hard suit jumped out of the ship and ran heavily toward the *Sultan*. He must have heard the *Preakness* coming in, but he ignored the chance that the Venerian ship would crush his plasma-fried ashes to the rock.

Gregg's lips pursed. He risked raising his visor for a moment to be sure. The stranger carried a repeating rifle, as ornately splendid as his metal hard suit. The suit, at least, was functional. It had just protected its wearer across a stretch of stone so hot it was tacky.

Gregg knew better than most what it took out of you to run in a hard suit, and how easy it was to trip with your helmet visor down. He strode down to the bottom of the ramp and offered the stranger a hand—a delicate way of warning the fellow of the raised lip.

The stranger caught his bootheel anyway and shouted curses in German loud enough to be heard above the *Preakness*' approach. With his left gauntlet in Gregg's right hand, they clomped into Cargo Three. It wasn't often Gregg met somebody bigger than he himself was.

Molts packed themselves tighter against the bulkheads to keep clear. The aliens understood human orders, even without the kicks that normally accompanied the words. Supposedly their mouth parts permitted them to use human speech, but Gregg hadn't heard one do so yet.

The ramp/hatchcover began to rise before Gregg and the stranger were fully clear of it, lowering the noise level abruptly. Piet Ricimer was at the control box.

The stranger opened his helmet. "So!" he said in Trade English. "I am *Kapitän*, that is Captain Schremp of Drillinghausen. My *Adler* has been here in orbit for a week, but the Federation bastards, they even shot at us when we tried to land. And you are?"

"The *Sultan* out of Betaport, Captain Choransky commanding," Ricimer said easily. "I think the captain—"

United Europe had not been involved in reopening the stars. Even now, the North American Federation and the Southern Cross were the only regions of Earth which showed a governmental interest in interstellar trade. Private ventures from the Rhine Basin were not uncommon, though.

From the rumors, the Germans' approach to trade was rough-and-ready, even by the standards Captain Choransky applied.

Choransky appeared at the ladder from the mid-deck. "What in God's name do you think you're playing at, landing at the same time as my *Dove*, you poxy bastard?" he roared at Schremp.

"I thought it was better to stay close to one of your ships until I had time to explain," Schremp said without embarrassment. His full beard was blacker than seemed natural for a man whose appearance otherwise was that of a fifty-year-old. "Explain that we are to be allies, yes? If we stay together, the pussies will be *glad* to deal with us, I'm sure!"

He smiled. The expression made Gregg think of the stories about German "trade."

—10—

Virginia

The orange berm of stabilized soil protecting the settlement was in sight, half a kilometer away. A uniformed Fed stood on it to watch the Venerians and Germans approach. He had either binoculars or an electronic magnifier.

Piet Ricimer knelt and teased a thorny plant loose from the margin of the grainfield surrounding the Fed settlement. "Stephen?" he said to Gregg. "Do you ever wonder what life was like before the Collapse?"

"What?" Gregg said. "Oh, you mean everybody rich with electronics? Well, sometimes."

He'd thought he was losing his fear of open spaces. Now that they'd left the dark trunks of the native forest for the cleared area supplying food for the settlement and the vessels that touched on it, he wasn't quite so sure.

Well, it wasn't really fear, just discomfort. And God knew that there was plenty of other discomfort, wearing armor and carrying a flashgun and still managing to lead a five-klick march.

"No, I meant . . ." Ricimer said. "See this? It's not a native plant, and I doubt the Feds brought it with them in the rediscovery."

The other spacers were coming up slowly, but nobody else was within a hundred meters of Ricimer and Gregg. The whole sixty or so in the party probably stretched a klick back into the forest.

"A thornbush?" Gregg said in puzzlement.

Two more Feds had joined the observer on the berm. One of them carried a megaphone. Despite its greater access to pre-Collapse sites on the outworlds, the North American Fed-

39

eration wasn't overall more technically advanced than Venus.

"Not a thornbush," Ricimer said. His finger carefully freed a full yellow bloom from the native foliage concealing it. "A rose."

"Stay where you are!" called the Fed with the megaphone. "Don't come any closer or we'll fire!"

"Right," said Leon, wheezing with the exertion of keeping up—almost—with the leaders. "And if that was the worst I had to worry about, I'd still die in bed."

"What you got, sir?" Tancred asked, squatting down beside Ricimer. "Hey! Artifacts!"

The young spacer carried a rifle. He used the barrel of the weapon to sweep back the vegetation. Underneath was half of a shallow porcelain bowl. Varicolored birds sang on a white field. The material had survived its millennium of exposure well enough, but Gregg didn't think it was up to the quality of current Venerian manufacture.

"Nothing valuable, though," Tancred said in disappointment. "You know, when I signed on, I kinda thought I'd, you know, pick up handfuls of chips when we got out-system."

"I think they're moving guns up behind the berm," Gregg said. "I can't see over, but there's some sort of commotion back there."

Two autogyros *pop-popped* in slow circles overhead. A line of diesel-powered ground vehicles rounded the edge of the ravelin shielding a gap in the berm. The spacers hadn't bothered to unload the trucks their vessels carried, because the forest was trackless and the tree boles averaged less than a meter and a half apart.

Choransky, Schremp, and a dozen men from each party joined the score of spacers who'd clustered around Ricimer and Gregg. As many more straggled along behind.

"I heard them shout," Choransky said. "What was it?"

"They told us not to come closer, sir," Ricimer said.

Schremp snorted. "Why should we want to do that?" he said. "When they're coming to us, and they don't have to walk like dogs."

The German leader wore only the torso and helmet from his hard suit. The face beneath his lifted visor was sweaty and bright red with exertion.

Gregg eyed the German's armor speculatively. The metal's bright finish—it appeared to be silver-plated, not just highly polished—would reflect energy better than Gregg's suit, and if the core was titanium alloy, it might be lighter as well. The métal couldn't be as effective a heat sink as Venerian ceramic, though, and Gregg was willing to bet his armor's higher hardness against metal's ability to deform under extreme stress instead of shattering.

Schremp glanced at Tancred. "Find anything valuable, kid?" he asked.

Tancred's face tightened. Before he could speak, Ricimer said, "Just the remains of somebody's garden, from a long time ago."

Schremp nodded and turned his attention to the oncoming vehicles that the other spacers were watching.

Rather than trucks, the Feds approached in three tracked, open-topped tractors, each towing a flatbed trailer in which forty or so figures rode. Figures, not "men", because half of the personnel were Molts and many of the humans wore coarse, bark-fabric clothing.

Though humans survived after a fashion on many outworlds, civilization did not. The men in indigenous dress were Rabbits, feral remnants of the pre-Collapse colonies.

The Rabbits and Molts were armed with cutting bars and even manual axes. None of them wore armor. There were half a dozen troops in Fed uniform on each vehicle. Not all of them had firearms, and only two wore head and torso armor.

"Huh!" said Jeude, scratching his neck with the edge of his cutting bar. "Those trucks're slower than glass flowing. I could walk as fast as that."

"They haul mats of timber processed at field stations," Ricimer explained. "They don't need to be fast."

"They're riding," Gregg guessed aloud, "because they want to show they've got vehicles and we're on foot."

"They got plasma guns in the fort," Leon said, eyeing the berm opposite the party of spacers. Metal glinted there without being raised quite high enough to make identification certain. "Them I'm willing to worry about."

Gregg spread and raised his flashgun's parasol. The meter-square solar cell swayed awkwardly in the breeze, making the weapon harder to control.

He didn't need to deploy the charger for any practical reason. He was carrying six extra batteries, and it was much faster to replace than recharge them in a firefight. The Feds weren't the only ones who could make silent threats, however.

Ten meters from the spacers, the tractor-trailers swung broadside and halted. A man wearing a white uniform and a number of medals got out of the cab of the leading tractor. He waited for two more officers, one of them female, and a pair of guards armed with rifles to get off the trailer behind him. With them in tow, he strode toward the spacers.

The whole party of Venerians and Germans surged forward across the wheat.

"Not so many!" the Fed leader cried, waggling his hand. He wore a pair of pistols completely swallowed by their cross-draw holsters. At careful inspection his uniform, though fancy enough, was frayed at the cuffs and noticeably dingy.

Choransky and Schremp muttered to one another for a moment. Choransky looked around. "You lot stay where you are!" he ordered. The two captains, accompanied by Platt and two Germans—as choice a pair of cutthroats as Gregg remembered seeing in his life—met the Feds between the waiting lines.

Choransky seized the initiative by blustering, "I want to know who you think you are, shooting at peaceful traders?"

"*I* am Port Commander Zaloga," the Fed leader blustered back, "and there'll be no trade with illegal interlopers like yourself on this planet or any planet of the North American Federation."

"North America is a thousand light-years away," said Captain Schremp in a surprisingly calm voice. "We are here with cargo your people need, slaves from my Venerian fellows there and the highest quality sauces and dairy solids aboard my *Adler*. Surely you must be tired of eating the bland mush you grow here, not so?"

"Your predecessor gave Captain Mostert a want list when he landed on Virginia last year," Choransky put in. "We brought our Molts here at your orders."

"My predecessor," Zaloga said, "was arrested for his trea-sonous dealings with interlopers like your Captain Mostert. You're not here at my orders. *My* orders are that you leave the planet at once. And as you see—"

He pointed toward the settlement. Half a dozen soldiers had lifted a small plasma cannon onto the top of the berm. The crew wore helmets, gauntlets, and padded coveralls against the effects of their own weapon.

"—I can enforce those orders!"

"Can you?" Schremp said with a sneer in his voice. "Take them," he added flatly.

Each of the Germans with him grabbed a Fed officer. Schremp himself caught Zaloga by the throat with his scarred left hand and squeezed hard enough to choke the port commander's protests into a startled bleat.

Choransky grasped the rifle of a Fed guard and prevented the man from lowering his weapon. Platt tried to do the same with the remaining guard, but he wasn't strong enough to overpower the fellow. They struggled for a moment.

Schremp, holding his repeater in one hand like a huge pistol, socketed the muzzle in the guard's ear and blew his brains out. The Fed's skull sagged sideways like a fruit dropped against concrete. Bits of colloid sprayed the female officer and the German who held her. She began to scream and kick hysterically.

"Stephen!" Ricimer shouted. His grip on Gregg's shoulder was as firm as a C-clamp. He pointed toward the plasma cannon with his rifle. He didn't bother to shoot because it was hopelessly out of his range. "Stop them!"

The half-armed militia on the trailers were too shocked by the violence to react, but the crew of the plasma gun were traversing their weapon squarely onto what had been the negotiating party. A bolt from that weapon—three or four centimeters in bore—would incinerate both command groups and probably a score of other spacers besides. The gunners might or might not fire—

But Piet Ricimer was right. The choice couldn't be left to them.

Gregg clashed his visor down and swore as the world blurred amber. The flashgun had a simple, four-post optical sight. He could only wish now that he'd checked the collimation, made sure that the point of aim was aligned with the point of impact, because at five-hundred meters you didn't have to be out by much to miss by a country klick.

The parasol swayed, twisting against the stock to which it was connected. One of the Feds on the berm raised his arm.

Gregg fired. The air snapped like the string of a powerful crossbow letting go. The line of the bolt was too sudden to see, but it left dazzling purple afterimages despite the filtering visor.

Light haloed the plasma cannon. Metal sublimed from the trunnion Gregg hit, flashing outward in a shockwave that ignited as it expanded. The ball of fire threw down the four crewmen on that side and behind the weapon. They lay where they fell. The remaining pair, untouched, vanished behind the berm.

Gregg lifted his visor. The air smelled burned. Half the members of the Fed militia had jumped behind the trailers. Those still visible had thrown down their weapons.

Gregg's flashgun whined as it started to recharge. The sound cut off when he opened the compartment in the stock and removed the discharged battery.

He thought he was fine, but his fingers fumbled and dropped the battery. He took a fresh charge from his side pocket and snapped it into the gun.

"That was necessary," Piet Ricimer murmured beside him. "Not this, what these *folk* are doing. But what you did, if we were to survive."

"Right!" said Captain Choransky. "Now, we're all going to trade like reasonable people. Isn't that right, Zaloga?"

Schremp transferred his grip to the port commander's shoulder. Zaloga was white-faced. He didn't attempt to speak, but he nodded agreement.

"That was easy, not so?" Schremp said cheerfully.

With the visor raised, Gregg could see a haze lift from the crew of the plasma cannon. Blazing metal vapor had ignited their clothing.

━11━

Venus

The probe dangling a hundred meters below the *Sultan* recorded the change in wind direction as it dipped into the third and final set of Hadley Cells layering the Venerian atmosphere. Warning bells clanged on the forward attitude-control workstations and, slightly distorted, from the stations in the next compartment.

"Oh, put a sock in it," Jeude muttered to his alarm.

"Think of it as welcoming us home, Jeude," Piet Ricimer said cheerfully. "This old girl could pretty well con herself into dock from here."

The *Sultan* twisted like a leaping fish when her hull passed through the discontinuity. Gregg felt a vague mushiness through his boots as the vessel continued her descent. Atmospheric density at this level was itself enough to slow a falling object appreciably.

The upper reaches of Venus' atmosphere roared from west to east at 450 kph, transferring heat from the sun-facing side of the planet to the cooler dark. Ships had to take wind direction and velocity into account during reentry.

But the top layer of sun-heated convection cells bottomed out and reversed course well above the planetary surface. Friction from the high-altitude cells formed an intermediate pattern of contra-rotating winds in the mid-atmosphere, but at much lower velocities.

When the convection pattern reversed again near the surface, completing the sequence of Hadley Cells, average wind velocity had dropped to 30 kph. That was scarcely a noticeable breeze to a craft which had managed to penetrate the crushing high-altitude violence.

"You know, Stephen, we should thank the Lord more often for our atmosphere," Ricimer said.

He was smiling, but Gregg knew Ricimer too well to think that anything the spacer said referencing God was a joke.

"As a warning of the Hell that awaits those who deny him?" Gregg suggested.

"For saving us during the Collapse," Ricimer explained. "All of the settlements on Venus were underground, so raiders didn't have any easy targets. And very few outplanet captains chose to hit us anyway. They knew that defensive vessels couldn't prevent hit-and-run attacks—but that if their ship attacked Venus, the planet herself would fight them. And the planet would win, as often as not, against inexperienced pilots."

"People died anyway," Gregg said. "Nine in ten died. Venus colony almost died!"

The harsh edge in his voice was a surprise even to him—especially to him. Many factorial families had their own records of the Collapse, and the journals of the Eryx County Greggs were particularly detailed. Stephen Gregg had found that reading about the deaths of your kin and ancestors by starvation, wall fractures, and manufacturing processes which desperation pushed beyond safe limits was not the same as "learning history."

Ricimer nodded. There was a tic of wariness though not fear in his expression. "Yes," he said, "the Lord scourged us. It had been easier to import some of our needs. When trade stopped, life almost stopped before we were able to expand food production sufficiently for the population."

"The surviving population," Gregg said. His voice was very soft, but it trembled.

Piet Ricimer rested his fingertips on the back of Gregg's right hand. "Never again, Stephen," he said quietly. "Trade must never fail. The tyrants who would stop it, President Pleyal and his toadies in Brisbane—the Lord won't let them stop free trade."

Gregg laughed and put his arm around the smaller man's shoulders. "And we're the instruments of the Lord?" he said, only half gibing. "Well, I don't usually think of myself that way, Piet."

As he spoke, Gregg realized that Piet Ricimer *did* usually think of himself as a tool of God. The odd thing from Gregg's viewpoint was that the holy types he'd met before always struck him as sanctimonious prigs, thoroughly unlikable . . .

"Prepare for landing," called Captain Choransky, hunched over a CRT loaded with scores of data readouts, each one crucially important in the moments of touchdown.

The vessel was coming down nearly empty since her main cargo, nearly 1,000 tonnes of cellulose base, had been unloaded in orbit. The mats had to be armored with a ceramic coating before purpose-built tugs brought them down through an atmosphere which would have consumed them utterly in their unprotected state.

The *Sultan* vibrated as the shockwaves from her thrusters echoed from the sides of the landing pit. Choransky chopped the feedlines, starving the thrusters an instant before the artificial intelligence would have done so.

The *Sultan* hit with a ringing impact. Gregg staggered but didn't fall against the workstations around him.

"Not really dangerous," Ricimer murmured, to Gregg and to himself. "The lower hull may want some reglazing . . . but after a long voyage, the torquing of so many transits, that'd be a good idea anyway."

Vibration continued even with the *Sultan*'s powerplant shut off. A huge dome rolled to cover the landing pit. When the pit's centrifugal pumps had dumped the Venerian atmosphere back into the hell where it belonged and the hull had cooled sufficiently, conveyor belts would haul the vessel into a storage dock. Betaport was a major facility with six landing pits, but the volume of trade she handled required that the pits be cleared as soon as possible.

The men at the attitude controls stood up and stretched. "C'mon, c'mon, c'mon," Jeude said toward a bulkhead. "Get that personnel bridge out here."

"I *got* my pay," Dole singsonged, "and I *want* somebody to spend it with. I do want that."

Lightbody looked at Dole. Ostentatiously, he took his Bible out of the pocket where he'd placed it on landing. He began to read, his lips forming the words as his right index finger traced the line.

The bridge console beeped. The CRT, blanked when Choransky shut down, filled with characters.

"What?" the captain demanded. "Are we getting hard copy of this?"

Bivens squinted at the screen. "This is message traffic from Captain Mostert," he said as he watched the data scroll upward.

"I know what it is," Choransky said angrily. He opened a cabinet beneath the CRT and threw a switch with no effect. "Are we getting hard copy of it, that's what I want to know?"

The duty of a ship's crewman was to do whatever a superior ordered him to do. It wasn't clear that a gentleman like Gregg *had* any superior aboard the *Sultan*; but he knew a great deal more about office equipment than anybody else on the ship did, and he didn't care to sit on his hands.

Gregg stepped past Choransky, knelt to study the installation for a moment, and reconnected the printer. It began spewing out copy as soon as he switched it on.

"There you go," he said to the captain. "Somebody probably got tired of the way it clucked every time the board switched mode." To the best of Gregg's knowledge, the printer hadn't been used at any previous point in the voyage.

The *Sultan* rocked.

"About d—" Jeude began. He caught Ricimer's eye. "About time the personnel bridge got here," he finished.

The vessel shuddered softly as ground staff evacuated the seal which clamped the enclosed walkway to the starship's hull.

"That message," Gregg said to Ricimer quietly. "Captain Mostert is summoning Choransky and his top officers to a meeting and party at his house in Ishtar City tomorrow morning. He's going to have potential investors for a larger voyage present. Some of them may be from the Governor's Council."

"Are you going?" Ricimer asked.

Gregg looked at him. "I suppose Uncle Benjamin will already have a representative chosen," he said. "If he's interested, that is."

"I doubt my cousin Alexi would leave you on his doorstep, though," Ricimer said.

A hatch sighed open. The air pressure increased minutely. Crewmen—none of them on the bridge—shouted "Yippee!" and "Yee-ha!"

"Why are you asking?" Gregg said. "Are you going yourself?"

"I'm not sure Alexi really expects me . . ." Ricimer explained. His grin flashed. "Though he *is* my cousin. I'm pretty sure his servants wouldn't bat an eyelash if I came with the nephew of Factor Benjamin Gregg, though."

Gregg began to laugh. He put his arm around Ricimer's shoulders again. "I'll tell you what," he said. "We'll go see my uncle. He's in Ishtar City and I need to report anyway. Then we'll play it by ear, just as we've been doing"—he gestured upward—"out there."

Gregg wondered as he spoke whether the reality of high-level politics would be as far from his expectations as the reality of trade in the Reaches had been.

Ricimer must have been thinking something similar, because he said, "In Ishtar City, they won't be trying to shoot us, at least."

—12—

Venus

Ricimer was darkly splendid when he emerged from the men's room outside the Western Rail Station in Ishtar City. The close-coupled spacer wore a tunic and beret of black velvet, set off by a gold sash and band respectively. His trousers were gray, pocketless and closely tailored. They fit into calf-height boots of natural leather, black and highly polished.

"I don't see why you had to waste time changing," Gregg said sourly.

Ricimer tucked a small duffel bag into the luggage on the porter's cart, then snugged the tie-down over it. "Why?" he asked. "We're not late, are we?"

The traffic of Ishtar City buffeted them without so much as a curse. Pedestrians; battery-powered carts like the one holding their luggage; occasionally a passenger vehicle carrying someone who chose to flaunt his wealth by riding, despite the punitive tax intended as much as a morality measure as it was for traffic control, though traffic control was necessary, especially here in the center of the Old Town. West Station served not only Betaport but the whole complex of hamlets and individual holds in Beta Regio and the plains southwest of Ishtar Terra.

The rail links were built before the Collapse, close beneath the surface. During the recovery, Ishtar City grew from the administrative capital of a colony to the heart of a resurgent, independent Venus. Housing and manufacturing expanded both downward and—much later, as ceramic techniques improved and fear of devastating war receded—into domes on the surface.

Rail communications across the planet were improved progressively rather than by a single, massive redesign. The traffic they carried continued to enter and leave the growing capital at the near-surface levels, creating conditions that were as crushingly tight as the living quarters of a starship on a long voyage.

Gregg had been raised in an outlying hold. He knew that the discomfort he felt in this crowding was making him irritable.

"No, it's not the time," he said, stolidly breasting the crowd, though his flesh crept from the repeated jarring on other humans. He knew the way to his uncle's house, so he led; it was as simple as that. "It's getting dressed up as if Uncle Ben was—" He started to say "God Almighty," but remembered his listener in time to twist the words into "—Governor Halys."

Ricimer laughed. "You're going to see Uncle Ben, my friend. I will meet Factor Gregg of Weyston—and no, before you say, 'Do you think you'll fool him that you're not the jumped-up sailor *I* know you are?'—no. But he'll recognize that I'm showing him the respect which is his due . . . from such as me."

Gregg grimaced. He was glad Ricimer couldn't see his face. "I never said you were a jumped-up sailor, Piet," he said.

"You both humored me *and* guarded our baggage while I changed, my friend," Ricimer said. "This is important to me. Important to God's plan for mankind, I believe, but certainly to me personally. I appreciate everything you're doing."

Many wealthy men, the Mostert brothers among them, now lived in the domed levels of Ishtar City where the ambience was relatively open. Uncle Ben's great wealth was a result of his own trading endeavors, but he had a conservative affection for the Old Town where the rich and powerful had lived when he was growing up. His townhouse was within a half kilometer of West Station.

By the time they'd made half that distance through twisting corridors cut by the first permanent human settlements on Venus, Gregg wished he was in armor and lugging his flashgun ten times as far in the forests of Virginia. The trees didn't shove their way into and past pedestrians.

"Stephen?" Ricimer said, breaking into Gregg's grim reverie.

"Uh?" Gregg said. "Oh, sorry." As he spoke, he realized he was apologizing for thoughts his friend couldn't read and which weren't directed to him specifically, just at cities and those who lived in them in general.

"When Captain Schremp spoke to the Federation officials, he referred to our cargo as slaves. Do you remember?"

There was a ceramic patch at the next intersection, and the dwellings kitty-corner across it were misaligned. When Gregg was a boy of three, there'd been a landslip that vented a portion of Ishtar City to the outer atmosphere. An error by a tunneling contractor, some believed, but there was too little left at the heart of the catastrophe to be sure.

Over a thousand people had died, despite Ishtar City's compartmentalization by corridor and the emergency seals in all dwellings. Uncle Ben had been able to pick up his present townhouse cheap, from heirs who'd been out of town when the disaster occurred.

"Schremp!" Gregg said in harsh dismissal. "The Molts aren't even human. They *can't* be slaves."

He pursed his lips. "The way the Feds treat the indigs, the Rabbits—maybe they're slaves. But that's nothing to do with us."

"Yes, well," Ricimer said. "I suppose you're right, Stephen."

Gregg looked back over his shoulder. His friend threw him a smile, but it wasn't a particularly bright one.

The facade of Uncle Ben's townhouse was glazed a dull slate-gray. The style and treatment were similar to other gray, dun, and russet buildings on the corridor, but it was unusually clean. The four red-uniformed attendants outside the doorway kept loungers and graffiti-scribblers away from the Factor's door.

The attendants straightened when they saw Gregg, suddenly conscious that he'd been on a train for twenty hours from Betaport, striding toward them. One of the men recognized the Factor's nephew and pushed the call button.

"Master Stephen Gregg!" he shouted at the intercom. He focused on Ricimer and the luggage, then added, "And companion."

There was no external door-switch. The valve itself was round, shaped like a section of a cone through the flats, and a meter-fifty in diameter across the inner face. If the Venerian atmosphere flooded the corridor, its pressure would wedge the door more tightly sealed until emergency crews could deal with the disaster.

Burt, a white-haired senior servant wearing street clothes of good quality, bowed to Gregg in the anteroom. Two red-suited underlings waited behind him to take the luggage from the porter.

"Sir, the Factor is expecting you and Mr. Ricimer in his office," Burt said. "Will you change first?"

"I don't think that will be necessary," Gregg said grimly. *For God's sake! This was Uncle Ben, who up until a few years ago traveled aboard his intrasystem traders on the Earth-Asteroids-Venus triangle to check them out!*

"Very good, sir," Burt said with another bow.

Uncle Ben had redone the anteroom mosaics since Gregg had last been to the townhouse. These were supposed to suggest a forest glade on Earth before toxins released during the Revolt finished what fifteen millennia of human fire-setting had begun.

Gregg thought of tramping through the woodlands of Virginia. He smiled. Uncle Ben, for all his wealth and success and ability, was in some ways more parochial than the young nephew who until recently hadn't been out of the Atalanta Plains for more than a week at a time.

Another liveried servant bowed and stepped away from the open door of the Factor's office.

In Old Town, corridors and dwellings were all as close to three meters high as the excavators could cut them. Ceilings were normally lowered to provide storage space or, in poorer housing, to double the number of available compartments. Gregg of Weyston's office was full height, paneled in bleached wood with a barely perceptible grain. The material was natural, rather than something reprocessed from cellulose base.

"Good to see you, Stephen," the Factor said. Through a tight smile he added, "I see you've had a hard journey."

Gregg glared at his uncle. "I'll change here, Uncle Ben," he said. "For G—for *pity'* s sake, I could have sent my dress suit by a servant to report to you, if that's what's important."

"My brother never saw much reason to dress like a gentleman either, Stephen," the Factor said. "That's perfectly all right—if you're going to bury yourself in the hinterlands with no one save family retainers to see you."

Gregg began to laugh. "May I present Mr. Ricimer, Uncle," he said. "An officer of Captain Choransky's company and a cousin of the Mosterts." He paused. "He gave me the same lecture on our way from the rail station."

Benjamin Gregg laughed also. He got up and reached over his broad desk to shake first his nephew's hand, then that of Piet Ricimer.

Gregg of Weyston was dark where his brother's side of the family, the Greggs of Eryx, were mostly fair, but he was as big as his nephew and had been both strong and active till back problems slowed him down. Even now, the weight he'd gained was under control except for a potbelly that resisted anything short of the girdle he wore on formal occasions.

The Factor gestured the younger men to chairs of the same blond wood as the paneling—as uncomfortable as they were obviously expensive—and sat down heavily again himself. "I've seen your report, Stephen," he said with a nod toward the sheaf of printouts on his desk. "It's as careful and precise as the accounts of Eryx always are. I'm impressed, though not surprised."

He pursed his lips. "Now," he went on, "what is it that you and Mr. Ricimer feel you need to add in person to the written account you transmitted when you landed at Betaport?"

"The Mosterts are giving a matinee this afternoon to launch plans for a larger expedition to the Reaches," Gregg said. "I suppose you've already made arrangements to be represented, but we'd like—I'd like—to be there on your behalf also, with Mr. Ricimer."

He flicked his eyes to his companion. Ricimer was seated in his chair with the poised, unmoving alertness of a guard dog.

The Factor nodded. "And why do you think I should be represented, Stephen?" he asked.

The question took Gregg aback. "What?" he blurted. "Why— for the profit, Uncle Ben. You're a merchant, and there are huge profits to be made in out-system trade."

The walls of the office were lined with books—hard-copy ledgers, some of them almost five decades old—and with memorabilia from the Factor's years of intrasystem trade. One of Gregg's earliest memories was of his uncle handing him a bit of clear crystal with waxy inclusions and saying that it was a relic of life from the asteroid belt before Earth had even coalesced as a planet.

But this was a different Uncle Ben. He lifted his nephew's itemized report. "Yes," he said. "Profit. One hundred twelve percent on my investment on Captain Choransky's voyage."

"Possibly a little less," Gregg said in a desire to be precise. "I'm assuming a low valuation for tariff purposes, in the belief that Governor Halys will want to minimize the amount of her investment profits that pass through the Exchequer. I may be wrong."

The Factor laughed. "You're not wrong, lad," he said. "If anything, you're overconservative. And in any event, over one hundred percent compares favorably with the thirty-three to thirty-five percent margin I try to run within the system."

Gregg nodded, allowing himself a wary smile while he waited for the hook.

"Until you factor in risk," Gregg of Weyston added, slapping the report down on his desk.

The Factor looked sharply at Ricimer. "Mr. Ricimer," he said crisply. "I can see you're a spaceman. How do you assess the possibility that one or all of Captain Choransky's vessels would have been lost on the voyage just completed?"

Ricimer lifted his chin to acknowledge the question. His eyes were bright.

"In-system, landings are the most dangerous part of a voyage," he said in a tone as cold and sharp as the blade of a cutting bar. "The risk varies from ship to ship, but say . . . three percent per vessel on the voyage in question because of the greater frequency of landings. Transits—again, that varies, but obviously the greater number of entries increases the possibility of system failure and of being caught in a pattern of rising gradients in which a vessel shakes its hull apart in trying to enter transit space."

The spacer tapped his right index finger on his chair arm while his eyes stared at a point beyond the Factor's ear. "I would say," he continued as his eyes locked with those of his questioner, "five percent on a well-found vessel, but I'll admit that the *Sultan* wasn't in the best condition, and I can't claim to have full confidence in the ship-handling abilities of the *Dove*'s officers."

Ricimer smiled bleakly. "You'll pardon me for frankness, sir," he said.

"I'll pardon you for anything except telling me damned lies, lad," the Factor said, "and there seems little risk of that. But—what about the Federation and the Southern Cross, then? I've had more reports of the voyage than this one, you know."

The older man brushed the sheaf of hard copy with his fingers. "It's all over Betaport, you see. My Stephen there"—he nodded, Uncle Ben again for the instant—"acquitted himself like a Gregg, and that surprises me no more than his accounts do. But one lucky bolt from a plasma cannon and there's your thrusters, your ship . . . and all hope of profit for your investors, lad."

His eyes were on his nephew now, not Ricimer. "And families at home to grieve besides."

Gregg jumped to his feet. "Christ's *wounds*, Uncle Ben!" he shouted. "Do you think I'm a, I'm a—" He shrugged angrily. "Some kind of a damned painting that's so delicate I'll fade if I'm put out in the light?"

"I think," the Factor said, "that I'm an old man, Stephen. When I die, I don't choose to explain to my late brother how I provided the rope with which his son hanged himself."

"I'll not be coddled!"

"I'm not offering to coddle you!" the Factor boomed. "Come and work for me, boy, and I'll grind you into all the hardest problems Gregg Trading falls against. *If* you can handle them, then—well, my brother had sons, and I have Gregg Trading. What I *won't* do is send you to swim with sharks."

Piet Ricimer stood up. He put his hand in the crook of Gregg's elbow. "Let me speak, Stephen," he said in a quiet, trembling voice.

Gregg turned his back on his uncle.

"Sir," Ricimer said. "You say you don't mind frankness, and I don't know any other way to be."

The Factor nodded curtly, a gesture much like that with which Ricimer had acknowledged the question a moment before.

"You'll survive and prosper if you hold to the in-system trade," the spacer said. "So will your heir and very likely his heir, if they're as able as you. What won't survive if you and the other leading merchants who respect you turn your backs on it is trade from Venus to the stars."

"Assuming that's true," Gregg of Weyston said carefully, "which I do *not* assume except for discussion—what of it? When humanity was at its height before the Collapse, ninety-eight percent of the humans in the universe were within the solar system. There'll always be trade for us here."

"There were twenty billion people on Earth before the Collapse," Ricimer replied evenly. "If there are twenty million

today, I'll be surprised. Earth is a poisoned hulk. Venus is—
the Lord put us on Venus to make us strong, sir, but nobody
can think our world is more than a way station on the path
of God's plan. The other in-system colonies breed men who
are freaks, too weak for lack of gravity to live on any normal
planet. We *need* the stars."

Gregg faced slowly around again. He was embarrassed by
his outburst. If there had been a way to ease back into his
chair, he would have done so.

"Man needs the stars, I accept," the Factor agreed with
another nod. "And man is retaking them. Now, I don't accept
Brisbane's dividing the Reaches between America and the
Southerns, either—as a matter of principle. But principle
makes a bad meal, and war makes for damned bad trade,
in-system as well as out. Let them have it if they want it so
bad. They'll still need manufactures from Venus, and it'll be
Venerian ships that dare *our* atmosphere nine times in ten."

Ricimer nodded with his lips pursed, not agreeing but rather
choosing his words. The skin was stretched as tightly over the
spacer's cheeks as it had been when he warned Gregg to shoot
on Virginia.

"The Southerns will do nothing, sir, as they've always done
nothing with their opportunities," he said. "The Feds, now . . .
the Feds will continue to strip the caches of microchips they
find in the Reaches. They'll try to run the few factories they
find still operable, but they won't do the work themselves,
they'll put Molts to it. And the Molts will do only what their
ancestors were taught to do a thousand years ago."

The Factor opened his mouth to speak. Ricimer forestalled
him with, "What they do get from the Reaches, they'll use
to strengthen themselves on Earth. They've been fighting the
rebels on their own west coast for a generation. Perhaps the
wealth they bring from the Reaches will permit them to finally
succeed. And they'll fight Europe, conquer Europe I shouldn't
doubt, because the Europeans can never conquer them and
President Pleyal won't stop while he has a single rival on
Earth."

"Venus can't be conquered," the Factor said, leaping a step
ahead in the argument and denying it harshly.

"Perhaps not," the spacer agreed. "But all mankind can
stagnate while President Pleyal forges an empire as rigid and
brittle as the one that shattered in the Collapse. And if we fall

back from the stars again . . . I don't believe the Lord will give
us a third chance."

The two fierce-eyed men stared at one another for a long
moment. The Factor shuddered and said in a surprisingly gentle tone, "Stephen? What's your opinion of all this?"

Gregg touched his lips with his tongue. He smiled wryly
and seated himself as he'd wanted to do for some while. "I'm
not a religious man, Uncle," he said, kneading his fingers
together on the edge of the desk and staring at them. "I
don't like transit, and I don't like"—he looked up—"some
of the ways trade's carried on beyond Pluto." The starkness
of his own voice startled him. "But I think I could learn to
like standing under an open sky. And I'm sure I'm going to
do that again."

His lips quirked. "God willing," he added, half in mockery.
Gregg's expression lost even the hint of humor. "Someone
will ship me, Uncle Ben. It doesn't have to be an expedition
in which Gregg Trading has invested."

The Factor glared at him. "Your father, boy," he said, "was
as stubborn as any man God put on Venus."

Gregg nodded. "He used to say the same of you, Uncle
Ben," he said.

Gregg of Weyston burst out laughing and reached across
the desk with both hands, clasping his nephew's. "Then I
suppose it runs in the family, lad. Go to your damned meeting,
then—I'll call ahead. And when you come back, we'll discuss
what you in your *business* judgment recommend for Gregg
Trading."

Piet Ricimer stood formally, with his heels near together and
his wrists crossed behind his back. There was the slightest of
smiles on his lips.

–13–

Venus

Gregg hadn't met Councilor Duneen before—he'd never *expected* to meet the head of the Bureau of External Relations—but there Duneen was at the side of Alexi Mostert, nodding affably and extending his hand. Siddons, by two years the elder Mostert brother, didn't appear to be present.

"So . . ." Duneen said. He was short and a trifle pudgy, but there was nothing soft about his eyes. "You'd be Gregg of Eryx, then?"

Gregg shook the councilor's hand. Duneen was only forty or so, younger than Gregg had expected in a man whom many said was Governor Halys' chief advisor. "That would be my brother, sir," he said.

"Mr. Gregg's here representing his uncle, Gregg of Weyston," Mostert put in quickly. "A major investor in the voyage just returned, and we hope in the present endeavor as well."

The Mostert brothers, Alexi and Siddons, had inherited a bustling shipping business from their father. They themselves had expanded the operations in various fashions. The politically powerful guests at this party were examples of the expansion as surely as the out-system trading ventures were.

"Allow me to introduce my friend Mr. Ricimer, Councilor," Gregg said. He noticed that Mostert's jaw tightened, but there was nothing the shipper could do about it. "One of Captain Choransky's officers on the recent voyage, and one of the major reasons for our success."

"A sailor indeed, Mr. Ricimer?" Duneen said approvingly. "I shouldn't have guessed it."

He nodded minusculy toward the bar. The captains and navigators from the recent voyage clustered there like six sheep floating amongst shark fins. The spacers were dressed in a mismatch of finery purchased for this event combined with roughly serviceable garb that would have been out of place in a good house in Betaport, much less Ishtar City.

Ricimer's turnout was stylish in an idiosyncratic way. For the party he'd kept the black tunic and boots, but he'd changed into taupe trousers and a matching neckerchief. His St. Christopher medal dangled across his chest on its massy chain, and he wore a ring whose similar metalwork clamped what was either a fire opal or something more exotic.

"Yes sir," Ricimer agreed promptly. "A sailor proud to serve a governor who understands the value of out-system trade to God's plan and the welfare of Venus."

Duneen shifted his feet slightly to close the conversation with Ricimer. Gregg started to put his hand out to his friend, but Ricimer already understood the signal and stepped away.

"A keen lad, Mostert," the councilor said. "We'll have use for him, I shouldn't wonder."

"Very keen indeed," Mostert replied with a touch of irritation.

Gregg glanced around the gathering. About half the forty or so present were gentlemen—or dressed like it. He didn't recognize them all. Most of the others were identifiable from the shipping trade: a mix of middle-aged men like Mostert himself and younger fellows, acting as Gregg was for a wealthy principal.

Councilor Duneen might have his own interests, but he was certainly here to represent Governor Halys as well. Out-system trade was a matter of state so long as President Pleyal claimed it infringed the sovereignty of the North American Federation.

The meeting room had ceilings three and a half meters high. The additional half meter wasn't functional; it simply proved that the Mosterts' mansion made use of the greater freedom permitted by buildings in the new domed quarters.

Out-system vegetation grew in niches along three of the walls. None of it was thriving: varied requirements for nutrition and light saw to that. Still, the display showed the breadth of the Mosterts' endeavors, which was probably all that it was intended to do.

Mostert stepped to a dais and rang a spoon in his glass for attention. "Councilor Duneen," he said, "gentlemen. As you all know, Mostert Trading is about to embark on a voyage promising levels and percentages of profit greater even than those of the voyage just returned under my subordinate, Captain Choransky. I've called you together as interested parties, so that all your questions can be answered."

"All right, Alexi," said a soberly-dressed man in his fifties; probably a shipper in the same order of business as the Mosterts, though Gregg didn't recognize him. "Are you talking about going to the Mirror this time, then?"

"No," Mostert said. "No, Paul, the time isn't right for that just yet. We'll be penetrating other portions of the Reaches for the first time, though—planets that aren't well served by the Feds themselves. We'll be able to skim the cream of the trade there."

"The cream," Paul rejoined, "is microchips, and that means going to the Mirror."

"The Feds won't trade for chips anywhere," somebody else objected morosely. "Pleyal knows how good a thing he's got there."

"We're talking about planets like Jewelhouse, Heartbreak, Desire," Mostert said loudly as he tried to get the discussion back on the track he desired. "Planets with valuable products of their own *and* the remains of extensive pre-Collapse colonies being discovered every day. There weren't microchip factories there, no, but those aren't the only ancient artifacts that can bring huge profits."

"The mirror worlds, all their settlements have forts and real soldiers," Captain Choransky said with the air of a man trying to explain why humans can't breathe water. "If we sashayed up to Umber, say, they'd just laugh at us."

"If they didn't blow our asses away," Bivens added, shaking his head in sad amazement. "That's what they'd do, you know."

Mostert grimaced. "We all know the orders President Pleyal has sent to his colonies," he said in brusque admission. "That won't last—it can't last. The colonies can't depend on Rabbits for labor. They need Molts to expand their operations, and they *want* to buy them from us. But—"

"They want to buy if there's a gun to their head," interjected Roon, who'd commanded the *Preakness*.

. "But that means we don't go where they've got guns of their own," Bivens said.

"They want to do most *anything* with guns to their heads," Roon added with a giggle.

Mostert's face was naturally ruddy, so the best clue to his mental state was the way he suddenly flung his glass to the side with a fierce motion. The vessel clinked against the wall but didn't break.

The clot of ships' officers, all of whom had drunk more than was good for them because they were nervous, grunted and looked away.

Gregg smothered a smile. Alexi Mostert had used better judgment when he bought tumblers for this gathering than when he made up the guest list.

Piet Ricimer swept the room with his eyes. "The best way to break the monopoly on out-system trade which the Feds and Southerns claim," he said in a clear voice, "will be for Venus to develop our own network of colonies, trading stations— perhaps our own routes across the Mirror or around it in transit space. But that will take time."

He stepped closer to the dais though not onto it. His back was to Mostert but he held the eyes of everyone else. Gregg watched their host over Ricimer's head. Mostert's expression was perfectly blank, but his fingers were bending the spoon into a tight spiral.

"For now," Ricimer continued, "we need to gain experience in out-system navigation in order to carry out what I'm convinced is God's plan. But—"

His smile was as dazzling as the ring on his finger. "— God doesn't forbid us to help ourselves while carrying out His will. The investors in the voyage just completed are wealthier by more than a hundred percent of their investments. Our mistress, Governor Halys"—Ricimer nodded to Duneen—"included. No one who's served with Captain Mostert can doubt that an argosy he commands in person will be even more successful."

. Gregg began to clap. He was only slightly surprised when light applause ran quickly across the room, like fire in cotton lint.

"For you gentlemen who don't know him," Mostert called from the dais, "this is my relative Captain Ricimer. He'll be commanding one of the vessels in the new endeavor."

There was another flurry of applause. Gregg raised an eyebrow. Ricimer acknowledged with something between a deep nod and a bow.

A servant entered the room carrying a round package nearly a meter in diameter. He scanned the crowd, then homed in on Ricimer.

"One moment, gentlemen," Ricimer said loudly to cut through the buzz of conversation following his speech and Mostert's.

He took the package and ripped the seal on the thin, light-scattering wrapper. All eyes were on him.

"Councilor Duneen," Ricimer continued, "we've spoken of the artifacts to be found beyond Pluto. I ask you to take this to Governor Halys, as my personal token of appreciation for her support of the voyage just ended."

He reached into the package and removed the fragment of porcelain birdbath Gregg had last seen in a garden on Virginia. Though carefully cleaned, the broad bowl was only half complete—and that badly worn.

There was a general gasp. Gregg's skin went cold. A flick of Mostert's wrist sent the spoon to follow the glass he'd thrown.

"And this as well," Ricimer continued loudly. His left hand shook the wrapping away. He raised a copy of the birdbath in its perfect state, the scalloped circuit whole and the colors as bright as Venerian ceramicists could form them.

Ricimer waved the ancient artifact in his right hand. "The past—" he cried.

He stepped onto the dais and waved his right hand. "And the glorious future of Venus and mankind! God for Venus! God for Governor Halys!"

Stephen Gregg clapped and cheered like everybody else in the meeting room. His eyes stung, and a part of him was angry at being manipulated.

But tears ran down the cheeks of Piet Ricimer as well, as the young spacer stood clasped by both Mostert and Duneen on the dais.

—14—

Above Punta Verde

"Featherboat *Peaches* landing in sequence," Ricimer said. "*Peaches* out."

He cradled the radio handset and engaged the artificial intelligence. "Hang on," he added with a grin over his shoulder, but even Gregg was an old enough sailor by now to have cinched his straps tight.

The thrusters fired, braking the 20-tonne featherboat from orbit, the last of Captain Mostert's argosy to do so. The deep green of Punta Verde's jungles swelled beneath them, though their landing spot was still on the other side of the planet.

The screens dissolved into colored snow for a moment, then snapped back to greater clarity than they'd managed in the stillness of freefall. Gregg swallowed his heart again.

Leon sat beside Gregg in the constricted cabin. He patted an outer bulkhead and muttered, "Silly old cow."

"You know, Piet," Gregg called over the vibration, "I never did ask you how you got that replica birdbath made so quickly."

"A friend in the industry," Ricimer replied without turning. "My, ah . . ."

He looked back at Gregg. "My father preaches in the Jamaica hamlet outside Betaport," he said. Gregg had to watch his friend's lips to be sure of the words. "But there were ten of us children, and now the new wife. He has a ceramic workshop. Mostly thruster nozzles for the port, but he can turn out special orders too."

Ricimer's voice grew louder. "He's as good a craftsman as you'll find on Venus. And that means anywhere in the universe!"

"Yes," Gregg said with a deep nod. "I was amazed at the high quality of the piece."

That was more or less true, but he'd have said as much if the bath looked like somebody'd fed a dog clay and then glazed the turds. A Gregg of Eryx understood family pride.

"You might," Gregg continued, changing the subject with a smile, "have parlayed it into something a little bigger than the *Peaches*. Your cousin really owed you for the way you put his voyage over with the investors. Councilor Duneen was impressed too, you know."

For a moment the featherboat trembled unpowered as her remaining velocity balanced the density of Punta Verde's atmosphere. The thrusters resumed firing at low output, providing the *Peaches* with controllable forward motion. The featherboat was now an atmosphere vessel. At best, the larger ships were more or less terminally-guided ballistic missiles.

"Ah, this is the ship to be in, Stephen," Ricimer said, no less serious for the laughter in his eyes. "Isn't that right, boys?"

"Beats the *Tollîver*, that's G-g-heaven's truth," Tancred agreed. "Leaks like a sieve, that one does. Wouldn't doubt they were all on oxygen bottles by now."

The featherboat could accept twenty men or so in reasonable comfort, but the six men from Ricimer's intrasystem trader were more than sufficient for the needs of the vessel. Gregg wondered if that was why his friend had accepted the tiny command when he might have pushed for the 100-tonne *Hawkwood* or even the slightly larger *Rose*. Piet Ricimer was a first-rate leader, but the business of *command* as opposed to leadership didn't come naturally to him.

"We ought to be coming up on a Molt city," Ricimer said, returning his attention to the viewscreen. As he spoke, the uniform green blurred by the featherboat's 200 kph gave way abruptly to beige. The Molts of Punta Verde used the trunks of living trees to support dwellings like giant shelf fungi. The smooth roofs underlay but did not displace the uppermost canopy, giving the city an organic appearance . . .

Which was justified. The Molts, though not indigenous to any of the worlds they were known to occupy, formed stable equilibria wherever man had placed them.

"We're coming up on the landing site," Ricimer warned. "It'd be nice if they'd cleared a patch for us, but don't count on it."

Plasma engines made communication between vessels during a landing impractical. The *Desire*, the argosy's other
featherboat, had barely shut down when Ricimer went in,
so the *Peaches* crew could only hope that matters had gone
as planned in orbit.

Ricimer overrode the AI, holding the *Peaches* in a staggering hover. The *Tolliver*, 500 tonnes burden and owned by the
government of Venus, was spherical rather than cigar-shaped.
Her dome stood as high as the canopy beyond the area her
thrusters had shattered. The 300-tonne *Grandcamp* was a good
kilometer away, while gaps in the jungle between the big ships
probably marked the *Rose* and *Hawkwood*.

At least none of the bigger ships had crashed. That wasn't
a given in the case of the *Tolliver*, eighty years old and at least
twenty years past her most recent rebuild. The big vessel was
intended to be serviced in orbit, but the state of her hull was
such that she leaked air faster than it could be ferried up to
her by boat.

The *Tolliver*'s size and armament were valuable additions,
though. The fact that the ancient vessel came from Governor
Halys made it a claim of official support—

As well as a difficult gift to refuse.

"We're going in," Ricimer said curtly as he reduced power
and swiveled the main thrusters. Leon and Dole, operating
without orders from their captain, pumped the nose high with
the attitude jets.

The *Peaches* lurched, balanced, and settled down on trees
smashed to matchsticks when the *Tolliver* landed a hundred
meters away. An instant before touchdown, the featherboat
was wobbling like a top about to fall over, but the landing
was as soft as a kiss.

"Nice work, Cap'n," Lightbody grunted.

"Only the best for my boys," Ricimer said with satisfaction.

The viewscreen provided a panorama of the *Peaches*' surroundings, though not a particularly crisp one. Heavily-armed
men disembarked from the flagship. One man, apparently closer than he cared to have been when the featherboat landed,
hurled a fruit or seedpod at the *Peaches*. Gregg heard a soggy
impact on the hull.

Leon and Bailey undogged the main hatch topside. The
Peaches had a forward hatch as well, but that was little more

than a gunport for the light plasma cannon.

Gregg frowned. "Shouldn't we let her cool?" he asked—aloud but carefully avoiding eye contact with the vessel's more experienced personnel.

"Aw, just watch what you grab hold of, sir," Tancred explained. "Featherboats like this, we braked on thrust, not friction pretty much."

"Will you pass the arms out as each man disembarks, Stephen?" Ricimer said. "You're the tallest, you see."

And also the most likely to grab a handgrip that would sear him down to the bone, Gregg thought. Having a gentleman dispensing the weapons was good form, but the only reason arms were segregated aboard the *Peaches* was to keep them from flying about the cabin during violent maneuvers.

Ricimer took another look at what was going on outside. A truckload of men seemed about ready to pull out, and additional crewmen were boarding two other vehicles.

"Leon, bring a rifle for me, will you?" Ricimer said sharply. He moved from the control console to the hatch and out in three lithe jumps. The viewscreen elongated the figure of the young officer bounding swiftly toward the flagship.

"He'll sort them out," Tancred said.

"Anybody who'd ship aboard a chamber pot like the *Tolliver*," Leon muttered, "hasn't got enough brains to keep his scalp inflated. And the *Grandcamp* isn't much better."

Gregg took his place beside the locker in the center of the ship. As each crewman hopped from the edge of the storage cabinet beneath the hatch—there was a ladder, but nobody used it—to the featherboat's outer hull, Gregg handed up a weapon.

Tancred took a rifle; there were cutting bars for the remainder of the crewmen. Besides his bar and the second rifle, Leon carried the torso and helmet of the captain's hard suit. He reached down from the hull to help Gregg.

Gregg wore his faceplate raised, but the chin bar still reduced his downward vision. He jumped into a mass of vegetation that smoldered and stank but was thankfully too wet to burn. The remainder of the crew had followed their captain, but the bosun solicitously waited for Gregg.

"I'm all right!" Gregg snapped.

"It's the flashgun and you wearing armor, sir," Leon said. He scuffed his feet in the mat of leaves, bark, and splintered wood. "That's a bad load in muck like this."

"Sorry," Gregg said sincerely. He knew that he'd spoken more sharply than he should have, because he *hadn't* been sure he was all right.

Piet Ricimer was having a discussion with Mostert and a group of other officers beside the leading truck. They had to speak loudly to be heard over the air-cooled rotary engine. The need to shout may have affected tempers as well. Platt, who'd been aboard the *Sultan*, hung out of the vehicle's cab with an angry expression on his face.

"But we can reconnoiter with the *Peaches*," Ricimer protested. "This isn't a planet we know anything about except its coordinates—"

"*And* the fact it's full of Molts, which is what the hell we're here for, Ricimer!" Platt snarled. Gregg suspected that Platt thought he rather than Ricimer should have been given a ship to command, though the officers hadn't gotten along particularly well during the previous voyage either.

"I just don't think we should jump in without investigating," Ricimer said. "There's no sign of Southerns here and—"

"Calm down, both of you," Alexi Mostert said in obvious irritation. His helmet and breastplate were gilded and engraved, and he carried a pistol as well as a repeating rifle. Sweat ran down the furrow between his thick eyebrows and dripped from his nose.

"We're not looking for Southerns, we're looking for Molts!" said Cseka of the *Desire*.

"Only the ones of us who've got balls," Platt added.

Gregg put his big left hand on Ricimer's shoulder. "I've got balls, Mr. Platt," he said in a deliberate voice that was loud enough to rattle glass. "And I think it's a good idea to know what we're doing before we do it."

Actually, a quick in-and-out raid seemed reasonable to Gregg. He'd have backed Ricimer in the argument if his friend said he thought they'd landed in a desert.

"Look, buddy!" Platt shouted. "You just sit back here on your butt if you want to. I don't have a rich daddy to feed my family if I'm too chicken to earn a living."

Captain Mostert stepped onto the running board of the cab and thrust, not shook, his fist under Platt's nose and moustache. "That's enough!" he said.

Platt jerked back, his face twitching nervously.

Mostert turned to look at the remainder of the officers around him. "This group goes now," he said. "Three trucks. Quile's sending fifty men from the *Grandcamp*, so we'll take the Molts from both sides. Surprise is more important than poking around."

He jumped down from the running board and glowered at Ricimer. "We *know* where the bloody city is, man," he added harshly.

Gregg still had a hand on his friend's shoulder. He felt Ricimer stiffen; much as Gregg himself had done when Platt suggested he was a coward.

The lead truck accelerated away, spewing bits of vegetation from its six driven wheels. The forest's multiple canopies starved the undergrowth of light, opening broad avenues among the boles of the giant trees. The other two truckloads of men followed. There were several officers besides Platt in the force, but it wasn't clear to Gregg who was in charge.

Piet Ricimer clasped his hand over Gregg's on his shoulder and turned around slowly.

"Come on, come on!" Mostert shouted. "Let's get the rest of these trucks set up."

"I wonder how surprised these Molts are going to be," Ricimer murmured to Gregg, "when they've heard six starships land within a klick of their city?"

─15─

Punta Verde

The jungle drank sound, but the clearing itself was bedlam.

The loudest portion of the racket came from the *Tolliver*'s pumps, refilling the old ship's air tanks. There was plenty of other noise as well. Piet Ricimer supervised a team probing for groundwater between the *Peaches* and the flagship. The rotary drill screamed through the friable stone of the forest floor. Nearby, crewmen argued as they loaded three more trucks to follow the lead element of Molt-hunters.

Gregg was only twenty meters from the featherboat. Even so, it wasn't till he turned idly and noticed Dole waving from the hatch that he heard the man shouting. "Sir! Get the captain! Platt, he's stepped on his dick for sure!"

Gregg opened his mouth to ask a question—but realized that whatever the details were, Ricimer needed to hear them worse than he did. He lumbered toward the drilling crew, feeling like a bowling ball with the burden of his weapon and armor.

Gregg felt out of place, both in the lush greenery surrounding the landing site and, at a human level, while watching knowledgeable sailors refit the vessels for the next hop. If he'd been among the crews off to snatch Molts for the ships' holds, Gregg would have a person of importance: better equipped and more skillful than the men around him, as well as being a leader by virtue of birth. He had no place in the argosy's peacetime occupations.

Rather than join the raiders on the second set of trucks, Piet Ricimer had pointedly taken charge of the drilling. The equipment was carried in the flagship's capacious holds, but Ricimer operated it with his own crew. A cable snaking from one of the *Tolliver*'s external outlets powered the auger's electric motors.

The ceramic bits had reached the subsurface water levels. The tailings, crumbly laterite somewhere between rock and soil, lay in a russet pile at the end of the drill's ejection pipe a few meters away. The crew—including Ricimer himself, Gregg was surprised to see—now manhandled sections of twenty centimeter hose to connect the well with the *Tolliver*'s reaction-mass tanks.

It struck Gregg that he could have stood radio watch, freeing Dole to help with the drilling, or he could have laid down his weapon for the moment and carried sections of hose. Because he was a gentleman, no one had suggested that . . . and the thought hadn't crossed *his* mind until now.

"Pict!" he called. "Dole's got something on the radio. There's been trouble with the raid."

Other operators than Dole had caught an emergency signal. As Gregg spoke, one of the ships distant in the forest honked its klaxon. The siren on top of the *Tolliver*'s dome began to wind up, setting nerves on edge and making it even more difficult to hear speech in the clearing below.

The raiding party had blown a gap in the tangle of trunks which the flagship knocked down on landing. Ricimer looked up at the curtain of foliage overhanging that, the only route by which the vehicles could return to the ships. Not so much as a leaf twitched in the still, humid air.

"Stephen," Ricimer said, "can you get four more rifles from the *Tolliver*? If I send one of the men, they'll be refused." He looked back from the jungle and made eye contact. "And I need to get the *Peaches* ready."

"Yes," Gregg said. He set off for the flagship's ramp at something between a long stride and a jog. The sweat soaking his tunic and scalp was suddenly cold, and his muscles trembled with the adrenaline rush.

"Bailey and Jeude, go along to carry," he heard Ricimer call behind him. "But *don't* get in his way. The rest of you, come on!"

Gregg had never been aboard the *Tolliver* before, but the men milling at the central pillar of the lower hold drew him to the arms locker. Incandescent bulbs in the ceiling left the rest of the enormous room dim by comparison with the daylight flooding through the open hatch behind Gregg. The air smelled sour, reeking with decades of abuse.

The *Tolliver* carried a crew of a hundred and sixty on this voyage. About half the men had joined the initial raiding party, but scores waited uncertainly about the arms locker and the trucks being assembled in the clearing.

Captain Mostert was neither place. He must have climbed six decks to the bridge when the alarm sounded.

Two sailors were handing out cutting bars under the observation of an officer Gregg didn't know by name. "You there!" Gregg said to one of the sailors. "I'm Gregg of Eryx and I need four rifles *now!*"

"But—" the sailor said.

"There aren't any rifles left, sir," said the other attendant, the man Gregg hadn't addressed.

"There may be some unassigned firearms still on the bridge, Mr. Gregg," the overseeing officer put in.

"May there indeed!" Gregg exploded. "Who in hell do you think I am, my man?"

He wasn't angry, but the soup of hormones in his blood gave his voice a trembling violence that counterfeited towering rage. Gregg was a big man in any case, the tallest in the hold. With the bulk of his helmet and body armor, he looked like a troll.

He looked at the men around him. The nearest started back from the gentleman's glare.

"You!" Gregg said, pointing to a man with a repeater. His eyes were beginning to adapt to the interior lights. "You—" another rifleman. "Y—" and the third man was holding out his breechloader to Gregg before the demand fully crossed his lips. Jeude and Bailey collected the weapons and bandoliers of sized ammunition without orders.

None of the other crewmen present held firearms.

Gregg focused on the officer. "You, you've got a rifle too. Quick, man!"

The man clutched the repeating carbine slung over his shoulder. "But I own this!" he protested.

"God strike you dead!" Gregg roared, raising the massive flashgun in his right hand as though he intended to preempt the deity. "We've got a battle to fight, man! Go up to the bridge if you need a gun!"

Jeude stepped to the officer's side and silently lifted the weapon by its sling. The man opened his mouth, then closed it again.

"Oh, for *God*'s sake!" he blurted. He ducked so that Gregg's two subordinates could remove both the carbine and the belt of cartridges looped in groups of five to match magazine capacity.

"Come along, you two!" Gregg said. He spoke to keep control of the situation. Bailey and Jeude were already ahead of him, silhouetted against sunlight. "There isn't much time!"

It occurred to Gregg as he spoke that there might not be much time, but he personally didn't have a clue as to what was going on. That didn't bother him. He'd carried out *his* task.

—16—

Punta Verde

A jet of foul steam spouted from around the *Peaches* as Gregg and his helpers lumbered toward the vessel. The thrusters had fired, barely enough to rock the hull. Leon and Dole were locking the bow hatch open to the outside hull. The muzzle of the 50-mm plasma cannon had been run out of the port.

"What's going on?" Bailey shouted to the visible crewmen.

A projectile struck the featherboat's bow hard enough to make the hull ring over the siren's continuing wail. Dole and Leon jumped back. Neither was injured, but there was a greenish smear across the ceramic.

The shot had come from above. Gregg paused, scanning the trees a hundred meters away at the clearing's edge. He couldn't see anything—

Bailey and Jeude had stopped when he did, looking nervous but waiting for orders. Another missile *whicked* into the matted vegetation between them at a 45° angle. The body of the shaft was smooth wood, thumb-thick and perhaps a meter long. An integral filament grew from the end of the shaft, stabilizing the missile in place of fletching.

"Get aboard!" Gregg shouted to the crewmen. "Now!"

He still couldn't see anyone in the high branches from which the projectiles must have come, but the foliage quivered. Gregg lowered his visor, aimed the flashgun, and fired.

Vegetation ripped apart in a blast of steam. Gregg threw up his visor to be able to scan for targets better as his hands performed the instinctive job of reloading. His mind was cold as ice, and his fingers exchanged batteries with mechanical crispness.

After ten or fifteen seconds, something dropped from the place where the laser bolt had scalloped the vegetation. Gregg couldn't make out a figure, but a flicker of mauve suggested the color of the Molts they'd loaded on Salute. The falling body made the second canopy, then the undergrowth, quiver.

Two more missiles snapped from the curtain on the other side of the trucks' passage. Gregg saw them, foreshortened into black dots as they sailed toward him. One missed his shoulder by a hand's breadth as he aimed the flashgun again.

He didn't have time to close the visor. He froze the sight picture, squeezed his eyes shut, and fired. The dazzle burned through the veils of mere skin and blood vessels and left purple afterimages when he tried to see what he'd accomplished.

"Mr. Gregg!" a voice called. "Mr. Gregg, *please*, get aboard, the captain says!"

Gregg ran back toward the *Peaches*. A projectile struck the hull in front of him and glanced away in two major pieces and a spray of splinters from the center of the shaft where it broke. He wondered if the arrows were poisoned.

He grabbed one of the handholds dished into the featherboat during casting and hauled himself up. Leon and Tancred aimed rifles out of the hatch. As Gregg rose above the curve of the hull, Tancred fired at the jungle behind him.

Bits of jacket metal and unburned powder bit Gregg's face like a swarm of gnats. He shouted, "God flay you, whore—"

A Molt projectile slammed into the middle of Gregg's back and shattered on his body armor. His breastplate banged forward into the hull, driving all the breath out of his lungs. Leon let his rifle fall into the featherboat's interior so that he could lean forward and catch the gasping gentleman's wrists.

"Take the flashgun," Gregg wheezed.

Tancred worked the bolt of his repeater and fired again. "Stubborn bastard," the bosun snarled, probably meaning Gregg, but he lifted the flashgun with one hand and dropped it behind him down the hatch while he supported Gregg with the other.

The *Peaches* lifted a meter or two with a wobbly, unbalanced motion. She rotated slowly about her vertical axis. Gregg saw another projectile as a flicker of motion in the corner of his eye, but it must have missed even the vessel.

Leon gave a loud grunt and hauled the gentleman up with a two-handed grip. Gregg managed to find a foothold and thrust

himself safely over the hatch coaming with no more grace or
control than a sack of grain. Bailey and Dole were waiting
inside to catch him.

Ricimer was at the controls. Lightbody and Jeude were
hunched forward, wearing helmets. Leon hopped down from
the hatch to pick up his rifle again.

The plasma cannon fired and recoiled. Vivid light across
and beyond the visual spectrum reflected through the gunport
and the open hatch. The thunderclap made the featherboat
lurch as though Ricimer had run them into a granite ledge.

"That'll make the bastards think!" Jeude crowed from the
bow. He opened the ammunition locker and took out another
round for the plasma cannon, though it would be minutes
before the weapon cooled to the point it could be safely
reloaded.

The egg-shaped shell was a miniature laser array with a
deuterium pellet at the heart of it. When the lasers fired, their
beams heated and compressed the deuterium into a fusion
explosion. The only way out in the microsecond before the
laser array vaporized was through the gap in the front of the
egg, aligned with the ceramic bore. The deuterium, converted
to sun-hot plasma by the energy of its own fusion, ripped down
the channel of the barrel and devoured everything in its path.

Gregg got to his feet. He found the flashgun and loaded a
fresh battery from the pack slapping against his chest.

"The Molts ambushed the trucks before they ever got to the
city," Leon shouted in explanation. "The buggers are up the
trees, Platt says."

"I noticed," Gregg said grimly as he stepped onto the storage locker again. A sharp pain in his ribs made him gasp. His
mouth tasted of blood, but he thought he must have bitten
his tongue when the arrow knocked him forward. Tancred
stood head and shoulders out of the hatch, trying awkwardly
to reload his rifle.

The *Peaches* was fifty meters above the ground, wobbling
greasily and moving at the speed of a fast walk. The plasma
bolt had blown a huge crater in the foliage. A dozen tree
trunks, stripped bare of bark and branches, blazed at the edge
of the stricken area.

Piet Ricimer kept the featherboat rising a meter for every
meter it slid forward. By the time the Venerians reached the
edge of the original clearing, they were high enough that their

thrusters seared the topmost canopy into blackened curls and steam.

Gregg stepped to the front of the long hatch and nudged Tancred aside. The young spacer grimaced but didn't protest aloud. Leon and Bailey, each holding a rifle, climbed onto the locker as well.

There were no targets. Indeed, from the topside hatch, nothing was visible over the bow save an occasional giant tree emerging from the general "landscape." Massed blooms added splotches of yellow, brown, and eye-catching scarlet to the normal green.

Accelerating very slightly, the *Peaches* proceeded in the direction the raiders' trucks had followed through the jungle. If there were Molt warriors beneath, they fled or died in the vessel's superheated exhaust.

Somebody tugged at the thigh of Gregg's trousers. He looked down.

"Sir," called Dole over the waterfall roar of the thrusters. "The captain, he needs you." He jerked his head toward Ricimer, facing forward over the control console.

Gregg knelt and stepped down into the featherboat's bay. He didn't duck low enough; his helmet cracked loudly against the hatch coaming, no harm done but an irritation. Between armor and the big flashgun in his arms, he was clumsy as a blind bear.

Despite the open hatch and gunport, the vessel's interior was much quieter than the outside. "Stephen," Ricimer said, "we're getting close to the vehicles. If I overfly them, they'll be broiled by our thrusters."

Ricimer's eyes were on the viewscreen. His hands moved as two separate living creatures across the controls, modifying thrust and vector. Dole seated himself at one of the attitude-jet panels, but from the rigidity of the crewman's face, he was afraid to do anything that might interfere with Ricimer's delicate adjustments.

"The only way I can think to break our people loose is to go down into the canopy and circle," Ricimer continued in a voice that was controlled to perfect flatness, not calm. "The men on the ground don't have any targets, but the Molts aren't camouflaged from their own level or a little above."

"Right," Gregg said. "Take us down." He turned.

"Stephen!" Ricimer said.

Gregg looked back. Ricimer risked a glance away from the viewscreens so their eyes could meet. "It will be very dangerous," Ricimer said. "And I have to stay here."

"Do your bloody job, man!" Gregg snapped in irritation. "Leave me to mine."

He climbed onto the locker again and moved Tancred aside. "Get ready," he ordered his fellow gunmen as he lowered his visor. "We're going down. Everybody take one side."

The *Peaches* shuddered and lost forward way for a moment. The stern dipped. The featherboat dropped into the canopy with its bow pitched up 20°, advancing at barely a fast walk. An arrow clanged against the underside.

Shadows and the faceshield's tint came dangerously close to blinding Gregg. He saw movement over the *Peaches*' bow, three Molts on a platform anchored where a pair of branches crossed between trunks. A catwalk of vine-lashed poles led into the green curtain to either side.

One Molt was cocking a shoulder-stocked weapon with a vertical throwing arm. Another fired his similar weapon at the featherboat's bow, not the men above the hatch. A crewman's rifle spoke.

Gregg squeezed off. The carapace of the Molt cocking his launcher exploded. The blast of vaporized flesh threw both his/her companions off the platform.

The *Peaches* nudged into a tree bole and crushed it over, tugging out the distant roots. The catwalk separated and fell away. Gregg saw poles flying from another walkway, unguessed until the moment of collapse. All his men were shooting, and he thought he heard muffled gunfire from the ground.

The laser was the wrong weapon for a close-quarter firefight like this. He couldn't see well enough with the visor down to react. "Give me a rif—" he shouted as he fed a fresh battery into the flashgun's stock.

The plasma cannon fired. The shockwave threw Gregg backward. If the *Peaches* hadn't bucked at the same time, he might have fallen flat. The directed thermonuclear explosion bored a cone of radiant hell hundreds of meters through the mid-canopy. Foliage to either side of the path withered and died.

Gregg saw a Molt plunging toward the ground like a flung torch. The aliens wore no clothing, but the creature's entire body had been ignited by the discharge.

Ricimer guided the featherboat along the ionized track. Molt constructions showed vividly where the leaves were burned away.

Gregg saw an alien clinging to the poles of a catwalk whose farther end had vanished. Instead of shooting the Molt he saw, he aimed at the high crotch where the poles were still attached. The flash of his bolt illuminated a pair of Molts crouching in the darkness. They hurtled to either side, while their fellow dropped in the tangle of his poles.

The featherboat nosed to starboard. Ricimer needed to encircle the site in order to free the raiders pinned down below. He or Dole had corrected the attitude to lower the bow. A gnarled, wrist-thick branch struck Gregg hard enough on the head to make his eyes water despite the helmet.

At least a dozen Molts fired a simultaneous volley. All the missiles were aimed at the gunmen this time. An arrow struck just in front of the hatch coaming and glanced upward into Gregg's chest. The impact stabbed daggers through his ribs.

A crewman screamed behind him. A pair of Molts reloaded on a catwalk only twenty meters ahead of the *Peaches*. The bow would throw them down in a moment. Gregg fired anyway and saw the bodies cartwheel away, one of them headless.

He flipped up his visor and turned. "A rifle!" he shouted. "Give me a—"

Leon was trying to keep Bailey from climbing out of the hatch. An arrow had plunged into Bailey's right eye and down, pinning his face to his left shoulder. The crewman gobbled bloody froth. His remaining eye was wild.

Tancred bellowed wordlessly as tears streamed down his cheeks. He didn't appear to be physically injured. He worked the bolt of his repeater and pulled the trigger, but the weapon's magazine was empty.

"Get down, all of you!" Gregg ordered. He dropped his flashgun and gripped the repeater at the balance. Tancred resisted momentarily. Gregg punched the boy in the pit of the stomach. He crumpled. Gregg snatched the bandolier and broke the strap free with the violence of his tug.

Bailey suddenly collapsed. Leon straightened and brought up his breechloader. Molt projectiles crossed in the air between Gregg and the bosun. "Get *down*!" Gregg repeated as he thumbed cartridges into the integral magazine.

The *Peaches* rocked into a series of tree trunks in quick succession. One splintered at the point of impact. The other trees pulled out of the thin soil and tilted crazily, half-supported by vines and branches interlocking with those of their neighbors. As the featherboat passed over the tangle, her superheated exhaust devoured those impediments and sent the trunks crashing the remainder of the way to the ground.

A Molt aimed his weapon down at the hatch. Gregg shot the creature through the body. Recoil brought a sharp reminder of the injured ribs. He chambered the next round, rotated to his left where motion shimmered in the corner of his eye, and smashed the triangular skull of an alien seventy meters away.

Leon fired. A projectile grazed the back of Gregg's helmet, making his vision blur.

"God rot your bones in Hell!" Gregg screamed in the bosun's face. "Get down and load for me! I've got armor!"

As he spoke, he fired the last round in his magazine. A Molt dropped his weapon to one side of a catwalk and fell to the other. He managed to grasp a guy rope of braided vine and cling there for the instant's notice Gregg had to give anything that wasn't immediately lethal.

He dropped the repeater. Tancred offered him a loaded rifle, stock-first, from the featherboat's bay. Leon ducked down as ordered. Either the words or the sense or the naked fury in Stephen Gregg's face had penetrated the bosun's consciousness.

With his visor up, Gregg felt like a god. He could see *everything*, and he couldn't miss. The *Peaches* was unstable at low speed even without grinding her hull into huge trees, which themselves weighed tonnes. It didn't matter. Gregg and the gunsights and each Molt were one until the *flash*/shock signaled the need to seek another alien target.

Two more arrows hit Gregg—on the right side and in the back, squarely over the smear where he'd been struck while boarding the featherboat. He was aware of the impacts the way he saw the black and green of vegetation—facts, but unimportant when only the mauve smudges of Molt bodies mattered.

He didn't bother to look down when he'd emptied a rifle, just dropped it and opened his hand to take the fresh weapon a crewman would slap there. The carbine from the *Tolliver*'s officer had a five-round magazine and was dead accurate.

Gregg used it to shoot the eye out of a Molt warrior at least a hundred meters away.

A corner of Gregg's mind noted two trucks glimpsed where the *Peaches* had cleared a sight line to the ground. Men huddled beneath the vehicles and behind nearby trees. A few of them waved. Molt projectiles stood out from the thin panels of the truck bodies like quills on a porcupine, and from sprawled men as well.

The featherboat yawed uneasily as Ricimer brought her bow onto a new heading. Gregg hadn't fired for—he didn't know how long. There weren't any targets, though occasionally he glimpsed an empty platform or catwalk.

The *Peaches* nosed onto the track her thrusters had cleared on the way to the ambush site. Over the bow Gregg saw the trucks again, all three of them, retreating toward the ships. They jounced over the buttress roots of trees at the best speed they were capable of. He realized he couldn't hear anything, not even the roaring thrusters, though he felt the vibration through his feet and the hatch coaming against which he braced his belly.

The clearing the *Tolliver* had blasted was a bright splotch without the shadow-dappling of the jungle beyond. The flagship had run out several of her big plasma cannon. Men rose from hasty barricades to greet the returning trucks.

"That's okay, sir," said a voice close to Gregg's ear. "We'll take over now."

A wet cloth dabbed at his forehead. He wasn't wearing his helmet anymore.

"Jesus God! What happened to his head?"

"Arrow must've hit right over the visor. Jesus!"

The last thing Gregg saw was the worried face of Piet Ricimer, framed by the hatch opening above him.

―17―

Punta Verde

Gregg didn't recognize the ceiling. He turned his head. A wave of nausea tried to turn his stomach inside out. Nothing came up except thin bile, but the spasms made his rib cage feel as though it was jacketed in molten glass.

Piet Ricimer leaned over him and gently mopped the vomit away with a sponge. "Welcome back," he said.

"I feel awful," Gregg whispered.

Ricimer shrugged. "Cracked ribs, a concussion, and unconscious for three days," he said. "You *ought* to feel awful, my friend."

"Three *days*?"

"I was beginning to worry a little," Ricimer said without emphasis. "The medic thought most of it was simple exhaustion, though. You were operating"—he smiled wryly—"well beyond redline, Stephen."

Gregg closed his eyes for a moment. "Christ's blood, I feel awful," he said. He looked up again. "Sorry."

"You've had quite a time," Ricimer said. "The Lord makes allowances, I'm sure."

"Where are—" Gregg began. He broke off, winced, and continued, "Just a bit. I'm going to sit up."

"The medics—" Ricimer said. Gregg lurched up on his right elbow and gasped. Ricimer slid an arm behind his friend's back but followed rather than lifted Gregg the rest of the way up.

The gentleman sat with his eyes closed, breathing in quick, shallow breaths. At last he resumed, "Where are we?"

"The argosy hasn't moved, if that's what you mean," Ricimer

said. "You and I are in a cabin on the *Tolliver*."

His smile had claws of memory. "They were going to put you in the sick bay," he added. "But I didn't think you ought to be disturbed by the other wounded men."

"I don't think I'm going to stand up just yet," Gregg said deliberately. He opened his eyes and saw the worry on Ricimer's face melt into a look of studied unconcern. "We're *going* to lift off, aren't we?" he pressed. "Mostert can't possibly think we can capture enough Molts here to be worth the, the cost."

"As a matter of fact . . ." Ricimer said. Gregg couldn't be sure of his tone. "The village we attacked—city, really, there are thousands of Molts living in it. The Molts were impressed. They've dealt with the Southerns before, but they'd never met anything like us."

Looking at a corner of the ceiling, Ricimer went on, "Leon's in the sick bay, you know. Splinters through the shoulder from an arrow that hit the hull beside him."

Gregg pursed his lips, remembering flashes of the way he'd shouted at the bosun. "I didn't know that," he said.

Ricimer shrugged. "He'll be all right. But I heard him telling a rating from the *Tolliver* in the next bed, 'Our Mr. Gregg, he's a right bastard. He went through them bugs like shit through a goose. As soon kill you as look at you, Mr. Gregg would.' "

"Lord, I'm sorry," Gregg whispered with his eyes closed. "I was . . ."

"He's proud of you, Stephen," Ricimer explained softly. "We all are. *Our* Mr. Gregg. And the Molts were so impressed that they want us to help them against their neighbors forty klicks away. In return, we get the prisoners."

"Well, I'll be damned," Gregg said.

"Not for what you did three days ago," Ricimer said. "Eight of the men with the trucks were killed, but none of them would have made it back except for us. Especially for you."

"Especially for you," Gregg corrected. He met his friend's eyes again. "Bailey?" he asked.

Ricimer shook his head minusculy. "No. But that's not— anyone's fault."

"When do we . . ." Gregg said. "The raid, the attack. When is it?"

"Three days from now," Ricimer said. "The Molts are getting their army, I suppose you'd call it, together. But Stephen, I don't think—"

"I'm going," Gregg said. He set his lips firmly together, then held out his hand toward his friend. "Now," he said. "Help me stand . . ."

—18—

Punta Verde

Because the four men stationed at the *Peaches'* hatch all wore body armor and helmets, Gregg knocked elbows when he twisted to either side. Even so, the hatchway was less crowded than the featherboat's bay in which twenty more heavily-armed men waited.

The *Hawkwood* at three hundred meters altitude led the expedition. She wobbled across the sky, losing or gaining twenty meters of elevation in an instant and slewing sideways by twice that much. The *Hawkwood* had a good enough thrust-to-weight ratio to make atmospheric flight a possible proposition, but not an especially practical one. They were using her because Mostert needed the firepower and the hundred men he could cram into the vessel's hull.

Four lifeboats, each with a dozen or more men aboard, veed out to the *Hawkwood*'s flanks. They skimmed the treetops, buttoned up but still washed dangerously by hot, electrically-excited exhaust from the leading vessel's thrusters. Occasionally one of them, buffeted or simply blinded when the *Hawkwood* slid to the side, dipped into the forest. As yet, none of them had been noticeably damaged by such mishaps.

The featherboats closed both arms of the vee. Gregg noted with grim amusement that the *Desire* to starboard porpoised almost as badly as the *Hawkwood* did, while Piet Ricimer kept the *Peaches* as steady as if she ran on tracks.

A kilometer ahead of the expedition's leading vessel, Gregg saw an incandescent rainbow: sun catching the plume of another spaceship's thrusters. The reason the Molts had allied themselves with the Venerians was that their rivals were in league with the Southerns, trading captives for firearms.

No one would hear Gregg if he shouted. The flashgunners in the hatch had their visors locked down against the retina-crisping dazzle of the *Hawkwood*'s exhaust. That and the engine roar isolated them as individuals. The other three came from the *Rose*. Gregg wouldn't recognize any of them with their helmets off.

Anyway, it wasn't the hatch crew which had to be warned but rather the vessels' captains. Their view was even blurrier than Gregg's through his filtered visor. It was possible that the distant vessel wasn't hostile . . . but it was equally possible that pigs flew on some undiscovered planet.

Gregg aimed his flashgun at the top of the distant plume where the other vessel had to be. He tried to steady his weapon. The shot was beyond human skill, but the vivid lance across the optics of the expedition vessels would at least call attention to the interloper.

The world fluoresced with a shockwave that felt for an instant like freefall. Forest vaporized in the bolt from the *Peaches*' plasma cannon. Despite the featherboat's distant position, Ricimer had seen the target as soon as Gregg did.

The interloper appeared startled, though it was untouched by the blast. It lifted from where it lurked in the upper canopy and ripped a series of brilliant sparks toward the *Hawkwood*. It appeared to mount a multishot laser rather than a plasma weapon.

The 14-cm Long Tom in the *Hawkwood*'s bow belched a sky-devouring gout of directed energy toward the interloper. Foliage exploded. Eighty meters of a giant tree leaped upward like a javelin, shedding leaves and branches as it rose. It had been struck near the base. The target dived to vanish within the forest again.

Mostert brought the *Hawkwood*'s bow around to starboard. He ignored the danger to the cutters on that side and the *Desire* in his eagerness to bring his port six-gun battery into play. These lighter weapons, 8- and 10-cm plasma cannon, had no target by the time they bore, but the gun captains loosed anyway. Gregg could imagine Piet Ricimer white-lipped at his controls as he watched his cousin's actions.

The squadron's destination was in sight: flat mushrooms rising beneath the topmost foliage. The city's extent seemed greater than that of the one Platt had tried to attack. These domes were mottled gray instead of being beige.

The *Peaches* swung wide and dipped as the other Venerian vessels homed in on the Molt stronghold. Ricimer was waiting for the Southern vessel to reappear. Gregg tightened his grip on the flashgun, then forced himself to relax so that he wouldn't be too keyed-up to react if he had to. The featherboat's plasma cannon was still too hot to reload, so it was up to him and his fellows if the target appeared.

It didn't. The Southerns had already shown more courage than Gregg would've expected, engaging a force that was so hugely more powerful.

The *Hawkwood* lowered toward the canopy, pitching and yawing. As she neared the treetops, her starboard battery fired. Four fireballs flared across the nearest Molt dome. Farther back across the stronghold, misdirected blasts blasted another structure and the topmost fifty meters from one of the forest's emergent giants.

The squadron's leader sank into the jungle at the edge of the stronghold in a barely-controlled slide. The cutters and the *Desire* settled in beside her.

The *Peaches* swept over the outer ring of domes and into the interior of the stronghold.

Gregg glanced down. The cellulose-based roof of the nearest dome was afire where the plasma discharges had struck it. Gangs of Molts sprayed the flames with a sticky fluid. Warriors on the roof of the structure fired point-blank at the featherboat with rifles as well as indigenous weapons. An arrow that missed the *Peaches* arched high over Gregg's head.

As he took her down, Ricimer rotated the *Peaches* on her vertical axis like a dog preparing its bed. The dome they'd overflown was completely alight from the plasma exhaust. Warriors and members of the firefighting team were dark sprawls within the sea of flame.

The Molts had cut away the undergrowth and mid-level vegetation within their stronghold. The boles of emergents split and corkscrewed as the thrusters seared them. Walkways connecting the domes burned brightly. The city stretched nearly a kilometer across its separate elements.

The featherboat grounded, then sank a meter lower when what appeared to be soil turned out to be the roof of a turf-and-laterite structure covering the interior of the stronghold. An unarmed Molt clawed its way through the broken surface, shrieking until one of the flashgunners shot him.

A warrior leaned from the crotch of an emergent, aiming his rifle at the *Peaches* seventy meters below. Gregg's hasty snap shot struck a meter below the Molt. The trunk blew apart with enough violence to fling the alien in one direction while the upper portion of the tree tilted slowly in the other.

Shouting men tried to push past Gregg. He lifted himself out of the hatch and toppled to the ground when his boot caught on the coaming. Armor and the flashgun made him top-heavy. Somebody jumped onto Gregg's back as he tried to rise. Finally he managed to roll sideways, then get his feet under him again.

The interior of the stronghold was as open as a manicured park. Here and there Molts popped to the surface from the underground shelter, but none of them were armed. Occasional warriors sniped from distant trees. The featherboat's thrusters had cleared the immediate area of catwalks by which the defenders might have approached dangerously close.

More—many more—Molts boiled from the lower levels of the burning dome. They were all warriors. The domes were actually the tops of towers rising from the ground. They were connected by gray vertical walls. At a close look, the material was wood pulp masticated with enzymes and allowed to solidify into something akin to concrete-hard *papier-mâché*.

Gregg reloaded his flashgun. Men leaped from the featherboat and hesitated. Those with rifles fired at Molts, but the disparity in their numbers compared to those of the aliens was shockingly apparent. Gunfire and cries could be heard through the stronghold's wall as if from a great distance.

"Follow me!" Gregg shouted as he fired his flashgun at a closed door in the base of the burning tower. His bolt shattered the panel and ignited it, as he'd hoped. He lumbered toward the nearest stretch of wall, reloading as he ran.

Three Molts swinging edged clubs rushed Gregg from the side. One wore a pink sash.

The battery Gregg was loading hung up in its compartment. When he tried to force it with his thumbs, the connectors bent.

A sailor Gregg didn't know aimed his rifle in the face of a Molt and squeezed the trigger. Nothing happened. The sailor bawled and flattened himself on the ground.

Gregg lunged forward, stepping inside the nearest alien's stroke instead of taking it on the side of his head. The Molt caromed away from Gregg's armored shoulder. As the warrior fell, Gregg saw the creature wore a pistol holster on its sash, but the weapon was missing.

Gregg clubbed his flashgun at the second Molt as the creature swung at him. Their blows, both right-handed, described the two halves of a circle. The flashgun's heavy barrel crunched a broad dent in the wedge-shaped skull. The alien's club was wooden, but dense and metal-hard. It rang on Gregg's helmet.

His limbs lost feeling. He slipped down on his right side. He could see and hear perfectly well, but his body seemed to belong to someone else. The third Molt stood splay-legged before him, raising his weapon for a vertical, two-handed chop. The Molts of this city had a tinge of yellow in their chitinous exoskeletons, unlike the smooth mauve of the clan with which the Venerians were now allied.

A bullet punched through the thorax of the Molt about to finish Gregg. The warrior fell backward in a splash of ichor. Piet Ricimer loaded a fresh round, butt-stroked the Molt beginning to rise from where the impact of Gregg's body had flung him, and bent to Gregg.

"Leon!" he shouted. "Help Mr. Gregg—"

Gregg twisted his body violently. As though the first motion broke a spell, he found he had control of his arms and legs again.

"C'mon," he said. He tried to shout, but the words came out in a slurred croak. The bosun gripped his shoulders to help him rise. "Gotta cut through the wall from this side."

The Venerian raiders wore half-armor or at least helmets for the assault. One man lay with a pair of arrows crossing through his throat, but that appeared to be the only fatality. A rifleman fired from the featherboat's open hatch. There might be a few others inside, either left for a guard or unwilling at the crisis to put themselves into open danger.

The rest of the force, eighteen or twenty men, was coalescing into a frightened group in the open area between the *Peaches* and the stronghold's wall. Most of them couldn't have realized where Ricimer was landing them. They'd spread momentarily when they jumped from the featherboat, but realization of how badly outnumbered they were drove the Venerians together again. Some of them were wounded.

For their own part, the Molts were equally confused by the series of events. A hundred or so warriors threatened the band

of Venerians, but they didn't press closer than five meters or
so in the face of gunfire. Relatively few of the aliens carried
projectile weapons. Gregg suspected the shooters had been
stationed high in the tower for a better field of fire. The
Peaches' thrusters had cooked most of those, though others
were bound to swarm to the point of attack from neighboring
towers.

"With me!" Ricimer shouted. "We'll cut through the wall!"
He waved his rifle in a great vertical arc as if it were a saber
and ran forward. Gregg felt like a hippo when he moved wearing armor. His friend sprinted as though he were in shoes and
a tunic.

Gregg took the jammed reload out of the flashgun's compartment and flung the battery as a dense missile at the nearest
Molt. He inserted a fresh battery. "Come on, Leon," he said
as he backed slowly with his face to the enemy. "I'm fine,
you bet."

Leon carried a cutting bar. He swung it in a showy figure
eight with the power on. The blade vibrated like a beam of
coherent light. He and Gregg were the rear guard. The wall
was thirty meters away. Gregg expected the Molts to rush
them, but instead warriors hopped uncertainly from one jointed
leg to another as the flashgun's muzzle flicked sideways.

Gregg's heel bumped something. He glanced down reflexively. An unseen marksman slammed an arrow into Gregg's
breastplate. He pitched backward over the body of an alien
eviscerated by a cutting bar. Thirty or forty warriors charged
in chittering fury. Gregg scrambled to his feet in a red haze
of pain and squeezed the flashgun's trigger.

The barrel had cracked when he used the weapon as a mace.
Instead of frying the Molt at the point of aim, it blew up like a
ceramic-cased bomb, hurling shrapnel forward and to all sides.
None of the fragments hit Gregg, but the concussion knocked
him on his back again.

Several Molts were down, though their exoskeletons were
relatively proof against small cuts. The rush halted in surprise,
though. A four-shot volley from the rest of the company
dropped several more aliens and turned the attack into a broken rout.

Piet Ricimer knelt beside Gregg and rose, lifting the whole
weight of the bigger man until the bosun grabbed the opposite
arm and helped.

"I'm not hurt!" Gregg shouted angrily. "I'm not hurt!" He wondered if that was true. He seemed to be standing a few centimeters away from his body, so that the edges of his flesh and soul didn't quite match.

The flashgun's barrel had disintegrated as completely as a hot filament suddenly exposed to oxygen. Gregg threw away the stock and picked up a repeater with Southern Cross markings. He didn't know whether it was a crewman's loot from an earlier voyage, or if a Molt had carried the weapon. There was an empty case in the chamber but two cartridges in the magazine.

A five-meter section of wall as high as a man sagged, then collapsed outward when crewmen kicked the panel to break the joins their hasty bar-cuts had left. Several armored Venerians burst through from outside the stronghold. Behind them were scores of allied Molts carrying projectile weapons and long wooden spears in place of the locals' edged clubs.

Gregg felt himself sway. He lifted his visor for the first time since he boarded the *Peaches* for the attack. He *knew* the air was steamy, but it touched his face like an icy shower. He thought of unlatching his body armor, but he wasn't sure he retained enough dexterity to work the catches.

Ricimer put a hand on Gregg's shoulder. "We did it," Ricimer croaked. "We've made the breakthrough. The Molts can carry the fight now."

He guided Gregg toward the featherboat. The tower was fully involved, a spire of flames leaping from the ground to twice the eighty-meter height of the structure that fed them. The radiant heat was a hammer. Gregg was too numb to connect cause and effect, so Ricimer led him clear.

The stronghold's defenders lay all about. Most of them were dead, but some twitched or even made attempts at connected motion. Allied Molts ripped open the ceiling of the underground chamber as soon as they were within the stronghold's walls, then disappeared from sight.

High-pitched screams came from distant portions of the city. The cries went on longer than human throats could have sustained. There had been other breakthroughs now that the Venerians had smashed the point at which the defenders concentrated against the assault. Gregg saw flames quiver upward through the sparse interior vegetation.

The Molt Gregg had bodychecked and Ricimer then clubbed was sitting up. It followed their approach with its eyes but did not move.

Gregg presented his rifle.

"Kill me, then, human," the Molt said in high-pitched but intelligible English.

"We're not here to kill p-p-p—" Ricimer began. "We're not here to kill you, we want workers."

A band of twenty or thirty defending warriors sprinted across the clearing the featherboat had made toward a neighboring tower. Allied Molts pursued them. Both sides paused and exchanged a volley of projectiles. A few fell. The survivors continued their race. Gregg covered the action with the rifle he'd appropriated, but he didn't bother to fire.

Ricimer put his hand on the shoulder of the Molt who had spoken. "Do you yield, then?" the spacer demanded.

"I yield to you, human," the Molt said calmly. "But the Y'Lyme will kill me and all my clan. We sold them to the slavers for a brood-year. Now they will kill us all."

"Nobody's going to kill you," Ricimer said harshly.

Smoke seeped from the soil in a dozen locations. Fires had started in the underground chambers. Allied Molts—Y'Lyme—came up, driving yellow-tinged locals ahead of them. Those hidden below were juveniles or cramped with age. Y'Lyme began to spear them to death. The victims seemed apathetic.

Ricimer's captive made a clicking sound that Gregg supposed was a laugh. "The slavers called me Guillermo," he said. "I was in charge of my clan's trade with them."

Platt jogged over to Ricimer and Gregg with three crewmen from the *Tolliver*. He carried a cutting bar. It and his breast-plate were smeared with brownish Molt internal juices. Behind Platt, Captain Mostert and other members of his headquarters group entered the stronghold through the gap the *Peaches* crew had cut.

"I'll get him!" Platt cried. He stepped to Guillermo and raised his howling bar.

"Hey!" Ricimer shouted. He stepped between Platt and his would-be victim. "What do you think you're doing?"

Platt shoved Ricimer aside. "Killing fucking Molts!" he said. "Till they all give up!"

Stephen Gregg extended his repeater like a long pistol. The barrel lay across Platt's Adam's apple; the muzzle pointed past his left shoulder.

Platt bleated. One of the men accompanying him aimed a rifle at Gregg's midriff. Out of the corner of Gregg's eye he saw Tancred, Dole, and Lightbody running toward the tableau.

"Look there, Platt," Gregg said. He jerked his chin to draw the officer's gaze along the line of the rifle.

A Molt thirty meters away sat up to aim a projectile weapon. A wooden arrow pinned the creature's thighs together.

The Molt fired. The missile whacked through the bridge of Platt's nose and lifted the officer's helmet from the inside.

Platt toppled backward. Gregg fired and missed. While other Venerians shouted and fired wildly, Gregg chambered his last round. He raised the rifle to his shoulder normally and fired. The Molt collapsed, thrashing.

Piet Ricimer surveyed his surroundings in a series of fierce jerks of his head. His fingertips rested on the head of the Molt who had yielded to him. His five crewmen and a promiscuous group of Venerians, from the *Peaches* and outside the stronghold, stared at him and Gregg, waiting for direction.

"All right!" Ricimer ordered. "Start rounding up prisoners. Don't let the, the others kill them. Do what you have to, to stop the killing."

His eyes met those of Stephen Gregg. Gregg stood like a tree. He was aware of what was going on around him, but his mind was no longer capable of taking an active part in it.

"In the name of God . . ." Piet Ricimer said. "*Stop* the killing!"

In all directions, the guard towers of the captured city blazed like Hell's pillars.

—19—

Sunrise

When the six Venerian captains conferred by radio about the moon they were orbiting, Piet Ricimer suggested the name Sunrise because of the way sunlight washed to a rose-purple color the gases belching from a huge volcano. The name stuck, at least for as long as the argosy refitted here. The next visitors, years or millennia hence, would give it their own name—if they even bothered.

Between the sun and the moon's primary, a gas giant on the verge of collapsing into a star, Sunrise was habitably warm though on the low side of comfortable. The atmosphere stank of sulphur, but it was breathable.

Cellular life had not arisen here, nor was it likely to arise. The primary raised tides in Sunrise's rocky core and swamped the moon's surface every few years with magma or volcanically-melted water which refroze as soon as the tremors paused.

The planet-sized moon was a useful staging point in the patterns of transit space connecting the Reaches with the worlds of the Mirror, where the sidereal universe doubled itself in close detail. There would be a Federation outpost on Sunrise—

Except for storms that battered the moon's atmosphere with a violence equal to the surges in the crust itself. Landing a large vessel on Sunrise would have been nearly suicidal for pilots who had not trained in the roiling hell of Venus.

For that matter, the *Tolliver*'s landing had been a close brush with disaster and the *Grandcamp* was still in orbit. Captain Kershaw's cutter ferried him down to attend the conference in person.

There hadn't been any choice about landing the flagship. Quite apart from the need to replenish the *Tolliver's* air supply, her disintegrating hull required repairs that could best be performed on the ground. Ricimer had hinted to Gregg that nothing that could be done outside a major dockyard was going to help the big vessel significantly, though.

"I say we head straight for home," said Fedders of the *Rose*. "We've got our profit and a dozen times over, what with the shell from Jewelhouse. The amount of risk we face if we try to move the last hundred Molts isn't worth it. And I'm talking about strain to the ships, irregardless of the Feds."

"We can't make a straight run for Venus," Kershaw protested. "I can't, at least. The gradients between transit universes are rising, and I tell you frankly—the *Grandcamp* isn't going to take the strain."

The buzz of crews overglazing the *Tolliver* provided a constant background to the discussion. Portable kilns crawled across the hull in regular bands, spraying vaporized rock onto the crumbling ceramic plates. The process returned the flagship to proper airtightness so long as she remained at rest. The stress of takeoff, followed by the repeated hammering of transit, would craze the surface anew.

"It's not the gradients—" said Fedders.

"The gradients *are* rising," Ricimer interjected quickly. "They're twenty percent above what the sailing directions we loaded on Jewelhouse indicate is normal."

"All right, they are," Fedders snapped, "but the real problem is the *Grandcamp*'s AI not making the insertions properly. And the Federation's Earth Convoy is due in the region any day now."

"That's enough squabbling about causes," Admiral Mostert said forcefully. "The situation is what's important. And the situation is that the *Tolliver* can't make a straight run home either. We're going to have to land on Biruta to refit and take on reaction mass."

Kelly of the *Hawkwood* muttered a curse. "Right," he said to his hands. They were clenched, knuckles to knuckles, on the opalglass conference table before him. "And what do we do if the Earth Convoy's waiting there for us? Pray they won't have heard how we traded on Jewelhouse?"

"*And* Bowman," Stephen Gregg murmured from his chair against the bulkhead behind Ricimer—Captain Ricimer—at the table. The aged flagship had few virtues, but the scale of her accommodations, including a full conference room as part of the admiral's suite, was one of them. "*And* Guelph. We didn't actually blow up any buildings either of those places, but the locals did business with us because forty plasma guns were trained on them."

A particularly strong gust of wind ripped across the surface of Sunrise. The *Tolliver* rocked and settled again. A similar blast when Gregg and Ricimer trekked from the *Peaches* to the flagship had skidded them thirty meters across a terrain of rock crevices filled with ice.

"I don't suppose there'd be another uncharted stopover we could use instead of Biruta, would there?" Fedders suggested plaintively. "I mean . . ."

Everyone in the conference room, the six captains and their chief aides and navigators, knew what Fedders meant. They also knew that Sunrise had been discovered only because of the *Peaches*' one-in-a-million piece of luck. Ricimer cast widely ahead of the remainder of the argosy, confident that he could rendezvous without constantly comparing positions the way the other navigators had to do.

The voyage thus far had been a stunning success. The Venerians loaded pre-Collapse artifacts from two Federation colonies, and on Jewelhouse they'd gained half a tonne of the shells that made the planet famous. The material came from deepwater snails which fluoresced vividly to stun prey in the black depths of the ocean trench they inhabited. Kilo for kilo, the shell was as valuable as purpose-designed microchips from factories operating across the Mirror.

When the voyage began, Mostert's men were willing to take risks for the chance of becoming wealthy. Now they *were* wealthy, all the officers in this room . . . if only they could get home with their takings. There was no longer a carrot to balance the stick of danger; and that stick was more and more a spiked club as the condition of the older vessels degraded from brutal use.

"We should be ahead of the Earth Convoy," Mostert said. His heavy face was without visible emotion, but the precise way his hands rested on the conference table suggested the control he exerted to retain that impassivity. "We'll load, repair, and be gone in a few days. We can offer the authorities on Biruta a fair price for using their graving docks. They need

Molt labor as badly as the other colonies."

"There's only one place to land a starship on Biruta," Fedders said with his eyes on a ceiling molding. "That's Island Able. And they'll have defenses there, the Feds will . . ."

A starship which committed to land on Biruta had no options if batteries at the port opened fire. The seas that wrapped the remainder of the planet would swallow any vessel which tried to avoid plasma bolts that would otherwise rip her belly out.

"They won't know we're from Venus," said Mostert. "I'll go in first with the guns ready for as soon as we're down."

He looked at his cousin. "Ricimer," he said. "You can bring your featherboat in at the same time the *Tolliver* lands, can't you?"

"Yes," Ricimer said softly. "We could do that. It'll confuse the garrison."

Mostert nodded. "If we give them enough to think about, they won't act. So that's what we'll do."

He looked around the conference table. "No further questions, then?" he said with a deliberate lack of subtlety.

No one spoke for a moment. The Venerians had accessed the data banks in the Jewelhouse Commandatura while they held the Fed governor and his wife under guard. The information there suggested that the annual Earth Convoy was due anytime within a standard week of the present . . .

"If there isn't any choice," Piet Ricimer said in the grim silence, "then—may the Lord shelter us in our necessity."

Gregg remembered the terror in the eyes of the wife of the Jewelhouse governor. He wondered if the Lord saw any reason to shelter the men in this room . . . including Stephen Gregg, who was of their number whether or not he approved of every action his company took.

—20—

Biruta

Biruta's atmosphere was notably calm. That, with the planet's location at the nearer edge (through transit space) of the Reaches and the huge expanse of water to provide reaction mass, made Biruta an ideal way station for starships staggering out from the solar system.

The *Peaches* had to come in at the worst part of the flagship's turbulence. She bucked and pitched like lint above an air vent. Ricimer and the men on the attitude jets, Leon and Lightbody this time, kept the featherboat on a reasonably even keel.

Jeude and Tancred in their hard suits hunched over the plasma cannon forward. They'd opened the gunport at three klicks of altitude, though they'd have to run the weapon out before they brought it into action.

Gregg smiled grimly as he gripped a stanchion and braced one boot against a bulkhead. He was getting better at this. And there were amusement parks where people paid money to have similar experiences.

Guillermo stood across the narrow hull from Gregg. From his first landing, the Molt rode as easily as if his jointed legs were the oil-filled struts of shock absorbers.

"Guillermo," Gregg called. "Did your genetic memory cover space flight? Landings, I mean."

"Yes, Mr. Gregg," the Molt said. "It does."

Gregg wasn't sure precisely what Guillermo's status was. So far as Mostert was concerned, Guillermo was an unsold part of the cargo loaded at Punta Verde. The larger vessels still carried fifty or sixty other Molts . . . who would be sold to the Feds here, if all went well.

To Gregg and the *Peaches* crewmen, the alien who'd taken over Bailey's duties in the course of the past four planetfalls wasn't simply merchandise. Gregg wasn't sure Guillermo had ever been merchandise to Piet Ricimer.

"What're them ships there?" Lightbody muttered as he peered at the viewscreen over his control consoles. "They're not big enough to be the Earth Convoy."

"Water buffalo," Leon said. "Liftships, laser-guided drones. The Feds' biggest ships boost to orbit with minimum reaction mass to keep the strain down. Liftships, they're just buckets to ferry water up to them."

Island Able was a ragged triangle with sides of about a kilometer each. A complex of buildings and two very small ships—featherboats or perhaps merely atmosphere vessels—were placed at the northern corner, protected by an artificial seawall.

Grounded near the eastern corner were the water buffalo, ships in the 50-to-80-tonne range. Until the bosun explained what they were, Gregg thought the vessels' simple outlines were a result of the screen's mediocre resolution.

On the third, western, corner, the Feds had built a fort with four roof turrets. Even as bad as the viewscreen was, Gregg should have been able to see the barrels of the guns if they were harmlessly lowered

"Captain," he said, glad to note there was no quaver in his voice. "I think the fort's guns are muzzle-on to us."

"They might track the *Tolliver,* Stephen," Ricimer said, "but I don't think they'd all four track us. I don't think the turrets have their guns mounted."

As he spoke, his hands played delicately with the thruster controls. The *Tolliver* rotated slowly on its vertical axis as it dropped. One or more of its attitude jets must be misaligned. Ricimer held the *Peaches* in a helix that kept the featherboat between the lobes of two of the flagship's huge thrusters.

The *Tolliver* settled close to the administration complex in a blast of steam and gravel. The featherboat hovered for a moment. When the flagship's cloud of stripped atoms dissipated suddenly like a rainbow overtaken by nightfall, Ricimer brought them in a hundred meters from the *Tolliver.* They flanked the direct path between the bigger ship and the Federation buildings.

It was probably not chance that the line at which the featherboat came to rest pointed her bow and plasma cannon at the fort a kilometer away.

Gregg and the Molt undogged the roof hatch. Steam billowed in like a slap with a hot towel. Jeude and Tancred remained at their gun, but the remainder of the crewmen got to their feet.

Gregg glanced at the viewscreen. Two Federation trucks drove close to the *Tolliver,* dragging hoses. "What—" he started to say.

The trucks suddenly bloomed with a mist of seawater. It paled to steam as it cooled the landing site and the vessel's hull. The hoses stretched to intakes out beyond the line of Island Able's gentle surf.

"They think we're the Earth Convoy," Ricimer said. It was only when he grinned broadly that Gregg realized how tense his friend had been beneath his outer calm. "They don't let their admirals sit aboard for an hour or so while the site cools naturally."

"They aren't going to bother with us, though, are they?" Dole grumbled. "*Not* that it looks like there's much entertainment on this gravel heap."

"I think if we suited up, Stephen," Ricimer said, "we could get to the *Tolliver* about the time they opened up for the local greeting party. Eh?"

"They got some platforms out a ways, fella told me on Jewelhouse," Jeude called in response to Dole's comment. "Not on the island, though. Not enough land."

"Sure," Gregg said. He thumped his armored chest. "I'd feel naked getting off a ship without a hard suit, the way things have been going. The leggings won't make much difference."

Guillermo opened the armor store and sorted out ceramic pieces, the full suit sized to Ricimer's body and the lower half of Gregg's. Ballistic protection alone didn't justify the awkwardness and burden of complete armor.

Piet Ricimer latched his torso armor over him, then paused. He looked around the featherboat's bay, even glancing at the suited gun crew behind him. In a clear, challenging voice, he said, "Guillermo, when we get back home, I'll have a suit made to fit you. I don't like carrying crewmen who don't have a way to stay alive in case we have to open the bay in vacuum."

"Too fucking right," Dole said, responding for the crew.

"And I'll chip in on the cost," Gregg said evenly, completing the answer of the question that nobody was willing to admit had been asked.

Ricimer's smile lit the bay. "Leon, you're in charge," he said. "Stephen, let's go watch my cousin negotiate."

─21─

Biruta

Five meters from the *Peaches,* the shingle was cool again. Gregg lifted his visor. Another Venerian ship dropped from orbit, but for the moment it was no more than a spark of high-altitude opalescence. The thunder of its approach had yet to reach the ground.

An airboat supported by three boom-mounted ducted props lifted from the administrative complex. Gregg tapped Ricimer's shoulder—armor on armor clacked loudly—and pointed. "Look," he said, "they're sending a courier to the outlying platforms."

Instead of heading off with a message that couldn't be radioed because of interference from starship thrusters, the airboat hummed a hundred and fifty yards across the shingle and settled again before the *Tolliver*'s lowering cargo ramp.

Piet Ricimer chuckled. "You wouldn't expect a Federation admiral to walk, would you, Stephen?" he said. "The locals expect high brass with the Earth Convoy, so they've sent a ride for them."

Four Federation officials descended from the airboat. They'd put on their uniforms in haste: one of them still wore grease-stained utility trousers, though his white dress tunic was in good shape.

The vehicle had only six seats. One of those was for the driver, who remained behind. Presumably some of the locals planned to walk back.

Gregg and Ricimer walked in front of the boat, following the officials to the flagship's ramp. The driver looked startled when he saw the two strangers were armed as well as wearing hard suits. Ricimer had a rifle, while Gregg carried a replacement for the flashgun that had failed at Punta Verde.

Ricimer eyed the driver through the windscreen, then raised a gauntleted index finger to his lips in a *shush* sign. The driver nodded furiously, too frightened even to duck behind the plastic bow of his vehicle.

"Administrator Carstensen?" called the leader of the local officials from the foot of the ramp. The *Tolliver*'s dark cargo bay showed only shadows where the crew awaited their visitors. "I'm Port Commander Dupuy. We're glad to welcome you to Biruta. I'm sure your stay will be enjoyable."

"I'm sure it will too, gentlemen," boomed Alexi Mostert. "I'm *absolutely* sure that you'll treat me and my ships as if we belonged to your own Federation."

"What?" said Dupuy. "What?"

The man in greasy trousers was either quicker on the uptake or more willing to act. He spun on his heel and started a long stride off the ramp

And froze. Between him and escape were the officers from the featherboat, huge in their stained white hard suits. The Fed official drew himself up straight, nodded formally to Ricimer and Gregg, and turned around again.

"I'm afraid I'll have to ask you gentlemen to be our guests for a time," Mostert continued. "We'll pay at normal rates with Molt laborers for the supplies we take, I assure you . . . but so that there aren't any misunderstandings, I'll be putting my own men in your fort and admin buildings. I'm sure you understand, Mr. Dupuy."

If the Federation official made any reply to Mostert, his words were lost in the roar of the *Hawkwood,* landing with her plasma cannon run out for use.

⎯22⎯

Biruta

"Easy, easy . . ." echoed Leon's voice through the fort's superstructure. Heavy masses of metal chinged, then clanged loudly together—the trunnions of a 15-cm plasma cannon dropping into the cheek pieces. "Lock 'em down!"

"Look at this," Ricimer murmured to Gregg in the control room below—and to Guillermo; at any rate, the Molt was present. Ricimer slowly turned a dial, increasing the magnification of the image in the holographic screen. "Just look at the resolution."

"Boardman, use the twenty-*four*-millimeter end, not the twenty-two!" Leon shouted. "D'ye have shit for brains?"

The bosun's twenty-man crew was completing the mounting of the fort's armament. The heavy plasma cannon had been delivered by a previous Earth Convoy. In three days, the Venerians had accomplished a job that Federation personnel on Biruta hadn't gotten around to in at least a year.

On the other hand, the Feds in their heart of hearts didn't expect to need the fort. The Venerians did.

"This is what we'll have on Venus soon," Ricimer said. "This is what all humanity will have, now that we have the stars again."

The five Venerian ships—the *Grandcamp* had vanished after the first series of transits, and only an optimist believed that she or her crew would ever be seen again—clustered together near the buildings at the north end of the island. Men were busy refitting the battered vessels for the long voyage back to Venus. They used Federation equipment as well as that carried by the argosy.

"All right," Leon ordered. "You four, torque her down tight. Loong, you and your lot are dismissed. Take the shearlegs and tackle back to the *Tolliver* with you. Anders, you're in charge here until you're relieved."

Ricimer had focused on the *Rose,* eight hundred meters across the island. At the present magnification, Gregg could identify some of the crewmen fitting new thruster nozzles beneath the vessel. The holds gaped open above them, letting the sea breeze flow through the vessel.

"We could see right into the ship if the light was a little better," Gregg agreed.

Guillermo said, "The third control from the right." His three jointed fingers together indicated the rotary switch he meant. "Up will increase light levels above ambient."

Ricimer touched the control, then rolled it upward. The edges of the display whited out with overload. Shadowed areas congealed into clarity beneath the ship, within the holds, and even through the open gunports.

"You've seen this sort of equipment before?" Ricimer asked.

The Molt flicked his fingers behind his palms in the equivalent of a shrug. "It's a standard design," he said. "My memory—"

"Memory" was a more or less satisfactory description of what amounted to genetic encoding.

"—includes identical designs."

"They'd have to be," Gregg realized aloud. "It's not as though the Feds built this. Their Molts did."

The huge advantage the North American Federation had over other states was its possession of planets whose automated factories had continued to produce microchips for years or even centuries after the Collapse. When the factories finally broke down, they left behind dispersed stockpiles of circuitry whose quality and miniaturization were beyond the capacity of the present age.

Fed electronics were not so much better than those of the Venerians as greatly more common. But Fed electronics were better also . . .

"Once Venus has its trade in hand," Ricimer said, "we'll do it properly. The Federation goes by rote—"

He nodded to Guillermo. Leon, muttering about the lazy frogspawn crewing some vessels he could name, clomped down the ladder serving the gun stations on the roof.

"—only doing what was done a thousand years ago. We'll build from where mankind was before the Rebellion—new ways through the Mirror, new planets with new products. Not just the same old ways."

"Old ways is right," Leon said as he entered the control room. "Those guns we mounted, they're alike as so many peas. Men didn't make them, Molts and machines did. The Feds just sit on their butts and let the work do itself—like people did before the Collapse."

Guillermo looked at the bosun. "Is work by itself good?" the Molt asked. "How can it matter whether you pull a rope or I pull a rope or a winch pulls the rope—so long as the rope is pulled?"

"Centralized production is sure enough *bad*," Leon said. "That's what caused the Collapse, after all. That and people having too much time to spend on politics, since they didn't do anything real."

"It's more than that," Piet Ricimer added. "Machines can't create. They'll make the same thing each time—whether it's a nozzle or a flashgun barrel or a birdbath. When my father or even one of his apprentices makes an item, it has . . ."

He smiled wryly to wipe the hint of blasphemy away from what he was about to say. "A *man's* work has what would be a soul, if the work were a man rather than a thing."

Guillermo's head moved from Leon to Ricimer, as if the neck were clicking between detents. "And my race has no soul," the Molt said. The words were too flat to be a question.

"If you do have souls," Ricimer replied after a moment's hesitation, "then in selling your fellows as merchandise, we're committing an unspeakable sin, Guillermo."

Man and Molt looked at one another in silence. The alien's face was impassive by virtue of its exoskeletal construction. Piet Ricimer's expression gave up equally little information.

Guillermo cocked his head in a gesture of amusement. "Things are things, Captain," he said. "But I'll admit that the number of things may be less important than how you use the things you have. And your Venus clan uses things very well."

The *Tolliver*'s siren began to wind.

"Damn the timing!" Gregg snarled. "Leon, did the men from the *Tolliver* leave in the truck?"

The bosun pursed his lips and nodded.

"All right," Gregg decided aloud. "Piet, I'll run across to the flagship and find out what's going on. You can—"

Ricimer smiled. "I think we can learn what's happening more easily than that, Stephen," he said.

As he spoke, he tapped pairs of numbers into a keypad on the console. Each touch switched the holographic display, either to a lustrous void or an image:

An office in the island's administrative complex, where half a dozen Venerians had put down their playing cards when the siren blew;

A panorama from a camera placed a hundred meters above the empty sea;

Another office, this one empty save for a chair over which was draped the uniform jacket of a Federation officer.

"Seventeen," Guillermo suggested, pointing.

Ricimer keyed in one-seven. The screen split, with Alexi Mostert on the left half, saying to the Federation officer on the right side, "Yes, your Administrator Carstensen, if he's in charge! And don't even *think* of trying to land without my permission!"

"I thought," Gregg said softly, "that we might manage to get away before the Earth Convoy arrived."

"It's no problem, sir," Leon said in mild surprise. "If they try to land, we'll rip 'em up the jacksies while they're braking. It's suicide for ships to attack plasma batteries on the surface."

"That's not the whole question, Leon," Piet Ricimer said. The right half of the screen had gone blank. On the left, Mostert was in profile as he spoke with subordinates. The Federation communications equipment completely muted all sound not directed toward it, so Mostert's lips moved silently.

The right side of the screen solidified into an image again. This time it was a heavy-jowled man in his fifties, wearing Federation court dress. He looked angry enough to chew nails. For the moment, he too was talking to someone outside the range of the pickup.

"Federation ships with Fed crews, they'll be in much worse shape than ours were," Ricimer continued in a bare whisper. "If we don't let them land, at least half of them will be lost . . . and that will mean war between Venus and the Federation."

"I'll fight a war if that's what they want, Mr. Ricimer," Leon said. He didn't raise his voice, but there was challenge in the set of his chin.

Gregg smiled tightly and squeezed the bosun's biceps in a friendly grip. "We'll all do what we have to, Leon," he said. "But war's bad for trade."

The Federation leader faced front. "I'm Henry Carstensen, Administrator of the Outer Ways by order of President Pleyal and the Federation Parliament," he said. "You wanted me and I'm here. Speak."

The crispness of both the visual and audio portions of the transmission were striking to men used to Venerian commo. There was no sign that Federation AIs made a better job of the complex equations governing transit, though . . .

"First, Your Excellency," Alexi Mostert said unctuously, "I want to apologize for this little awkward—"

"Stop your nonsense," Carstensen snapped. "You're holding a Federation port against Federation vessels. Is it war, then, between Venus and Earth—or are you a pirate, operating against the will of Governor Halys?"

"Neither, Excellency," Mostert said. "If I can explain—"

"I'm not interested in explanations!" Carstensen said. "I have ships in immediate need of landing. If one of them is lost, if one *crewman* dies, then the only thing that will prevent the forces of Earth from *devastating* your planet is your head on a platter, Mostert. Do you understand? My ships must be allowed to land *now*."

The Venerian commander bent his head and pressed his fingertips firmly against his forehead.

"Cousin Alexi's going at it the wrong way," Ricimer said dispassionately. "With a man like Carstensen, you negotiate from strength or you don't negotiate at all."

"I'll see how they're coming on the fourth gun," Leon said abruptly. He bolted from the control room.

Mostert lifted his head. "Then listen," he said. "These are the terms on which I—"

"You have no right to set terms!" Carstensen shouted.

"Don't talk to me about rights, mister!" said Alexi Mostert. "I've got enough firepower to scour every Federation platform off the surface of this world. I can fry your ships even if you stay in orbit. If you try to come down there won't be bits big enough to splash when they finally hit the water. These are my terms! Are you ready to listen?"

"Much better, cousin," Piet Ricimer murmured.

Administrator Carstensen lifted his chin in acceptance.

"Your eight ships will be allowed to land," Mostert said. "Their guns will be shuttered. As soon as they're on the ground, the crews will be transported to outlying platforms. There will be no Federation personnel on Island Able until my argosy has finished refitting and left."

"That's impractical," Carstensen said.

"These are my terms!"

"I understand that," Carstensen said calmly. It was as though the Federation official who started the negotiation had been replaced by a wholly different man. "But some of my vessels are in very bad shape. They need immediate repairs or there'll be major fires and probably a powerplant explosion. I need to keep maintenance personnel and a few officers aboard to avoid disaster."

The Venerian commander's lips sucked in and out as he thought. "All right," he said. "But in that case I'll need liaison officers from you. Six of them. They'll be entertained in comfort for the few remaining days that my ships need to complete their refit."

Carstensen sniffed. "Hostages, you mean. Well, as you've pointed out, *Admiral* Mostert, you're holding a gun to the heads of nearly a thousand innocent men and women as it is. I accept your conditions."

Mostert licked at the dryness of his lips. "Very well," he said. "Do you swear by God and your hope of salvation to keep these terms, sir?"

"I swear," Carstensen said in the same cool tones which had characterized his latter half of the negotiations.

Carstensen stood up. His console's pickup lengthened its viewing field automatically. The administrator was surprisingly tall, a big man rather than simply a broad one. "And I swear also, Admiral," he said, "that when President Pleyal hears of this, then your Governor Halys will hear; and you will hear of it again yourself."

The convoy's side of the screen went blank.

"I'm not worried," Mostert said to the pearl emptiness. His side of the transmission blanked out as well.

Piet Ricimer turned to Gregg with an unreadable smile. "What do you think, Stephen?" he asked.

"I think if your cousin isn't worried," Gregg replied, "then he's a very stupid man."

─23─

Biruta

"Slow down," Gregg said to Tancred, who was driving the guards back from the fort at the end of their watch. He peered into the darkness behind the brilliant cone of the truck's ceramic headlamps and the softer, yellower gleam of lights from the Federation vessels. "That looks like—stop, it's Mr. Ricimer."

Tancred brought the vehicle to a squealing halt. "Christ's blood!" he said. "I don't care what oaths those Feds swore. This is no safe place for one of our people alone."

The Earth Convoy lay across the center of Island Able. The straggling line was as close a group as the vessels' condition and their pilots' skill permitted. The Feds were well separated from the five Venerian ships at the north end of the island, but the metal-built vessels controlled the route between there and the fort on the western corner.

Changing the guard at the fort required driving through the midst of the Federation fleet. That didn't feel a bit comfortable, even for twenty armed men in a vehicle; and as Tancred said, it was no place for a Venerian on foot.

"He's not alone," Gregg said, clutching the flashgun closer to his breastplate so that it wouldn't clack against the cab frame as he got down. "He's with me. Leon?" he added to the men in amorphous shadow in the truck bed. "You're in charge till we get back."

Ignoring the crewmen's protests, Gregg jumped to the shingle and crunched toward his friend. After a moment, the truck drove on.

The sea breeze sighed. It was surprisingly peaceful when the truck engine had whined itself downwind, toward the

110

administrative complex and Venerian ships. Work proceeded round the clock on several Federation ships, but the uniformly open horizon absorbed sound better than anechoic paneling.

"What in the name of heaven do you think you're doing here, Piet?" Gregg demanded softly. "Trying to be the spark that turns this business into a shooting war?"

"I'm just looking at things, Stephen," Ricimer answered. "But not for trouble, no."

Though Gregg thought at first that his friend was a deliberate provocation, standing in the very middle of the ragged Federation line, he realized that except for the moment Ricimer was swept by the truck's headlights he was well shielded by darkness. The young captain wasn't going to be noticed and attacked by a squad of Federation engine fitters who objected to his presence.

"It's a good place to find trouble anyway," Gregg grumbled. "Look, let's get back to where we belong."

"Listen," Ricimer said. A large airboat approached low over the sea with a throb of ducted fans. A landing officer used a hand strobe to guide the vehicle down beside the Federation flagship three hundred meters from Gregg and Ricimer. It landed on the south side of the vessel so that the latter's 800-tonne bulk was between the airboat and the Venerian ships.

"Well, they've been bringing in supplies," Gregg said. "Taking cargo off too, I shouldn't wonder."

"*Listen,*" Ricimer repeated more sharply.

Gregg heard voices on the breeze. They were too low to be intelligible, and from the timbre the speakers had nothing important to say anyway.

But there were a lot of them. Several score of men, very likely. And they had disembarked on the north side of the airboat so that *it* blocked the view from the Venerians and the night vision equipment in the fort.

"Oh," Gregg said. "I see."

"Boats came in the same way last night," Ricimer explained. "Three loads. I thought I ought to be sure before I—told my cousin something that he's not going to want to hear."

Gregg grimaced in the darkness. "Let's get on back," he said. "Look, we leave tomorrow morning. It'll be all right."

Ricimer nodded or shrugged, the gesture uncertain in the darkness. "We'd best get back," he agreed.

• • •

"No, the admiral's still up in his cabin," said the steward who'd turned angrily from the midst of banquet preparations. The man calmed instantly when he saw that two officers and not a fellow crewman had interrupted him. "Captain Fedders is in with him and some others."

Level Four, the higher of the *Tolliver*'s two gun decks, was bustling chaos. The flagship was pierced for fifty guns and carried twenty on the present voyage. The eight on this level were run out of their ports to provide more deck space for banquet tables. Officers' servants from the three larger vessels combined on the flagship to prepare and present the celebratory dinner.

The *Tolliver*'s vertical core was taken up by tanks of air and reaction mass. The remaining space, even when undivided as now on Level Four, wasn't really suitable for a large gathering, but it was the best available aboard the ships themselves.

Fed structures on Island Able provided minimal shelter for low-ranking service personnel. No buildings could be solid enough to survive the crash of a starship, so all comfortable facilities were on artificial platforms at a distance from the island. The barracks, the only large building in the administrative complex, was a flimsy barn with no kitchen. It smelled as much of its previous Molt occupants as the holds of the Venerian vessels did.

Guests—the officers and gentlemen from the other vessels—had already drifted to the flagship's banquet area, getting in the way of the men who were trying to prepare it.

The ships had been repaired to the degree possible outside a major dockyard. The only people on duty were the stewards, a port watch on each vessel, and the guard detachment in the fort—supplied by the Tolliver for this final night on Biruta.

In the morning the argosy would lift for Venus, carrying cargo of enough value to make every officer rich, and every crewman popular for three days or a week, until he'd spent or been robbed of his share. The investors, Gregg of Weyston among them, would have their stakes returned tenfold. Even assuming the *Grandcamp* had come apart in the strain of forcing her way between bubble universes as the energy gradients separating them rose, the voyage had been a stunning success.

Gregg followed Piet Ricimer up the companionway to the bridge on Level Six. Behind them, coming from barracks in the administrative complex, were Administrator Carstensen's six hostages and the Venerian gentlemen watching over them. Mostert had invited the "liaison officers" to the banquet, although it had become obvious by the second day that the Feds were not nearly of the rank their titles and uniforms claimed.

Alexi Mostert, wearing trousers of red plush but still holding the matching jacket in his hand, stood in the doorway of his cabin, partitioned off from the bridge proper, and shouted, "God grind your bones to *dust*, Fedders! Don't you know an order when you hear one?"

Three officers of the flagship, Mostert's personal servant, and Fedders of the *Rose* were part of the tableau surrounding the admiral. Two crewmen, detailed to the port watch while their fellows partied on a lesser scale than their leaders, listened from behind one of the pair of plasma cannon mounted vertically in the bow.

"Don't you know danger when you see it, Mostert?" Fedders shouted back. "I tell you, they're cutting gunports in the side of the big freighter facing us. What d'ye think they're planning to do from them? Wave us goodbye?"

Unlike the other officers on the bridge, Fedders wore shipboard clothing of synthetic canvas and carried a ceramic helmet instead of dress headgear. The fact that Fedders was fully clothed and had forced himself on Mostert while changing was an implicit threat that made the admiral certain to explode, but the discussion probably would have gone wrong anyway.

Mostert clutched his tunic with both hands. The hair on the admiral's chest was white though his hair and beard were generally brown. For an instant, Gregg thought from the way Mostert's pectoral muscles bunched that he was going to rip the garment across.

Instead he deliberately unclenched his hands and said, "All right, Fedders, I'll put a special watch on what our Terran friends are doing. You. Report to your ship immediately and don't leave her again until we land in Betaport."

"Punishing me isn't going to stop the Feds from blasting the hell out of us as we lift, Mostert!" Fedders said. "What we need to do is take over their ships right now and put every damned soul of them off the island before it's too late!"

"He's right, Admiral," Piet Ricimer said, careful to stay a non-threatening distance from Mostert.

"Christ bugger you both for fools!" Mostert bellowed. He tugged at the tunic, unable to tear the fabric but pulling it all out of shape or the possibility of wearing. "Both of you! To your ships! *Now,* or God blind me if I don't have you shot for treason!"

Galliard, the *Toliiver*'s navigator, was a friend of Fedders'. He took the *Rose*'s captain by the elbows and half guided, half pushed him toward the companionway.

"Sir," said Ricimer, "blasphemy now is—"

"You canting preacher!" Mostert said. "I've enough chaplains aboard already. Get to your ship—and see if you can find some courage along the way!"

Ricimer's face went white.

Gregg set his flashgun down to balance on its broad muzzle. He stepped deliberately between his friend and Mostert. "Admiral Mostert," he said in a voice pared to the bone by anger. "If a man were to address me in that fashion, I would demand that he meet me in the field so that I might recover my honor."

The cold fury in the gentleman's voice slapped Mostert out of his own state. The admiral wasn't afraid of Gregg, but neither was he a mere spacer with money. There was no profit in making Gregg of Weyston's nephew an enemy.

"I assure you, Mr. Gregg," he said, "that no part of my comments were directed at you."

"Come away, Stephen," Ricimer said, drawing Gregg around to break his eye contact with Admiral Mostert.

"The *Tolliver* will lift last of the argosy," Mostert said in a gruffly reasonable voice. "We'll have our guns run out. At the least hint of trouble we'll clear the island!"

Ricimer picked up the flashgun by its butt. Gregg reached for it numbly but his friend twitched the weapon to his side.

"We've gotten this far without having trouble that the Governor, that Governor Halys can't forgive," Mostert said. He sounded wistful, almost desperate. "We're not going to start a war now!"

"You'll need to change for the banquet," Ricimer said as he directed Gregg down the companionway ahead of him. "The *Peaches* should have some representative there, after all."

-24-

Biruta

"To the further expansion of trade across the universe!" Alexi Mostert called from the head table. He raised the glass in his right hand. That was the only part of the admiral which Gregg could see from where he sat, a third of the way around the curve of the deck.

"Expansion of trade," murmured the gathered officers and gentlemen in a slurred attempt at unison. The night's heavy drinking hadn't begun. A combination of relief at going home and fear of another series of transits like the set which had devoured the *Grandcamp* had given some of those present a head start on the festivities, however.

The banquet was served on rectangular tables, each of which cut an arc of the circular deck space. The sixty or so diners sat on the hull side, while stewards served them from the inner curve. The *Tolliver*'s galley was on Level Three, and the two companionways were built into the vessel's central core.

The hostages were spaced out among the Venerians. The older man beside Mostert, supposedly the deputy commander of a Fed warship but probably a clerk of some sort, looked gloomy. The female Gregg could see on almost the opposite side of Level Four was terrified and slobberingly drunk. To Gregg's immediate left sat a man named Tilbury, younger than Gregg himself. He was keyed to such a bright-eyed pitch that Gregg wondered if he was using some drug other than alcohol.

Well, perhaps the hostages thought they would be slaughtered when the argosy left—or as bad from their viewpoint, carried off to the sulphurous caves of Venus.

"Sir," said a steward. *"Sir."* To get Gregg's attention, the fellow leaned across the remains of a savory prepared from canned fruit. "There's an urgent call for you on the bridge. From your ship."

Walking would feel good. Gregg was muzzy from the meal, more drink than normal, and reaction to the scene on the bridge two hours before. He still trembled when he thought about that . . .

"All right," he muttered, and slid his chair back. The breech of a 20-cm plasma cannon blocked his path to the right. Even run out, the heavy weapons took up a great deal of space. He could go to his left and maybe creep between the corners of two tables, but that would be tight. Tilbury looked ready to explode if awakened from his glittering dreamworld to move.

Gregg ducked under the table. He knocked his head by rising too quickly and found himself on the other side with something greasy smeared on the knees of his dress trousers. They were gray-green silk shot with silver filaments, and they'd be the very devil to clean.

Cursing his stupidity, not the call that summoned him, Gregg strode to the companionway and climbed the helical stairs three treads at a time.

The bridge felt shockingly comfortable. The petty officer and two crewmen on watch had opened the horizontal gunports. The mild cross-breeze made Gregg realize how hot and crowded Level Four was.

"Here you go, sir," the petty officer said as he gave Gregg the handset. It would have been nice if they could have stripped the Federation communications system out of the port buildings . . . but this was a trading voyage.

"Go ahead," Gregg said into the handset. At least it was a dual frequency unit, so the two carrier waves didn't step on one another if the parties spoke simultaneously.

"Stephen," said Piet Ricimer's crackling voice, "I don't think the Feds are going to wait till tomorrow. Their three warships are clearing their gunports, and airboats have been ferrying more men onto the island all night."

Gregg moved to an open gunport within the five-meter length of the handset's flex. He peered out. The circular port looked south. He couldn't see the *Peaches,* but the Federation convoy bulked across the night sky like a herd of sleeping monsters.

"What do you . . ." Gregg said. He shook his head, wishing

that he could think more clearly. The bridge watch watched him covertly. " . . . want me to do?"

Biruta's moon was a jagged chunk of rock. Even full, as now, it did little to illuminate the landscape. The silhouettes of Federation ships were speckled by light. The Feds were opening, then closing their gunports to be sure that the shutters wouldn't jam when the order came to run the guns out for use.

"Stephen," Ricimer said tautly, "you've *got* to convince Mostert to take some action immediately. I know what I'm asking, but there's no choice."

"Right," said Gregg. He put down the handset and glanced around for the petty officer.

He didn't know the man's name. "You," he said, pointing. "Sound the general alarm now. *Now!*"

"What?" said the petty officer. One of the crewmen threw a large knife-switch attached to a stanchion. The flagship's siren began slowly to wind.

A plasma cannon fired from one of the Federation vessels.

Gregg was fully alert and alive. "Get those guns slewed!" he cried as he jumped into the companionway. With his right hand on the rail, he took the fifteen steps in three huge, spiraling jumps and burst out onto the banquet room again.

Men were looking up, alarmed by the siren and drawn to the electric *crashTHUMP* of the plasma discharge.

"We're being attacked!" Gregg shouted. "Get to your—"

Tilbury rose from his seat, looking toward Admiral Mostert as though the two of them were the only people in all the universe. The Federation hostage lifted the short-barreled shotgun which had been strapped to his right calf.

Gregg dived over the table at him. As he did so, three guns salvoed from the *Rose*, lighting the night with their iridescence. The metal hull of the Federation flagship bloomed with white fireballs which merged into a three-headed monster.

Gregg hit Tilbury. The shotgun fired into the ceiling. Lead pellets splashed from the hard ceramic.

Gregg slammed the smaller Terran into the bulkhead hard enough to crush ribs, but he couldn't wrest away Tilbury's shotgun as they wrestled on the deck in a welter of food and broken crockery. Tilbury giggled wildly.

Gregg suddenly realized that the weapon was a single-shot. He released it, gripped Tilbury's short hair, and used the strength of both arms to slam the hostage's head against the deck until the victim went limp.

Something crashed dazzlingly into the *Tolliver*. A portion of the hull shattered. The rainbow light was so intense that it flared through the gunports open to the east, south, and west together. Gregg couldn't tell where they'd been hit.

"Stand clear!" somebody roared as he switched on the gunnery controls for the weapon Gregg sprawled under.

Gregg jumped to his feet. There was already a crush of men at the nearer companionway. Gregg fought into them. He was bigger than most, and adrenaline had already brought his instincts to full, murderous life.

A 20-cm gun, *beside* the one whose captain had given a warning, fired at the Fed convoy. The cannon recoiled, pistoning the air in a searing flash.

Under normal circumstances, plasma cannon were fired by crews wearing hard suits, in sections of the vessel partitioned off to protect nonarmored personnel from the weapons' ravening violence. There was neither time nor inclination to rig the ship for battle now.

The blast knocked down the men nearest to the gun. Ribbons and the gauze ornaments of their clothing smoldered. The other south-facing cannon fired also. Three Fed bolts raked the *Tolliver*. A red-hot spark shot up the center of the companionway.

By the time Gregg reached Level Three, there was only one officer ahead of him. That fellow stumbled midway down the next winding flight, and Gregg jumped his cursing form.

The *Tolliver*'s crewmen were running forward the Level Two plasma cannon; the shutters had already been raised for ventilation. The internal lights had gone off. A glowing hole in the outer hull showed where a Federation bolt had gotten home. The air stank of insulation, ionized gases, and burning flesh.

Gregg dropped into the hold and ran down the ramp. His hard suit and flashgun were on the featherboat. In his urge to get to familiar equipment and his friends, he hadn't thought about arming himself aboard the flagship. Now he felt naked.

Plasma spurted from the flank of a 100-tonne Federation warship. There were four bolts, but they were light ones. Two struck the *Rose*, throwing up sparks of white-hot ceramic slivers. The *Delight* bucked, then collapsed into separate bow and stern fragments with only glowing slag between them.

The *Hawkwood,* lying slightly to the north of all the Venerian ships save the *Peaches,* had not been hit by the cannonading thus far. Five 10-cm plasma cannon along her starboard side volleyed. The bolts converged squarely amidships of the spherical Federation flagship. White-hot metal erupted as if from a horizontal volcano.

For several seconds, steam from blown reaction-mass tanks wreathed the vessel. The vapor was so hot that it didn't cool to visibility until it was several meters beyond the hull. A secondary explosion, either a store of plasma shells or compressed flammables, spewed fire suddenly from every port and hatchway on the huge vessel.

Gregg was running toward the *Peaches.* The concussion knocked him down. He looked over his shoulder. The Federation warship's thick hull gleamed yellow as it lost strength and slumped toward the shingle.

Gregg scrambled forward, dabbing his hands down before he got his feet properly under him. Carstensen's disintegrating flagship threw a soft radiance across the island. Most of the plasma cannon on both sides had fired and were cooling before they could be reloaded. Twin shocks from the *Tolliver* indicated the guns on the lower level had been brought into action.

Gravel spat from beneath the *Peaches*; Ricimer had lighted the thrusters. A pebble stung Gregg's thigh. "Wait for me!" he screamed. He could barely hear his own voice over the roar of the incandescent Federation flagship.

A handheld spotlight spiked Gregg from the featherboat's hatch. It blinded him, so he didn't see the rope flung to him until it slapped him in the face. "Quick! Quick!" a voice warned faintly.

Gregg braced his boot against the curve of the hull and began to pull himself upward, hand over hand. As he did so, the thrusters fired at mid-output. The *Peaches* lifted a meter and began to swing.

Two of the fort's plasma cannon fired simultaneously. A large airboat approaching from the west blew apart only a few meters above the sea, showering the surface with debris, bodies, and blazing kerosene. A second airboat, slanting down parallel to the first, ground to a halt beside the fort.

Federation soldiers, humans and Molts together, jumped out of the vehicle. Rifles flashed and spat, mostly aimed at the Venerian defenders. More Federation troops spilled from nearby cargo vessels and ran toward the fort.

Gregg flopped over the hatch coaming and into the featherboat's bay like a fish being landed. Internal lights were on, but his retinas were too stunned by plasma discharges for him to be able to see more than shadows and the purple blotches across his retinas.

"Give me my flashgun!" he cried as he tried to stand up. "And a helmet, Christ's blood!"

The *Peaches'* bow gun fired, jolting the hovering featherboat into a wild yaw. Somebody lowered a helmet onto Gregg's head, visor down. Leon said, "Here you go, Mr. Gregg," and pressed the familiar angles of a flashgun into his hands.

"Ammo!" Gregg demanded as he jumped on top of the storage locker to aim out the hatch. Even as he spoke, he realized that Leon had slung a bandolier heavy with charged batteries over the laser's receiver.

Bullets or gravel spit by other thrusters clicked against the featherboat's hull. The *Rose* was under way, swinging to bring her portside guns to bear on the Federation convoy.

Three bolts from Fed ships punched the *Rose* as she slowly rotated. Sections of ceramic hull blew out in bright showers. The third hit doused internal lighting over the forward half of the vessel: Then her six-gun port battery cut loose in a volley timed to half-second intervals.

During the truce, the Feds had mounted guns in their largest ship, a cylindrical cargo hauler of 1,000 tonnes. It was the vessel closest to the Venerian ships and its fire had been galling. Now the freighter's hull plating, thinner than that of a warship, vaporized under the point-blank salvo. The last of the six bolts blew through the ship's far side. Flame-shot gases gushed from both bow and stern.

The *Tolliver* and three surviving ships of the Earth Convoy settled into a series of punch and counterpunch. Individual bolts from the Venerian flagship's heavy guns were answered by double or triple discharges from lighter Federation weapons.

A yellow-orange spot on the hull of a Fed warship indicated where a plasma cannon had been run out again after being fired. The barrel, stellite rather than ceramic in normal Terran

usage, still glowed from the previous discharge. Gregg used
it as his aiming point and fired.

His flashgun couldn't damage the vessel's hull, but the laser
bolt might snap through the open port. Even better, a bolt that
passed down the cannon's bore would detonate the shell out
of sequence, turning it into a miniature fusion bomb instead
of a directed-energy weapon. That would require amazing luck
under the present conditions—

But the Venerian argosy was going to need amazing luck if
any of them were to survive this treacherous attack.

The *Tolliver*'s bow guns fired. Scratch crews had pivoted
the weapons from vertical to horizontal gunports.

Each hit on a Fed hull belched gouts of flaming metal, but
the ships continued to work their guns. Bubbles of glowing
vapor flashed through the interior of the vessels. Even with
partitions rigged within the compartments to limit blast effects,
Terran casualties must have been horrendous.

Federation troops rushed from the two freighters toward
the *Tolliver*. Harsh shadows from plasma weapons confused
their numbers: there may have been a few score, there may
have been over a hundred. Some were Molts, angular and
thin-limbed.

Gregg fired, trying to keep his aim low. The flashgun wasn't
a particularly good weapon against troops well spaced across
an empty plain. A laser bolt striking in front of the ragged line
would spray gravel across the attackers. That provided some
hope of casualties and considerable psychological effect.

Ricimer slewed the *Peaches* eastward, keeping the featherboat's bow toward the hostile vessels. Gregg wondered if his
friend was taking them out of the battle. A single plasma bolt
could gut the featherboat. All that had saved them thus far was
being some distance from the fighting and therefore ignored
by Federation cannoneers.

Gregg fired again. Tancred was beside him with a repeater,
a better choice for the task. Rifles and a flashgun flashed
from the *Tolliver*'s holds where crewmen prepared to meet the
Federation attack. The Venerians were badly outnumbered.

The *Peaches*' bow gun fired. Ricimer had swung the
featherboat to a position that enfiladed the line of Federation troops. The plasma bolt flashed the length of the
attackers, killing half a dozen of them outright and throwing
the survivors back in panic. Burning bodies and the sparks of

detonating ammunition littered the shingle.

One rifleman—a Molt—stood silhouetted against the blazing freighter and aimed at the featherboat. The alien soldier was almost four hundred meters away. Gregg aimed as if the boat quivering beneath him were the bedrock solidity of a target range.

The Molt fired and missed. Gregg's laser lighted the Molt's instantaneous death. The creature's torso exploded as its body fluids flashed to steam.

Why had it fought to preserve Federation claims?

Why did anybody fight for anything?

The fort's heavy guns fired in pairs. The *Rose* flared like the filament of a lightbulb. Because the Venerian ship had risen to fifty meters, her underside was exposed. One bolt shattered half her forward thrusters.

Captain Fedders and the *Rose*'s AI tried to keep control. A quick switch of the angle of the surviving thruster nozzles kept the ship from augering in under power, but nothing could prevent a crash.

The *Rose* nosed into the shingle at a walking pace, yawing to port as she did so. Fragments of ceramic stressed beyond several strength moduli flew about in razor-edged profusion, far more dangerous than the spray of gravel gouged from the ground. The stern of the vessel came to rest in fairly complete condition, but the bow disintegrated into shards of a few square meters or less.

Light winked toward the *Peaches* from a port open onto the flagship's bridge. For a moment Gregg thought someone had mistaken them for a Fed vessel; then he realized that Mostert or one of his men was using a handheld talk-between-ships unit to communicate with the featherboat. The TBS used a modulated laser beam which wasn't affected by plasma cannon and thrusters radiating across all the radio bands.

Ricimer brought the *Peaches* in tight behind the *Tolliver*. The *Hawkwood* was already there. A line of men transferred crates and bales of goods from the flagship's holds to the lighter vessel.

The guns of the recaptured fort hammered the *Tolliver*. The plasma bolts blew pieces of the west-facing hull high above the vessel, glittering in the light of burning ships. Gregg grunted as though he'd been struck by medicine balls, even though the flagship's mass was between him and the bolts' impact.

The featherboat grounded hard. Gregg didn't have any targets because they were behind the *Tolliver*. He felt as though he'd come to shelter after a terrible storm. His bandolier was empty. He was sure there had been six spare batteries in it at first, and he didn't remember firing that many rounds.

His laser's ceramic barrel glowed dull red.

Crewmen in one of the *Tolliver*'s holds extended a boarding bridge to the featherboat. The end clanged down in front of Gregg. Tancred and Dole clamped it to the coaming. Gregg moved back, out of the way. He stumbled off the closed locker and into the vessel's bay.

Guillermo caught him; the Molt's hard-surfaced grip was unmistakable. Gregg was blind until he remembered to raise his helmet's visor. The featherboat's interior was a reeking side-corridor of Hell.

Forward, the plasma cannon's barrel threw a soft light that silhouetted the figures of the armored crewmen who were to load a third round. The bore must still be dangerously hot, but needs must when the Devil drives.

Piet Ricimer got up from the main console. "Stephen, you're all right?" he called.

The seats before the attitude-control boards weren't occupied. Guillermo and Lightbody had run them until the *Peaches* grounded. Now Lightbody caught and stowed bales of cargo that the men at the hatch swung down to him.

"We're going to take aboard men and valuables from the *Tolliver*," Ricimer said. "She's lost, she can't lift with—"

A drumroll interrupted him. It started with a further exchange by plasma cannon and ended in the cataclysmic destruction of another Federation vessel. Light from plasma bolts reflected through the *Tolliver*'s interior and brightened the image of the flagship's holds on the viewscreen behind Ricimer.

"We're all lost," Gregg said. Ionized air had stripped the mucus from his throat. He wasn't sure he had any voice left.

"No!" Piet Ricimer cried. Perhaps he'd read Gregg's lips. "We're not lost and we're not quitting!"

Gregg pawed at a bandolier hanging from a hook. Its pockets were filled with rifle cartridges, but the satchel beneath it held more flashgun batteries. He lifted the satchel free, only vaguely aware that the bandolier dropped into the litter on the deck when he did so.

"Who said quitting?" he muttered through cracked lips.

—25—

Biruta

If it had been Mostert's ships against the Earth Convoy alone, the Venerians would have ruled Island Able at the end of the fight. Better crews, heavier guns, and the refractory ceramic hulls made the argosy far superior even to Carstensen's warships. The thin-skinned freighters were little better than targets. All of them were gapped and blazing by now.

But possession of the fort was decisive. Its meters-thick walls could withstand the *Tolliver*'s heavy plasma cannon, and the separately-mounted guns could be destroyed only one at a time by direct hits. The only way to take the fort was as the Feds had done, by a sudden infantry assault that ignored casualties. The Venerians had neither the personnel nor a chance of surprise to reverse the situation.

The flagship fired a plasma cannon directly over the *Peaches*. Men transferring cargo screamed as the iridescent light shadowed the bones through their flesh. Tancred wasn't wearing a helmet. He fell into the featherboat, batting at the orange flames licking from his hair.

The concussion threw Gregg forward. His mouth opened, but his bludgeoned mind couldn't find a curse vile enough for the gunner who fired in a direction where there were no hostile targets.

"Look—" Ricimer said/mouthed, and turned from Gregg to point at the viewscreen's fuzzy panorama.

One of the remotely-controlled water buffalo had lifted from the station at the far end of the island. It slid slowly toward the three surviving Venerian ships, only a few meters above the ground.

The *Tolliver* fired another 20-cm plasma cannon at the water buffalo. Though the gunport was next to that of the first weapon, the discharge seemed a pale echo of the unexpected previous bolt. At impact, steam blasted a hundred meters in every direction. Moments later the unmanned vessel emerged from the cloud, spewing water from a second huge gap in its bow plating.

The Federation drone was full of seawater, nearly a hundred tonnes of it. Guns that fired at the water buffalo bow-on, even weapons as powerful as those of the *Tolliver,* could only convert part of that reaction mass to steam. The bolts couldn't reach the thrusters, the only part of the simple vessel that was vulnerable.

The amount of kinetic energy involved in a loaded water buffalo hitting the *Tolliver* would be comparable to that liberated by a nuclear weapon.

Ricimer bent to put his lips to Gregg's ear and shouted, "Stephen, if I bring us alongside, can you hit a nozzle with—"

"Do it!" Gregg said, turning away as soon as he understood. *We'll do what we have to.*

Crewmen cursing and shouting for medical attention hunched beneath the roof hatch. Cargo, more than a dozen cases of valuables transferred from the flagship in the minutes before the gun fired overhead, choked the narrow confines. Gregg bulled his way through, treating people and goods with the same ruthless abandon.

If he didn't do his job, it wouldn't matter how badly his fellows had been injured by the ravening ions. If he did do his job, it might not matter anyway . . .

The featherboat lifted. Guillermo was alone at the attitude controls. Lightbody must have been one of those flayed by the side-scatter of ions. Nevertheless, the *Peaches* spun on her vertical axis with a slow grace that belied her short staffing.

The liftship came on like Juggernaut, moving slowly but with an inexorable majesty. It was already within five hundred meters of the Venerian ships. Plasma cannon clawed at one another to the south, but the gunfire was no longer significant to the outcome.

The *Peaches* pulled away from the flagship. The boarding bridge cracked loose, bits of clamp ricocheting like shrapnel off the featherboat's inner bulkheads. There'd been a few bales of cargo on the walkway, but the crewmen carrying them had either jumped or been flung off when the cannon fired above them.

Gregg aimed, over the barrel of his flashgun rather than through its sights for the moment. He didn't want to focus down too early and miss some crucial aspect of the tableau. He wouldn't get another chance. None of them would get another chance.

The *Peaches* swung into line with the water buffalo. Leon and Jeude fired their plasma cannon, a dart of light through Gregg's filtered visor. The featherboat's bow lit like a display piece. A line of ionized air bound the two vessels. At the point of impact, a section of steel belly plates became blazing gas.

The drone's thrusters were undamaged.

Gregg felt the *Peaches* buck beneath him. His bare hands stung from stripped atoms, but he didn't hear the crash of the discharge. His brain began shutting down extraneous senses. Cotton batting swaddled sound. Objects faded to vague flickers beyond the tunnel connecting him to his target.

"Reloads, Mr. Gregg," said a voice that was almost within Gregg's consciousness. Tancred stood beside him in the hatch. He held a battery vertically in his left hand, three more in his right.

The featherboat was on a nearly converging course with the water buffalo. Neither vessel moved at more than 8 kph.

Did the Feds think they were going to ram? That wouldn't work. The heavily laden drone would carry on, locked with the featherboat, and finish the job by driving the *Hawkwood* into the flagship in a blast that would light a hemisphere of the planet.

Three hundred meters.

Water spurted in great gulps from the drone's bow. The plasma bolts had hit low, so each surge drew a vacuum within the water tank and choked the outflow until air forced its way through the holes.

Two hundred meters. Ricimer's course was nearly a recip- rocal of his target's.

The water buffalo sailed on a cloud of plasma from which flew pebbles the thrusters kicked up. The nozzles were white glows within the rainbow ambience of their exhaust.

The Fed controller kept his clumsy vessel within a few meters of the ground. He was very good, but as the *Peaches* closed he tried to lower the water buffalo still further.

One hundred meters. At this pace, the featherboat would slide ahead of the drone by the thickness of the rust on the steel plating. They would pass starboard-to-starboard.

The water buffalo grazed the shingle, then lifted upward on a surge of reflected thrust. Its eight nozzles were clear ovals with hearts of consuming radiance.

Gregg fired. He was aware both of the contacts closing within the flashgun's trigger mechanism and of the jolt to his shoulder as the weapon released.

The laser bolt touched the rim of the second nozzle back on the starboard side. The asymmetric heating of metal already stressed to its thermal limits blew the nozzle apart.

There was no sound.

Gregg's fingers unlatched the flashgun's butt, flicked out the discharged battery, and snapped in the fresh load. He didn't bother to look at what he was doing. He knew where everything in the necessary universe was.

Tancred shifted another battery into the ready position in his left hand.

The drone's bow dropped, both from loss of the thruster and because the vessel had risen high enough to lose ground effect. It was beginning to slew to starboard.

Fifty meters.

Only the leading nozzles were visible, white dashes alternately rippled and clear as water gushed over the bow just ahead of them. The drone was a curved steel wall, crushing forward relentlessly.

There was no sound or movement. The rim of the starboard nozzle was a line only a centimeter thick at this angle. The sight posts centered on it.

Trigger contacts closed.

The universe rang with light so intense it was palpable. Gunners in the fort had tried desperately to hit the featherboat but not the drone almost in line with it. They missed both, but the jet of plasma ripped less than the height of a man's head above the *Peaches*.

The water buffalo yawed and nosed in, much as the *Rose* had done minutes before. At this altitude, the Fed controller couldn't correct for the failure of both thrusters in the same quadrant.

The roar went on forever. Steam drenched the impact site, but bits of white-hot metal from the disintegrating engines sailed in dazzling arcs above the gray cloud.

Piet Ricimer slammed the featherboat's thrusters to full power. Guillermo at the attitude jets rolled the vessel almost onto her port side. The *Peaches* blasted past to safety as the ruin of the Federation drone crumpled toward her. For a moment, the featherboat was bathed in warm steam that smothered the stench of air burned to plasma.

Gregg didn't lose consciousness. He lay on his back. Someone removed his helmet, but when Lightbody tried to take the flashgun from his hands, Gregg's eyes rotated to track him. Lightbody jumped away.

There were voices. Gregg understood the words, but they didn't touch him.

We're low on reaction mass.

When the cannon's cool enough to reload, we'll choose one of the outlying platforms and top off. They must be down to skeleton crews, with all the force they threw into the attack.

Then?

Then we go back.

Gregg knew that if he moved, he would break into tiny shards; become a pile of sand that would sift down through the crates on which he lay. Hands gentle beneath their calluses rubbed ointment onto his skin. The back of Gregg's neck was raw fire. The pain didn't touch him either.

How is he?

He wasn't hit, but . . . take a look, why don't you, sir? I'll con.

Stephen.

"Stephen?"

Everything he had felt for the past ten minutes flooded past the barriers Gregg's brain had set up. His chest arched. He would have screamed except that the convulsion didn't permit him to draw in a breath.

"Oh, God, Piet," he wheezed when the shock left him and the only pain he felt was that of the present moment. "Oh, God."

His fingers relaxed. Lightbody lifted away the flashgun.

"I think," Gregg said carefully, "that you'd better give me more pain blocker."

Piet Ricimer nodded. Without turning his head, Gregg couldn't see which of the crewmen bent and injected something into his right biceps. Turning his head would have hurt too much to be contemplated.

He closed his eyes. Because of where he lay, he couldn't avoid seeing Tancred. The young crewman's body remained in a crouch at the hatchway despite the featherboat's violent maneuvers. The plasma bolt had fused his torso to the coaming.

When the water baked out of Tancred's arms, his contracting muscles drew up as if he were trying to cover his face with his hands. His skeletal grip still held reloads for the laser, but the battery casings had ruptured with the heat.

Tancred's head and neck were gone. Simply gone.

—26—

Biruta

When the *Peaches* returned to Island Able with full tanks
and her bow gun ready, the *Hawkwood* had vanished and
the *Tolliver* was a glowing ruin, the southern side shattered
by scores of unanswered plasma bolts. By the time the fort's
guns rotated to track the featherboat, Piet Ricimer had ducked
under the horizon again.

Stephen Gregg was drugged numb for most of the long
transit home, but by the time they prepared for landing at
Betaport, he could move around the strait cabin again.

He didn't talk much. None of them did.

—27—

Venus

Stephen Gregg walked along Dock Street with the deliberation of a much older man who fears that he may injure himself irreparably if he falls. Four months of medical treatment had repaired most of the physical damage which the near miss had done, but the mental effects still remained.

You couldn't doubt your own mortality while you remembered the blackened trunk of the man beside you. Gregg would remember *that* for the rest of his life.

The docks area of Betaport was crowded but neither dangerous nor particularly dirty. The community's trade had reached a new high for each year of the past generation. Accommodations were tight, but money and a vibrant air of success infused the community. The despair that led to squalor was absent, and there were nearly as many sailors' hostels as there were bordellos in the area.

On the opposite side of the passage was the port proper, the airlocks through which spacers and their cargoes entered Betaport. The Blue Rose Tavern—its internally-lighted sign was a compass rose, not a flower—nestled between a clothing store/pawnshop and a large ship chandlery with forty meters of corridor frontage. The public bar was packed with spacers and gentlemen's servants.

The ocher fabric of Gregg's garments shifted to gray as the eye traveled down it from shoulders to boots. He was so obviously a gentleman that the bartender's opening was, "Looking for the meeting, sir? That's in the back." He gestured with his thumb.

"Good day to you, Mr. Gregg!" Guillermo called from the doorway. The Molt wore a sash and sabretache of red silk and cloth of gold. His chitinous form blocked the opening, though he didn't precisely guard it. "Good to have you back, sir."

Men drinking in the public bar watched curiously. Many of the spacers had seen Molts during their voyages, but the aliens weren't common on Venus.

"Good to see you also, Guillermo," Gregg said as he passed into the inner room. He wondered if the Molt realized how cautious his choice of words had been.

There were nearly twenty men and one middle-aged woman in the private room. Piet Ricimer got up from the table when Guillermo announced Gregg. Leaving the navigational projector and the six-person inner circle seated at the table, he said, "Stephen! Very glad you could come. You're getting along well?"

"Very well," Gregg said, wondering to what degree the statement was true. "But go on with your presentation. I'm I regret being late."

Gregg never consciously considered turning down his friend's invitation—but he hadn't gotten around to making travel arrangements until just after the last minute.

Ricimer turned around. "Mr. Gregg represents Gregg of Weyston," he said to the seated group. "Stephen, you know Councilor Duneen and Mr. Mostert—"

Siddons Mostert was a year older than his brother. He shared Alexi's facial structure, but his body was spare rather than blocky and he didn't radiate energy the way his brother did.

The way his brother did when alive. After four months, the *Hawkwood* had to be assumed to have been lost.

"Factors Wiley and Blanc—"

Very wealthy men, well connected at court; though not major shippers so far as Gregg knew.

"Comptroller Murillo—"

The sole female, and the person who administered Governor Halys' private fortune. She nodded to Gregg with a look of cold appraisal.

"And Mr. Capellupo, whose principal prefers to be anonymous. We've just started to discuss the profits, financial and otherwise, to be made from a voyage to the Mirror."

"And I'm Adrien Ricimer," interrupted a youth who leaned forward and extended his hand to Gregg. "This voyage, I'm going along to keep my big brother's shoulder to the wheel."

Gregg winced for his friend. Adrien, who looked about nineteen years old, had no conception of the wealth and power concentrated in this little room. This was a gathering that Gregg himself wouldn't have been comfortable joining were it not that he *did* represent his uncle.

"Adrien," Piet Ricimer said tonelessly, "please be silent."

Brightening again, Ricimer resumed, "This is the Mirror."

He flourished a gesture toward the chart projected above the table. "This is the core of the empire by which President Pleyal intends to strangle mankind . . . and it's the spring from which Venus can draw the wealth to accomplish God's plan!"

The navigational display was of the highest quality, Venerian craftsmanship using purpose-built chips which the Feds had produced in a pre-Collapse factory across the Mirror. The unit was set to project a view of stars as they aligned through transit space, not in the sidereal universe.

In most cases, only very sensitive equipment could view one of the stars from the vicinity of another. For ships in transit through the bubble universes, the highlighted stars were neighbors—

And they all lay along the Mirror.

The holographic chart indicated the Mirror as a film, thin and iridescent as the wall of a soap bubble. In reality, the Mirror was a juncture rather than a barrier. Matter as understood in the sidereal universe existed in only one portion of transit space: across the Mirror, in a bubble which had begun as a reciprocal of the sidereal universe. The two had diverged only slightly, even after billions of years.

There were two ways to reach the mirrorside from the solar system. One was by transit, a voyage that took six months if conditions and the captain's skill were favorable and more than a lifetime if they were not.

The other method required going *through* the Mirror, on one of the planets which existed partly in the sidereal universe and partly as a reflected copy mirrorside. The interior of the Mirror was a labyrinth as complex as a section of charcoal. Like charcoal it acted as a filter, passing objects of two hundred kilograms or less and rejecting everything larger without apparent contact.

There was no evidence that intelligent life had arisen on the mirrorside. Human settlement there had begun less than a generation before the Collapse, and none of those proto-colonies survived beyond the first winter on their own. Because men had vanished so suddenly, they hadn't had time to disrupt the colonies' automatic factories in vain, desperate battles. Some of the sites continued to produce microchips for centuries, creating huge dumps of their products.

Some factories were designed with custom lines to tailor limited runs to the colony's local needs. Often those lines had been shut down at the time their supervisors fled or were killed, so the equipment had not worn itself out in the intervening centuries. With the proper knowledge, those lines could be restarted.

Molts carried that genetically-encoded knowledge. The Federation had begun to bring some of the factories back in service.

"That's where the wealth is, all right," said Murillo. "But President Pleyal has no intention of giving any but his own creatures a chance to bring it back."

"We need the governor's authorization to redress damages the Federation caused by its treacherous attack," Siddons Mostert said forcefully, his eyes on Councilor Duneen. "The ships, the lives—my brother's life! We can't bring back the dead, but we can take the money value of the losses out of the hides of their treacherous murderers."

Gregg's mouth quirked in something between a smile and a nervous tic. He understood perfectly well how to reduce injuries to monetary terms. Life expectancy times earnings, reduced by the value of the interest on the lump-sum payment. He'd done the calculation scores of times for the relicts of laborers killed on the family holdings.

He thought that if Administrator Carstensen appeared in person with the mulct for Tancred—and a very modest amount it would be—he, Stephen Gregg, would *chew* through Carstensen's neck if no better weapon presented itself.

"No," said Duneen. He looked around the gathering. Though a passionate man, the councilor's voice was for the moment as cold as chilled steel. "Governor Halys *absolutely* will not authorize an act of war against the North American Federation."

"But all I ask is leave to organize a trading expedition," Piet Ricimer said quietly. His index finger idly pointed from one point on the chart to another. Prize, Benison, Cauldron; Heartbreak, Rondelet, Umber. Names for a trader to conjure with. The source of the Federation's wealth, and the core of the empire President Pleyal schemed to build.

Damn him, Gregg thought. Only when startled eyes glanced around did he realize he had spoken aloud.

"I beg your pardon, gentlemen," he said. "Milady."

He nodded with cold formality, then continued, "Mr. Ricimer. Factor Benjamin Gregg, my principal, was extremely pleased on his return from your recent voyage. Despite the difficulty and losses at the end of it. I'm confident that he'll be willing to subscribe a portion of any new venture you plan."

"What are we talking about precisely?" Capellupo demanded bluntly. "A fleet? Five ships? Ten?"

"Two," Piet Ricimer said. "And they needn't—shouldn't, in fact—be large."

"Two?" Murillo said in surprise. She looked at Mostert, who sat beside her.

The shipper shrugged and made a wry face. "It wasn't my, ah, first thought either, madam. But Mr. Ricimer has very settled notions. And he's been on the scene, of course."

"He hasn't been to the Mirror," Capellupo said flatly. The agent wasn't precisely hostile, but he obviously regarded it as his duty to press the points that others might be willing to slough. The stories that returned aboard the *Peaches* made Piet Ricimer a hero in Betaport; and to the local spacefaring community, President Pleyal was Satan's brother if he wasn't the Devil himself.

"My brother's been to the gates of Hell!" Adrien Ricimer burst out angrily. "*That's* where—"

"Adrien!" Piet Ricimer said.

"I just . . ." Adrien began. He stopped, a syllable before something would have happened—an order to leave, that might or might not have been obeyed; a scuffle, with Stephen Gregg doing what had to be done if the conference were to continue.

"You're quite right, Mr. Capellupo," Piet Ricimer resumed smoothly. "Things that are true for other parts of the Reaches don't necessarily hold for Federation outposts on the Mirror. We'll reconnoiter the region before we proceed further, staging out of an undeveloped world Admiral Mostert explored on the voyage just ended."

Sunrise . . . Gregg thought. *Which Ricimer and the* Peaches *had discovered.*

"The need to keep a low profile while gathering information along the Mirror is one of the reasons I think a modest force is the best choice for this voyage," Ricimer continued. "The *Peaches*, a featherboat which I own in partnership with Factor Mostert—"

He nodded toward Siddons. *Piet must have bought part of the little vessel with his share of the cargo packed aboard her in the last moments on Biruta.*

"—and another vessel a little larger, say fifty to a hundred tonnes. That and fifty men should be sufficient."

Factor Wiley, a stooped man known both for his piety and his ruthlessness in business transactions, frowned. "Mostert, you could fund a business this small yourself," he said. "Why is it you've called this lot together? I thought you must be planning a full-scale expedition to capture some of the planets Pleyal's heathens try to bar us from."

Councilor Duneen looked at him. "I don't know that so public a gathering—"

He glanced at the men standing around the walls of the modest room. Gregg knew that many of them or their principals were major shipping figures; in Duneen's terms, they were rabble.

"—is the best place to discuss such matters."

"This is where we are, Councilor," Murillo said with unexpected harshness. Gregg's eyes flicked to her from Duneen. There was clearly no love lost between Governor Halys' chief public and personal advisors.

Murillo jerked her chin toward Mostert in a peremptory fashion. "Go on, say it out loud. You want to compromise as many powerful people as you can, so that you'll be protected when President Pleyal asks the governor for your head."

"I want as many successful people as possible," said Piet Ricimer, speaking before Siddons Mostert could frame the answer demanded of him, "because I intend to make everyone who invests in this voyage extremely wealthy. Wealth even in the governor's terms, milady."

He flashed Comptroller Murillo a hard smile, not the joyous one Gregg had seen on his friend's face before.

"I want to bring wealth to so many of you," he continued forcefully, "because this won't be the last voyage. There'll be scores of others, hundreds of others. Voyages that you send out yourselves, because of the profit you see is waiting beyond

Pluto. Voyages that no one here will be concerned in, because others will see the staggering wealth, the inconceivable wealth, and want some for themselves. And they'll find it! It's waiting there, for us and for Venus and for mankind—with the help of God!"

"Venus and God!" Duneen cried, turning toward Murillo to make his words an undeserved slap.

Hear hear/Venus and God crackled through the room. Gregg did not speak.

"And no, milady," Ricimer said as the cheers faded, "I don't expect investors on Venus to bring me safety. I saw what safety Admiral Mostert gained by being in the governor's own ship when he met Federation treachery. There'll be no safety beyond Pluto until decent men wrest the universe from President Pleyal and his murderers!"

"Which we will do!" Murillo cried as she rose to her feet, anticipating the cheers that would otherwise have been directed against her. Neither she nor her mistress would have survived in a male-dominated society without knowing how to turn political necessity into a virtue.

"Factor Mostert will discuss shares in the venture with you, milady and gentlemen," Ricimer said when the applause had settled enough for him to be heard by at least those nearest to him. "I need to talk over some personal matters with my old shipmate here, Mr. Gregg."

They stepped together into the public bar. Sailors watched them with open curiosity, while the gentlemen's liveried attendants tried to conceal their interest in the enthusiasm from the back room.

"Marvin?" Ricimer asked the bartender. "May we use your office?"

"Of course, Mr. Ricimer," the bartender replied. He lifted the bar leaf to pass them through to the combined office/storeroom behind the rack of ready-use supplies.

Part of Gregg's mind found leisure to be amused. Ricimer had set this meeting not in a townhouse but on ground where he had an advantage over the nobles who were attending.

Ricimer closed the door. "What do you think, Stephen?" he asked.

Gregg shrugged. "You have them eating out of your hand," he said. "Even though they know you're going as a raider this time, not to trade."

Ricimer lifted his jaw a millimeter. "President Pleyal can't be allowed to trap mankind within the solar system again," he said. "Nobody can be allowed to do that. Whatever God's will requires *shall* be done."

He quirked a wry grin toward Gregg. "But that isn't what I was asking, Stephen. As you know."

"Of course Uncle Ben will support this," Gregg said. As an excuse for not meeting his friend's eyes, he turned to survey the kegs and crates of bottles. The Blue Rose had its beer delivered instead of brewing on-premises, as taverns in less expensive locations normally did.

"I . . . was afraid that would be your answer," Ricimer said quietly. "When you didn't contact me after we got back. Well, I'm sorry, but I understand."

Gregg turned. "Do you understand, Piet?" he demanded. "Tell me—how many people do you think I've killed since you met me? You don't have to count Molts."

"I do count Molts, Stephen," Ricimer said. He crossed his wrists behind his back and looked directly into Gregg's angry gaze. "You killed because it was necessary to save your own life and those of your friends. We all did, whoever's finger was on the trigger."

"It was necessary because I went beyond Pluto," Gregg said. He didn't shout, but the way his voice trembled would have frightened anyone who didn't trust Gregg's control. "So I'm not going to do that again."

"I can't force you, Stephen," Ricimer said. "But I want you to know that I don't think of you as merely an investor or even as a friend. Your abilities may be necessary to our success."

"You know, Piet," Gregg said, "I don't care if you think I'm a coward. I suppose I am. . . . But what I'm afraid of is me."

"Stephen, you're not a coward," Ricimer said. He tried to take Gregg's right hand in his, but the bigger man jerked it away.

"I don't hate killing," Gregg shouted. "I like it, Piet. I'm good at it, and I really like it! The only problem is, that makes me hate myself."

"Stephen—" Ricimer said, then twisted away. He clenched his fists, opened them again, and pressed his fingertips against the wall of living rock. "The Lord won't let His purpose fail," he whispered.

Ricimer turned around again. He gave Gregg a genuine smile, though tears glittered in the corners of his eyes. "You'll be taking that troubleshooting job your uncle offered you?" he asked.

Gregg nodded. "We haven't discussed it formally," he said. "Probably, yes."

He hugged the smaller man to him. "Look, Piet," he said. "If you needed me . . . But you don't. There's plenty of gunmen out there."

Ricimer squeezed Gregg's shoulder as they broke apart. "There's plenty of gunmen out there," he repeated without agreement.

An outcry from the street redoubled when the men within the tavern took it up. Feet and furniture shuffled.

Gregg opened the office door. The sailors were already gone. The gentlemen from the back room were crowding toward the street in turn, accompanied by their servants. The bartender himself rubbed his hands on his apron as if thinking of leaving himself.

"Marvin?" Ricimer asked.

"The *Hawkwood*'s landed, Mr. Ricimer," the bartender blurted. "They're bringing the crew through the airlocks right now, what there's left of them."

"The *Hawkwood*?" Gregg said in amazement.

"Yessir," Marvin agreed with a furious nod. "But the crew, they're in terrible shape! The port warden says they loaded two hundred men on Biruta and there's not but fifteen alive!"

Guillermo followed as Ricimer and Gregg pushed out onto Dock Street. Ricimer's status as a local hero cleared them a path through the gathering mob. The gentlemen who'd attended the meeting had to fight their way to the front with the help of their servants.

The airlock serving Dock Three, directly across the corridor from the tavern, rumbled open. A whiff of sulphurous fumes from the outer atmosphere dissipated across the crowd. Port personnel carrying stretchers, some of them fashioned from tarpaulin-wrapped rifles, filled the lock's interior.

"Alexi!" Siddons Mostert cried as he knelt beside his supine brother. An ambulance clanged in the near distance, trying to make its way through the people filling the corridor. "Ricimer and I thought that avenging you was all we could offer your memory!"

Alexi Mostert lurched upright on his stretcher. He looked like a carving of hollow-cheeked Death. His skin had a grayish sheen, and all his teeth had fallen out. "Ricimer?" he croaked. "That traitor!"

Ricimer stood beside Siddons Mostert. It was only when Ricimer jerked at the accusation that Alexi's wild eyes actually focused on him.

"Traitor!" Alexi repeated. He tried to point at Ricimer, but the effort was too great and he fell back again.

Spectators looked from the *Hawkwood*'s hideously wasted survivors to the man Mostert was accusing—and edged away. Ricimer drew himself up stiffly.

Gregg had lagged a step behind Ricimer. Now he moved to his friend's side.

"What's this?" Factor Wiley demanded. "Traitor?"

"He abandoned us," Alexi Mostert said, closing his eyes to concentrate his energy on his words. "Half our thrusters were shot out before we could transit. We had only a week's food for as many people as we'd taken aboard, and only half the thrusters to carry us. He—"

Mostert opened his eyes. This time he managed to point a finger bony as a chicken's claw at Piet Ricimer. "He ran off and left us to starve!"

"No!" Stephen Gregg shouted. "No! That's not what happened!"

The crowd surged as the ambulance finally arrived. Men who'd heard Mostert bellowed the accusation to those farther back. Soon the corridor thundered with inarticulate rage.

Gregg shouted himself hoarse, though he couldn't hear his own voice over the general din. When he thought to look around for his friend, he saw no sign of either Piet Ricimer or his Molt attendant.

28

Venus

"Mr. Gregg, gentlemen," said the servant in fawn livery. He bowed Gregg into the Mostert brothers' drawing room, then closed the door behind the visitor.

"Very good to see you again, Mr. Gregg," Siddons Mostert said with a shade too much enthusiasm. He rose from the couch and extended his hand.

"And that in spades from me, Gregg," said his brother. "But I won't get up just this moment, if it's all the same with you."

A month of food and medical care had made a considerable improvement in Alexi Mostert. If Gregg hadn't seen the survivors as they were carried into Betaport, though, he would have said the shipowner was on the point of death. Alexi sat in a wheelchair with a robe over his legs. His hands and face had filled out, but there was a degree of stiffness to all his motions.

"I'm glad to see you looking so well, sir," Gregg said as he leaned over to shake Alexi's hand. "And I appreciate you both giving me this audience. I know you must be very busy."

The drawing room was spacious but furnished in a deliberately sparse fashion. Room was the ultimate luxury on Venus, where habitable volume had to be armored against elements as violent as those of any human-occupied world.

As if to underscore that fact, the room's sole decoration was the mural on the long wall facing the door. In reds and grays and oranges, a storm ripped over the sculptured basalt of the Venerian surface. In the background, a curve overlaid by yellow-brown swirls of sulphuric acid might have been either the Betaport dome which protected the Mosterts' townhouse—or the whim of an atmosphere dense enough to cut with a knife.

"Pour yourself a drink and sit down, lad," Alexi said. He gestured toward the glasses, bottles, and carafe of water on the serving table along the short wall to his left.

Gregg nodded and stepped toward the table. When his back was turned, Alexi continued, "I was planning to call on you, you know, as soon as I got my pins under me properly. I'm told that you were the fellow who saved my life by bringing down that Fed drone."

"Saved the lives of everyone who was saved," Siddons said primly. "*And* saved the cargo loaded on the *Hawkwood,* which is quite a nice amount."

He cleared his throat. "Ah, the share-out on the cargo isn't quite complete yet," he added. "But if your uncle is concerned about the delay, I'm sure . . . ?"

Gregg turned to his hosts holding a shot of greenish-gray liquor in one hand and a water chaser in the other. He sipped the liquor, then water. "Uncle Benjamin trusts you implicitly, gentlemen," he said. "We await the accounting with interest, but you needn't hurry such a complex matter on our part."

Every factory on Venus distilled its own version of algal liquor, slash, according to recipes handed down since before the Collapse. The Mosterts' sideboard contained wines and liquors imported from Earth at heavy expense, but it was slash that Stephen Gregg grew up with. This version was all right, though it hadn't the resinous aftertaste of Eryx slash that made outsiders wince.

"We were actually wondering whether it was business or pleasure that brought you to us tonight, Gregg," Alexi said carefully. "You're welcome for either reason, of course, shipmate."

There was a glass of whiskey on the arm of his wheelchair. The level didn't change noticeably when he lifted it to his lips and set it down again.

Gregg barked out a laugh. "Oh, business," he said, "indeed business. I thought I'd relax at Eryx for a time, you know, when we got back. But that didn't work very well."

"Your brother's the factor, I believe?" Siddons said.

Gregg nodded and looked at the shot glass. It was empty. "Dead soldier," he said.

He flipped the glass into a waste container across the room. Neither the glass nor the ceramic basket broke, but they rang in different keys for some seconds.

Gregg giggled. "Sorry," he apologized. "I shouldn't have done that." He rotated on his heel and poured slash into a fresh tumbler. With his back to his hosts he continued, "My brother August was very kind, but I could tell he wasn't, well, comfortable around me."

His arm lifted and his head jerked back. He put down the shot glass, refilled it, and faced the Mosterts again.

"He'd talked to my doctors, August had," Gregg said, "and they—well, you know about doctors, Admiral. I shouldn't have told them about the dreams. They don't understand. You know that."

Gregg smiled. The smile slowly softened. His eyes were focused on the mural rather than the two seated men.

"Ah . . ." Siddons said. "This is Gregg of Weyston's business that you've come to us with, Mr. Gregg?"

"No," said Gregg. "No." He gave an exaggerated shake of his head. "This is my own business."

He looked at Alexi Mostert with absolutely no expression in his eyes. "You've been getting a better perspective on what happened at Biruta, have you, Admiral? Than you had right when you docked, I mean."

"I hope nothing I may have said when I was delirious, Mr. Gregg . . ." Alexi said. The fingers of his right hand opened and closed on the whiskey glass. " . . . could have been construed as an insult directed toward you. To be honest, I don't recall anything from docking until I awakened in hospital three days later."

"It wasn't until my brother read the report compiled for Governor Halys that the details of that very confused business became clear, Mr. Gregg," Siddons said.

"Nobody insulted me, Admiral," Gregg said. "Besides, I wouldn't kill anybody just because of words. Not anymore."

He giggled. "My brother didn't like it when I said it was *fun* to kill people. He thought I was making a bad joke."

Siddons got up from the couch, then sat again before he'd reached a full standing position. "The compilation of accounts from all the survivors—including those of the *Peaches,* of course—created a degree of understanding that, ah, individuals didn't have while lost in their personal problems."

"You understand that, don't you, shipmate?" Alexi said. "It was Hell. Hell. There's no other word for it."

Gregg tossed off his shot. "I understand Hell," he said. He smiled again.

"I suspect I owe my cousin an apology," Alexi said heavily, looking at his glass. "During the whole trip home, all I could see in my mind was the featherboat running off instead of staying to help us."

"He knows now that you loaded reaction mass and came back," Siddons put in with a forced grin. "It was all a very tragic time."

"Ricimer's a friend of yours, I believe, Mr. Gregg?" Alexi said.

"Best friend I've ever had," Gregg agreed nonchalantly. "I wonder if he has the dreams, do you think, Admiral?"

He hurled the shot glass into the waste container. Both glasses and the container rang together. "Sorry, I didn't mean to do that."

Gregg turned to the serving table. "I don't think an apology really does much good," he said as he tilted the decanter of slash. "Do you, gentlemen?"

"You're here on Mr. Ricimer's behalf, is that it?" Siddons said.

Gregg glanced over his shoulder and grinned. "Nope," he said.

He looked down, raised the glass to his lips, and poured again before he faced around. "I'm here on my own. Piet, he's trying to put together an expedition still. He's having trouble even buying a featherboat, though."

"I believe one of my secretaries made problems about my cousin buying the remaining share in the *Peaches*," Alexi said. "I'll put that right immediately."

"A lot of people won't touch Piet because of the trouble when the *Hawkwood* landed, you know," Gregg said. He hadn't drunk any of the chaser since his first sip on pouring it. "Stories travel better than corrections do. You know how it is."

He threw back his head and emptied the shot glass.

"I'm not responsible for anything that happened while I was delirious!" Alexi Mostert shouted from his wheelchair.

"We're all responsible for everything we do, Admiral," Gregg said through his smile. "D'ye sometimes dream about things you haven't done yet? I do."

He looked at Siddons. "You don't have the dreams, do you, Master Siddons? You're lucky, but you're missing some interesting things, too. You know, a man's head can be there and then *poof!* gone, not an eyeblink between them. Right beside you, a man's head is just *gone*."

Alexi's glass fell onto the floor of polished stone. Both brothers jumped. Gregg chuckled and returned to the serving table.

"What do you think might be a fair recompense for the inconvenience I've caused my cousin, Mr. Gregg?" Alexi Mostert said hoarsely.

"Well, it occurs to me that a simple commercial proposition might turn out to everybody's benefit," Gregg said toward the wall.

He swung around. "For his expedition, Piet wanted a featherboat, which he could provide himself, and a bigger ship. If Mostert Trading provided an eighty tonner, with crew and all expenses—why, that'd prove the stories about Piet betraying you on Biruta were false. Wouldn't it, Admiral?"

Siddons leaned forward on the couch. He took a memorandum book from his waist pouch. "What share-out do you propose?" he asked.

"For the vessels," said Gregg, "equal shares. Officers and crewmen sharing from a single pool, with full shares for those who—"

Gregg's unfocused eyes made his grin even more horrible.

"—don't make it back."

Alexi Mostert leaned back in his wheelchair and forced a laugh. "So *that* was the business that brought you here," he said.

"Oh, no, Admiral," said Stephen Gregg. His voice was as soft as the quiver of wind against the dome far overhead. "But if this commercial transaction goes ahead, then there won't be any need for my business."

Gregg turned his chaser over. Water splashed his boots and the floor. He walked to the stone wall and twisted the tumbler against it.

The glass held for a moment. Then a scratch from the harder basalt destroyed the integrity of the man-made material. The tumbler shattered into powder and spewed between Gregg's fingers.

He looked at the brothers. "Sooner or later, they always break," he said. "Everything does, you know?"

"We accept your terms," said Alexi Mostert without expression. "Will you notify Mr. Ricimer so that we can formalize the agreement?"

Gregg dusted his hands together. Because his right palm was wet, shards too tiny to be seen except as a glitter stuck to the skin.

He shook his head. "No, gentlemen," he said, "that's for you and Piet to work out together. He doesn't have any idea that I'm here, you see. I'd like it to stay that way."

Gregg cocked an eyebrow. Siddons looked up from his notebook. Alexi Mostert nodded minusculy in agreement.

"Then I'll take my leave of you," Gregg said. "I appreciate you giving me your time."

He put his hand on the door. As soon as the panel quivered at his touch, the servant in the hall swept it fully open. "And I hope our next meeting," Gregg concluded, "will be at the share-out party when Mr. Ricimer's expedition returns."

"Mr. Gregg?" Alexi Mostert called.

Gregg turned in the hallway. "Sir?"

"Will you be accompanying the expedition yourself?"

"That's right," Gregg said. "I've decided that's where I belong. Beyond Pluto."

Mostert nodded stiffly. Gregg disappeared down the hall behind the footman.

"That's odd," Siddons Mostert said. "The level of slash in the decanter doesn't seem to have gone down as much as it should have."

"That young gentleman may not have been drunk," his brother said, "but you won't convince me that he's not crazy. Not after I saw him in action on Biruta. I think we'd best take him at his word."

"Yes," Siddons said as he rose to his feet. "I'll call Ricimer. Shall we offer the *Dalriada*, do you think?"

29

Benison

Ricimer brought the *Peaches* to a near halt a meter above the ground, then slid her forward between the boles of the broadleaf trees. The yellow-rimmed hole the thrusters seared on entering the forest would be obvious from the air. If the featherboat herself was concealed, though, an observer might assume the interlopers had taken off again.

Gregg and the new crewman, Coye, flung the main hatch open. Benison's atmosphere was sweet and pleasantly cool in comparison to the fug within the *Peaches* after a voyage of seventeen days.

"Not so very bad, Piet," Gregg said approvingly as he raised his visor. He lifted himself out on the featherboat's deck, glancing around with the nervous quickness of a mouse on the floor of a ballroom. The flashgun was a useless burden in this pastoral woodland.

"I don't see the piles of microchips, though," Coye muttered. Gregg didn't know the sailor well enough to be sure that he was making a joke, but he chuckled anyway.

As armed crewmen hopped up to join Gregg, waiting for the lower hull to cool, Piet Ricimer talked to Captain Dulcie of the *Dalriada*. When Gregg bought the remaining half share in the *Peaches'* hull from the Mostert brothers, Ricimer invested some of his capital thus freed into first-class electronics for the featherboat. Her viewscreen and voice radio were now both enhanced to diamond clarity.

"Find a landing site at least fifty klicks from here, Dulcie," Ricimer ordered. "And stay away from the cultivated fields. There's no sign of Fed patrols, but they can't very well miss a ship the size of the *Dalriada* if it drops on top of them. Over."

"Weren't we coming in alongside the Mirror, sir?" Leon said quietly to Gregg. The bosun peered about him as if expecting to see a glittering wall in the near distance.

"I can't imagine that Mr. Ricimer didn't land us where he intended to, Leon," Gregg replied. Dulcie's reply was an inaudible murmur within the vessel. "I suppose we're here on Benison because he wants to get experience of the Mirror where it's safer to do that."

Piet wasn't forthcoming with his plans. Gregg didn't like to press, because he was pretty sure his friend wouldn't tell him anything useful anyway. It wasn't as though any of them needed to know, after all.

Adrien Ricimer had equipped himself with helmet, torso armor, and a slung cutting bar as well as the repeater he carried. He called, "The fields are that way!" and leaped to the ground. He sprawled full length, overborne by his load.

Gregg jumped down beside him. In the guise of helping the boy up, he kept a grip on him. "When your brother's finished administrative chores," he said to Adrien, "it'll be time to go exploring."

Adrien gave an angry shrug and found that it had absolutely no effect on the bigger man's grip. When he relaxed, Gregg let him go. The rest of the crew joined them, moving a few steps into the forest to get clear of ground which the thrusters had baked.

Benison was three-quarters of an Earthlike world with a diameter of 14,000 kilometers. Three-quarters, because a section centered in the planet's northern hemisphere didn't exist either in the sidereal universe or across the Mirror. The mirrorside of Benison was an identical three-quarters of a planet, orbiting an identical sun and clothed in similar though genetically distinct native vegetation.

The juncture that turned a single world into a near duplicate of itself was not in the three-dimensional universe. Benison's orbit and planetary rotation had no effect on the boundary that separated the sidereal universe from the bubble that mimicked it across the Mirror.

It had been noted, though not explained, that the apparent thickness of the boundary layer was directly proportional to the percentage of planetary mass that existed in the paired universes. It was possible to cross the Mirror on Benison, but the length of the route made it impractical to carry any significant quantity of goods from side to side that way. Umber, the 5,000 kilometer disk of a planet whose calculated diameter would have been over 12,000 kilometers, carried virtually all of the direct trade between mirrorside and the sidereal universe.

Ricimer and Guillermo jumped down from the featherboat. "Dulcie says that apart from air and reaction mass, the *Dalriada*'s in perfect condition," Ricimer explained, obviously pleased with the situation. "He'll keep his crew close by the ship and relax while we do what exploring there is."

The men stiffened, waiting for direction. Ricimer went on, "Stephen and I will cover Guillermo while he talks to field workers. Leon, you're in charge of the ship until we return. If that's more than two hours, I'll radio."

He patted the flat radio hanging from the right side of his belt, where it balanced the forty rounds of rifle ammunition on the left.

"You're leaving me under *him*?" Adrien said in amazement.

Piet looked at him. "No," he said with scarcely a hint of hesitation. "You'll come with us, Adrien . . . But leave the rifle, that's too much to carry."

Gregg nodded mentally. Adrien couldn't get into too much trouble with a cutting bar.

"Look, I'll take off my armor instead. I—"

"*Leave the rifle,* Adrien," Ricimer repeated, very clearly the captain.

Adrien's handsome face scrunched up, but he obeyed without further comment.

Benison's open woodlands were as alien to Gregg as anything beyond the corridors of Venus, but he found they had a friendly feel. The leaves overhead provided a ceiling of sorts, but they didn't have the overpowering immensity of Punta Verde's layered forests.

Small animals chirped and mewed, unseen. Sometimes the ankle-high ground cover—neither moss nor ferns, but similar to both—quivered ahead of the party.

Guillermo led, carrying a fist-sized direction finder. The Molt slung a holstered revolver from a pink sash like the one he'd worn on Punta Verde when he was captured. Piet was next in line. Twice Adrien tried to come abreast of his brother and talk, but Piet brushed him back.

Gregg brought up the rear with his flashgun and bleak thoughts. He was nervous around Adrien Ricimer. He was afraid of his own temper, afraid that one day he was going to crush the boy like a bug.

Afraid that jealousy was as much a reason for his anger as Adrien's brashness.

They came to the verge of cultivated fields a quarter klick from the landing site. Hectares of waist-high sorghum stretched for as far as Gregg could see. Stripes and wedges of native vegetation, taller and a brighter green, marked patches too wet or rocky for gang plows.

A pair of high-wheeled cultivators crawled across the fields in the middle distance. Guillermo immediately entered the open area, pushing through the saw-edged leaves with chitin-clad ease.

"Wait!" Gregg said. "Shouldn't you take your, your sash off?"

The Molt's triangular head turned almost directly backward though his torso didn't move. "Any human observer will think I'm a supervisor, Mr. Gregg," he said. "A thousand years ago, his ancestors would have thought the same."

Guillermo resumed his swift progress toward the Federation equipment. Gregg sighted on the nearer vehicle, but his laser's 1.5x scope didn't provide enough magnification to tell whether the driver was a Molt or perhaps a Rabbit.

It hadn't occurred to him until Guillermo spoke that *all* the aspects of Molt-human interaction had been set before the Collapse. The thought made him a little queasy. He had a vision of eighty generations of Stephen Greggs sighting their flashguns toward treetops full of defiant warriors . . .

"The *Dalriada*'s truly a first-class ship," Piet Ricimer murmured as the three men watched Guillermo from the forest-edge undergrowth. "I suppose it's my cousins' way of making apology for the business when the *Hawkwood* landed. Though after that ordeal, nobody could blame Alexi for wild talk."

"I wanted to call him out!" Adrien snarled.

Neither of the older men spoke. Had the Mosterts bothered to respond, they would have sent servants to beat the pup within an inch of his life—or beyond. Betaport would have applauded that handling of lower-class scum who insulted his betters by claiming the right of challenge.

A red film lowered over Gregg's eyes. He pointed the flashgun toward the ground. He didn't want an accident because his trigger finger trembled.

Guillermo jumped off the cultivator he'd mounted and returned toward the waiting humans. The vehicle had never paused in its slow progress across the sorghum.

"Frankly, I did my cousins an injustice," Piet continued. "I expected them to, well, ignore that they'd been mistaken. Instead, well—I couldn't have hoped for a finer ship than the one they provided. I'd hoped to involve more of the . . . upper levels of the nation in this expedition than I've done. But that will come next time."

"Sometimes people come through when they come right up against it," Gregg said. "I'm glad your cousins did."

His voice was hoarse. He coughed, as if to clear his throat.

Guillermo rejoined them. The Molt's chestplate pumped with exertion, sucking and expelling air from the breathing holes along the lateral lines of his torso. "They'll meet us tonight," he said.

"Those will?" Adrien asked. "The workers?"

"Not them," his brother explained. "Their kindred, who've escaped and hide along the Mirror. The only food available is what's grown here on the plantations, so I was sure that there'd be contact between free Molts and the slaves."

He nodded toward the *Peaches* to start the party walking back. "I want to understand the Mirror better before I make final plans. That means I need someone to guide me through."

━30━

Benison

Coye waggled Gregg's booted foot to awaken him before going on to each next man in the lean-to and doing the same. Gregg pulled his helmet on as he got up. He was already fully dressed, with the flashgun sling over his right arm.

The sky was faintly pale where it could be glimpsed through the foliage, but it did nothing to illuminate the forest floor. Even the featherboat's off-white hull was easier to sense than see in the first moments of wakefulness.

Gregg was stiff in odd places. The bed of springy boughs had seemed comfortable when he lay on it, but it had locked his body into one posture as the thin pad over the *Peaches'* decking hadn't done during the voyage. His sinuses were stuffy from pollen, either native or drifting from the nearby plantation.

And he was afraid. Clambering up the side of the featherboat was good for the fear. The massive solidity of the *Peaches'* hull soothed Gregg in a fashion that the personal weapon he carried could not.

In the hatchway Leon, who'd shared the watch with Coye, whispered to Piet Ricimer. Clipped to the coaming was the sonic scanner, another piece of hardware purchased with the profits of Mostert's disastrous voyage. Rather than magnifying sounds for the operator to classify, the scanner plotted an ambient and indicated changes above that baseline on a screen. It didn't tell the operator what a sound was, but it gave volume and vector.

Gregg glanced at the readout. He lay across the hull beside the hatch and aimed his weapon toward the line of peaks

153

which the scanner had noted—footsteps or brush rustling past an oncoming body.

Ricimer laid his left hand across the eyepiece of the flashgun's sight. "Guillermo's out there," he whispered. "He's meeting them."

"Sirs?" the Molt called in a clear voice. "Our friends are here. We're coming in."

Gregg glimpsed the movement of several bodies. Faint light bloomed. Three strange Molts accompanied Guillermo. One of them brought a phosphorescent twig out of the pot which had covered it. In this near-total darkness, the bioluminescent sheen was as good as a magnesium flare.

The strange Molts were noticeably bulkier though not taller than Guillermo. One carried a breechloader, while the others had one-armed "bows" similar in design to those the Venerians had faced on Punta Verde.

Piet Ricimer swung his legs over the hatch coaming and jumped to the ground in front of the Molts.

"This is K'Jax," Guillermo said, dipping both forelimbs toward the rifleman in a gesture of respect. "I have told him that you need a guide through the Mirror."

"Why?" said K'Jax. His eyes and those of his fellows tracked quickly across the humans facing them, hesitating minutely at each weapon they noted.

"Because I need to know more about the Mirror in order to determine how best to take from the Federation the wealth belonging to all persons," Ricimer replied calmly. Gregg noted that his friend had left his rifle in the featherboat. "Wealth which the Feds claim as their own."

"So you want us to be your servants," K'Jax said flatly.

The Molt leader spoke unaccented English, but his intonations were as mechanical as those of a synthesizer. By contrast, Guillermo's voice couldn't be told from that of a human except that the Molt clipped his labials slightly.

"I want you to be our allies," Ricimer said. "The Feds are your enemies as well as ours. We can provide you with weapons. A few now, more after we're successful and return—though that will be sometime hence, perhaps as much as a year. But I *will* return."

K'Jax clucked. "I am the chieftain of Clan Deel," he said. "They burned my limbs when I would not work for them. I fled as others have fled."

The Molt leader glanced around, at his silent fellows and the forest which surrounded him. He had a look of rocklike solidity, a soul that could be pulverized but never changed in essence.

"If they let us grow our own crops," K'Jax continued, "we would ignore them. When we clear fields, they find us and attack, and they hunt us with planes. So we raid their fields. We kill them when we can. One day we will kill them all."

His chitinous fingers caressed his Federation breechloader, designed for human hands but adaptable to those of a Molt.

K'Jax clucked again. The sound was that of a repeater chambering the next round. "If you're the enemy of the Federation, human," he said, "then you don't have to pay me or mine for our help. When do you want to pass through the Mirror?"

"Now?" said Ricimer.

"Now," K'Jax agreed. He and his fellows turned.

Gregg jumped down from the featherboat. He was pleased and a little surprised to land squarely on his feet without stumbling. The satchel of spare batteries slapped his thigh.

"Leon, you're in charge," Ricimer said. "Guillermo and Mr. Gregg accompany me."

"I'm going too!" cried his brother, stepping forward.

"Adrien," Piet Ricimer said sharply, "you will stay with the vessel and obey Leon's directions."

The bosun tossed a rifle and bandolier from the hatch. Despite the poor light, Ricimer caught the gear in the air.

The Molts paused five meters off in the darkness. Ricimer glanced at them, then said to Leon, "If we're not back in four days, use your judgment. But we should be back."

He strode swiftly after K'Jax with Gregg and Guillermo flanking him. Gregg was glad when the local Molt covered his glowing wand, because only then could they be sure Adrien Ricimer would not be able to follow.

—31—

Benison

"This is the Mirror," said K'Jax.

The words brought Gregg up like a brick wall. He'd gotten into a rhythm in the darkness, tramping along close to Guillermo. The concept of distance vanished when each stride became a blind venture. The Molt's night vision was better than a human's, though occasionally Guillermo brushed a shadowed tree bole and Gregg collided with him.

Gregg edged closer with his left hand advanced. He instinctively gripped the flashgun close to his body and pointing forward, though his conscious mind realized there was no material threat before him.

His hand felt cold. He saw nothing, absolutely nothing, until the Molt uncovered the torch again. Gregg's left arm had vanished to the elbow. Only the degree of shock he felt kept him from shouting.

One of K'Jax's fellows must have gone ahead. The transition was hard to see because an image of the sidereal universe shimmered on it in perfect fidelity. The reflected forest appeared as real as the one through which Gregg had just stumbled.

"We've laid poles along the ground within," the Molt leader said. He pointed down. The crudely-chopped end of a sapling about a hundred millimeters in diameter protruded from the transition. "Touch one foot against them to keep your direction."

He clucked. The sound must be equivalent to a laugh. "Don't disarrange the poles," he added. "You can walk forever in the Mirror."

He vanished through the boundary. His fellow with the light followed, then Guillermo.

"Stephen?" Ricimer said.

"Sure," said Gregg. He stepped into nothingness, feeling as detached as he had when he aimed at the oncoming water buffalo.

The interior of the Mirror was not only lightless but empty. There was a feeling of presence everywhere in the sidereal universe, the echo from surrounding existence of the observer's being. Nothing echoed here, nothing *was* here. Gregg had to be standing on something, but there was no feeling of pressure against the balls of his feet when he flexed his body upward as an experiment.

He slid his left foot sideways, suddenly aware that he wasn't sure of direction. When his foot stopped, he knew that he must be in contact with the pole, but he couldn't feel even that.

"God our help in ages past," Gregg whispered. He shuffled forward, picking up the pace. Now that he had begun, there was nothing in life that he wanted so much as to be out of this *place.* "God who saved Eryx when the ground shook and the sky rained fire. Be with me, Lord. Be with me . . ."

There was a gap between one sapling and the next. Gregg was a vessel for another's will, the will of the man who had stepped into the Mirror seconds ago. He wasn't afraid for the instant his boot wandered unchecked, only doubtful. It was as if he were falling, painless and even exhilarating until the shock that would pulp him, bones and spirit together.

He touched the next pole in sequence and stepped on.

Gregg's skin began to prickle. He wasn't sure whether the sensation was real or, like the flashes of purple and orange that crossed his vision, merely neuroreceptors tripping in the absence of normal stimuli.

Needles of ice. Needles driving into every cell of his skin. Needles sinking deeper, probing, penetrating his bone marrow and the very core of his brain. He could no longer tell if he still carried the flashgun. He felt nothing when he patted his left palm in the direction where his chest should be.

Gregg knew now why men so rarely entered the Mirror. Part of his mind wondered whether he would have the courage to cross the barrier again to return to realside, but only part. For the most part, his intellect was resigned to spending eternity within the Hell that was the Mirror.

The shock of the tree trunk was utter and complete. Gregg shouted and grasped the coarse bark that had bloodied his lip. The air was warm and there was enough light to read by, enough light to see Guillermo reaching in surprise to steady the young gentleman who had walked straight into a tree several meters beyond the edge of the Mirror.

Piet Ricimer appeared from nowhere, his eyes open and staring. Only when he tripped on a sprawling runner and flew forward did awareness flame back into his expression. Ricimer hit the ground, wheezing and chuckling in a joy that echoed Gregg's own.

The Molts watched, Guillermo and the locals together. Their expressionless faces could have been so many grotesque masks.

"How long were we . . ." Ricimer asked as Guillermo helped him to his feet. Gregg held onto the tree with which he'd collided. He thought he would probably fall if he let go. "In there. In the Mirror."

Guillermo and the Benison Molts talked for a moment in a clicking language nothing like Trade English. "About four hours," Guillermo finally said to Ricimer. "It's nearly dawn on the other side as well as here."

Gregg tried to understand how long he'd been walking. His mind glanced off the concept of duration the way light reflects from a wall of ice. The experience had been eternal, in one sense, but—his thigh muscles didn't ache the way they should have done after so long a hike. Perhaps brain functions slowed within the Mirror . . .

"How far is the nearest Federation colony on this side?" Ricimer asked. He tried to clean away the loam sticking to the front of his tunic, but after a few pats he stopped and closed his eyes for a moment.

Gregg deliberately let go of the tree and squeezed his cut lip between his thumb and forefinger. The tingling pain helped to clear his brain of the icy cobwebs in which the Mirror had shrouded it.

"Two kilometers," K'Jax said. He pointed his free hand eastward. "They build spaceships there. There are a few mines, some crops. Most of the settlements are on the other side."

The Molt leader nodded to indicate his fellows. "We stay on the other side, because the fields there are too extensive for the humans to guard well. When they bring in extra troops and hunt us there, we cross to here."

"Let's take a look at the settlement," Ricimer said. "I think I can walk." He looked at Gregg. "Are you all right, Stephen?"

"I'll do," Gregg said. Maybe. He wasn't sure that he could walk two klicks, but his intellect realized that he'd probably be better off for moving.

He wasn't sure he could bear to reenter the Mirror, either; and perhaps that would be possible also.

K'Jax and his fellows set off without comment, as they had done earlier at the *Peaches*. To them, the decision appeared to be the act. Gregg wondered whether Guillermo's less abrupt manner was a response learned as an individual when he was liaison to the Southerns for his clan rather than a genetic memory.

Ricimer threw himself after the Molts. Guillermo hung at his side, but after the first staggering steps both humans were back in control of their limbs.

"Don't the Feds conduct combined operations?" Ricimer asked. "Hunting you on both sides of the Mirror at once?"

"They try," K'Jax replied. "Their timing isn't good enough."

"Humans don't enter the Mirror," another of the local Molts added unexpectedly. "*They* send us as couriers. Molts." He made the clucking noise Gregg had decided was laughter.

The vegetation here was nothing like that on the sidereal side of the Mirror. The trees grew in clumps from a common base, like enlarged grasses. The foliage formed a dense net overhead, but the volume beneath was divided into conical vaults rather than the cathedral aisles of a forest whose trees grew as individual vertical columns.

After a time, Gregg shifted the flashgun from his right arm to his left. The weapon was less accessible there, but he couldn't bring himself to believe they were in serious danger of ambush. He wasn't a good judge of distances, certainly not in gullied forest like this.

Everything seemed profitless: this hike, this expedition; life itself. Passage through the Mirror had blighted his mind like a field ripped by black frost. He could only pray that the effect would wear off—or that the Feds would anticipate his own sinful consideration of looking down the short, fat barrel of his laser as his thumb stroked the trigger.

"K'Jax?" Gregg called suddenly. He supposed they shouldn't make any more noise than necessary, but it *was* necessary for him to blast his thoughts out of their current channel. "Does the Mirror bother you Molts? Does it make you feel as if . . ."

"As if your mind had been coated in wax and sectioned for slides?" Piet Ricimer offered. It hadn't occurred to Gregg to ask his friend.

"Yes," said the Molt leader flatly.

"Does it go away?" Gregg demanded.

"Mostly," said K'Jax. He continued striding ahead, not bothering to look back as he spoke. The Molts took swifter, shorter strides than humans of similar height.

"Until the next time," said another of the locals. "We enter the Mirror only when we must, so it doesn't matter what it costs."

"But you entered it for us," said Ricimer.

"You are enemies of our enemies," the Molt explained.

From the head of the line, K'Jax stopped, knelt, and announced, "The settlement is just ahead. The humans call it Cedrao."

Gregg eased forward in a crouch to bring himself parallel with K'Jax. He noticed that one of the local Molts turned to watch their backtrail, his projectile weapon ready.

The trees grew up to the edge of a twenty-meter drop. From that point, the ground fell away in a series of a dozen comparable steps, about as broad as they were deep. The *Peaches* had overflown similar country as Piet brought her in, but it didn't lie within fifty kilometers of their eventual landing point. Divergence on the mirrorside of Benison included details of tectonics as well as biology.

Below the escarpment, the tilted remains of ancient sediments, lay a broad valley. Sunrise painted into a pink squiggle half a kilometer distant the river that had cut through the rocks over ages.

On the near bank was a straggle of two or three hundred houses. The community stank of human and industrial wastes even at this distance.

"Cedrao," K'Jax repeated.

Ricimer sighted through the hand-sized electronic magnifier which he carried. Gregg suspected that a simple optical telescope would have been nearly as effective and considerably more rugged, but Piet liked modern toys.

A steam whistle blew from a long shed at one end of the community. An autogyro was parked behind the cast-concrete building that appeared to be the Commandatura. A few pedestrians wandered the street between the river and the dwellings. All of those Gregg could see through the flashgun's sight were Molts.

Ricimer backed away from the edge of the bluff and stood up. "How many humans live in Cedrao?" he asked.

"A few score," K'Jax said. "Transients when a ship lands. And a few human slaves."

"Rabbits," Guillermo explained.

"You could capture the town by a surprise attack," Gregg said/suggested.

"If we attacked," said the Molt watching their backtrail, "the Molts down there would fight us too. They aren't Deels. They won't hunt us in the woods, but they'll resist an attempt on *their* clan."

"K'Jax and his fellows ran away from humans and formed their own clan," Guillermo said. "Others of my folk bond to their supervisors." He clucked as the locals had done.

Guillermo himself had bonded to his supervisor—as he knew very well.

Ricimer shook himself. "We can go now," he said. "Though—Stephen, would you prefer to, ah, rest on this side before we cross the Mirror again?"

"I don't want to think about it," Gregg said in a voice as pale as hoarfrost. "If I thought about it for a day, I'd, I'd . . . It'd be harder."

K'Jax strode off in the lead as brusquely as he'd executed each previous decision of the human leader. The others fell into line behind him.

"Piet?" Gregg said.

"Um?" his friend said, grinning wryly back over his shoulder.

"Why did we come here at all?"

Ricimer looked front again and nodded his head. "Because I had to see," he said at last. "See the Mirror, and see how President Pleyal was really developing the worlds he claims."

He looked back at Gregg again. All the humor was gone from his face. "They can't be allowed to continue, Stephen," he said. "Everything here, everything on Jewelhouse and Biruta and everywhere the Federation squats—slavery, cruelty, and no chance of survival if there's the least shock to the home government. Mankind *will* return to the stars. President Pleyal and his henchmen can't be allowed to stop it, no matter what it takes."

"Oh, I know what it'll take," Stephen Gregg said, as much to himself as to his friend. His right hand rested on the grip of his flashgun, while his left gently rubbed the weapon's barrel. "And it can be arranged, you bet."

―32―

Near Rondelet

"We ought to go down and get them," said Adrien Ricimer. "There's probably a dozen ships on Rondelet for the taking."

He turned. Because everyone aboard the *Peaches* wore his hard suit, there was much less room than usual in the featherboat's interior. Adrien's elbow clacked against the back of Gregg's suit. For an instant, Gregg's right fist bunched. He didn't look around. After a moment, he relaxed.

"I watched the *Rose* come down with her thrusters shot away, boy," Dole said from the scanner readout. "I don't much want to watch from the inside when another drops."

The featherboat slowly orbited Rondelet at ten light-seconds distance; the *Dalriada* kept station a little less than a light-second away. Piet had narrowed the viewscreen field to the image of the planet alone, since a spherical panorama was useless on this scale, but even so Rondelet was no more than a cloud streaked blue bead.

Radar and even optical magnifiers on the planet *could* find the ships. There was no reason to assume that would happen so long as the Venerians kept their thrusters and transit apparatus shut down. Chances were good that an incoming Federation vessel would spend a number of close orbits trying to raise an operator on the planet's surface who could supply landing information.

"Ionization track," said Dole.

Coye, crewing the plasma weapon with Leon, reacted by latching down his faceshield. There was no need for that yet, but the slap *click* startled Gregg into doing the same thing. Gregg quickly reopened his visor, embarrassed but obscurely

163

happy to have something to do with his hands at a moment he had no duties.

"Adrien," Piet Ricimer ordered his brother, "get the *Dalriada*. We'll handle this, but they're to be ready to support us. Leon, don't run the gun out until I order. Everyone, check your suit now before we open up."

As Ricimer spoke, his fingers accessed scanner data and imported it to the AI's navigational software. The AI would set a course for interception, updating it regularly as further information came in.

Gregg peered over the console toward the viewscreen, trying to make out the target they were hunting. It might not have registered as yet on the small-scale optical display.

"I'm lighting the thrusters," Piet Ricimer said.

The featherboat shook like a wet dog as the separate engines came on-line at fractionally different moments. Ricimer held the thrusters to low output, just enough to give the *Peaches* maneuvering way.

Gregg shook his head and laughed harshly. Jeude, crouched across the central chest from Gregg, looked at him in concern. The two of them would be the boarding party, if and when it came to that.

Behind Gregg, Adrien talked excitedly to Captain Dulcie of their consort. "Don't worry about me," Gregg said. "I just want it to happen. But it'll happen soon enough."

"I'm about to engage the AI," Piet Ricimer said. His voice was clear and calm—but also loud enough to be heard throughout a larger vessel than the *Peaches*.

Gregg clamped his armored left arm to a stanchion. He held the flashgun to his chest with his right, so that it wouldn't flail around under acceleration. He should have checked his satchel of reloads again, but there would be time for that . . .

"Enga—"

Gregg's tripes everted repeatedly in a series that had by now become familiar if not comfortable. It was like watching an acrobat do backflips, only these were in four dimensions and he *was* them.

"—ging."

Rondelet vanished from the viewscreen. A fleck of light grew between intervals of transit, when grayness blinked like a camera shutter across the screen. At the sixth jump, the fleck was a ship for the instant before disappearing through transit space.

On the seventh jump, the *Peaches* and its target were parallel and so apparently close on the screen that Gregg imagined that he could pucker and spit across to the other vessel's metal hull. He closed his visor, though for the moment he left the vents open to save the hard suit's air bottle.

"I'll take the communicator, Adrien," Piet said. He lifted the handset from his brother's half-resisting grip and switched it from radio to modulated laser.

The screen blanked and cleared. The vessels retained the same alignment, though they must have shifted some distance within the sidereal universe. The featherboat's AI had locked courses with the Federation ship. For the moment, the Fed crew was probably unaware that they had company, but they had no chance now of escaping.

There were infinite possible actions but only one best solution. Given the task of predicting what another navigational computer would do, an AI with sufficient data could find the correct answer every time.

"Federation cargo vessel," Ricimer said in a voice punctuated by intervals of transit. "Shut down your drives and prepare for boarding. If you cooperate, you won't be harmed. Shut down your drives."

"Sir," said Leon. "I want to run the gun out."

"Go ahead, Leon," Ricimer agreed calmly.

The bosun activated the hydraulics which opened the bow port and slid the muzzle of the plasma cannon clear of the hull. A flexible gaiter made an attempt at sealing the gap between hull and gun tube, but it leaked so badly that Dole shut down the *Peaches*' environmental system as soon as Ricimer ordered the gun brought to battery.

Pressure in the featherboat's hull dropped abruptly. The vents in Gregg's suit closed automatically and he began to breathe dry bottled air. Sound came through his feet.

Another jump. Another. The Federation vessel was no longer on the viewscreen. Adrien swore.

Another jump and there was the target again, the four thrusters podded on its belly brilliant. At this range the *Peaches*' 50-mm plasma cannon would shatter all the nozzles and probably open the hull besides.

The Fed ship wasn't very prepossessing. Judging from hull fittings of standard size, particularly the personnel hatch, it was barely larger than the featherboat—30 tonnes burden at most. It was a simple vessel, even crude. Gregg suspected it had been built here in the Reaches in a plant like the one they'd viewed on the mirrorside of Benison.

"Take the heathens, sir!" Lightbody said from the attitude controls. The processor in Gregg's helmet flattened the voice transmitted by infrared intercom.

"Federation vessel—" Ricimer began. As he spoke, vacuum drank the target's exhaust flare. For a moment, the nozzles stood out, cooling visibly against the hull their glow lighted. The Feds vanished again; the *Peaches* jumped and they did not.

The featherboat's AI corrected. After a final, gut-wrenching motion, the *Peaches* lay alongside the target. The thrusters and transit drives of both vessels were shut down.

"Boarders away," Piet Ricimer said.

"Boarders away!" Gregg echoed as he and Dole threw the undogging levers that opened the featherboat's main hatch.

Dole stepped onto the coaming and checked his lifeline. The Federation ship hung above them, a section of its hull framed by the *Peaches*' hatch. He flexed his knees slightly and jumped.

Gregg climbed onto the hull. He couldn't see Rondelet or even the yellow sun the planet orbited. Perhaps they were below the featherboat. The metal skin of the Federation vessel was a shimmer of highlights, not a shape. He'd never been outside a ship in vacuum before.

"I'm anchored, sir," Dole's voice called. Gregg couldn't see the crewman. "Hold my line and come on."

Gregg hooked his right arm, his flashgun arm, across the end of Dole's lifeline. The multistrand fiber was white where the featherboat's internal lighting touched it. A few meters beyond the vessel, it vanished in darkness.

"I'm coming," said Stephen Gregg. He pushed off, too hard. His mouth was open. His limbs held their initial grotesque posture as though he were a dancer painted on the wall of a tomb.

The pull of the line in the crook of Gregg's arm made him turn a lazy pinwheel. The Fed ship rotated away. He saw the featherboat beneath him as a blur of grays and lightlessness.

The brilliant star beyond was Rondelet's sun. The few transits the Feds made before the *Peaches* brought them to had not taken the vessels beyond the local solar system.

Gregg hit, feet down by accident. His legs flexed to take the shock. "Good job, sir!" Dole cried as he steadied Gregg, attributing to skill what luck had achieved.

The boots of the hard suit had both electromagnets and suction grippers, staged to permit the same movements as gravity would. The suction system held here, as it would have done on a ceramic hull. The Fed ship was made of nonferrous alloys, probably aluminum. A plasma bolt would have made half the hull blaze like a torch. No wonder the crew had shut down as soon as they were aware they were under threat.

"Open them up, Dole," Jeude called. "They don't have suits, just an escape bubble, so they say they can't work the controls."

Jeude must have stuck his head out of the featherboat's hatch in order to use the IR intercom. Gregg thought he could see a vague movement against the straight lines of the coaming when he looked back, but that might have been imagination. He felt very much alone.

Large ships were normally fitted with airlocks for operations in vacuum. Small vessels didn't have space for them. In the case of *this* flimsy craft, cost had probably been a factor as well.

Dole twisted the wheel in the center of the hatch. It was mechanical rather than electronic. He had to spin it three full circuits before an icy twinkle of air puffed over him, shifting the hatch on its hinges at the same time.

As soon as the hatch had opened sufficiently for his armored form, Stephen Gregg pulled himself into the captured vessel behind his flashgun. He was unutterably glad to have a job he could do.

The three Fed crewmen cowered within the milky fabric of an escape bubble. Such translucent envelopes provided a modicum of protection at very little cost in terms of money or internal space. Inflated, they could keep one or two—three was stretching it, literally—persons alive so long as the air supply and CO_2 scrubbers held out.

One of the two humans in the bubble was a Rabbit. The

remaining crewman was a Molt. Alone of the three, the Molt didn't flinch when the laser's fat muzzle prodded toward the bubble.

Dole scrambled in behind Gregg. "The captain's coming," he said. "Leave the hatch open."

The speaker on the vessel's control panel was useless without air to carry the sounds to the boarding party. Piet must have used radio or intercom to alert the crewman while he was still out on the hull.

The cabin of the captured ship was small. It was partitioned off from the cargo spaces with no direct internal communication. The Venerian featherboat was cramped and simple, but this ship had the crudity of a concrete slab.

A third armored figure slid through the hatchway, carrying a rough coil over his shoulder: Dole's lifeline, which Ricimer had unhooked from the *Peaches* before he launched himself toward the captive. Dole reached out and drew the hatch closed.

When the dogs were seated but the air system had only begun repressurizing the cabin, Piet Ricimer opened his visor. "Gentlemen," he announced in a voice made tinny by the rarefied atmosphere, "when you've answered my questions, I'll set you down on the surface of Rondelet where your friends can rescue you. But you *will* answer my questions."

Another man would have added a curse or a threat, Gregg thought. Piet Ricimer did neither.

Though with the flashgun aimed at the captives from point-blank range, threatening words wouldn't have added a lot.

—33—

Sunrise

"The meeting's in ten minutes," said Piet Ricimer, wobbling as a long gust typical of Sunrise stuttered to a lull. Though the two men were within arm's length of one another, he used the intercom in order to be heard. "Time we were getting back."

"You're in charge," Gregg said. There were no real hills in this landscape. He'd found a hummock of harder rock to sit down on. There was enough rise for his heels to grip and steady his torso against the omnipresent wind. "The meeting won't start until you get there."

A three-meter rivulet of light rippled toward them across the rocks and thin snow. The creature was a transparent red like that of a pomegranate cell. Twice its length from the humans, it dived like an otter into the rock and vanished.

Gregg's trigger finger relaxed slightly. He leaned on his left hand to look behind him, but there was no threat in that direction either.

The *Peaches, Dalriada,* and the prize Ricimer had named the *Halys* were a few hundred meters away. The ships had already gathered drifts in the lee of the prevailing winds. Temporary outbuildings housed the crusher and kiln with which the crews applied hull patches, though neither Venerian vessel was in serious need of refit.

On a less hostile world, men would have built huts for themselves as well. On Sunrise, they slept in the ships.

"What do you think, Stephen?" Ricimer asked. He faced out, toward a horizon as empty as the plain on which he stood. Occasionally a tremble of light marked another of the planet's indigenous life forms.

169

Gregg shrugged within his hard suit. "You do the thinking, Piet," he said. "I'll back you up."

Ricimer turned abruptly. He staggered before he came to terms with the wind from this attitude. "Don't pretend to be stupid!" he said. "If you think I'm making a mistake, tell me!"

"I'm not stupid, Piet," Gregg said. He was glad he was seated. Contact with the ground calmed him against the atmosphere's volatility. "I don't care. About where we go, about how we hit the Feds. You'll decide, and I'll help you execute whatever you do decide."

A creature of light so richly azure that it was almost material quivered across the snow between the two men and vanished again. Gregg restrained himself from an urge to prod the rippling form with his boot toe.

Ricimer laughed wryly. "So it's up to me and God, is it, Stephen?" He clasped his arms closer to his armored torso. "I hope God is with me. I pray He is."

Gregg said nothing. He had been raised to believe in God and God's will, though without the particular emphasis his friend had received. Now—

He supposed he still believed in them. But he couldn't believe that the smoking bodies Stephen Gregg had left in his wake were any part of the will of God.

"I'm going to go back there and give orders," Ricimer continued. His face nodded behind the visor, though the suit's locked helmet didn't move. "There's a risk that my plan will fail disastrously. Even if it succeeds, some of my men will almost certainly die. Stephen, *you* may die."

"All my ancestors have," Gregg said. "I don't expect to be any different."

He raised his gauntleted hand to watch the fingers clench and unclench. "Piet," he said, "I trust you to do the best job you can. And to do a better job than anybody else could."

Ricimer laughed again, this time with more humor. "Do you, Stephen? Well, I suppose you must, or you wouldn't be here."

He put out a hand to help his friend stand. "Then let's go back to *Peaches,* since until I do my job of laying out the plan, none of the rest of you can do yours."

Sunrise

The command group met on the featherboat rather than the much larger *Dalriada* because of the electronics with which Ricimer had outfitted the vessel he and Gregg owned personally. The planning kernel which coupled to the AI was the most important of these toys at the moment. It converted navigational information into cartographic data and projected the result onto the *Peaches'* viewscreen.

An image of Umber, simplified into a tawny pancake marked with standard symbols, filled the screen now.

There were ten humans—the gentlemen and officers of the expedition—and two Molts packed into the featherboat's bay. John, the Molt captured aboard the *Halys,* had asked and been allowed to join the Venerians.

John's recent knowledge of Umber was an obvious advantage for the raid; Guillermo operated the display with a skill that none of the humans on the expedition could have equaled. Nonetheless, several of the *Dalriada*'s gentlemen looked askance at seeing aliens included in the command group.

"There's only one community on this side of Umber," Ricimer said as Guillermo focused the screen onto the upper edge of the pancake. "It's paired with a single community across the Mirror. The planetary surface is entirely desert on both sides, lifeless except for imported species."

From straight on like this, Umber appeared to be a normal planet with a diameter of about 5,000 kilometers. Instead, it was a section from the surface of a spheroid 12,000 klicks in diameter—had the remainder of the planet existed.

Umber's gravitational attraction was normal for the calculated size and density of the complete planet—slightly below that of Venus. There was no mass in realside, mirrorside, or *anywhere* to account for that gravity.

"Umber City is built along the Mirror," Ricimer continued. "The population varies, but there are usually about a thousand persons present."

"Both sides?" asked Wassail, the *Dalriada*'s navigator. Gregg had already been impressed by the way Wassail showed interest in new concepts. Dulcie, the *Dalriada*'s captain, was competent but as dull as his vessel's artificial intelligence.

"This side only," Ricimer said. "The community on mirrorside is much smaller and ninety percent of the residents are Molts. On realside, up to a third at any given time are human Federation personnel."

"One Venerian's worth six of those Fed pussies any day," Adrien interjected. "We'll go right through them!"

"We aren't here to fight," his brother said sharply. "We're going to take them by surprise, load with chips, and be away before they understand what's happened."

His lips pursed, then flattened into a smile of sorts. "Our task is somewhat complicated by the fact that another vessel attacked a freighter as it was starting to land on Umber two weeks ago."

Ricimer nodded toward John to source the data. "The attempt was unsuccessful—the attacker pursued into the atmosphere, and guns from the fort drove the hostile vessel off. It was sufficient to alarm the entire region, however. Umber sent couriers to neighboring planets and to Earth itself."

"A ship from Venus?" asked Bong. He was a younger son, like Gregg, but from an Ishtar City family.

"It was metal-hulled," Ricimer said. "In all likihood Germans from United Europe."

He turned to face the screen in order to discourage further questions. "The spaceport is here," he said, pointing at the lower edge of the developed area.

The port area was bounded by four large water tanks on the right. They held reaction mass brought from Rondelet on purpose-built tankers. Artesian wells supplied the town with drinking water, but such local reserves couldn't match the needs of the thrusters arriving at a major port.

The fort, a circle smaller than those of the water tanks, was sited below the lowest rank of dwellings. Below it in turn were the outlines of six starships, ranging from 20 to about 100 tonnes burden.

The ships, typical of the traffic Umber expected at any given time, were a symptom of a problem with the planning kernel. Its precision was a lie.

The kernel assembled data on Umber from the *Halys'* navigational files and from interrogations of two of the Fed crewmen. The third, the Rabbit, hadn't said a word from the time he was captured until Ricimer landed him, as promised, back on Rondelet.

The sum of that information was very slight. The kernel fleshed it out according to stored paradigms, creating streets and individual buildings in patterns which fit the specific data. It was easier for humans to visualize acting in a sketched city than in a shading marked DEVELOPED AREA, but that very feeling of knowledge had a dangerous side.

"The fort mounts four heavy guns," Ricimer went on. "They can be aimed and fired from inside the citadel, but there are no turrets or shields for the loading crews."

"Molts," John said.

Ricimer nodded. "The guns will certainly be manned, though two weeks without further trouble is long enough for some of the increased watchfulness to fade away.

"In the center of the community is a park fifty meters by seventy-five," Ricimer continued, "parallel to the Mirror. It's stocked with Terran vegetation, mostly grasses and shrubs. No large trees. The Commandatura faces it."

He tapped the screen. "All the colony's control and communications are centered in the Commandatura, and valuables are frequently stored in the vaults in the basement."

"Chips?" Wassail asked.

"Chips, valuable artifacts," Ricimer agreed. "They're brought across the Mirror here"—he indicated the "eastern" end of town, assuming north was up—"by a sectioned tramway laid through the Mirror. Molts push the cars through from mirrorside and back."

Guillermo murmured to John, who said, "No Molts are allowed to live west of the park. They use Rabbits for house servants." The click he added at the end of the statement was clearly the equivalent of a human spitting.

Piet Ricimer bowed his head, a pause or a silent prayer. "We'll proceed as follows," he resumed. "The *Halys* will land an hour after full darkness. Mr. Gregg will command."

Adrien Ricimer jumped to his feet. "No!" he said. "Let me lead the attack, Piet! I'm your brother!"

Everyone stared at him. No one spoke. Gregg began to smile, though it wasn't a pleasant expression.

"Adrien," Piet Ricimer said through dry lips, "please sit down. You're embarrassing me. You will be my second-in-command for the assault on the Commandatura."

Adrien's face set itself in a rictus. He hunched back into his seat.

"Stephen," Ricimer continued, "you'll have Dole as your bosun—is that satisfactory?"

"Yes."

"As well as John and four men from the *Dalriada*. Captain Dulcie, you will provide Mr. Gregg with four of your most trustworthy people. Do you understand?"

"I'll pick the men, sir," Wassail volunteered. "You'll want trained gunners?"

Ricimer nodded. "Yes, that's a good idea. Now, when the *Halys* has captured the fort . . ."

Stephen Gregg's mind wrapped itself in a crackling reverie that smothered the remainder of his friend's words. He would go over the complete plan at leisure. For now, all Gregg could focus on was the initial attack that might be the end of his involvement in the operation, and in life itself.

—35—

Umber

The *Halys* lurched into freefall. Dole cursed and reached for the main fuel feed.

"Don't," Gregg snapped, "touch that, Mr. Dole."

The thrusters fired under direction from the artificial intelligence. The vessel yawed violently before she came to balance and resumed a measured descent. John, crewing both sets of attitude controls, didn't move during the commotion.

"Christ's *blood*, sir!" Dole protested. "That's rough as a cob. I could do better than that!"

"We're here to look like Feds landing," Gregg said coolly. "That's what we're going to do"—he gave Dole a tight smile—"if it kills us. That means we let the AI bring us in, as coarse as it is and as crude as the thrusters it controls."

Gregg looked at the Molt on the attitude controls. "Is this how you would have landed if it had been you and your regular captain, John?" he asked.

"Yes," the alien said.

The *Halys*' viewscreen was raster-scanned. Synchronous problems divided the display into horizontal thirds, and the image within those segments was bad to begin with. Nor did it help visuals that a windstorm was blowing dust across Umber City as the raiders came in.

The four men from the *Dalriada* braced themselves against stanchions and tried to keep their cutting bars from flopping. They seemed a solid crew. The three common sailors showed a natural tendency to look to the fourth, a gunner's mate named Stampfer, when orders were given, but they'd showed no signs of deliberately rejecting either Gregg's authority or Dole's.

That was as well for them. Stephen Gregg might not trust himself at piloting a starship, but he could damned well see to it that his orders were obeyed the second time.

The viewscreen's jagged images of sandy soil and the three ships already docked on Umber vanished suddenly in a wash of dust. "Hang on, boys," Gregg said. "Here it comes."

The thrusters slammed up to three-quarter power. Two of the attitude jets fired, controlling the yaw from the thrusters' asymmetry. The corrections were so harsh and violent that it was a moment before Gregg realized that the final shock had been the landing legs grounding.

He let go of the stanchion and flexed life back into his left hand. His right biceps had twinges also, from the way he'd clamped the flashgun against his chest.

He gave a broad grin. "Gentlemen," he said, "I can't begin to tell you how glad I am that's over."

For a moment, none of the crewmen spoke. Then Stampfer broke into a grin of his own and said, "Too fucking right, sir!"

Dole got up from the thruster controls. He nodded toward the hatch. "Shall I?"

Gregg switched off the *Halys*' internal lights. "Just crack it," he ordered. "Enough to check the local conditions. We aren't going anywhere for . . . fifteen minutes, that'll let them go back to sleep in the fort."

Dole swung the hatch far enough to provide a twenty-centimeter opening. The six humans instinctively formed a tight arc, shoulder-to-shoulder, to look out. One of the Dalriadans eased the hatch a little farther outward; Gregg didn't object.

Dust blew in. It created yellow swirls in the glow above instrument telltales. The outside light of the fort was a similar blur, scarcely brighter though it was less than a hundred meters away. Gregg couldn't see the docked ships from this angle, but they'd shown no signs of life from above.

Dole covered the breech of his rifle with a rag. Even so, the chance of the second round jamming when he tried to reload was considerable. Gregg consciously avoided checking his laser's battery, because he'd get nonconducting grit on the contacts sure as Satan loved sinners.

Well, even one shot would be too much. If a threat wasn't sufficient, they were going to need a warship's guns; and they didn't have a warship.

"I'll lead," he said, repeating the plan aloud to fill time, his and his men's, rather than because he thought any of them had forgotten it. "They'll be expecting us to register for tariff . . ."

The door beneath the light was steel and closed. It didn't open when Gregg pushed the latchplate. He pounded the panel with the heel of his left hand. Nothing happened.

He was terrified, not of death, but of failing so completely that he became a laughingstock for the expedition.

Dole muttered something to John. The Molt reached past Gregg, rapped the latch sharply to clear it of dust, and slammed the panel with the full weight of his body. Chitin rapped against the metal.

The door gave. Gregg pushed it violently inward with his left boot, bringing the flashgun up to his shoulder as he did so.

One of the six Molts in the room beyond had gotten up to deal with the door. He fell flat on the concrete floor when he saw he was looking down a laser's muzzle. The others froze where they sat at the desk they were using as a dining table.

Gregg jumped into the room so that his crew could follow him. "Who else?" he demanded in a harsh whisper. John chittered something in his own language.

A seated Molt pointed toward the inner door. He used only half his limb as though fearing that a broader gesture would leave his carapace blasted across the wall behind him. Things like that happened when the man at the trigger of a flashgun was keyed-up enough.

"One human," John said. "Perhaps asleep." He indicated the ladder through the ceiling. "There's no one in the gun room."

"Stampfer, check it out," Gregg whispered. "One of you, open the door for me."

He slid into position. The door panel was thermoplastic foam with a slick surface coating, no real obstacle. It opened outward.

A Dalriadan touched the handle, well aware that gobs of molten plastic would spray him if the flashgun fired *into* the panel. He jerked it open as Stampfer and two men clattered up the ladder.

Gregg pivoted in behind his flashgun. His visor was up, despite the risk to his retinas if he had to fire, but even so he couldn't find a target in a room lighted only by what spilled from the chamber behind him.

Something blurred. "What? What?" cried a woman's voice.

Dole found the light switch. A young woman, pig ugly by the standards of anyone who hadn't spent the past month in a male-crewed starship, sat up in a cot that was the only piece of furniture in the room. She looked terrified.

Gregg let out his breath in a sigh of relief that told him just how tense he had been. "Madam," he said, "you'll have to be tied up, but you will not be harmed in any way. You are a prisoner of the Free State of Venus."

"What?" she repeated. She tugged at her sheet. It was caught somewhere and tore. The hem covered her collarbones like a stripper's boa, leaving her breasts and navel bare.

"Tie her, Dole," Gregg said as he turned to leave. "And *no* problems! We're not animals."

"Of course not, sir," the bosun said. His voice was so meek that Gregg knew he'd been right to be concerned.

"While I go call down Piet and the others," Gregg added to himself. "May God be with them."

36

Umber

The *Peaches* grounded hard; Leon at the control console understood that speed was not only more important than grace, speed was the *only* important thing.

Lightbody and Jeude threw the undogging levers, and a big Dalriadan hurled the hatch open with a lift of his shoulders. Dirt which the featherboat had gouged from the park as it landed dribbled through the opening.

"Follow me!" Piet Ricimer cried. He stepped to the coaming and pushed off in a leap that carried him clear of the plasma-blasted ground. He sprawled onto all fours, jabbing the knuckles of his rifle hand on a bush which exhaust had seared into a knot of spikes. "Follow me!"

His men were following, squirting from the hatchway like somebody spitting watermelon seeds. He'd stripped the *Peaches*' interior for the operation, even shipping the bow gun onto the *Dalriada*. Sixteen armed men were still a claustrophobically full load for a landing from orbit.

The Commandatura was a stuccoed two-story building with an arching false front to give the impression of greater height. There were no lights on inside, but windows in neighboring structures began to brighten. There was surprisingly little interest, given that the featherboat had landed squarely in the center of town. The spaceport was close enough that residents must be used to the roar of thrusters at all hours of the day and night.

The entrance doors were double glass panels in frames of baroque metalwork. Blowing sand had etched the glass into milky translucence.

Ricimer pushed the door. It didn't give.

179

"I got it!" bellowed the torso-armored Dalriadan who'd lifted the hatch. He hit the doors shoulder-first. Glass disintegrated into dangerous shards—

Terran ceramics! sneered a back part of Ricimer's mind.

—and the Dalriadan crashed through into a terrazzo lobby. The empty hinges clicked back and forth from the impact. They were intended to open outward.

A Molt wearing a dingy sash of office, probably a janitor, stepped from a side room, then fled back inside. A Venerian swept his cutting bar through the door and kicked the remnants aside as he and two fellows pursued.

Ricimer took the stairs to the second floor three at a time. He used his left hand to pull himself even faster by the balustrade. He fought to keep his eyes on the top of the stairs, not the step he was striding for as instinct would draw them. One of his men found the main light switch and brought the building to brilliant life.

"Somebody watch these rooms!" Ricimer called as he rounded the newel-post on the second floor and started up the black metal stairs to the communications center on the roof.

Every member of the landing party had been briefed on his job during the assault. Despite that, it was still possible that in the rush of the moment the men told off for cellars, ground-, and second-floor duties were all going to follow their commander to the roof.

The latch turned but the door at the top of the stair tower resisted. Ricimer put his shoulder against it. He was panting. The panel whipped away from him, pulled by the same strong wind that had held it closed.

The roof was a thicket of antennas and the guy wires that kept them upright. Lamps around the roof coping, ankle-height on three sides and taller than a man in front, cast a dust-dimmed illumination across the tangle. The antenna leads merged at the three-by-three-meter shed on a back corner of the roof. Ricimer ran to the structure, hopping like a spastic dancer to clear guys crossing his path.

The *Dalriada* was coming down, three minutes behind the featherboat, as planned. Gusts of wind compressed the roar of her thrusters into a throbbing pulse.

"Let me, sir," Leon cried as Ricimer reached for the door.

Ricimer nodded, knelt, and presented his rifle. The bosun leaned past him and gripped the latch in his left hand while his right held a cutting bar ready to strike. He jerked the door open.

The man inside the commo shack was asleep in his chair. His right hand trailed to the floor. A bottle had rolled away from him. Wind rattled another bottle, empty, against legs of the console.

Leon sniffed the fluid in the partial bottle and said, "Phew! I'd sooner drink hydraulic fluid!"

"Find the emergency channels," Ricimer ordered. "Start broadcasting that everyone should get into their bomb shelters immediately."

"Do they have bomb shelters, sir?" asked Marek, one of the pair of Dalriadans who had followed Ricimer to the roof as they were supposed to do.

"If they don't," Ricimer said, "they'll be even more frightened than if they do."

Leon pulled the radioman from his swivel chair and slung him out of the shack. The fellow still didn't awaken. Ricimer had heard him snore, so he wasn't dead of alcohol poisoning. Not yet, at any rate.

The lot to the east of the Commandatura was a fenced vehicle store. The building beyond it was two story, with lines as simple as those of a concrete block. Lights went on behind the bank of curtained windows on the upper floor, but they went off again almost instantly.

Ricimer frowned. That showed an undesirable degree of alertness on somebody's part.

The *Dalriada* shook the city. The vertical glare of her eight small thrusters stood every vertical form in a pool of its own shadow. Moving with the ease of a featherboat, the 70-tonne vessel lowered beside the *Peaches*, demolishing the remainder of the park. Clods of imported dirt and the stony bedrock beneath pelted the Commandatura's facade and the other buildings nearby.

The thrusters shut off with a sucked-in *hiss*, hugely loud in the silence that followed. Guillermo handed Ricimer unasked the portable radio he could use now that plasma exhaust didn't blanket the RF spectrum.

As Ricimer put the modular unit to his mouth and ear, Leon came out of the commo shack and said, "I put Marek on the horn, sir." He thumbed toward the console. The Dalriadan had arranged three microphones before him on the ledge. He spoke earnestly into all of them at the same time. "What next?"

Ricimer opened his mouth to speak. Something glimmered on the upper floor of the building across the parking lot. "Watch—" he said.

At least a dozen rifles volleyed from the other building. Leon pitched forward, blood spraying from his mouth. Something punched Ricimer's right thigh below his body armor; another round slammed high on his left shoulder. The bullet splashed on the ceramic, but its shock threw Ricimer down. Bits of red-hot jacket metal stung his cheek.

A bullet-severed guy wire howled a sour chord. The antenna it braced fell over.

Adrien was yammering something on his radio. Ricimer's own unit was the command set. He held the radio above his face as he lay on his back and switched it to the glowing purple override setting.

"Ricimer to Dulcie!" he called. He wasn't shouting. "Hit the building across the parking lot from us. It's a barracks. Use your cannon to—"

The *Dalriada* had landed with her eight 10-cm weapons run out to port and starboard. The crash of the first gun to fire cut Ricimer's orders short.

The point-blank bolt punched low through the front of the building and blew out all the ground-floor windows. Glass and framing shotgunned in all directions, driven by a rainbow-hued fireball.

The barracks walls were thermoplastic sheathing on a metal frame. They were beginning to sag outward when a second plasma cannon fired into the upper story.

The Feds' armory exploded in a numbing blast. Chunks of roof lifted and rained down from a black mushroom cloud. The remainder of the barracks flattened across the immediate neighborhood like a crushed puffball.

Marek stumbled out of the commo shack. The secondary explosion had wrecked the equipment and torn off three walls, but the Dalriadan seemed unhurt. Lights all over the city went out when the barracks exploded.

Guillermo examined Leon with a pencil flash. Ricimer glanced over. The bosun wasn't wearing a gorget to lock his helmet and body armor together. A bullet had drilled through the back of Leon's neck and exited where his nose had been until that instant.

Guillermo switched off the light.

It must have been instantaneous. All things were with God.

Ricimer rolled to his knees. He thought he was okay, though a double spasm shook his right thigh as he moved. He rotated the radio's control to its green setting, normal send-and-receive.

"—basement vault open," Adrien's voice was saying. *Did the boy even realize he'd been locked out of the net?* "But the real value, the purpose-built chips, they're at the tramhead. Let's go get them now. They're worth ten times the old pre-Collapse run! Answer me, Piet!"

"Ricimer to Adrien," Piet said. He stood up unaided, but he had to grasp Guillermo's shoulder an instant later when his thigh spasmed again. "Stay where you are. I'm coming down. Break. Ricimer to Dulcie, over."

"Go ahead, sir," the *Dalriada*'s captain caroled back. "Did you see how we blasted those bastards? Ah, over."

"Don't release your follow-up party until further orders," Ricimer said. He was feeling dizzy. Perhaps that was why Dulcie's delight in the—necessary, and ordered—slaughter struck him so wrong. "Ricimer out."

He released the sending key and handed the radio back to Guillermo. It would be some minutes before the ground beneath the *Dalriada* cooled enough for the second sixteen-man team to disembark, but Ricimer didn't want them scattering before he determined how best to deploy them. The expedition had only three handheld radios—his, Adrien's, and the one with Stephen's party in the fort. When the additional crewmen left the *Dalriada*, they were out of touch except by shouted commands.

"Come on," Ricimer said to Marck and Guillermo. "There's nothing more for us up here."

The Dalriadan glanced down at Leon.

Ricimer was already heading for the stair tower. Their duties were to the living. The dead were in the hands of God.

―37―

Umber

The Commandatura basement was divided by concrete walls into a larger and a smaller volume. The former was a jumble of general storage, unsorted and in large measure junk. The smaller room was intended as a vault, but the open door couldn't have been closed until some of the boxes piled around it were removed.

A man in Federation whites cowered against the wall outside the vault. A Dalriadan held a flashlight on him, while another waved a cutting bar close to the prisoner's face. When the Venerian saw Ricimer appear at the foot of the stairs, he triggered the bar. Its whine brought a howl of terror from the captive.

"Stop that," Ricimer ordered sharply.

His brother came out of the vault, holding a handful of loose microchips. "See Piet?" he said, waving his booty through a flashlight's beam. "They're old production here, and it'll take forever to load them with the power out. You! Heathen! Tell my brother about the new stock."

The prisoner had opened his eyes a crack when the cutting bar went off. "Sirs," he whimpered, "the latest production, they're just now being brought across the Mirror. It's only two weeks till the Earth Convoy arrives, so they're being stored in the blockhouse at the head of the tramway."

"Why?" Ricimer demanded. He shook his head to try and clear it. His sight and hearing were both sharp, but all sensory impressions came to him as if from a distance.

"So as not to have to shift it twice, sirs," the prisoner said. His sleeve insignia marked him as a mid-level specialist of some sort, probably a clerk pulling night duty. He'd opened his eyes fully and had even straightened up a little against the wall. "The blockhouse is safe enough for a few days, surely."

"Not now it isn't!" Adrien cried exultantly. "Let's go clear it out now! Right, Piet?"

A Dalriadan crashed down the stairs so quickly that he almost bowled Ricimer out of the way. Guillermo's presence brought him at the last instant to the realization the man with his back to the stairs was his commander.

"Schmitt and Lucius got two of the trucks running, sir!" the man shouted. "The windshield's blown off, but they run. Do we go?"

Ricimer started to shake his head, still trying to clear it. He pressed his hands to his face instead when he realized the gesture would be misinterpreted. He wished he could think. He must have left his rifle on the roof, or was that one of the weapons Guillermo now carried?

"Yes, all right," he said through his hands. "I'll have the second team begin loading these as soon as they can open the *Dalriada*. I wish—"

He didn't know how he'd meant to finish the sentence.

Adrien and the Dalriadans bolted up the stairs. Ricimer wobbled as he started to follow. He got his stride under control and shook away the Molt's offered hand.

He wished Stephen were here.

Jeude met him at the ground-floor stairhead. "We're getting the navigational data out of the computers, sir," he said, waving a sheaf of flat transfer chips. "Lightbody's finishing up. We got the emergency backup running when the mains power blew. Hey, what was that bang?"

"Leon's dead," Piet Ricimer said inconsequently. "I—you two stay here, finish your work. It's important. We'll be back. Tell—"

He shook his head. "Guillermo, give him the radio. Adrien has one already. Tell Captain Dulcie to put the second team to loading the vault's contents as soon as they can. We're going after purpose-built chips at the, at the tramhead."

"Piet!" Adrien's voice echoed faintly through the wrecked doorway. "Come on if you're coming!"

"We're coming," Piet Ricimer mumbled as he staggered forward. Guillermo paced him. One jointed arm curved about

the commander's waist, not touching him but ready to grasp
should Ricimer fall.

Jeude watched them with a worried expression.

As the first truck roared out of the parking lot, a Dalriadan
helped lift Piet Ricimer onto the bed of the second while
Guillermo lifted him from behind. He was very tired. The
truck driver accelerated after Adrien in the leading vehicle.
The Molt had to run along behind for a few steps before he
could jump aboard.

Though the wind had abated, the lead truck lifted freshly-
deposited dust from the street and spun it back in the follower's
headlights in a double whorl. The diffused illumination joined
them as a bar of opaque yellow.

Occasionally the edges of murky light touched a Molt standing in front of a building, watching the vehicles. Once a human
ran out into the street ahead, shouting and waving his arms.
He jumped to safety when Adrien's truck didn't slow. The
Dalriadan beside Ricimer fired at the sprawling figure but
missed.

Instead of being laid out in a straight line, the street to the
tramway kinked like a watercourse. The trucks, diesel stake
beds, were clumsy, and even the leading driver's visibility
was marginal. The modest pace, grinding gears, and frequent
jolting direction changes hammered Ricimer into a kind of
waking nightmare.

Something changed, but Ricimer wasn't sure what it was.
Then he realized the vehicles had pulled up at a line of steel
bollards. Beyond the waist-high barrier was a low building with
several meters of frontage. One leaf of the front double door
was open. The facade was pierced by four loopholes besides.

"Master, are you all right?" someone/Guillermo murmured
in Ricimer's ear.

Men jumped out of the trucks. Adrien swung from the cab
of the other vehicle and strode to the bollards. Beyond the
blockhouse, the Mirror could be sensed but not seen.

"I'm—" Piet Ricimer said. He pitched sideways, off the
truck bed. Guillermo tried to grab him but failed.

Ricimer knew that he'd hit the pavement, but he felt no
pain. His right leg was cold. The trousers were glued to his
skin by blood from the thigh wound that he only noticed now.
He couldn't make his limbs move.

A Molt wearing a Federation sash stepped out of the block-house. "Halt!" he ordered in Trade English. "Who are you?"

Adrien shot the alien in the head. "C'mon, boys!" he cried. "They're just Molts!"

The wall gun mounted at one of the loopholes fired a 1-kg explosive shell into Adrien's chest. Ricimer saw his brother's body hurled back in a red blast. Adrien's helmet and bits of his shattered breastplate gleamed in the flash of the second gun, which fired from the other side of the door. The round hit a Dalriadan, blowing off both legs and lifting his armored torso several meters in the air.

Guillermo knelt and lifted Piet Ricimer in a fireman's carry. The Molt had discarded his weapons to free both arms.

Rifle bullets pecked craters in the surface of the blockhouse. A Venerian jumped into the cab of the other truck. A shell struck the engine compartment and blew blazing kerosene across the men falling back in confusion. The cannons' muzzle flashes were yellow-orange, brighter than those of the bursting charges.

Guillermo jogged down the dusty street. Only the wall guns were firing. A crewman passed them, screaming, "Jesusjesusjesus!" Ricimer saw the man was missing his right arm.

That was the last thing he noticed before night stooped down on him with yellow pinions.

-38-

Umber

Flame burped over the roofs of the darkened city. The light was gone before Gregg could jerk his head around to watch it directly. The sound which came a moment later was hollow, *choong* rather than a bang.

"What was that, sir?" Dole called from the control room. "Was it a bomb?"

A post-mounted tannoy and omnidirectional microphone connected the unprotected gun deck on the fort's roof with the thick-walled citadel set off in a corner below. The latter had room for only the battery controls and one person, the fort's human officer.

The emergency generator had fired up without hesitation when external power failed after the explosion. It was a ceramic diesel of Venerian manufacture. Trade would have been a lot simpler.

Gregg stared at Umber City. The center of the community was a rose and magenta glow, though the flames were too low to be seen above the buildings on the southern side of town. "No," he said.

He realized that his bosun couldn't hear him. He turned and called loudly toward the microphone array, "No, it was probably a fuel tank rupturing in the heat. Don't bother us with questions, Mr. Dole."

"Watch it! Watch it!" Stampfer cried.

A cutting bar's note rose to a high scream as the gun mount twisted enough to free the sides of the blade. Gregg pressed himself against the roof's chest-high windscreen. The light metal bonged from the pressure.

A Dalriadan tugged his cutting bar hard to free it and

jumped clear. A tag of metal fractured. The heavy plasma cannon sagged slowly toward the deck, restrained but not supported by the remaining mount.

"There we are!" the crewman said triumphantly. "Let 'em try to use that one as we take off."

"One down," Stampfer said, "three to go. Get at it."

He looked over to Gregg. "We're not equipped for this, sir," he added apologetically. "It's a job for a machine shop, not cutting bars."

"Do what you can," Gregg said. "Likely that the Feds'll have other things on their minds by the time we lift."

"I wish they'd tell us what was going on," one of the Dalriadans said wistfully.

"They've got their own duties!" Gregg blazed. "So do you! Get to it!"

He turned, more to hide his embarrassment at overreacting than to look at the city. He wished somebody'd tell him what was going on too. The sophisticated handheld radios Ricimer had bought for the expedition couldn't listen in on calls on the net that weren't directed to them.

When the *Dalriada* fired its main battery and the target went up in a gigantic secondary explosion, Gregg and his outlying squad spent nearly a minute convinced there'd been a catastrophe. Dulcie had finally responded to Gregg's call, but he didn't know anything about what Piet and the landing party were doing either.

Stampfer, the two crewmen on deck with him, and John changed batteries in their cutting bars and sawed at a mount of another 20-cm cannon. Gregg had expected to disable the guns as he left the fort by blasting the control room. Though the fort did have director control, the individual cannon each had a mechanical triggering system that was too simple and sturdy to be easily destroyed.

That meant they had to cut the gun mounts—properly a third-echelon job, as Stampfer said. But you did what you had to do.

Gunfire thumped from the east end of town. Gregg squinted in an attempt to see what was happening—nothing at this distance, not even the flicker of muzzle flashes.

He glanced back at his men. They hadn't heard the shooting over the howl of their bars, and they probably wouldn't have understood the significance anyway.

The weapons firing were bigger than handheld rifles. The expedition hadn't brought any projectile weapons that big.

A car with a rectangular central headlight sped toward the fort from the west end of town. The vehicle wasn't following a road. It jounced wildly and occasionally slewed in deep sand.

"Watch it!" Gregg cried. "We've got company. Dole, Gallois, can you hear me?"

"Yessir-ir," crackled the tannoy. One Dalriadan guarded the prisoners in the ready room, while Dole kept track of distant threats in the control room. All they needed for this to become an epic disaster was for the Earth Convoy to arrive while the raid was going on . . .

"Don't shoot!" he added. "They may be our people."

They might be a party of whirling dervishes from the Moon, for all he knew. Why the *hell* didn't anybody communicate?

"Stampfer!" he said. "Cut away this fucking shield for me, will you?"

He kicked the windscreen; it flexed and rang. "It won't stop spit, but *I* can't shoot through it with a laser."

Stampfer triggered his bar and swept it through the screen in a parabola, taking a deep scallop out of the thin metal. The windscreen depended on integrity and a rolled rim for stiffening. The edges of the cut flapped inward, shivering like distant thunder.

The car swung to a halt beside the door on the fort's north side. It was an open vehicle with three people aboard, all of them human. They were armed.

"Hold it!" Gregg called, aiming the flashgun. The flat roof was three meters above the ground.

"You idiots!" screamed the woman who jumped from the left side of the car. "We're under attack! Are you blind?"

She waved a pistol in Gregg's direction.

"Drop your guns!" Gregg ordered. "Now!"

His visor was down, but the light outside the fort was good enough that he could see the woman's expression change from anger to open-eyed amazement.

The two men climbing from the other side of the car put their hands in the air. The woman fired at Gregg.

He didn't know where the bullet went. It didn't hit him. He put a bolt from his flashgun into the fuel tank of the car. The tank must have been nearly empty, a good mix of air and hydrocarbons, because it went off like a bomb instead of merely bursting in a slow gush of flame.

The shock threw the woman against the fort's wall and straightened Gregg as he groped for a reload. She was screaming. Gregg raised his visor and tried to locate the others. Somebody was running back toward Umber City. He couldn't see the remaining Fed; he was probably in the ring of burning diesel.

A bullet whanged through the north and south sides of the windscreen but managed to miss everything else. The shooter was in one of the houses, but the twinkling muzzle flash didn't give Gregg a good target.

He keyed the radio. "Gregg to Ricimer!" he shouted. "We're under attack. What is your status? Over!"

A shot winked from one of the houses only a hundred and fifty meters away. The bullet slapped the concrete and ricocheted upward.

Gregg sighted, closed his eyes because he hadn't time to fool with the visor, and squeezed. His bolt cracked through an open window, liberated its energy on an interior wall, and turned somebody's bedroom into a belching inferno.

Nobody answered him on the radio. More Feds were shooting. A bullet that glanced from one of the plasma cannon splashed bits onto Gregg's hand as he reached for his battery satchel. Pity the fort's architect had made sure the big guns couldn't be trained on the city.

Dole knelt beside Gregg, fired, and reloaded. He must have cleaned his rifle of grit while he had time.

"Stampfer," Gregg called without looking behind him. "How long to disable all the guns?"

"Jesus, sir—"

Something moved between buildings. Gregg's snap shot was instinctive. Only when the rattling explosion followed his bolt did he realize that he'd hit another vehicle. This one was loaded with enough ammunition to flatten both the adjacent structures. He blinked as if he could wipe the afterimages of his own shot from the surface of his eyes.

"—at least a fucking hour!"

"Hey!" shouted a Dalriadan. "Hey, that Molt of ours just jumped off the roof and run away!"

"So let him go," Gregg snarled. "Dole, get back to the *Halys*. Don't light her up, I don't want to lose the radio—"

It seemed he'd already lost the fucking radio, so far as everybody in the main party was concerned.

"—but be ready to go. Leave me your rifle! Stampfer, can that gun you cut loose still fire?"

"You bet!"

"Get down in the control room. Send your men off with Dole, they're no good now. Don't worry about the prisoners, the tape'll hold long enough. *Move*, everybody!"

Dole fired again toward the city. "Sir," he said, "I don't want to leave—"

A bullet struck the center of Gregg's breastplate. His chest went numb with the *whack*! The inside of both arms burned as though they'd been scraped with a saw blade.

"Get the *fuck* out, you whoreson!" Gregg screamed as he lurched to his feet. He fired into the night, without a conscious target. A figure flung its rifle away and fell from a second-story window. It was a Molt. It lay on the ground, its Federation trappings burning brightly enough to illuminate the body.

Everyone else had left the roof. Gregg ducked below the level of the windscreen, no protection but it blocked his opponents' view.

The dismounted plasma cannon was already pointed generally to the north. Gregg put his shoulder against the barrel and tried to slew it more nearly in line with the houses from which the rifle fire came. The gun wouldn't move. His boots slipped on the deck.

"*Dalriada* to Gregg!" the radio flopping against his side shrilled. The voice might have been Dulcie's, though it was an octave higher than Gregg had heard before from Dulcie's throat. "For God's sake save yourself! Mr. Ricimer's dead and—"

Two plasma cannon blasted from the center of town, backlighting rooftops like a strobe light. Even as the second blast rang out, thruster exhaust blanketed the RF spectrum.

Gregg's radio roared with static. He prodded at it with a finger, trying to find the power switch. The static pulsed as he switched bands uselessly instead. He smashed the unit with the edge of his hand, using his torso armor as the anvil to his rage. Fragments of thermoplastic and electronic components prickled his skin.

The *Dalriada* rose on a huge billow of plasma, shaking the world. A moment later, the *Peaches* followed, dancing like lint above an air vent because of the larger vessel's exhaust.

Gregg screamed in fury, backed a step, and kicked the twisted gun mount with his bootheel. Metal creaked. He pushed again at the barrel, planting his hands as close to the muzzle as he could to maximize his leverage. The massive weapon slid a millimeter, then jounced across the decking for half a meter before it locked up again. The edge of the muzzle scored a bright line in the concrete.

Gregg jumped into the stairway to the ready room and hunched there. "Go ahead, Stampfer!" he shouted. He didn't have time to close the armored door above him. He'd seen figures scuttling toward the fort out of the corner of his eye. "Shoot! Shoo—"

The plasma cannon fired. The bolt, the residue of a directed thermonuclear explosion, struck the deck at a flat angle and sprayed out over a 120° arc. The portion of windscreen in the blast's path vaporized; the shockwave blew the rest of it off the fort's roof, along with everything else smaller than the other cannon. The rifle and bandolier Dole left according to orders were gone forever.

Scattered backflare seared Gregg's hands even though he huddled below roof level and clasped them against his chest. The cannon recoiled hard, shearing the remaining mount and dumping the weapon itself over the lip of the building.

Stampfer stumbled out of the control citadel. He mouthed words, but Gregg couldn't hear them. Gregg waved the gunner ahead and climbed after him to the blast-scarred roof.

The line of thirty houses facing the fort was on fire, every one of them. Some were built of concrete, but the surge of ions had ignited their interiors as surely as those of houses built of less refractory materials.

For a moment Gregg thought he was still being shot at. No bullets sparked or whined around him. Rifle ammunition was cooking off in the blaze.

There were still three mounted plasma cannon. Gregg stared at them transfixed. *He could hold the fort himself while the Halys lifted the rest of his party to safety.*

Stampfer seized Gregg by the hand and rotated him so that they were face-to-face. The Dalriadan patted the nearest plasma cannon with his free hand.

"C'mon!" he said, speaking with exaggerated lip movements to make himself more comprehensible to his half-deafened commander. "These're fucked good by the backblast. The training gear's welded. Let's get out while we can!"

Stampfer jumped off the south side of the deck, keeping the fort's bulk between him and the burning city.

Gregg followed. When he threw his arms out to balance him, pain lancing across his pectoral muscles stopped the motion. He fell on his face and had to shuffle his knees forward to rise.

He began running, ten paces behind Stampfer. The vessel's side hatch was open, and the glow of her idling thrusters was a beacon to safety.

━39━

Sunrise

Dole waited poised at the controls while a gust of unusual violence even for Sunrise channeled between the hulls of the *Dalriada* and that of the metal-built ship lying parallel to her. The wind settled to 15 or 20 kph.

"There!" the *Halys*' bosun said as he shut the thrusters down with a flourish. "*That's* greasing her in!"

"I'll go see what I can learn about why we were abandoned on Umber that way," said Stephen Gregg in an expressionless voice. He reached for the hatch control.

"Sir?" Dole said, sharply enough to draw Gregg's attention back from its bleak reverie. "Ah—d'ye think you're going to need the flashgun you're carrying?"

Gregg stared at him. "That depends on what I learn," he said evenly.

"Right, right," said Dole as he rose from the console. "So wait for a minute while I get my gear on too, okay?"

Stampfer got up from the attitude controls. He laced his fingers together over his head and stretched them against the normal direction of the joints. "I guess we'll all go, sir," he said toward the bulkhead. "It was all our asses they left to swing in the breeze, wasn't it?"

"Too right," murmured Gallois, already half into his hard suit.

"Say," said another of the Dalriadans plaintively as he donned his armor, "does anybody know what that other ship's doing here with our two?"

"I don't know what it's doing," Gregg said as he waited for his men to equip themselves, "but I'm pretty sure what it is, is the *Adler*. They're Germans from United Europe."

He paused while he remembered Virginia. "The captain's a man named Schremp," he added. "I could have lived a good deal longer without seeing him again."

Dole had brought the *Halys* in between two ships lying within a hundred meters of one another. It was a form of bragging, proving how much better he could do than the *Halys*' AI.

It had also been dangerous, but Gregg felt too bloody-minded to care if misjudgment sent them crashing through the side of the *Dalriada*. Anyway, it was a short walk hatch-to-hatch in the brutal wind.

The ramp to the *Dalriada*'s forward hold dropped as soon as Gregg opened the *Halys*. He and his crew started toward the larger vessel. A single man waited for them in the hold. He raised his visor as they entered.

It was Piet Ricimer.

"Good Christ!" Gregg blurted. "Piet, I—Dulcie told me you were dead."

"Thanks to the goodness of Christ," Ricimer said, a reproof so gentle you had to know him well to recognize it, "nothing happened to me that rest and a great deal of blood plasma couldn't cure."

He glanced toward the ramp. "I'm going to close the hatch now," he said, reaching for the control. "You'd better step forward, Gallois."

Gregg embraced him. Their suits clashed together loudly.

"I thought you were, were lost too, Stephen," Ricimer murmured. "When I came to, I asked where you were. They said they were sure you'd lifted off of Umber, but you hadn't joined them on the run to Sunrise."

"Them bastards took off like scalded cats!" Dole snarled. "And us in a Federation pig that thinks it's a miracle to come within four zeros of her setting on a transit. Of *course* we were going to be a couple days behind, if the bastards didn't wait up on us!"

"I've got something to discuss with Captain Dulcie," Gregg said in a voice as pale as winter dawn. He clapped his friend on the back and moved toward the companionway to the bridge.

Ricimer stepped in front of him. "No, Stephen," he said. "I made the plans, I gave the orders. The fault was mine."

"You were unconscious!" Gregg shouted.

"I was responsible!" Ricimer shouted. They were chest-to-chest. "I *am* responsible, under God, for the future success of this voyage. Me!"

Both men eased back by half-steps. They were breathing hard. "Stephen," Ricimer said softly. "What's done is done. It's the future that counts. Those mistakes won't happen again."

Gregg smiled savagely. "So, it's forgive and forget, is that it, Piet?" he said.

"No, Stephen," Ricimer said. "Just forgive." He wet his lips with his tongue. "It was good enough for our Lord, after all."

Gregg laughed. He turned to his crew. "How do you men feel about that?" he asked mildly.

Men shrugged within their hard suits. "Whatever you say, sir," Stampfer said.

Gregg put his flashgun muzzle-down on the deck. "What I say," he said, "is that we all swore an oath to obey Captain Ricimer when we signed on for this voyage. So I guess we'd better do that."

He grinned lopsidedly at his friend.

Ricimer unlatched his hard suit. "We can leave all the gear here," he said. "I'll be going back aboard the *Peaches* after the meeting myself."

"Meeting?" Gregg repeated as he began to strip off his armor also.

"Yes," Ricimer said. "You're just in time for it. Captain Schremp has a crewman who was aboard the *Tolliver* when we refitted here on the previous voyage. As a result he located us, and he wants us to join forces with him on the next stage of our operations . . ."

━40━

Sunrise

A dozen members of the *Dalriada* crew bent over equipment in the compartment adjoining the bridge and captain's suite. They weren't precisely lurking; even after the casualties on Umber, space aboard the 70-tonne vessel was tight. There was no question that the men's nervous attention was directed toward the meeting in the next chamber.

Besides the Dalriadans, three metal hard suits stood in pools of condensate. One of the suits was silvered, and the rifle slung from it was the ornate, pump-action repeater Gregg had seen Captain Schremp carrying.

Ricimer led Gregg onto the bridge. The ten men already there crowded it. Only Wassail among the *Dalriada*'s officers would meet Gregg's cold eyes, but the Germans nodded to the newcomers.

To Gregg's surprise, Schremp clearly recognized him. Of course, Gregg hadn't forgotten Captain Schremp . . .

"Rondelet," the German captain boomed before Ricimer had seated himself again at the head of the chart table. "There's a hundred occupied islands with Fed ships at a score of them at any given time. None of them are defended to the degree that'll be a problem to you and me together."

He waved a hairy, powerful hand. "Umber was suicide. You were lucky to get out of it as well as you did, Ricimer."

"Umber might not have been such a problem," said Stephen Gregg from where he stood by the hatch, "except some idiot had botched a raid two weeks before and roused the whole region."

One of the Germans muttered a curse and started to get up from his chair. Schremp waved him down with a curt gesture

198

and said, "We needed a featherboat on Umber, that is so. On Rondelet your featherboat comes in low, eliminates the defense battery, and the larger ships drop down and finish the job. Together, it's easy."

"Our raid on Umber wasn't such a failure as it may have appeared to outsiders," Ricimer said coolly. "I've reviewed the pilotry data we gathered there, and it's clear that the Federation holds Rondelet in considerable strength. Each of the magnates there has an armed airship of his own . . . and as you've pointed out, Captain Schremp, there are more than a hundred of these individual fiefdoms."

"They're spread out," insisted one of Schremp's henchmen, a squat fellow with blond hair on his head but a full red beard. "We pick an island where a ship is loading, strip the place, and we're gone before the neighbors wake up."

"Or," Ricimer said, "we're a few seconds late in lifting off, and there's a score of airships circling the island, waiting to put plasma bolts into our thrusters when we're a thousand meters up. I think not."

Schremp's hands clenched on the chart table. He deliberately opened them and forced his face into a smile. "Come now, Captain Ricimer," he said in a falsely jocular tone. "There are always risks, of course, but these Principals as they call themselves—they live like kings on their little islands, yes, but they don't have armies. A dozen or so armed Molts for show, that is all. *They* won't fight."

"My late brother," Ricimer said with a perfect absence of emotion, "was saying something very similar when a Molt killed him."

Gregg's face went as blank as his friend's. *He'd wondered why Adrien wasn't present* . . . He reached over, regardless of the others, and squeezed Ricimer's shoulder.

"The Earth Convoy will top off and refit on Rondelet on its way to Umber," Wassail put in. He'd obviously studied and understood the data lifted from Umber's Commandatura also. "It's due anytime now."

"All right," snarled the blond German, "what do you propose we do? Calisthenics on the beautiful beaches outside and then go home?"

"No, Mr. Groener," Ricimer said. "My men and I are going to Benison. What your party does is of course your own affair."

"Benison?" Schremp cried. "Benison! There's nothing but

local trade there. *Food* ships to Rondelet and Umber. Where's the profit there?"

"A ship itself is worth something," said Dulcie, "when you pay for it at the point of a gun." The *Dalriada*'s captain had brightened noticeably when Ricimer said they weren't going to attack another well-defended target.

Schremp stood up. His right fist pumped three times, ending each stroke millimeters above the tabletop. "Are you all cowards?" he demanded. "Did you all have your balls shot off on Umber, is that it?"

He turned and pointed at Gregg. "You, Mr. Gregg," he said. "Will you come with me? *You're* not a coward."

Gregg had been leaning against the hatchway. He rocked himself fully upright by flexing his shoulders. "My enemies have generally come to that conclusion, Captain," he said. "Neither am I a deserter, or a fool."

Schremp didn't flinch at Gregg's tone, but Dulcie stared at his hands in horror.

"So be it!" Schremp said. Everyone in the room was standing. "You will not help us, so we will help ourselves."

He led his entourage off the bridge, bumping between chairs and Venerians pressed against the bulkhead. At the hatch Schremp turned and said, "Captain Ricimer, for your further endeavors, I wish you even better fortune than you had on Umber!"

Gregg closed the hatch behind the Germans. They would be several minutes in the next compartment donning their hard suits—unless they were angry enough to face Sunrise weather unprotected as they returned to the *Adler*.

The Venerians looked at one another, visibly relaxing. "Well," said Dulcie, breaking the silence, "I think picking up the local trade on Benison is far the best idea."

Ricimer gave him a lopsided smile. "Oh," he said, "that isn't my plan at all, Captain Dulcie. Though we *are* going to Benison."

—41—

Benison

Lightbody would be watching the panel, but Gregg had set the sonic scanner to provide an audio signal before he let himself doze off in the featherboat's bay. The *peep-peep-peep* of the alarm wakened him instantly, even though when he came alert the tiny sound was lost in the shriek of a saw fifty meters away cutting into the frame of the *Halys*.

Lightbody, bending down to arouse Gregg, seemed surprised he was already up. "Somebody's coming from the east, sir," he whispered. "I think it must be the captain coming back."

"I think so too," Gregg said. He checked the satchel of reloads, aimed his flashgun, and then tested his faceshield's detents to be sure that it would snap closed easily if he needed the protection. Daylight through the foliage had a soft, golden tinge.

The saw stopped. Somebody cheered in satisfaction. The men were treating their work as if it were a normal shipwright's task, ignoring the fact they were on a hostile planet. Realistically, there was no silent way to remove a thruster and the transit system from a ship built as a single module; besides, five hundred meters of the dense forest would drink the noise anyway. The comfortable, even carefree manner of the men under his temporary command irritated Gregg nonetheless.

"I'm coming in," called Piet Ricimer. He was out of sight, to prevent a nervous bullet or laser bolt. "I'm alone, and I'm coming in."

"Thank God for that!" Gregg said. He jumped down and met his friend ten meters from the *Peaches*. They shook, left hand to left hand, because Gregg held the flashgun to his side on its muzzle-forward patrol sling.

"Where's Guillermo?" Gregg asked.

"With K'Jax and his, well, Clan Deel," Ricimer explained as they walked back to the featherboat. "There's fifty or sixty of them coming. I came on ahead."

"We need that many?" Gregg said.

"For portage," his friend replied. "I don't want more than one trip through the Mirror. I'll only need a few of our people, humans; specialists. Ah, I want you to remain in charge of the base party and the vessels."

They'd reached the *Peaches*. Men without specific tasks—and Dulcie, who was supposed to be overseeing work on the *Halys*—strode toward their commander along the paths trampled to mud beneath the trees.

"I want to be able to flap my arms and fly," said Gregg evenly. "That's not going to happen either."

"We've got the AI dismounted and we're almost done sectioning it for carriage, Captain Ricimer," Dulcie boomed with enthusiasm. "And the powerplant, thrusters and plumbing, that's already complete. The ship's pretty well junked, though."

Ricimer nodded absently to him. "The *Halys* wasn't a great deal to begin with," he said. "But she'll do. Stephen—"

Gregg shook his head. "There was work to be done here," he said. "Fine, I stayed while you went off to find the Molts. I'd sooner have gone, but I understood the need."

"And—" began Ricimer.

"Now," Gregg continued forcefully, "the operation's on the other side of the Mirror, and there's nothing to do here but wait. I'm sure Captain Dulcie can wait just as well as I could."

He nodded pleasantly at the *Dalriada*'s captain. Dulcie blinked, suspicious that he was being insulted but relieved at the implication that he wouldn't be expected to take a front rank in the coming raid. "Well, I'm sure you can depend on me to do my duty, gentlemen," he said.

"An autogyro patrolling the fields came close enough we could hear it," Gregg said. "The camouflage net over the *Dalriada* did the job. That's the *only* threat in the past three days. Don't tell me you're not going to need a shooter worse on mirrorside. Because if you do, I'll call you a liar, Piet."

Ricimer shook his head. "Well," he said, "we can't have that. I think six of the men will be sufficient. How did those with you aboard the *Halys* work out, Stephen?"

"None of them were problems," Gregg said without hesitation. "Dole and Stampfer I'd take with me anywhere."

"Then we'll take them on this operation," Ricimer said. He smiled. "I'm not sure they'll find it so great an honor after they've had personal experience with the Mirror."

Ricimer's face hardened. "I'll inspect the supplies and equipment for the operation now," he added crisply. "If possible, I'd like to leave as soon as Guillermo gets here with our allies."

"I've got them," Gregg called up to the Molt invisible in the treetop as the wicker basket wobbled down into his arms.

Gregg transferred handfuls of recharged batteries from the basket to an empty satchel, then replaced them with another dozen that had been run flat with the tree cutting and shaping. The bark-fiber rope was looped around the basket handle and spliced instead of simply being tied off. Otherwise it would have been simpler to trade baskets rather than empty and refill the one.

"Ready to go!" he called. He stepped back as the Molt hoisted away.

The solar collector had to be above the foliage to work. It was easier to lift batteries up to the collector than it would have been to haul fifty meters of electrical cable through the Mirror so that the rest of the charging system could be at ground level.

"And so, I think, are we, Stephen," Piet Ricimer said, shocking Gregg as he turned without realizing his friend had walked over to him as he stared up into the tree.

"Ready?" Gregg said in surprise. He looked toward the starship in the center of the circle that had been cleared to provide the vessel's framework.

The portable kiln still chugged like a cat preparing to vomit, grinding, heating, and spraying out the sand and rock dumped into its feed hopper. The routine of work over the past week had been so unchanging that Gregg was subconsciously convinced it would never change.

"Lightbody and Stampfer are clearing the kiln," Ricimer said. He smiled wanly. "My father would never forgive me if I put up a kiln with the output lines full of glass. That can cause backflow through the feed chute the next time you use the equipment."

Side by side, the two officers walked toward the ship, which was possibly the ugliest human artifact Stephen Gregg had ever seen in his life. He was about to entrust his life to her.

The crewmen waited expectantly. The Molts who aided them when possible—Venerian ceramic technology belonged to the post-Collapse era, so it was not genetically coded into the aliens' cells—were ready to begin loading the ship with the piled equipment and supplies, but no one had given the order to begin.

"Gentlemen," Piet Ricimer said loudly. Everyone's attention was on him already.

The ship was a framework of wooden beams, covered with planks sawn from the neighboring forest with cutting bars. She was less than twenty meters long.

"We're men of action, not ceremony," Ricimer continued. "Nonetheless, I thought we should pause for a moment, to pray and to name the vessel we have built."

The rough-hewn planks were sealed and friction-proofed with a ceramic coating applied by one of the portable kilns the expedition carried to make repairs. It was the largest item the Molts had had to carry through the Mirror. Gregg couldn't imagine how K'Jax, who took the load himself, had managed.

"I considered calling our ship the *Avenger*," Ricimer said. His voice, strong from the beginning, grew firmer and clearer yet. Gregg recalled Piet mentioning that his father was a lay preacher. "But vengeance is for the Lord. Our eyes must be on the benefit to all men that will occur when our profit leads our fellows to join in breaking the Federation monopoly."

They'd installed the artificial intelligence and transit apparatus from the *Halys* in the flimsy wooden vessel. By comparison with this construction, the shoddy Federation prize was a marvel of strength and craftsmanship.

"And I thought of naming her the *Biruta*," Piet continued. "It was on Biruta that the treachery of the Federation authorities proved to us all that the Federation had to be fought and defeated if men were to live as God wills among the stars. But Biruta was the past, and we must view the future."

For power and direction, they had a single thruster from the *Halys*, gimballed with ceramic bearings held in hardwood journals. If anyone but Piet Ricimer had offered to take off in such a contraption, Gregg would have made sure to be out of the probable impact zone. Instead, he would be aboard her.

"The future is Umber—the unprotected mirrorside where Pleyal's henchmen store the chips that will launch a hundred further vessels when we return laden with them," Ricimer said. "Therefore, under God, I name this ship the *Umber*. May she bear us to triumph!"

The tanks of reaction mass were wood partitions sealed with glass, much like the hull itself. Air was a greater problem. They couldn't build high-pressure tanks, so the crew would have to breathe from bottles attached to their hard suits for the entire voyage. They were taking along all the expedition's containers. At best, it would be very close.

"Friends and allies," Ricimer concluded. "Friends! Let us pray."

He bowed his head.

God help us all, thought Stephen Gregg.

━42━

Mirrorside, near Umber

The *Umber* trembled in the atmosphere like a bubble deforming in a breeze. Umber's tawny planetary disk shuddered past in the viewscreen. There was no sign that the ship was descending.

Guillermo was in what appeared to be a state of suspended animation. Gregg hadn't realized that Molts could slow their metabolism at will. For Guillermo, the entire voyage would be a blank filled with whatever dreams Molts dream.

For the humans aboard the *Umber*, the voyage was a living Hell.

"Get on with it!" Coye whimpered. "For God's own sake, set her *down*!"

Lightbody snicked open a knife and put the point of its ceramic blade to the throat of his fellow crewman. "Blaspheme again," he said in a voice husky with tension and pain, "and it won't matter to you if we never touch down!"

Gregg knocked up Lightbody's hand with the toe of his boot. Dole was lurching upright with his rifle reversed to club the butt. Gregg caught the bosun's eye; Dole forced a grin and sat down again.

The *Umber* bucked harder than usual. Gregg lost his feet but managed to sit with a suggestion of control by letting his hand slide down one of the poles cross-bracing the interior. He wanted to stand up; he *would* stand up. But not for a moment yet.

Ricimer bent over the control console, hunched forward from the wicker back of his chair—the *Umber*'s sole piece of cabin furniture. Piet had to balance thrust, the slight reaction mass remaining in the tanks, and the vessel's wooden frame. At a slight excess of atmospheric braking, the hull would flex and the ceramic coating would scale off like bits of shell from a hard-boiled egg.

If the *Umber* wasn't opened to a breathable atmosphere soon, everybody aboard her was going to die from lack of oxygen.

"Oh, God," Coye moaned. He raised his air bottle to his mouth and squeezed the release vainly again. He hurled the empty container away from him. It hit Stampfer. The gunner either ignored it or didn't feel the impact.

The *Umber* tracked across the planetary surface in a reciprocal of her previous direction. Gregg hadn't felt a transition, but they had reversed at the Mirror.

The ship had slowed. The ragged settlement looked larger as it passed through the viewscreen.

Gregg stood up. His head hammered as though each pulse threatened to burst it wide open. He wanted desperately to sip air from the bottle. Instead he walked over to Coye, ducking under a brace that was in the way.

Gregg put the bottle to the crewman's lips. Coye tried to trigger the release himself. Gregg slapped away Coye's greedy hand and gave him a measured shot of air.

It was the hardest act that Gregg remembered ever having performed.

Filters scrubbed CO_2 from the jerry-built vessel's atmosphere, but that did nothing to replenish the converted oxygen. Rather than release the contents of the air bottles directly into the ship's interior, Gregg doled them out on a schedule to the individual crewmen. Human lungs absorbed only a small percentage of the oxygen in a breath, so the exhaled volume increased the breathability of the cabin air.

To a degree.

Everyone was on his last bottle. Most of them had finished theirs. It was going to be very close.

Piet Ricimer adjusted the fuel feed and thruster angle. Gregg swayed forward from deceleration. Through the cross brace, he felt the *Umber* creak with strain.

He wondered if the ship was going to disintegrate so close to their goal. Part of his mind noted that if impact with the atmosphere converted his body to flaked meat, the pain in his head would stop.

Very deliberately, he took a swig from his air bottle. The feeling of cold as gas expanded against his tongue eased his pain somewhat, even before the whiff of oxygen could diffuse into his blood . . . but the bottle emptied before his finger released the trigger.

Umber's natural surface was too uniform for Gregg to be able to judge their velocity against it. When the Federation settlement came in sight again, it was clear that Piet now had the wooden vessel in controlled flight rather than a braking orbit.

Umber City on the planet's realside wasn't prepossessing. The community here on the mirrorside was a dingy slum.

Two small freighters sat on the exhaust-fused landing field. They resembled the *Halys*; like her, they had been built in the Reaches, very possibly in the yards on Benison. Memory of the prize he had so recently commanded made Gregg dizzy from recalled luxury: the ability to fill his lungs without feeling he was being suffocated with a pillow.

There were six human-built structures. Four of them were large enough to be warehouses, constructed of sheet metal. A smaller metal building stood between the larger pairs, at the head of the tramline crossing the Mirror.

A large circular tank formed the center of the landing field. Like the similar structures on realside, it held reaction mass for the ships that landed here. Dedicated tankers shuttled back and forth between Umber and the nearest water world, replenishing the reservoir. The local groundwater was barely sufficient for drinking purposes.

A small barracks and an individual dwelling built of concrete each had a peaked metal roof while all the other structures were flat. There was no need of roof slope in a climate as dry as Umber's; someone had decided on the design for esthetic reasons, probably to differentiate human habitations from those of the alien slaves.

The Molt dwellings looked like a junkyard or, at best, a series of metal-roofed anthills. Walls of sandbags woven from scrap cloth supported sheet-metal plates. Loose sand was heaped onto the plates to anchor them against the wind.

On Punta Verde and among K'Jax' folk on Benison, Molts adapted their buildings to varied sorts of locally available raw materials. Gregg was sure that they would have occupied a neat community on Umber's mirrorside, if their human masters had allowed them basics. The sand could be stabilized by cement powder, heat-setting plastic with a simple applicator, or portable kilns of the sort any modest Venerian spaceship carried—and would trade away for a handful of microchips.

The Federation administrators weren't saving money by condemning the aliens to this squalor: they were making a political statement. Duty on the mirrorside of Umber was worse than a prison sentence for the humans involved. They felt a need to prove they were better than somebody else.

It was, in its way, a rare example of the Feds treating Molts as something other than objects. The Molts became persons for the purpose of being discriminated against.

"There . . ." Ricimer murmured. He eased back a millimeter the fuel feed. The image advancing on the viewscreen slowed still further, then began to expand. The *Umber* dropped against the pilot's precisely-measured thrust. The landing field was directly beneath the vessel.

Gregg turned from the viewscreen to the hatch. He stared at it for some seconds before the oxygen-starved higher levels of his mind responded to what his lizard brain was trying to tell him. He staggered across the bay, avoiding the frame members but tripping on Jeude's sprawled feet on the way.

The hatch was a half meter across. They'd had to bring large fittings into the *Umber* before the hull was sealed. The wooden edges of the hatch and jamb were beveled to mate under internal pressure. They were ceramic-coated and smeared with the milky, resilient sap of a mirrorside climbing vine immediately before the ship was closed for liftoff.

The square panel was wedged closed on the inside. Gregg grabbed the handle of one wedge and strained against it. It didn't move. He grunted in frustration.

"The other way, sir!" Jeude croaked. "You're pushing it home."

That's exactly what he was doing.

Dole had gotten cautiously to his feet, but he swayed where he stood. It was hard to imagine that in the recent past the crew had enough energy to fight.

Gregg didn't need help, now that Jeude had oriented him. The closures were paired, one on each of the four surfaces. Stampfer knocked them home with a mallet on Benison. Gregg used his left hand on the forward handle to anchor his pull on the wedge opposite. The right side gave, the top gave—

He switched the power grip to his left hand, because his right fingers were bleeding from pressure cuts. The forward closure pulled out. Gregg lost his balance with it and fell backward.

Dole, Jeude, and Lightbody reached over him, grabbed the hatch crossbar, and tugged inward with their combined strength. Though the bottom wedge was still in place, the hatch jumped from its jamb and tilted inward.

The air that blasted past it was dusty and tinged with ions from the thruster's exhaust. Its touch was as close to heaven as Gregg expected ever to know.

"Coming in!" said Piet Ricimer, his voice high-pitched and trembling with relief.

The *Umber* grounded in a controlled crash and immediately rolled onto her portside. She'd been launched from a cradle. Hydraulically-extended landing legs to stabilize the craft on the ground were out of the question, and fixed outriggers would have put too much strain on the hull during atmospheric braking.

The hatch was nearly overhead. Gregg stepped to a cross brace—he was still too logy to jump—and thrust his flashgun through the opening. Ricimer stroked Guillermo awake. The Molt was strapped to what now was the starboard bulkhead.

"Follow me!" Gregg cried as he crawled through the hatch. His battery satchel, slung at hip level, caught on the jamb. A crewman below gave Gregg a boost. He slid down the hull and hit Umber's mirrorside on his shoulder and chest.

He didn't care. He was breathing in deep lungfuls of air, and it would be a long time before any injuries outweighed the pleasure of that feeling.

A pair of Molts stared at the *Umber* from the open door of the warehouse two hundred meters away. Other Molts clustered near the tramhead, apparently intent on their own thoughts. Gregg didn't see any humans.

He glanced over his shoulder. Dole had squirmed through the hatch with a repeater held high to keep it from knocking the hull as he dropped to the ground. Gregg reached up to help control the bosun's fall.

The *Umber* herself was in amazingly good condition. The ceramic coating had flaked away in patches from her underside when she scraped onto the landing field, but the rest of the hull appeared intact. She could be made to fly with a little effort.

It would take much greater effort to convince any of the present complement to crew her again, though.

Piet Ricimer was the third man out. He must have used his rank to press ahead of the other men. Gregg and Dole together caught him as he slid down.

"Let's go," Ricimer said as he unslung his rifle. He grinned. Guillermo hopped easily to the ground beside them. "Since we don't have a battalion to back us up, I think we'd best depend on speed."

The four of them spread into a loose skirmish line as they moved toward the tramhead. Jeude climbed through the hatch, jumped to the ground, and fell. He brushed off his rifle's receiver as he jogged to a place between Dole and Ricimer.

The warehouses were on the left, with the Molt hovels straggling against the Mirror beyond. Gregg took the right side of the Venerian formation, toward the barracks and house. None of Umber's structures seemed to have windows. The doors to the residences were on the far side.

The wind blew hard enough to sting sand against Gregg's bare hands, but it didn't raise a pall the way the storm had during the assault on realside. At least the weather was cooperating. He really wished there'd been time to don his body armor, but there wasn't. Suits for the whole crew were stored in the *Umber*, but removing them would mean dismantling the ship.

Lightbody joined them. Gregg looked back. Stampfer was climbing through the hatch. All the men carried rifles. Besides a cutting bar, Guillermo wore a holstered pistol, but Gregg wasn't sure how serious a weapon it was meant to be.

The Molts at the tramhead watched the Venerians. Many of them turned only their heads, giving the crowd an uncanny resemblance to an array of mechanical toys.

The line reached the buildings. The Molts in the warehouse doorway had moved only their heads to track the Venerians. Ricimer turned and gestured toward Coye, running to catch up with them. "Coye!" he called, aided by the breeze. "Watch that pair!"

Gregg stepped smoothly around the corner of the barracks, the nearer of the two buildings on his end, and presented his laser. The doors in the middle of both buildings were closed tightly against the windblown sand. There were no windows on this side either.

Nothing to see, and no one to impress by pomp.

"Who is in charge here?" Ricimer called to the Molts at the tramhead.

None of them reacted until Guillermo chittered something in his own speech. One of the Molts said in English, "Our supervisors have gone across the Mirror for the celebration. Who are you?"

Guillermo continued to talk in quick, clattering vocables. The local Molts moved, slight shifts of position that relieved the Venerians' tension at the abnormal stillness of a moment before. Ricimer approached the group. His men hung back by a step or a half-step each, so that the line of humans became a shallow vee. None of the aliens was armed or appeared hostile.

Guillermo turned to Ricimer and explained, "The Earth Convoy has arrived on the realside. There will be a party in Umber City. The humans from here have crossed the Mirror to join it."

"Most of the humans," said the Molt who had spoken before. He wore a sash of office, gray from a distance but grease-smeared white when Gregg saw it closer. "Under-clerk Elkinghorn is—there she is."

The Molt pointed. Gregg was already turning. The barracks door had opened. The woman who'd started toward the tramhead had failed to latch it properly behind her: as Gregg watched, the door blew open again, then slammed with a bang deadened by the adverse wind.

"Hey!" she called. She wore uniform trousers and tunic, but she had on house slippers rather than boots. "Hey! Who are you?"

"Hold it right where you are!" Dole shouted as he aimed his rifle.

"Don't!" Piet Ricimer cried. "Don't shoot!"

The woman turned and ran back toward the door from which she'd come. A bottle flew out of the pocket of her tunic and broke on the ground. It was half full of amber liquor.

Elkinghorn was ten meters away. Gregg aimed. He was coldly furious with himself for not having continued to watch the residence buildings.

"Stephen!" Ricimer called. "Don't shoot her!"

Elkinghorn threw open the door. Gregg fired past her head, into the partition wall opposite.

Elkinghorn flung herself backward, onto the ground. The laser bolt converted paint and insulation to blazing gas. It blew the door shut and bulged the sides of the barracks.

"I think," said Gregg as he clicked a fresh battery into his flashgun, "that she'll be in a mood to answer our questions now."

Umber

"Not a thing!" Jeude snarled as he stamped into the secretary's residence. "Not a *damned* thing."

"There's food," said Stampfer, closing the outer door behind himself and his partner in searching the nearer warehouse. The gunner sucked on a hard-cored fruit so lush that juice dripped into his beard. With his free hand, he pulled another fruit from his bulging pocket. He offered it to Ricimer, Gregg, and the Fed captive promiscuously. "Want one?"

Gregg shook his head at Stampfer and said to Jeude, "Maybe Dole and Coye had better luck."

"It's not up to date," Elkinghorn said miserably from the outpost's central computer. "I know it shows twelve cases of Class A chips here, but as God is my witness, they've all been trucked across. All of them."

She squeezed her forehead with her right hand, then resumed advancing the manifest with the light pen in her left, master, hand. She was trembling badly.

Ricimer had refused to give the prisoner more liquor. She'd been drinking herself comatose in irritation at being left behind, "in charge", while the rest of the outpost's complement crossed to Umber City for the celebration. The laser bolt had shocked her sober, but she wasn't happy about the fact.

"That other warehouse, Dole's looking, but it's not going to do a bit of good," Jeude replied. "Supplies, machinery—trade goods for other colonies on the mirrorside, that's all there is."

Stampfer dropped his pit on the coarse rug. He began eating the fruit in his left hand.

Lightbody came in the door, carrying his cutting bar in his hand. "I got through the sidewall of the barracks," he announced, "but it wasn't any good. You torched her right and proper, sir."

He nodded to Gregg. "Fully involved. *Zip*, I cut through the wall, and *boom*, the roof lifts off because air got to the inside that had about smothered itself out."

Gregg shrugged sheepishly. "I thought she might have a gun inside," he said.

"There's no guns here," the prisoner said. "There's nothing but Christ-bitten *desert* here, so what's to shoot?"

Anger raised her blood pressure. She dropped the light pen and pressed both hands to her temples. "Oh, God, I need a drink so bad," she groaned.

Ricimer stood. "Tie her," he said to Lightbody. At the tramhead, the Venerians had found a coil of rope woven somewhere on mirrorside. The Molt laborers said they used it to bind bulky loads onto the cars. "And give her a drink, if there is one."

Jeude shrugged and took a bottle out of his sabretache.

The door opened and banged closed again. Dole and Coye came into the office with a drift of sand despite the near airlock.

"It's all outgoing stuff, sir," the bosun said, echoing Jeude of a moment before. "There's not a chip in the settlement."

He noticed the office console and pointed his breechloader at it. "Besides whatever's in that unit, I guess."

Ricimer looked at his men. Greg winced mentally to see his friend's haggard face. While the rest of them simply tried not to scream during the slow suffocation of the *Umber*'s approach, Piet brought the jerry-built vessel down softly by the standards of a manual landing on a proper ship.

"We've gotten here too late to find the chips I'd hoped," he said quietly. "Over the past week, the stockpile was taken across the Mirror in anticipation of the Earth Convoy's arrival."

He licked his lips, chapped by sand blown on the dry wind. "The chips haven't vanished. With the celebration going on, officials of Umber City and the convoy won't have had time to complete loading the ships. They may not even have started yet."

Ricimer's voice grew louder, stronger. Gregg grinned coldly to see gray tension vanish from his friend's face and his eyes brighten again.

"To get the chips, we would have to cross the Mirror again," he said. "To return to Umber City. You all know the risks. You all know—"

His voice would have filled a room of ten times the volume of this office.

"—that I failed before, that many of our f-friends and loved ones were killed because of my miscalculation. The risks are even greater now, because the convoy and all its personnel will be in Umber City."

"Hey, it's not that dangerous," Jeude protested. "The Feds won't be expecting us this direction, right?"

Ricimer's head rotated like a lathe turret. "They didn't *expect* us before," he said harshly to Jeude. "That didn't prevent them from reacting effectively."

He scanned his assembled men. "Guillermo tells me the labor force here will help us, run the trams the way they do for their masters. He's organizing that now. In exchange, we will take every *slave* off this planet. We can't return them to their home planets, but they'll be able to live free on Benison with K'Jax."

"Gonna be tight . . ." Dole muttered. Catching himself, he added quickly, "Not that we're not used to it. No problem."

Free with K'Jax, Gregg thought. He was willing to grant that Molts were "human", whatever that meant. He hadn't seen anything to suggest they were saints, though; or that K'Jax would be considered a particularly benevolent leader of *any* race.

"I won't order you men to go to Umber City again with me," Ricimer went on fiercely. "I won't think the less of anyone who wants to stay. But I'm going across, and with the help of God I hope this time to succeed."

Stampfer dropped the second fruit pit on the floor. "I haven't come all this way to go home poor," he said.

Yeah/Sure/Count me in from the remainder of the crew.

Gregg said nothing. He was smiling slightly, and his eyes were light-years distant.

"Stephen?" Piet Ricimer said.

Gregg shook himself to wakefulness. "If the Earth Convoy's in, then so is Administrator Carstensen," he said in a trembling, gentle voice. "I'd like to meet him and discuss Biruta. For a time."

Coye, who hadn't been around Stephen Gregg as long as some of the others, swore softly and turned away from the expression on the young gentleman's face.

Umber

The tramcars were constructed of wire netting on light metal frames. Each car's weight and that of the Molt pushing it had to be subtracted from the potential payload.

Gregg eyed a car dubiously. "A motor wouldn't weigh as much as a, a person," he said. "If you've got tracks through the Mirror, then they'll guide the car whether or not there's somebody behind it pushing."

"Motors will not work in the Mirror," said the Molt leader. Her name was Ch'Kan.

"Electric motors?" Ricimer asked.

"Diesel, electric—even flywheels," Ch'Kan said. "None of them work in the Mirror."

She clicked her mandibles to indicate some emotion or other. "We work in the Mirror. Until we die."

The tracks ran from the warehouses to the lambent surface of the Mirror. The rails were solid and spiked deep into the surface of Umber for as far as the eye could follow them. Beyond the transition zone, the rails were laid with short gaps between ends. They weren't attached because there was no ground within the Mirror, merely a level which objects could not penetrate.

The Molts said that sometimes cars tilted off the rails. The slave pushing the vehicle could usually find his way to one end of the tramway or the other by following the tracks.

If he or she abandoned the load within the Mirror, the Federation supervisors whipped the creature to death for sabotage.

Ricimer clambered into a tramcar. It creaked under his weight.

"I'd better go in the first one," Gregg said. He climbed into a car in a siding beside his friend's. The main line split to

217

serve both warehouses, and there were a dozen lay-bys on each branch to allow cars to pass and be sorted.

The Feds had left a dozen Molts on mirrorside for routine tasks. Most of the labor force had crossed with their masters to handle cargo for and from the Earth Convoy. Their heads rotated from one human officer to the other, waiting for clear directions. The Venerian crewmen watched in silence also.

"I'll lead, Stephen," Ricimer said with a touch of iron in his voice. The sun had set. Pole-mounted lights at the tramhead threw vertical shadows down across his face.

Gregg smiled and shook his head. "When you get a flashgun," he said, "and learn to use it the way I can use this one—"

He nodded his weapon's muzzle in the air. He handled the flashgun as easily as another man might have waved a pistol.

"Then you can lead. For now, we need as much firepower up front as we can get. And that's me, Piet—not so?"

Ricimer shrugged tightly. "Go ahead, then," he said.

The crewmen got into cars like those of their leaders. Stampfer's almost upset from a combination of his short legs and weight, but two Molts balanced the vehicle for him.

The Molt leader threw a switch lever, then stepped around behind Gregg's car and began to push it forward. He heard the wheels squeaking, a loud pulse at the end of each full turn. Gregg concentrated on that so completely that he barely started to tremble by the moment his face gleamed at him and the terrible cold turned his soul inside out.

Only the cold. Utterly the cold.

The car wheels clacked at the gaps between rails. If Gregg could have counted the jolts, he would have known the length of the trip. The tracks were no longer straight, though. They curved, and the rails were seconds clicking on a circular dial that would take him back to zero before starting again.

Only the cold.

The change was sudden and much sooner than Gregg expected. Time and space within the Mirror were not constants. However the temporal or spatial distance between realside and mirrorside was measured, it was shorter on Umber than had been the case on Benison.

The tramcar plunged Gregg into the sidereal universe. The shock was like a bath in magma. Floodlights overhead and the fireworks streaking the sky toward the center of Umber City merged with the patterns of frozen color which Gregg's optic nerves fired to his brain in the frozen emptiness.

Gregg gasped and threw himself sideways. The tramcar tipped over, as he intended. He wasn't sure he had enough motor control to climb out of the car normally.

He had to get clear of its confinement *now*.

Gregg hadn't been within a klick of the realside tramhead during the raid on Umber City, and Piet's fainting recollections of shots and chaos were of limited help for visualizing the place. Gregg hit the stone pavement, pointing his flashgun and trying to look in all directions at once.

The blockhouse was set three meters forward of the Mirror to provide space for the tracks to split and curve right and left of the building. Instead of individual switched sidings, the architect who laid out the tramway on realside used these two fifty-meter tails of trackway to store empties. At the moment, the lengths of track were nearly full of cars.

Rather than a wall, the rear face of the blockhouse was protected by a grille that was now rolled up to the roofline. The building's interior was stacked with rough wooden cases whose volume ranged from a quarter cubic meter down to half that size. There was a narrow passageway to the open door in the front wall, but Gregg couldn't tell if the loopholes to either side were blocked.

Cases of more irregular size were stacked to either side of the blockhouse. There were others between it and the bollards which formed a deadline separating the stored valuables and Umber City. Twenty or more Molts, singly or in pairs, poised to lift containers.

The diesel trucks that would normally have transported cargo to the landing field were burnt skeletons in front of the bollards. They'd been dragged out of the immediate way but not removed from where the defenders' own fire had destroyed them during the previous raid.

A human cradling a double-barreled shotgun oversaw the gang of Molt porters. Another human stood beside the back corner of the blockhouse, watching aliens work. A radio hung from the second man's belt. His weapon, a brightly decorated rifle, leaned against the wall beside him.

The shock of hitting the ground broke Gregg's mind free of the frozen constraints that bound it until that moment. The clatter as his tram toppled drew the eyes of Molts and human officials together. One of Gregg's trouser legs was caught in the wire mesh.

"*Don't move!*" he shouted. The short trip through the Mirror hadn't numbed him, but it sharpened his voice to an edge of hysteria more disquieting than the fat muzzle of his laser.

The man by the blockhouse stiffened as though he'd been given a jolt of electricity. His hip bumped the ornate rifle and knocked it down. As it rattled away from him, he threw both hands in front of his face and screamed, "Lord Jesus Christ preserve me!"

Ch'Kan called to her fellows in a sequence of liquid trills. A second car squealed out of the transition behind Gregg, but his attention had focused down on the man with the shotgun. Everything beyond the Fed's face and torso vanished behind a mental curtain as gray as a sight ring.

The fellow's uniform was white with blue epaulets instead of the yellow of Federation ground personnel. He was big, almost as tall as Gregg and much bulkier. The short-barreled weapon in his hands looked like a child's toy. His teeth were bared in a snarl in the midst of his neatly-cropped beard and moustache, and he spun to bring the shotgun to bear.

To Gregg's adrenaline-speeded senses, the Fed was turning in slow motion. Gregg felt his trigger reach its release point beneath the pad of his index finger.

The target, bathed in vivid coherent light, flipped optically into the photographic negative of a human being. The Fed's shout turned into an elephantine grunt as all the air in his lungs exploded out his open mouth. The body toppled. The head and shoulders lay at an angle kinked from that of the legs and lower chest. A smoldering tatter of cloth and flesh joined the portions.

Gregg kicked hard. His trouser leg tore. He got to his feet, keeping the flashgun pointed at the remaining Federation official while the fingers of his right hand switched the discharged battery for a fresh one.

" . . . now and at the hour of our death," the Fed mumbled. His eyes were open, but he'd only half lowered his hands. He was swaying and seemed about to fall.

Ricimer carefully got out of the cart that had brought him across the Mirror. He glanced at the rifle in his hands as though he'd never seen anything like it before, then pointed an index finger toward the corpse.

"Get that into the building and out of sight," he said in a firm, clear voice.

Two of the Molts immediately obeyed. The rest of the labor party moved slightly away from the piled crates, distancing themselves from their duties for the Federation. A car with Dole aboard shimmered through the transition layer. The bosun's face was set, and his eyes stared vacantly.

Gregg stepped over to the Fed official. The man was in his early twenties. He had fine features and blond hair that was already starting to thin. Gregg gripped the Fed's shoulder with his left hand, to immobilize the fellow and to focus his horror-struck attention.

Ch'Kan pointed to Ricimer. "Here is the man who will take us away from this place," she said. Now that the immediate crisis was past, she had switched to Trade English. "We will load the cargo on carts and take it back to mirrorside for him."

A gush of fireworks streaked above the city. The vessels of the Earth Convoy were hidden by darkness and the buildings, but some of them played searchlights with colored filters into the air.

A party of Molts trudged up the central street toward the bollards. In the uncertain illumination, Gregg couldn't spot the armed guard who he was sure accompanied the group to prevent pilferage and malingering. He squinted, holding the flashgun down at his side where its unexpected outline wouldn't cause alarm.

"Whether or not you help us," Piet Ricimer said to the Molts who stared at him, "I'll take any of you who want to go to Benison and release you with your own free fellows. If you *do* help me and my men, though, you bring closer the day that we can smash the Federation's grip on the stars and free *all* your fellows."

Not so very long ago, Gregg thought, *you and I were in the business of supplying crews just like this one. But times change, and men change . . . and maybe occasionally they change for the better.*

Coye came out of the Mirror. Stampfer's cart followed on the heels of the Molt pushing Coye. Dole's expression was one of blinking awareness, but he still stood in the car while a Molt looked on from behind.

"Dole!" Gregg called. "Come watch this guy. Tie him or something."

"You're going to be fine," he added to the prisoner. "Just don't play any games. Because I'll smash your skull all over the stones if you do."

Gregg didn't speak loudly. He knew he was very close to the edge. If he'd shouted the threat, it might have triggered his arm to move, swinging the laser's heavy butt. And anyway, he didn't need to shout to be believable.

Dole and the Molt who'd pushed him took the white-faced prisoner and began to secure him with pieces of rope from the coil they'd brought. Under Guillermo's direction, Molts were loading the empty tramcars. They concentrated on the smaller cases stenciled as new-run chips.

Ricimer patted Gregg on the back as he strode past. "I'm going to see what else is in here," he explained. "Keep a watch on that gang coming, though they don't seem in much of a hurry."

Gregg peered around the back corner of the blockhouse. "Coye," he called. "Stampfer. Keep down, will you? Behind the stacks of cases or inside the building."

It didn't much matter whether Feds saw Guillermo and the Molts reloading the cars—no one was likely to pay enough attention to note that the chips were going in the wrong direction. Too many armed humans around the blockhouse could be more of a problem.

The ground on which the blockhouse stood was slightly higher than that of Umber City and the spaceport beyond, though the slope would have been imperceptible on a surface less flat than the present one. Because the city was so full of transients, illuminated windows marked the roads though there was no streetlighting as such.

The floodlit Commandatura stood out in white glory. The park and the street between it and the building were hidden behind intervening structures. Tricolored bunting and the Federation's maple leaf emblem hung between the windows of the second floor.

Besides the fireworks at the park, occasional shots whacked the air. That could mean either "happy shooting" toward the starless sky or the quarrels of drunken sailors getting out of hand. Whichever, it was useful cover if there was trouble with the party nearing the blockhouse.

The guard walked beside her charges, near the front but generally hidden by the line of alien bodies. Glimpses showed

Gregg that she had reddish hair, no cap, and carried a weapon
slung muzzle-down over her right shoulder.

"Sir," Dole said tensely. "This guy's—"

"Not now," Gregg whispered. Only the right side of his face
projected beyond the corner of the blockhouse. His flashgun,
muzzle-up, was withdrawn to his side so that the oncoming
party wouldn't see it.

"There's a radio back there," Ricimer said as he came from
the front of the building, "but the loopholes are both covered
by box—"

He continued to speak for a moment. Gregg's mind turned
the words into background buzz. It was no more than the hiss
of the breeze and the sting of sand on his neck.

The oncoming Molts reached the line of bollards. Guillermo
trilled to them in their own language. The remainder of the co-
opted aliens continued to load cars. Now that all the Venerians
had crossed on the single track, the Molts could begin taking
chips over to mirrorside.

"Blauer?" the Fed guard called. Besides the slung carbine,
she carried a quirt in her right hand. She slapped the shaft
against her left palm. "Hey! Blauer!"

The Molts nearest to her flattened to the pavement. Gregg
stepped around the corner and leveled his flashgun. "Don't,"
he said in a high, distant voice.

The woman blinked, held by the laser's sight line like a
beetle pinned to a board. She dropped the quirt, then shrugged
carefully to let the carbine sling slide off her shoulder without
her hands coming anywhere near the weapon.

"Now come forward," Gregg ordered quietly. He nodded to
Stampfer, poising behind a loaded tramcar. Stampfer ran out
to pick up the carbine while Lightbody and Coye secured the
new prisoner.

She didn't speak, but her eyes glared hatred at everything
her gaze touched.

"Jesus!" Gregg said, letting his breath out for the first time
in too long. The air stank of cooked filth, the effluvium of the
torso shot into the previous guard. His hands were shaking and
he almost gagged.

Molts were widening the narrow aisle into the blockhouse.
Piet put a comforting hand on Gregg's arm. "I want to clear the
loopholes inside," he said. "We may need them before we're
done."

"Right," Gregg said. He looked down at the receiver of his flashgun. The present locked into focus again.

"Right," he repeated. "I can't believe they blocked those wall guns off. You'd think the Feds would've learned a lesson from our first raid, wouldn't you?"

"They learned they didn't have to be afraid of raiders," Ricimer said with a slight grin. "Not every lesson is the right lesson."

"There's more coming, sir," Stampfer called from the shelter to which he'd returned. "Molts, anyhow."

"We'll handle them the same way," Ricimer replied. "Maybe we won't have any real problems with this."

"Captain!" Jeude called from inside the blockhouse. "There's somebody on the radio, wondering where his cargo is."

"I'll handle it," Ricimer said, brushing past a Molt coming out of the building with a case of chips.

"Look at this, Mr. Gregg," Dole murmured, holding up their first captive's rifle. "Don't it look like it's . . . ?"

"It sure does . . ." Gregg agreed. He handed his flashgun to Dole and took the richly-carved pump gun. The chance of there being another rifle so much like Captain Schremp's wasn't high enough to consider.

The blond captive lay on his side, with his ankles and wrists tied together behind his back. Gregg knelt beside him, waggled the ornate weapon in his face, and then touched the muzzle to the prisoner's knee.

"Tell me exactly how you got this rifle," he said. His finger took up the slack on the trigger. He hadn't checked to be sure there was a round in the chamber, but they'd learn that quickly enough when the hammer fell.

"I bought it!" the Fed screamed. "From the flagship's purser! I swear to God I bought it!"

Gregg eased off the trigger very slightly. He tapped again with the muzzle. "All right," he said. "Where did the purser get it?"

"Oh, God, I just wanted a rifle," the blond man moaned. He squeezed his eyes shut, but he couldn't escape the caress of the weapon. It would blow his leg off at this range. "I don't know, I just asked around when the convoy landed. They all do a little business on the side, you know how it is, and I had a few chips saved back. Oh God oh God."

"Blauer, you make me want to puke," sneered the female prisoner unexpectedly. She turned her head from her fellow to Gregg. "You want to know where it came from? From a pirate like you!"

"Go on," Gregg said. He raised the repeater's muzzle and handed the weapon back to Dole. Threatening the woman would be counterproductive; and anyway, she had balls.

"We caught them on Rondelet," she said. "They were attacking a mansion when we came out of transit. We smashed their ship from orbit and they all surrendered. Were they friends of yours?"

Piet joined the tableau. He didn't interrupt.

"Not really," Gregg said. By habit, he checked the flashgun Dole returned to him. "What happened then?"

"Then we hanged them all," the woman said. "*After* we'd convinced them to talk. Too bad they weren't friends!"

Gregg stood up. "Well," he said mildly to Ricimer. "We know what Schremp did after he left us. I can't say I'm sorry he's gone."

Ricimer nodded. "We can get to one of the wall guns now," he said. "It's a one-kilogram. There's only a few shells for it."

Molts pushed laden tramcars into the Mirror one after the other. They moved at a measured, almost mechanical pace, a skill learned to prevent them from running up on each other's heels in the hellish void beyond the transition layer.

Ricimer stepped past Gregg to peer at the labor party trudging up from Umber City. "They'll be here in a few minutes," he said.

Gregg smiled tightly. He indicated the female prisoner with the toe of his boot. "Gag that one," he said to Dole. "Or she'll try to warn the next batch. And I don't want to kill her."

Piet Ricimer squeezed his friend's shoulder again.

—45—

Umber

The Umber tramway had thirty-four cars. There'd been thirty-five when the Venerians arrived, but Gregg had bent the trucks of the one that carried him when he kicked his way free. He didn't remember anything so violent occurring, but his right leg ached as though a piano'd fallen on it.

The Molts were starting a second round trip to mirrorside. Because there was only a single trackway, none of the cars could return until all had gone across. The blockhouse was nearly emptied; five bound and gagged Federation guards lay out of sight within it.

Lightbody had draped a tarpaulin over the corpse. Gregg hadn't killed anybody since that one. The sudden dissolution of the man's chest had merged with the soul-freezing trip through the Mirror in a shadowland that Gregg would revisit only when he dreamed.

The front of the blockhouse was pierced by four loopholes, though there were only two wall guns. Ricimer watched Umber City from one of the clear openings while he responded to radio traffic with a throat mike and plug earphone.

Gregg remained at the right rear corner of the structure. Ricimer looked back over his shoulder at his friend with a wan smile and tapped the earphone. "The watch officer on the *Triple Tiara*'s getting pretty insistent about where his cargo is," he said. "He doesn't get to join the party until it's delivered."

Gregg tried to grin. The result was more of a tic, and his eyes returned to the street beyond immediately. "That's Carstensen's flagship?" he said.

"Yeah. I told him I had the same problem, but once the porters left here, there wasn't a thing I could do about how fast they marched."

The fireworks had ended. Snatches of music drifted up when the breeze was right. The captured guards said there was always a banquet when the convoy arrived: a sit-down meal in the Commandatura for the brass, and an open-air orgy in the park for common sailors and the journeymen of the community's service industries.

Both sites had suffered during the previous raid. If anything, that would increase the sense of celebratory relief.

Gregg heard the ringing sound of a distant engine. A green, then a red and a green light wobbled into the sky beyond the rooftops.

"They're coming!" Gregg called. "One of the ships just launched an autogyro."

Four of the Venerian enlisted men were with Piet inside the blockhouse, crewing the 1-kaygees. Jeude squatted behind one of the shrinking stacks of boxes. Like Gregg, he wore a white jumper stripped from a prisoner. He kept out of sight because the guards with the two remaining labor gangs might nonetheless realize that he wasn't one of their number.

An autogyro wasn't a threat. One of the watch officers was sending a scout to track down the missing cargo. No problem.

Ricimer murmured to the gun crews, then handed the communications set to Dole. He strode back to Gregg and eyed the situation himself.

"Jeude," Gregg said. "Stand up—don't look like you're hiding. If he lands, we'll pick him up just like the guards. No shooting."

He looked at Piet. "Right?"

"Right . . ." Ricimer said with an appraising frown. "That would be the best result we can hope for."

The appearance of things at the tramhead shouldn't arouse much concern. The raiders had been sending excess Molt laborers back to mirrorside to load the ships under Guillermo's direction. Ch'Kan acted as straw boss here. If shooting started, Guillermo could be better spared than any of the Venerians—though Gregg wouldn't have minded the presence of K'Jax and a few of his warriors.

Piet looked over the remaining cargo and pursed his lips. "We shouldn't get greedy and stay too long," he said.

"We'll be all right for a while yet," Gregg said.

Gregg's mouth spoke for him. His mind was in a disconnected state between the future and past, unable to touch the present.

His eyes tracked the path of the autogyro, visible only as running lights angling toward the blockhouse at fifty meters altitude. Its engine and the hiss of its slotted rotor were occasionally audible. There was no place to fly on Umber, but the ships of the Earth Convoy were equipped for worlds like Rondelet and Biruta, where solid ground was scattered in patches of a few hectares each.

In Gregg's mind, humans and Molts exploded in the sight picture of his flashgun. Every one a unique individual up to the instant of the bolt: the snarling guard here, the woman beneath the fort trying to shoot him; a dozen, a score, perhaps a hundred others.

All of them identical carrion after Stephen Gregg's light-swift touch.

More to come when the present impinged again. *Lord God of hosts, deliver me.*

Ricimer touched the back of his friend's hand. "Why don't you go into the blockhouse, Stephen?" he suggested. "We shouldn't have more than two humans visible."

"I'll handle it," Gregg said. He watched as the autogyro turned parallel to the Mirror and approached the tramhead from the west. "I'm dressed for it."

He plucked at the commandeered tunic with his free hand. He held the flashgun close to the ceiling of the blockhouse so that it couldn't be seen from above.

Ricimer nodded and moved back.

The Federation aircraft zoomed overhead, its engine singing. The sweet, stomach-turning odor of diesel exhaust wafted down.

The Molts hefted cases, pretending they were about to carry them to the spaceport. The last of the tramcars had disappeared into the Mirror some minutes before, so the crew had no real work. A few of them looked up.

Jeude waved. Gregg raised his free hand, ostensibly to shade his eyes from the floodlights but actually to hide his face. Two faces peered down from the autogyro's in-line cockpits.

"Fooled them that time, Mr. Gregg!" Jeude called.

"So far," Gregg said to the men within the blockhouse, "so good."

His expression changed. "They're coming back," he added. "I think they're going to land."

The note of the diesel changed as the pilot coarsened the prop pitch. He was bringing the autogyro down, very low and slow, between the rear of the blockhouse and the Mirror.

They couldn't land there because of the tracks . . .

The autogyro swept by with its fixed landing gear barely skimming the pavement. The fuselage was robin's-egg blue, and the rotor turning slowly on its mast was painted yellow with red maple leaves near the tips. Both the pilot and the observer wore goggles, but there was no mistaking the shock on their faces when they saw the number of humans, standing and lying bound, within the blockhouse.

The diesel belched a ring of black smoke as the pilot brought it to full power. He banked hard, swinging the nose toward the city. The observer craned his head back over the autogyro's tail as he held a microphone to his lips.

"We're fucked!" Dole shouted from the blockhouse radio. "They've spotted—"

The fuselage faded to gray, but reflection from the pavement still lighted the rotor blades a rich yellow-orange. The flashgun was tight against Gregg's shoulder. Though the autogyro was turning away from him, it wasn't quite a zero-deflection shot yet. He swung through the tail surfaces and continued the graceful motion even after his trigger finger stroked with the sights centered between the forward cockpit and the glittering dial of the prop.

All he'd wanted to do was to bring the aircraft down, to punch his laser through the thin plastic hull and smash the engine block. The fuel tank was directly behind the diesel. It ruptured, hurling a ball of blazing kerosene over hundreds of square meters of the nearest buildings.

The pilot and observer were the two largest pieces of debris from the explosion. They were burning as they fell, but impact with the ground would have been instantly fatal even if they'd survived the blast.

"Now we'd better leave," Gregg said as he reloaded.

"Not yet!" Ricimer said crisply.

He clicked off the interior light, then pointed to the blond prisoner wearing ground-personnel flashes. "You! How do we turn out these area lights?" Though Ricimer was inside the blockhouse, the toss of his head adequately indicated the four pole-mounted floodlights bathing the site.

"There's no switch!" the Fed bleated. "It's got a sensor, it goes on and off with sunlight!"

The Commandatura darkened suddenly as a Federation official had the same idea and executed it with dispatch.

Jeude stood up. He still carried the repeating carbine he'd liberated from a Venerian officer on Punta Verde. He shot out the first bulb, worked the bolt, and missed the second. The reflector whanged as the bullet pierced its rim.

Jeude finished the job with the remaining three cartridges in his magazine. The blockhouse and its surroundings weren't in the dark, but now the illumination came from the burning buildings fifty meters beyond the bollards.

"Why don't we go back now, Piet?" Gregg asked in much the voice that he'd have offered a cup of coffee. He had four charged batteries remaining, plus the one in the laser. His fingertip ticked over the corner of each in the satchel. He didn't touch the battery contacts, because the sweat on his skin would minuscuely corrode them.

The siren on the Commandatura began to sound.

"Because if we go back now . . ." Ricimer said. His voice seemed calm rather than controlled, and he spoke no louder than he needed to for Jeude and the wall gun crews all to hear him. " . . . we meet the empty cars returning from mirrorside. We have to wait until they've all come through."

"Christ's blood!" Dole said as he realized how long *that* would take.

Ricimer turned on the bosun like an avenging angel. "Mr. Dole!" he said. "I suggest that you remember that the next words we speak may be those we have on our lips when we go to meet our God. Do you understand?"

Dole swallowed and fell to his knees. He pressed his palms together, but his face was still lifted toward his captain with a look of supplication.

Ricimer shook himself and bent to lift Dole to his feet. "He'll understand," Ricimer muttered. "As He'll understand the fear that causes me to lose my temper."

A bullet, fired from somewhere within the town, slapped the front of the blockhouse. Gregg didn't hear the shot, and he couldn't spot the muzzle flash through the glare of burning buildings either. The nearest portion of the street was lighted by the houses and scattered pools of kerosene, but beyond that the pavement was curtained in darkness.

"Madam Ch'Kan," Ricimer called to the Molt leader. "Get your people to cover. There's room for most of you in the blockhouse without affecting our ability to fight. Jeude—if you stay there to the side, you won't be as well covered when it comes time to run for the tramline."

Jeude shook his head. "Those loopholes, they're nothing but bull's-eyes. I'll take my chances here, thank'ee kindly."

He patted the waist-high breastwork of boxed microchips which hadn't been carried back to mirrorside yet.

The Molt leader chittered to her fellows. Four of them lay behind crates the way Jeude had. The rest—there were about twenty on this side of the Mirror—shuffled quickly into the blockhouse and knelt, beneath the level of the loopholes.

Another bullet sang past nearby. The sound ended abruptly as the projectile vanished into the Mirror. *At least they didn't have to worry about ricochets from behind.*

Lightbody flinched instinctively. Stampfer muttered a curse, and the frozen stillness of the other crewmen showed that they too were affected by the unseen snipers.

All of the Federation guards had carried firearms. Piet Ricimer chose a captured weapon, a long-barreled breech-loader, and the owner's cross-belts with about fifty tapered cartridges in the loops. He carried the gear over to Jeude, deliberately sauntering. Gregg chuckled.

Crewmen watched Ricimer through the loopholes in the side of the blockhouse. He set the rifle beside Jeude and said loudly, "Here. I don't like to trust repeaters not to jam."

Fed soldiers volleyed. There were six or eight of them, sited on a three-story rooftop some two hundred meters away. This time a breeze parted the curtain of flame enough for Gregg to see the nervous yellow winking of muzzle flashes. The structure beneath them was dark, but Gregg knew where it must be.

"Gunners!" he shouted as he locked down his visor. "*Here's* your aiming point!"

The flashgun jolted in his hands. Smoke may have scattered the coherent light somewhat, but not to a great enough degree to prevent the bolt's impact from shattering the concrete roof coping.

White-hot lime in the cement hadn't faded below yellow when Jeude fired toward it with his carbine. Stampfer, professionally quick and angry with himself for feeling windy a moment before, was almost as fast. The 1-kg shell burst with a bright flash that hurled a Fed soldier backward.

The *whop!* of the bursting charge echoed the muzzle blast of the short-barreled wall gun. Dole, firing the other weapon of the pair a moment later, put his round a meter or two low. The aiming error was a useful one, because the shell went off within the building and set the contents of a room on fire.

Gregg stepped back into the blockhouse as he changed batteries in his laser. The breechblocks of the wall guns clanged as the gunners cammed them open, then closed again after the loaders dropped in fresh rounds. Propellant residues from the shell casings smelled like hot wax.

An empty cart emerged from the transition layer. The Molt pushing it took three steps forward, numbed by the Mirror, before he noticed the battle going on around him. He gaped.

Ch'Kan shouted to the laborer. He broke into a multijointed trot, pushing the car to the end of the branch. There it was out of the way of later comers like the one already entering realside.

A bullet struck one of the metal bollards and howled horribly away. None of the Venerians seemed to notice. The wall guns banged.

Piet and Jeude aimed out over their breastwork. The crewman fired as fast as he could work his carbine's bolt, then picked up the powerful single-shot. Ricimer watched as much as he aimed, but after a moment he fired. Gregg saw shards of glass fly into the street from a window eighty meters away.

Gregg raised his visor to scan for a worthy target. He had only four charges left, and the flashgun was too valuable a weapon to empty with indiscriminate firing. He thought of taking one of the captured rifles, but instinct told him not to put the laser down.

Movement beyond the smoke.

Something was coming around the corner where the street leading to the tramhead kinked and hid whatever preparations went on beyond it. The flashgun came up. Gregg closed his eyes over the sight picture and fired.

Actinics from the bolt pulsed orange through the skin of Gregg's eyelids. The blockhouse shuddered behind a puff of dust and smoke. The Feds had brought up a landing array from one of the ships, three 4-cm barrels on a single wheeled carriage. The shells were comparable to those thrown by the wall guns in the blockhouse.

Only one tube fired before Gregg's laser stabbed into the open magazine attached to the trail of the array's carriage.

The blast was red and went on for a considerable while, like a man coughing to clear phlegm. Some shells burst like grenades against walls and rooftops where the initial explosion hurled them. The bodies of the crew, Molts and humans both, lay around the ruined weapon. Burning scraps of clothes and shell spacer lighted them.

The Fed round hit the door in the center of the blockhouse facade and sprang it. The hinges and the staple of the closure bar held, but acrid smoke from the shellburst oozed around the edges of the armored panel. The inner face of the door bulged, and the center of the dent glowed faintly.

Umber

The wall guns were silent. Dole swung his out of the way to fire through the loophole with a rifle while Coye used the other opening to the left of the door. Stampfer and Lightbody took turns at the loophole on their side, but the gunner had left his 1-kg in position. He'd saved a shell back for special need, where Dole had fired off the entire stock of ammunition.

Tramcars continued to reappear from the Mirror. Ch'Kan called directions to each blinking laborer who followed a car.

Occasionally the newcomer stumbled away when his faculties warmed enough to realize what was going on around him. One Molt even plunged back into the Mirror in a blind panic that must have ended only when he starved in the interdimensional maze. Ch'Kan herself pushed abandoned cars out of the way or simply toppled them off the rails.

Molts in the blockhouse reloaded rifles for the Venerians to fire through the loopholes. Gregg saw two of the aliens, solemn as judges, using their delicate "fingers" to work loose a cartridge case that had ruptured instead of extracting from the hot breech of a repeater.

Gregg slung his flashgun. Its barrel was shimmering. If he'd laid the weapon down on the cold stone, the ceramic might have shattered. The Molts had left Schremp's rifle beside Gregg by chance or intent. He took it and let his cold killer's soul search for movement.

A bullet sparked through the wire sides of a cart being pushed toward the line of those stored on Gregg's side of the blockhouse. A second bullet shattered the head of the Molt pushing the cart. Her body continued to pace forward.

Gregg spotted the shooter at a ground-floor window of a nearby building whose roof was ablaze. He aimed through the post-and-ring sight, squeezed into the third muzzle flash, and felt the concrete explode beside his left ear as the Fed soldier fired at the glint of Schremp's silvered receiver.

Grit and bullet fragments slapped Gregg's head sideways. His helmet twisted and flew off. He knelt and patted his face with his left hand. His cheek felt cold and his hand came away sticky.

"This is the last!" Ch'Kan called in the high, carrying treble to which Molt voices rose at high amplitudes.

Piet Ricimer turned from where he crouched behind the row of crates. The breech of his rifle was open and streaming gray powder gases. "Ch'Kan!" he ordered. "Start your people through. Fast! We're safe when we're into the Mirror!"

"They're coming!" Stampfer warned.

Gregg looked toward the city. He didn't have binocular vision, but he only needed one eye for the sights. Shadows approached through the smoke, moving with the doll-like jerkiness of men in hard suits.

Stampfer's wall gun banged. A figure fell back in a red flash. Gregg pumped his rifle's action, aimed low, and fired. Maybe the Feds were wearing only head and torso armor rather than complete suits. Flexible joints might not stop a bullet at this range, and a hammerblow on a knee could drop a man even if the projectile didn't penetrate.

The target fell. The man or woman fell, but that didn't matter, wouldn't matter until the dreams came. Gregg pumped the slide again, very smooth, and dropped another Fed. Schremp had bought a first-rate *weapon,* if only he hadn't turned it into a sighting point for every hostile in the world.

The sniper who'd almost nailed Gregg from the window didn't fire again. Close only counts in horseshoes . . .

Half the attackers were down; the others crowded close to the buildings instead of advancing. The Molts who'd brought the carts through had mostly returned to the Mirror, though nearly a dozen alien bodies lay or thrashed on the pavement. There hadn't been much cover for them, and they'd been silhouetted against the Mirror for Feds who wanted soft targets. Molts in the blockhouse poised to leave under Ch'Kan's fluting direction.

Gregg shot at a Fed and spun him, though for a moment the target didn't seem willing to go down. The pump gun shucked out the empty case, but there wasn't quite enough resistance as the breech slapped home again. It hadn't picked up a fresh round because the tubular magazine was empty. Gregg reached down for the shoulder belt that came with the rifle, slung with pockets each holding five rounds.

Rainbow light erupted from the spaceport. It silhouetted buildings for an instant before the vessel rose too high. Gregg got a good view of the craft while it was illuminated by the reflection of its own exhaust from the ground. It was a ship's boat, a cutter; but a large one, nearly the size of the *Peaches*.

Gregg dropped the rifle and ammo belt to unsling his flashgun. The cutter's hull would be proof against the amount of energy the laser delivered, but if the vessel tried to overfly the blockhouse and fry the raiders with its exhaust—well, Gregg had smashed thruster nozzles under more difficult conditions.

Molts streamed from the shelter of the blockhouse at a measured trot. A part of Gregg's mind wondered about sending aliens to safety while humans remained at risk; but the Venerians were needed as a rear guard until the last instant . . . and anyway, Piet didn't think in terms of men and not-men.

Neither did Gregg at the moment. His universe was a place in which targets would appear if only he waited.

The cutter slanted slowly upward to fifty meters, turning on its vertical axis. The starboard side swung parallel to the front of the blockhouse a kilometer away. At this distance, Gregg didn't have an angle to hit a thruster no matter how steady his aim was.

A few Feds still fired from the town. Venerians shot back, but the crewmen were tensed to follow the Molts in a moment or two. Quick, scuttling movement beyond the screening smoke indicated that the Feds planned *something,* but there were no good targets just now.

"By God, we're going to make—" Jeude cried in a tone of burgeoning triumph.

Because the cutter was illuminated from below, Gregg didn't guess the existence of the vessel's large side-opening hatch until the Fed gunner opened fire with the laser mounted in the hold. It was a powerful weapon, pumped by the cutter's fusion drive. The tube tripped six or eight times a second to keep from overloading individual components.

The gunner's aim was good for line. Though he started low, the cutter was rolling on its horizontal axis and walked the burst on. A bollard blazed like a magnesium flare. Pavement between there and the blockhouse shattered into shrapnel of fist size and smaller, flying in all directions. It was no danger to Gregg at the rear corner of the structure.

The laser hit the front of the blockhouse and blew off meters of the concrete facing. The grid of reinforcing wires acted as a cleavage line, saving the inner ten centimeters of thickness, but a pulse of coherent light streamed through a loophole unhindered.

Coye blew apart in a flash of painful density. Dole, a meter away, screamed from the burst of live steam that had been his loader an instant before. Gregg felt something splash his left ankle. He didn't look down to see what it was.

It didn't matter. He had a target.

Gregg aimed as the Fed laser ripped across the last of the Molts entering the Mirror. Parts of three or more of the aliens—the destruction was too great to be sure of the number—sprayed out in a white-hot dazzle.

Shouting to encourage themselves, fifty or more Fed soldiers rose and charged the blockhouse. Piet Ricimer's rifle cracked alone to meet them.

The target was a klick away; Stephen Gregg was using a handheld weapon. He had no doubt at all that he would hit. He and the flashgun and the cutter's hatch were beads on a wire that would be straight though it stretched to infinity. He squeezed.

The hatch flared, becoming a rectangle of momentary white against the dark hull. Gregg's bolt had punched a bulkhead inside the cutter, converting an egg-sized dollop of metal to blazing gas. The shock hurled one of the weapon's crew forward, out of the hatch.

The laser slewed left and down but continued to fire. Gouts of flame leaped each time a pulse stabbed into Umber City. The Fed infantry paused, looking back at what had been their hope.

The laser's wild firing stopped after a few seconds. Reflected light glimmered as the gunner swiveled his tube back on target.

Gregg swung his reloaded flashgun up to his shoulder. *Beads on a wire.* He squeezed the trigger.

The second bolt's impact was a brief flash, followed by ropes of coruscating blue fire that grew brighter as they ate the metal away from all four sides of the hatch. Gregg had severed one of the armored conduits which powered the laser's pumping system. The generator's full output dumped into the cutter's hull through a dead short.

"Run for it!" Ricimer cried. He stood and swept his rifle's barrel toward the tramline like a cavalryman gesturing with his saber. "Stay between the rails!"

Stephen Gregg locked the lid of the butt compartment down over his last charged battery.

Jeude ran hunched over, carrying the heavy rifle in his right hand and dragging his carbine by its sling in his left. The three Venerians surviving within the blockhouse ran for the tramline also. Coye's legs to the pelvis, baked to the consistency of wood, remained standing behind them. Piet waited till his men were clear, then followed.

The Federation cutter rolled over on its back and plunged out of sight. The flash and the shockwave three seconds later were much greater than a vessel so small could have caused by hitting the ground. The cutter must have dived into one of the starships, perhaps the one which had launched it.

"Stephen!"

Gregg aimed his flashgun.

He was hard to see against the concrete, but some of the Fed soldiers had now reached the bollards. Several of them fired simultaneously. Something *hot* stabbed Gregg's lower abdomen and his right foot kicked out behind.

He squeezed. The bolt from the flashgun illuminated the figure who stood at the central window of the blacked-out Commandatura. The target existed only for the instant of the shot, high-intensity light converted to heat in the flesh of a man's chest.

Gregg turned to run. A bullet had carried away the heel of his right boot. He fell over. When he tried to get up, he found his arms had no strength.

Half a dozen Fed soldiers continued their assault even after the cutter's crash broke the glass out of all the remaining windows in Umber City. They'd ducked as Gregg leveled his lethal flashgun, but they came on again when he fell.

Gregg levered his torso off the ground. It was over. He couldn't move beyond that.

"On my *soul* you won't have him!" Piet Ricimer screamed. He held the short-barreled shotgun a Fed guard had carried. It belched twice, bottle-shaped flares of powder gases burning ahead of the muzzle. A soldier staggered backward at either shot. The unexpected flashes and roars did as much to stop the attack as the actual damage did.

Gregg felt arms around him. He knew they must be Piet's, but he couldn't see his friend for the pulsing orange light that swelled silently around him.

The orange suddenly flipped to cyan. Then there was nothing.

Nothing but the cold.

—47—

Above Benison

"Lift the suit around me and latch it," Gregg said. "I'll be fine with it carried on my shoulders. I just don't want to bend to pick it up."

Weightlessness in orbit above Benison made his guts shift into attitudes slightly different from those of the gravity well in which he'd been wounded. The result wasn't so much painful as terrifying. Part of Gregg's mind kept expecting ropes of intestine to suddenly spill out, twisting around his shocked companions.

His left eye was undamaged. Blood from his cut brow had gummed it shut during the blockhouse fight.

"Stephen," Ricimer said, "you can't do any good in your present condition. You'll only get in the way. Besides, the mirrorside authorities don't have the strength to interfere with us and K'Jax' people together, if they so much as notice us land."

"Lightbody," Gregg said. "Pick up my body armor and latch it around me." He glared at Ricimer.

The Venerians hadn't bothered to formally name the ships they captured on Umber's mirrorside. Because you had to call them something, the other vessel was *Dum* and this one, *Dee*. Lightbody looked from Gregg to Ricimer and fingered his pocket Bible. The three of them were the only humans aboard.

Ricimer sighed. "No, I'll take care of it," he said to the crewman. He reflexively crooked his leg around a stanchion to hold him as he lifted the torso of the hard suit. "Is it just that you want to die?"

"I'm sorry," Gregg said. He stretched his arms out to his side so that Ricimer could slide the right armhole over him.

The movement was controlled by his fear of the consequences. "I—if I give in to it, I will die, I think. I don't want to push too hard, really. But I can't just. Lie back."

"Okay, now lower them," Ricimer said. The backplate was solid, with hinges on the sides and the breastplate split along an overlapping seam in the middle. Ricimer closed the left half of the plate carefully over the bandaged wound.

One of the Molts from Umber was a surgeon. It was typical of Federation behavior that she and other specialists had been sent to the labor crews when there was need to carry crates to the spaceport.

Because the surgeon had survived the firefight, and because there was a reasonably-equipped clinic on Umber's mirrorside, Gregg had survived also.

When Gregg awakened halfway through the voyage back to Benison, Lightbody offered him the bullet. He'd taken the battered slug because he was still too woozy from analgesics to refuse, but now he was looking forward to tossing it away discretely as soon as they were on a planet again.

"*Dum* has arrived," Guillermo called from the control console, where he watched the rudimentary navigational equipment. "Shall I radio her?"

He was one of the half dozen Molts awake on the two vessels together. The rest were in suspended animation. Air wasn't a problem this time, but there were limited provisions available. Besides, with all the cargo, there was no space to move around as it was.

"Yes, of course," Ricimer said. "Tell Dole that we'll set down first, but I'll wait till he's ready to follow immediately."

"If there's no trouble with the locals, Piet," Gregg said quietly, "then it won't matter whether I'm holding a rifle or not. If there *is* trouble, then I'm still the best you've got."

His lips smiled. "Even now."

Ricimer latched the strap over Gregg's left shoulder. "You never explained why you waited to fire that last shot," he said, his eyes resolutely on his work. "After you brought the cutter down."

"It was an idea I had," Gregg said. A Molt who had been watching the proceedings without speaking handed him the helmet that replaced the one Gregg had lost beside the blockhouse. Coye hadn't worn his through the Mirror, and he had no need of one now.

"I thought that Carstensen would be watching the . . . proceedings," Gregg continued.

"You thought?" Ricimer said sharply.

"I felt he was," Gregg said. He was embarrassed to explain something he didn't understand himself. "Sometimes when, when there's . . ."

His voice trailed off. Piet met his gaze from centimeters away.

"Sometimes when I've got a gun in my hands," Gregg continued coldly, "I know things that I can't see. I saved one charge in the flashgun. And I was willing for whatever happened later if I'd sent that bastard to Hell to greet me."

He licked his dry lips. "I'm not really thinking when I'm like that, Piet," he said. "And I don't care to remember it later."

But I do remember.

"Yes," said Ricimer. "Do you want to wear the rest of the suit?"

Gregg shook his head. "This'll be fine," he said. "It's really a security blanket, you know."

"Mr. Dole reports they're ready to land," Guillermo called.

"All right," Ricimer said. "I'll take the console for landing."

He handed Gregg the breechloader and cross-belts Jeude had brought back through the Mirror because he was too single-minded to think of throwing them down.

"The Lord has mercy for all who love Him, Stephen," he added softly as he turned away.

48

Benison

Piet shut off the thrusters. The *Dum* dropped the last meter and pogoed back on the shock absorbers, simply springs rather than oleo struts, of her landing outrigger.

Gregg jounced in the hammock that was all the mirrorside builders had provided in the way of acceleration couches. Everything felt all right; though he didn't suppose there'd be nerves to tell him that the stitches holding his guts together had all let go. He got up, carefully but trying to hide his concern.

"Sorry," Ricimer said as he undid his harness. "I was getting so irregular a backwash from the ground that I shut down sooner than I cared to do."

"Any one you walk away from, sir," Lightbody said cheerfully. He stood and stretched at the rudimentary attitude-control panel. He'd let the AI do the work, wisely and at Ricimer's direction. "Not as though we're going to need these again, anyhow."

"That's not a way I like to think, Mr. Lightbody," Piet said tartly. He latched on his own body armor. The suits were too confining to wear safely while piloting.

The two Molts from Umber went into the *Dum*'s single hold to wake their fellows. Guillermo stepped to the personnel hatch in the cockpit bulkhead and undogged it.

Ricimer glanced at the viewscreen. It was almost useless. If you knew what the terrain of Benison's mirrorside looked like, you could just make out the skeletons of multitrunked trees, burned bare by the exhaust.

Gregg checked the chamber to make sure his rifle was loaded. It was a falling-block weapon. He would have preferred a turn-bolt with more power to cam a bulged or corroded

243

case home. *Beggars can't be choosers.*

"I'm ready," he said aloud.

Guillermo dragged the hatch inward hard. Hot air surged in; heat waves rippled from the baked soil beyond. K'Jax rose into sight twenty meters away, just beyond the burned area. Both of his bodyguards now carried firearms.

"Any trouble here, K'Jax?" Ricimer called. The relief in his voice was as evident as that which Gregg felt at seeing the situation they had planned on.

A glint in the upper atmosphere indicated Dole was bringing the *Dee* down right on their heels. The nearest Federation settlement was hundreds of klicks away, so the chance of being disturbed really hadn't been very high. It was only paranoia, Gregg supposed, that had made him so fearful ever since they reached orbit.

"None here," said the Molt leader. "But across the Mirror, the humans came and attacked your ships. One was destroyed, and the other two fled."

—49—

Benison

"You're all right now, Mr. Gregg," said the black-bearded Federation guard whose chest was a tangle of charred bone. The corpse gripped Gregg with icy hands. "You've passed through the Mirror, sir."

Gregg shouted or screamed, he wasn't sure which. He swung. The butt of the rifle he was carrying struck a tree and spun the weapon out of his hands. The Molt who'd tried to stop Gregg, already five paces from the edge of the Mirror, ducked away from the rifle and Gregg's flailing hands.

"Oh!" Gregg said. "Oh." He took a deep breath, closed his eyes, and said, "I'm all right now," before he opened them again.

It was overcast on Benison's realside. Gregg had traveled enough by now that open skies bothered him less than they once had, but the tight gray clouds were a relief after another episode with the Mirror.

The Molt he'd swung at was T'Leen, whom K'Jax had sent with Ricimer and Gregg as a guide. He picked up the rifle, examined it—a smear of russet bark on the stock, but no cracks or serious damage. He gave the weapon back to Gregg.

"I'm sorry," Gregg said. "I don't handle the Mirror well." *And I'm getting worse, like a man sensitized to an allergen.*

Piet sat on the stump of a tree burned off close to the ground by a plasma bolt. Guillermo stood beside him, ready to grab if his master toppled from what couldn't have been a comfortable seat.

The Mirror took it out of a fellow. Even on Umber where the boundary was shallower, what must it have been like to carry a man the size of Stephen Gregg through in your arms?

Gregg forced himself to walk toward Ricimer. He felt increasingly human with every consciously-directed step. The wound in his lower abdomen was a frozen lump, but that was better than the twist of fiery needles he'd been living with since he awakened during transit.

Piet smiled and started to get up. His face went blank. Guillermo reached down, but Ricimer managed to lurch to his feet unaided. He smiled again, this time with a mixture of relief and triumph.

"There's no sign that the Feds harmed either the *Peaches* or *Dalriada*," he said. "After all, we'd dismantled the *Halys* ourselves before we crossed to mirrorside."

A party of armed Molts appeared from the forest surrounding the blasted area. T'Leen clicked reassuringly to them. K'Jax remained on mirrorside for the moment, greeting and working out power arrangements with the newcomers from Umber.

A plasma bolt had struck the bow of the *Halys*. It came from a powerful weapon, but the depth of atmosphere between target and the bombarding vessel in orbit dispersed the effect over several square meters. An oxidized crust of thin metal plated the soil around the point of impact. Metal icicles jagged where they'd cooled on lower portions of the hull.

A dozen other bolts had vaporized chunks of forest in the immediate neighborhood. That didn't say a great deal for the Feds' fire direction, though Gregg realized there were severe problems in hitting anything with a packet of charged particles that had to pass through kilometers of atmosphere.

"How did they find us, do you think?" he asked Ricimer.

Piet clambered aboard the *Halys*. The hatch, open when the bolt hit, had crumpled in on itself like foil held too close to a flame.

He looked back. "Schremp, I suppose," he said. "Or one of his men. I said we were going to Benison to mislead them."

Ricimer grinned. "Without lying, you see. Carstensen must have sent a warship from Rondelet to check out the report."

His grin became bleak. "The next time," he said, "I'll lie."

T'Leen returned to the humans with others of the clan in tow. "Fire came from the sky," he said. "Eight days ago, in the morning. It killed two of our people."

He pointed in the general direction where the *Dalriada* had been berthed in the forest.

"Were the ships hit?" Ricimer asked.

"No, not then," the Molt said. T'Leen's voice lacked human inflections, but the vocabulary of Trade English was close to the surface of his mind, in contrast to the impression Gregg had of K'Jax.

"The fire came again, nine times," T'Leen went on. "It didn't hit any of us, or the ships. We ran into the Mirror, all but K'Jax and I and S'Tan. The large ship fired guns into the sky."

T'Leen cocked his head to one side, then the other, in a gesture Gregg couldn't read. "We have never seen guns like those used before. If we had guns like those, we would drive the humans off this world."

Gregg mentally translated "human" as "Fed" when members of K'Jax' clan used the word. At moments like this, he was less than certain that the Molts didn't mean exactly what they said.

"The fire from the sky stopped when the large vessel began to shoot," T'Leen said. "The ships took off, the little one and then the large one."

He pointed to the *Halys*. "This they left. S'Tan would have gone back to bring the clan from mirrorside, but the fire came again. Here."

His chitinous fingertips clicked against the ruined hull. "Then soldiers came on vehicles and aircraft, and we went across the Mirror too," T'Leen said. "There was nothing more here."

"Well," Gregg said. "They got away, at least. Dulcie and the crews did."

He wondered how much of the chill in his guts was physical and how much came from the realization that he might spend the rest of his life on Benison.

"It was my fault," Ricimer said as he examined the vessel's cockpit.

Though the dispersed bolt had opened the *Halys* as completely as a pathologist does a skull before brain removal, the interior of what remained wasn't in too bad a condition. That was partly because the Venerians themselves had gutted her thoroughly to create the *Umber,* abandoned on the mirrorside of her namesake.

"The fire that did this," T'Leen said. "And burned the forest. That was from guns like those on your ship?"

Gregg nodded. "Yeah," he said. "Plasma cannon. Probably bigger ones than the *Dalriada* mounts. Not so well served, though."

"We thought so," said T'Leen. "One day we will have such guns."

Gregg sighed and wiped the stock of his rifle with the palm of his hand. How many times would he have to run into the Mirror to save himself from Fed hunters?

"A ship in orbit's at a disadvantage in a fight with ground batteries," he said to divert his mind from an icy future. "The Feds didn't get lucky when they sprang their surprise, so they eased off and let our people get away."

He snorted. "I've got a suspicion the *Halys* will be promoted to a Venerian dreadnought in that Fed captain's report."

"Stephen!" Ricimer said. "Switch your radio on to Channel Three!"

"Huh?" said Gregg. The helmet radio was designed for use by men in vacuum wearing gauntlets. He clicked the dial on the right temple from Channel One, intercom, to Channel Three which the squadron used for general talk-between-ships, then pressed the dial to turn the unit on.

"*. . . to Ricimer, we've been attacked by the enemy. We'll remain in orbit for another day. Call us when you return. Dulcie to Ricimer. We've been attacked—*"

Gregg switched his radio off. The static-broken voice, a recording that presumably played in segments interspersed with dead air for a reply, was the most welcome sound he'd ever heard.

"Piet!" he said. "We're saved!"

A cold as terrible as that of the Mirror flooded back into his soul. "Except we *can't* call them," he said. "These helmet intercoms won't punch a signal through the atmosphere. Stripping the commo system out of *Dee* or *Dum* and setting it up in working order will take a lot more than a day with the tools and personnel we've got."

"Yes," Ricimer said crisply. He looked down at their Molt guide. "T'Leen," he said, "please recross the Mirror and tell the personnel there to immediately begin bringing the cargo over to this side. First of all, send across all of my crewmen. I'll need their skills for the work."

T'Leen flexed his elbow joints out in his equivalent of a nod. He stepped toward the transition layer.

"What work, Piet?" Gregg asked.

It was possible to travel from mirrorside to realside through normal transits, though it was a brutal voyage that might take years. *Dum* and *Dee* would never survive it, but they could capture a larger ship—

Six humans and perhaps a few Molt volunteers. Most of their weapons abandoned on the realside of Umber. Capturing a ship that could journey home from the mirrorside.

Right. And perhaps the angels would come down in all their glory and carry Stephen Gregg to Eryx without need for a ship at all.

"To put the *Halys* in shape to lift off," Ricimer said.

"What? Piet, we gutted her before we left. She's got three thrusters, no AI, and she's been torn to Hell besides!"

"Yes," Ricimer said. "But if she lifts me to orbit, then I think I can raise our friends with my helmet radio."

Gregg stared at the ruined vessel. They'd cut frame members to remove the thruster. "Piet," he said. "She'll twist, flip over, and come in like a bomb."

Like the Federation cutter he'd brought down on Umber.

Ricimer smiled gently. "If that's God's will, Stephen," he said, "so it shall. But if we give up hope in the Lord's help, then we're already lost."

Gregg opened his mouth. He couldn't think of anything to say, so he turned away quickly before Piet could see his tears of frustration.

Benison

The thrusters crashed to life. The *Halys* yawed nose-down to starboard as her stern came unstuck. The Venerians had removed the starboard stern unit to power the *Umber*. Ricimer, a suited doll in the open cockpit, seemed to have overcompensated for the imbalance.

"Forward throttle, sir!" Dole screamed. Piet couldn't hear him over the exhaust's crackling roar, and it wasn't as though the deathtrap's pilot didn't know what the problem was.

Besides, Gregg knew instinctively that Dole's advice was wrong. Gregg couldn't pilot a boat in a bathtub himself, but he knew from marksmanship that you were better off carrying through with a plan than to try to reprogram your actions in mid-execution.

You'd probably gotten it right when you had leisure to consider. Your muscles couldn't react quickly enough to follow each flash of ephemeral data. If you kept your swing and squeeze constant, the chances were that the shot and the target would intersect downrange.

If you were as good a shot as Stephen Gregg.

Ricimer was at least as good a pilot as his friend was a gunman.

The *Halys* continued to lift with her nose low. Her bow drifted to starboard so that as the blasted vessel climbed, she also wheeled slowly.

"You've got her, Piet," Gregg whispered. "You've *got* her, you do!"

They'd rigged manual controls to the *Halys*' remaining thrusters, using what remained of the reel of monocrystal line they'd left on mirrorside after the *Umber* was complete. They couldn't fit her with a collective: they didn't have a test facility in which to check alignments and power delivery, so that a single control could change speed and attitude in a unified fashion. Flying the *Halys* now was like walking three dogs on separate leashes—through a roomful of cats.

"He's got it!" Stampfer shouted, clapping his big hands together in enthusiasm. "I didn't think—"

He didn't finish the sentence. He didn't have to. Lightbody read his Bible with his back to the launch. Jeude squatted beside him. His eyes drifted toward the book, but every time they did, he set his mouth firmly and looked away.

Cased microchips stood in neat piles just within the edge of the undamaged forest. The only Molt present was Guillermo. The aliens had shifted the cargo through the Mirror more than an hour before the Venerians finished rerigging the *Halys*. K'Jax immediately gathered both Clan Deel and the new-comers from Umber and whisked them away.

He claimed he was doing that because the spaceship's liftoff would call Feds to the site. That might well be true, but Gregg suspected K'Jax wanted to absorb the new immigrants beyond human interference. Absorb them, and assert his own dominance.

The Feds had eased K'Jax' difficulties. The cutter's weapon had caught Ch'Kan, last of her people to run for the Mirror and safety.

Gregg's momentary shiver of hatred for K'Jax wasn't fair, wasn't even sane. The clan chief hadn't created the situation from which he was profiting. He was simply a politician handed an opportunity. A single strong clan under a leader with experience of Benison's conditions was to the benefit of all the race . . .

With the exception of one or two of the newcomers who would balk, and who would become examples for the rest.

Gregg stroked the fore-end of his rifle. His feelings were quite insane; but it was just as well that K'Jax, a faithful ally, was nowhere around just now.

The *Halys* rose slowly. Her nozzles were toed outward, because if they'd been aligned truly parallel Piet would have had insufficient lateral stability. Half the attitude jets had been destroyed or plugged when the plasma bolt hit. Manually-controlled thrusters were as much as one man could hope to handle anyway.

As much or more.

The *Halys* reached the cloud base and disappeared. The throb of the thrusters faded more slowly.

A patch of cloud glowed for some moments. Lightning licked within the overcast. The charged exhaust had created imbalances that nature sought to rectify.

Gregg looked at his command: a Molt and five humans, himself included. Four firearms if you counted Guillermo's pistol, and four cutting bars.

None of the personnel in perfect condition, and Gregg able to move only by walking slowly. If he'd been physically able to survive the shock of takeoff, he'd have been in the *Halys* with Piet; but he couldn't.

"Mr. Dole," he said crisply. "You, Lightbody and Jeude position yourselves at the edge of the clearing there."

Between the *Halys*' exhaust on landing and takeoff, and the plasma bolts the Feds had directed at her from orbit, fires had burned an irregular swatch a hundred meters by three hundred into the forest. Large trees spiked up as blackened trunks, but in general you could see across the area. Gregg pointed to the center of one long side.

"Stampfer, Guillermo and I will wait across the clearing," he continued. "That way we'll have any intruders in a cross fire."

Jeude glanced at the party's equipment. "Some cross fire," he muttered.

Gregg smiled tightly. He hefted the heavy rifle Jeude himself had brought back from Umber City. "I'd prefer to have a flashgun, Mr. Jeude," he said. "But if the need arises, I'll endeavor to give a good account of myself with what's available. As shall we all, I'm confident."

The smile disappeared; his face looked human again. "Let's go," he said as he turned.

He heard Dole murmur as the parties separated, "If it's him with a sharp stick and the Feds with plasma guns, Jeude, I know where *my* money lies."

—51—

Benison

"They're coming!" Stampfer said. He clicked his channel selector across the detents, making sure that the increasing crackle of static blanketed the RF spectrum. "Mr. Gregg, they're coming! I can hear the thrusters!"

"Mr. Dole," Gregg said, speaking loudly on intercom mode, though he knew that wouldn't really help carry his voice over the hash of plasma exhaust. "Don't show yourselves until we're sure this is friendly."

He cut off the helmet radio and looked at Stampfer Guillermo wasn't going to run out into the middle of the clearing waving his arms. "Us too," he said. "We don't know it's Piet. We don't even know it's a spaceship."

"Aw, *sir*," the gunner said. The thrusters were a growing rumble rather than just white noise on the radio. "It couldn't be anybody else!"

He craned his neck skyward.

The vessel overflew the clearing at a thousand meters. Its speed was in the high subsonic range. It was a ship's boat. From the hull's metallic glint it was of Terran manufacture.

Perversely, Gregg's first reaction was an urge to smirk knowingly at Stampfer, who had been so sure the news had to be good. Next he wondered what they could do about it . . . and the answer was probably nothing, though he'd see.

"It may be a boat they've captured, like the *Halys*," Gregg said aloud.

"The larger settlements on Benison usually have a cutter available," Guillermo said. "This craft comes from the direction of Fianna, which is the nearest settlement."

"Or it could be from orbit," said Stampfer, as gloomy now as he had been enthusiastic a moment before. "The Fed warship that drove them away before—Dulcie may not be the only one that came back and waited for something to happen."

The sound of the thruster had died away to a shadow of itself. Now it rose again, the sharper pulses syncopating the dying echoes of the previous pass. The boat was coming back.

"I doubt a warship from the Earth Convoy has been wasting the past week and a half in orbit here, Mr. Stampfer," Gregg snapped. He wasn't so much frightened as completely at a loss for anything to do. The local Feds had noticed Piet's liftoff. They'd sent a cutter to scout the location.

The boat roared over the clearing again, this time within a hundred meters of the ground. It had slowed considerably, but not even Gregg could have hit the vessel in the instant it was visible overhead. A rifle bullet wouldn't have done any damage to a spacegoing hull, but the Feds might be concerned about laser bolts.

If only he hadn't lost the flashgun . . .

"Stampfer and Guillermo," Gregg said. "Go directly across the clearing to Mr. Dole's force and inform him that all of you are to run for the Mirror immediately. Go!"

Neither of them moved. "Hey," said Stampfer. "We can still fight."

"God's blood, you fool, there won't *be* a fight!" Gregg shouted. "They'll come over on the deck and fry us with their exhaust. Go!"

Stampfer looked at the Molt, then back at Gregg.

"His injury won't permit him to run," Guillermo said to the gunner.

"We'll help him," Stampfer said. He forcibly wrapped Gregg's left arm across his shoulders.

"No, there's not enough—" Gregg began, and then it truly was too late. The boat was coming back, very fast and traveling parallel with the clearing's long axis. The pilot wanted to get the maximum effect now that he'd identified the target by the waiting crates.

Did he know what the crates contained? Probably not, but it wouldn't matter. Though the cargo was hugely valuable, none of it was going into the pockets of the boat's crew. They would be far more concerned about their own safety, especially if

word of the bloodbath in Umber City had reached Benison
by now.

"Let go of me," Gregg said. He had to shout to be heard.
"I'll get one shot at least. Guillermo, you shoot too."

Gregg aimed, wondering which side of the clearing the Feds
would ignite on their first pass. Either way, it wouldn't be long
before they finished the job.

Guillermo took the pistol from his holster. He pointed it
vaguely toward the north end of the clearing. His head rotated
to stare at Gregg rather than the sight picture.

Was the pilot perhaps a Molt too?

The boat, transonic again, glinted over the rifle sight. Gregg
squeezed.

The boat's hull crumpled around an iridescent fireball. The
bow section cartwheeled through the sky, shedding sparkling
bits of itself as it went. The stern dissolved in what was less
a secondary explosion than a gigantic plasma flare involving
the vessel's powerplant. The initial thunderclap knocked Gregg
and his companions down, but the hissing roar continued for
several seconds.

"Metal hulls," said Stampfer, seated with his hands out
behind him to prop his torso. "Never trust them. Good ceramic
wouldn't have failed that way to a fifty-mike-mike popgun."

The *Peaches* boomed across the clearing, moving too fast to
land on this pass. Gregg saw the featherboat bank to return.

"Not bad shooting, though," Stampfer added. "Not bad at
all."

Gregg didn't have the strength to sit up just at the moment.
He tried to reload the rifle by holding it above his chest, but
after fumbling twice to get a cartridge out of its loop, he gave
that up too.

"Only the best for Piet's boys," he said, knowing the words
were lost in the sound of the featherboat returning to land.

—52—

Venus

The personnel bridge shocked against the hull of the *Peaches.* The featherboat rocked and chattered as the tube's lip tried to grip the hot ceramic around the roof hatch. A hiss indicated the Betaport staff was purging the bridge even though they didn't have a good seal yet.

"Boy, they're in a hurry for us!" Dole said with a chuckle. "When Customs sent *our* manifest down from orbit, that got some action, didn't it?"

"What do you figure the value is, Captain?" Jeude asked. "All those chips—"

He gestured, careful both because he wore a hard suit in anticipation of landing and because of the featherboat's packed interior. They'd skimped on rations for the return voyage in order to find space for more crated microchips.

"I never *saw* so many, just here. And the *Dalriada,* it's as full as we are for all she's so much bigger."

Ricimer looked at Gregg and raised an eyebrow.

Rather than quote a figure in Venerian consols, Gregg said, "I'd estimate the value of our cargo is in the order of half or two-thirds of the planetary budget, Jeude."

His mouth quirked in something like a smile. It was amusing to be asked to be an accountant again. It was amazing to realize that he *was* still an accountant, a part of him. Humans were like panels of stained glass, each colored segment partitioned from the others by impassable black bars.

"Of course," he added, still an accountant, "the quantity of chips we're bringing is great enough that they'll depress the value of the class on the market if they're all released at the same time."

"They will be," Ricimer said, his eyes on the future beyond the *Peaches*' hatch. "To build more starships for Venus, to give them the best controls and optics as they've already got the best hulls and crews."

He looked at his men. "The best crews God ever gave a captain in His service," he said.

"What'll a personal share be then, Mr. Gregg?" Lightbody asked. His right hand absently stroked his breastplate, beneath which he carried his pocket Bible. "Ah—for a sailor, I mean, is all."

"*If* they let us keep it," Stampfer said. "You know how the gentlemen do—begging your pardon, Mr. Gregg, I don't mean *you*. But it may mean a war, and it may be they don't want that."

"It was a war on fucking Biruta, wasn't it?" Jeude said. "Nobody cared about that but the widows!"

"I cared," Gregg said without emphasis. And at the end, Henry Carstensen cared; though perhaps not for long.

"Well, we all cared," Jeude said, "and all Betaport cared. But the gent—the people in Ishtar City, they let it go by."

He gave Gregg a pleading look. "The governor, she won't give our cargo back, will she, sir?"

Gregg looked at Ricimer, who shrugged. Gregg smiled coldly and said, "No, Jeude, she won't. Her own share's too great, and the value to the planet's industrial capacity is too great. Pleyal's government will threaten, and they'll sue for recovery . . . but they'll have to sue in our courts, and I doubt they can even prove ownership."

Ricimer looked surprised.

Gregg laughed. "You're too innocent to be a merchant, Piet," he said.

He rapped a case with his armored knuckles. "How much of this do you think was properly manifested on Umber—and so subject to Federation taxes and customs? My guess is ten percent. A quarter at the outside. And they'll play hell getting proper documentation on *that*."

"And our share, Mr. Gregg?" Lightbody repeated.

"Enough to buy a tavern in Betaport," Gregg said. "Enough to buy a third share in a boat like the *Peaches*, if that's what you want to do."

Enough to stay drunk for a month, with the best friends of any man on Venus during that month. Lightbody might not be the one to spend his share that way, but you can't always guess how a man would act until he had the consols in his hands.

"I want to go out with the cap'n again," Dole said. "And you, Mr. Gregg."

Gregg gripped the back of the bosun's hand and squeezed it.

"Open your hatch," a voice crackled on the intercom. The featherboat's ceramic hull didn't form a Faraday cage the way a metal vessel's did, but sulphur compounds baked on during the descent through Venus' atmosphere were conductive enough to diffuse even short-range radio communications. "Captain Ricimer and Mr. Gregg are to proceed to the personnel lock, where an escort is waiting."

"Hey, the royal treatment!" Jeude crowed as he reached for one of the undogging levers. "Not just coming in like the cargo, *we* aren't."

"We" would do just that, enter Betaport when the landing pit cooled enough for machinery to haul the *Peaches* into a storage dock. Jeude thought of his officers as representing all the crew.

In a manner of speaking, he could be right.

Gregg started to lock down his faceshield. Ricimer put out a hand. "I think the tube will be bearable without that," he said. "Not comfortable, but bearable for a short time."

"Sure," Gregg said.

Positive pressure in the personnel bridge rammed a blast of air into the *Peaches* when the hatch unsealed. The influx must have started out cool and pure, but at this end of the tube the hot reek made Gregg sneeze and his eyes water.

The crewmen didn't seem to be affected. Gregg noticed that none of them had bothered to close up, as they could have done.

Ricimer murmured something to Guillermo and climbed into the bridge. He extended a hand that Gregg refused. An upward pull would stress his guts the wrong way.

A crewman pushed from behind, welcome help.

The two men walked along the slightly resilient surface of the personnel bridge. With their faceshields up they could talk without using radio intercom, but at first neither of them spoke.

"I don't suppose they understand," Ricimer said. "Do you think they do, Stephen?"

"That Governor Halys could find her life a lot simpler if she handed a couple of high-ranking scapegoats to the Federation for trial?" Gregg said. "No, I doubt it."

He snorted. "As Stampfer implied, sailors don't think the way gentlemen do. And rulers. But I don't think she'd bother throwing the men to Pleyal as well."

"It'll go on, what we've started," Ricimer said. The side-walls of the tube had a faint red glow, but there was a white light-source at the distant end. "When they see, when all Venus sees the wealth out there, there'll be no keeping us back from the stars. This time it won't be a single empire that shatters into another Collapse. Man will *have* the stars!"

Gregg would have chuckled, but his throat caught in the harsh atmosphere. "You don't have to preach to me, Piet," he said when he'd hacked his voice clear again.

Ricimer looked at him. "What do you believe in, Stephen?" he asked.

Gregg looked back. He lifted a hand to wipe his eyes and remembered that he wore armored gauntlets. "I believe," he said, "that when I'm—the way I get. That I can hit anything I aim at. Anything."

Ricimer nodded, sad-eyed. "And God?" he asked. "Do you believe in God?"

"Not the way you do, Piet," Gregg said flatly. Time was too short to spend it in lies.

"Yes," Ricimer said. "But almost as much as I believe in God, Stephen, I believe in the stars. And I believe He means mankind to have the stars."

Gregg laughed and broke into wheezing coughs again. He bent to lessen the strain on his wound.

His friend put out an arm to steady him. Their armored hands locked. "I believe in you, Piet," Gregg said at last. "That's been enough this far."

They'd reached the personnel lock set into one panel of the huge cargo doors. Ricimer pushed the latchplate.

The portal slid sideways. The men waiting for them within the main lock wore hard suits of black ceramic: members of the Governor's Guard. Their visors were down. They weren't armed, but there were six of them.

"This way, please, gentlemen," said a voice on the intercom. A guard gestured to the inner lock as the other portal sealed again. "Precede us, if you will."

The guards were anonymous in their armor. They weren't normally stationed in Betaport, but there'd been plenty of time since the *Peaches* and *Dalriada* made Venus orbit to send a contingent from the capital.

Piet Ricimer straightened. "It was really worth it, Stephen," he said. "Please believe that."

"It was worth it for me," Gregg said. His eyes were still watering from the sulphur in the boarding tube.

A guard touched the door latch. The portal slid open. Gregg stepped through behind Ricimer.

Three more guards stood to either side of the lock. Beyond them, Dock Street was full of people: citizens of Betaport, factors from Beta Regio and even farther, and a large contingent of brilliantly-garbed court officials.

In the midst of the court officials was a small woman. Stephen Gregg could barely make her out because of his tears and the bodies of twelve more of her black-armored guards.

They were cheering. The whole crowd was cheering, every soul of them.

Author's Afterword: Drake's Drake

Truth is something each individual holds within his heart. It differs from person to person, and it can't really be expressed to anyone else.

Having said that, I try to write fiction about people who behave as closely as possible to the way people do in my internal version of truth. One of the ways I achieve that end is to use historical events as the paradigm for my fiction: if somebody did something, another person at least *might* act that way under similar circumstances.

In the present instance, I've built *Igniting the Reaches* on an armature of events from the early life of Francis Drake (including acts of his contemporaries, particularly the Hawkins brothers and John Oxenham). This isn't biography or even exegesis. Still, I wound up with a better understanding of the period than I had when I started researching it, and I hope I was able to pass some of that feel on to readers.

My research involved a quantity of secondary sources ranging from biographies to treatises on ship construction by naval architects. These were necessary to give me both an overview and an acquaintance with matters that were too familiar to contemporary writers for them to bother providing explanations.

The heart of my reading, however, was *The Principall Navigations of the English Nation*, the 1598 edition, edited by Richard Hakluyt: *Hakluyt's Voyages*. I've owned the eight-volume set since I was in law school many years ago and have dipped into it on occasion, but this time I had an excuse to read the volumes straight through and take notes. The *Voyages* provided not only facts but a wonderful evocation of the knowledge and attitudes of their time.

The authors of the accounts varied from simple sailors to some of the most polished writers of the day (Sir Walter Raleigh, whatever else he may have been, was and remains a model of English prose style). I appreciated the period far better for the careful way two sailors described coconuts—because people back home wouldn't have the faintest idea of what they were talking about. (Another writer's description of what is clearly a West African manatee concludes, "It tasteth like the best Beef"; which also told me something about attitudes.)

When one views the Age of Discovery from a modern viewpoint, one tends to assume that those involved in the events knew what they were doing. In general, they didn't. It's useful to realize that Raleigh, for example, consistently confused the theatre of his activities on the Orinoco with explorations of the Amazon by Spaniards starting in the latter river's Andean headwaters. Indeed, Drake was practically unique in having a well-considered plan which he attempted to execute. (That didn't keep the wheels from coming off, much as described in this novel.)

I'll add here a statement that experience has taught me will not be obvious to everyone who reads my fiction: I'm writing about characters who are generally brave and occasionally heroes, but I'm not describing saints. Some of the attitudes and the fashions in which my characters behave are very regrettable.

I would like to believe that in the distant future, people will be perfect—tolerant, peaceful, nonsexist. Events of the twentieth century do not, unfortunately, suggest to me that we've improved significantly in the four hundred years since the time of the paradigm I've used here.

Let's work to do better; but we *won't* solve problems in human behavior if we attempt to ignore the realities of the past and present.

Dave Drake
Chatham County, N.C.